PRAISE FOR LISA APPIGNANESI

"An intriguing novel — richer and stranger than a mere thriller"

— THE GUARDIAN

"A cleverly conceived plot about the strange and terrifying power of love"

— GLOBE AND MAIL

"A chilling study in male obsession"

— NATIONAL POST

"A classic tale of suspense . . . one of the finest you'll read in its genre . . . a lyrical page turner and a rare creation."

— OTTAWA CITIZEN

"At once a murder mystery, a psychological study of obsessive jealousy, and a meditation on gender relations and political ideals, this book aims high and hits its targets with deadly accuracy. This is a novel of real depth, and, I suspect, lasting impact."

— MONTREAL REVIEW OF BOOKS

"Appignanesi's fifth novel explores love and jealousy, image and reality, and confirms her reputation as a compelling writer."

— THE TIMES

"I stayed up until 3 a.m. reading right through."

— GLOBE AND MAIL

Also by Lisa Appignanesi
from McArthur & Company

Sanctuary

Dead of Winter

A Good Woman

Losing the Dead

PARIS
REQUIEM

PARIS REQUIEM

Lisa Appignanesi

McArthur & Company
Toronto

Published in Canada in 2001 by
McArthur & Company
322 King Street West, Suite 402
Toronto, ON M5V 1J2

National Library of Canada Cataloguing in Publication Data

Appignanesi, Lisa
Paris requiem

ISBN 1-55278-250-6

I. Title.

PS8551.P656P37 2001 C813'.54 C2001-901637-9
PR9199.3.A66P37 2001

Design & Composition: *Mad Dog Design*

Cover Concept & f/x: *Mad Dog Design*

Printed in Canada by *Transcontinental Printing Inc.*

The publisher would like to acknowledge the financial support of the Government of Canada through the Book Publishing Industry Development Program (BPIDP) and the Canada Council for our publishing activities. The publisher further wishes to acknowledge the financial support of the Ontario Arts Council for our publishing program.

10 9 8 7 6 5 4 3 2 1

For my daughter, Katrina —
a thoroughly modern woman
in the making.

1900, the Belle Époque, like Janus, wears two faces — one that sings and one that cries . . . Paris is a cesspool below and fireworks above. Everything moves, standing still. Nothing gets done, but everything is planned. Something wants to be born and tries to free itself — that something is what we call 'modernity', in other words, the ephemeral.

HUBERT JUIN

Live all you can; it's a mistake not to. It doesn't so much matter what you do in particular, so long as you have your life. If you haven't had that what have *you had?*

HENRY JAMES, *The Ambassadors*

3ie serie *Paris, le 3 Mai, 1899*

Le Journal

From our Crime Correspondent:

In the early hours of the morning of 29 May, police pulled an unidentified woman's body from the Canal St. Martin. About twenty years old, dark-haired and wrapped in a dress which might once have been blue, the woman bore the marks of severe beating, which police ascribe to the collision of her body with the numerous barges which crowd the canal. While the police carry out their investigations, it is unclear whether the woman jumped to her death or was already dead when her body was thrown to the waters.

This marks the sixth suspicious death in half the months of a hapless young woman in our capital. The Seine, the shafts of the still unfinished Metropolitain, the shrubs bordering the river at Auteuil near the Auberge Boileau, all have provided last stops for these ill-fated women, two of them barely old enough to leave their mothers' care.

Police are quick to attribute these deaths to suicide. Why not? After all, two of the women were listed prostitutes whose degenerate lives, according to our guardians of morality, deserve no better end. Two others were homeless vagabonds. But what if prostitution and vagabondage are the symptoms of their plight and not its cause?

As republicans, we need to address the larger question: what is it in the tumultuous hub of modernity which is Paris that drives young women to confront their maker in such violent ways?

There is also a secondary matter which the police must confront. Were the lives of these women really worth so little that they could fling them away? Or are there foul forces at play here — as foul and murderous as those which condemned Captain Dreyfus — that have conspired violently to cut short these women's days?

PART ONE

ONE

Paris sizzled with the spectres of past and future danger. The Gare Saint-Lazare was a hellhole. The air burned. Engines hissed. Smoke billowed. Whistles shrieked. Trains clanged and clattered like weary mechanical beasts. Everywhere was heat and noise and the crush of humanity.

James Alexander Norton hesitated at the open door of his compartment. The truth was that he hadn't wanted to come. He hadn't wanted to see these women with their scarlet slashes of mouths patting handkerchiefs to brows and plunging bodices. He hadn't wanted to hear these perspiring men shouting orders, nor the cabin trunks clanking to the porters' wild gesticulations nor the children screaming, their cries amplified by the slaps of solemn-gowned governesses.

He had barely wanted to leave the quiet of his study at the Harvard Law School and make the trek across the Charles River into Boston, let alone travel from his native city to New York. Still less had he wanted to board a liner and spend mindless days staring out at an eternity of waves.

He had reached the age, he told himself, where habits were preferable to change, and travel a trying diversion. He also had — though the very concept irked him since he was an imminently rational man — what he was forced to call a premonition: a lurking sense that no good could ever come from his return to this city.

He hid his reluctance with skill. As he leapt off the boat train onto the platform and mingled with the throng, the impression he gave was hardly that of a man who felt his future was all behind him. His jaw wore a determined forward thrust. There was an alacrity to his step. His cheeks were ruddy from the sea wind, his deep-set eyes an icy blue. In his well-brushed linen suit, his sparkling white shirt and carefully knotted tie, he looked like what he also was: a man in his prime. A thirty-five-year-old American with a mission. A stubborn, secret man, who had learned to keep his emotions in check.

He scanned the platform and waited for the anticipated face to emerge from the crowd, if a little late. When it didn't he pulled out his pocket watch in an impatient gesture.

The sound of his name, audible beneath a foreign inflection, made him turn. He saw the conductor pointing in his direction. A slight, cloth-capped youth wove his way through the fray and stopped in front of him. Large, dark-lashed eyes examined him from a grimy face.

'Monsieur Norton?'

James nodded. A stream of words poured from the boy's lips. Amidst the noise, he couldn't quite follow them. But the envelope which found its way into his hands was decipherable enough despite the smudge of a fingerprint across his name.

He tore it open and made out his brother's hasty scrawl.

'Forgive. Forgive. Something urgent has come up. Rooms reserved for you at the Grand. And a friend's carriage is at your disposal. Antoine will guide you to it. Until tomorrow, I hope. R.W.N.'

When James looked up, the youth he decided must be Antoine was already negotiating a porter to his trunk and urging James along the platform.

James shrugged off his irritation. Typical of his wayward little brother to have business more pressing than that of coming to meet him — though it was for him he was here. He should have predicted it.

Rafael William Norton, known to his near ones as Raf, hadn't bothered to respond to the telegram announcing James's arrival. Nor, indeed, had he written more than the most cursory of letters home for some months. If they wanted to read Raf, they now had to turn to those pages of the *New York Times* which charted the clamorous progress of French politics and the murky in's and out's of the everlasting Dreyfus Affair. That was what had seduced a holidaying Raf to stay in Paris in the first place and what had brought him back, this time with their sister, Ellie, some ten months ago.

A prod at his back forced James to adjust his face. He turned with a hovering smile to see the bustling, matronly girth of one of his dinner companions from La Bretagne.

'Hotel Mercure. Don't forget, Mr. Norton. Charlotte and I count on you.'

James nodded, bowed, extricated himself from the lingering sidelong glance the young Miss Elliott cast on him, and let the two women pass, the daughter as tall and angular as the mother was short and stout. He waited until they had disappeared into the teeming main hall of the station and then battled through the crowd, amplified now by a motley assortment of ragged vendors and cheeky flower girls, all shouting their wares. He caught up with Antoine at the street doors.

A whiff of sewage mingled with the cloying odour of fresh dung rose to his nostrils. A hundred hoofs clacked over cobbles. Cabs squealed and rattled. Whips cracked. The air itself crackled with electricity, jolting everyone into jangling speed. Feeling his own heart beat faster, James paused for a moment to take in this first taste of the city. Paris, as this nineteenth century hurtled towards its end, was distinctly nervous.

On the opposite side of the street, a tight rank of blue-clad policemen in stiff, rounded caps held back a braying mob of demonstrators. Mustachioed ruffians in thick shapeless jackets shook their fists and shouted in orchestrated menace. Soberly garbed citizens, straw boaters slightly askew, lifted threatening canes into the air. Flags and banners billowed above massed heads. Bullhorns blared a torrent of words he couldn't quite make out. But he could read the banners.

'Death to the traitor Dreyfus, the German's lackey.' 'NO to the re-trial.' 'Long live the French Army.'

James had a sudden sharp sense of danger. It rose from this thronging mass of disorderly humanity like the high reek of uncontrollable hatred.

Antoine tugged at his sleeve and pointed him towards a street to the right. The lad wanted to get away before the inevitable brawl erupted. James hurried after him and clambered into the designated carriage.

As the horses executed a sharp turn away from the tumult of the station, he leaned into surprisingly comfortable leather cushions and relaxed to the half-remembered sights of the city. Impressions poured over him. The bustle of a marketplace. Vast tubs of vivid flowers beneath the pale bulk of the Madeleine. The Baron Haussmann's majestic boulevards, perfectly tuned to the march of armies. The dark, reckless passion in the face of a man dashing across a street. The weight of history clinging to the stone buildings like the pervasive soot and bare-bosomed statuary. Yes, he had come back to Paris after all these years and despite himself, his senses seemed to sharpen into a forgotten wakefulness which bore all the trappings of excitement.

Gilded empire elegance reigned in the lobby of the Grand Hotel. Like some stage set resurrected from former times, it demanded appropriate mannerisms, muting voices, eliciting a decorum which shunned the frenzy of the streets.

James cleared his throat and announced himself. The manikin of a clerk behind the gleaming counter looked up from his registers with a theatrical beam of a smile.

'Ah Monsieur Norton, the older. Yes, your brother told us. Un grand avocat. Lawyer. De Boston.'

James nodded and wished that Raf wasn't so garrulous. But the clerk was both pleasant and efficient and within minutes, James had been given his room number and key and shown not only the restaurant where diners already gathered, but the telephone cabin from which he put a call through to his siblings' number. He waited and waited, to no avail. Neither his brother, nor, more suprisingly, his sister, it seemed, was eager for his arrival. It would make his mission all the more difficult.

He rode up to the fourth floor in the mirrored elevator. His old love of architecture, a profession he had once wished to pursue, drew him to the windows of his room before anything else. He allowed himself to feed on the spectacle of the well-proportioned square dominated by the imposing façade of Garnier's recent neo-Baroque Opera. His eyes played over the stately harmony of the whole, then rose slowly across detail and towards the winged victories which perched atop the edifice. In this light, their stoney faces brought his mother to mind. He looked away abruptly.

It was his mother's increasing distress which had propelled him on his mission to Paris. The absent Raf was her favourite. His visit home the preceding summer had rejuvenated her. Under his appraising eye, she had shed her stern greys and blacks and on occasion come down to dinner in pale frocks James didn't believe he had seen since before his father's death over six years ago now. And she had assumed that Raf was home for good. Even when the new publisher of the *New York Times* had asked his brother to cover the Paris peace conference which marked the end of the United States' protracted war with Spain, it hadn't crossed her mind that her youngest might choose to linger and linger in the distant city. She had sent Ellie along, not only as a treat and distraction for her long-suffering daughter, but as an extra assurance that the two would be back before Christmas.

But the end of the peace conference did not mark the end of the siblings' stay in the capital of temptation. Instead, delaying letters arrived. Ellie stated that it seemed best to prolong their time since she felt ever so much better here and Raf really shouldn't be pulled away from such a stimulating terrain for his writing. Raf's letters, on the other hand, intimated that Ellie was in no condition for winter seas, though her mood was good, and that it would be wise to extend their stay in what were fine quarters.

The extension seemed to have no boundary. Their mother's disappointment had turned to ire and then, as letters became infrequent, unassuageable anxiety. She was convinced things were being kept from her. There were hidden reasons for her children's interminable absence which had little to do either with Ellie's health or Raf's work. She had begun to disapprove of the tenor of that, too.

She could think of nothing but the absent pair. Her usual round of charitable endeavours fell away. So too did meetings with friends, except those who might have heard some gossip from Paris. For the rest, she fretted and worried, pacing the length and breadth of her front room, covering miles, pausing only to gaze out the windows with the gaunt face of a Hecuba whose offspring had been lost to fate.

Some four weeks ago, she had grasped at James's hand like some life raft, clawed at it. 'I know now. Ellie's finally confessed. He's entangled. Entangled with . . .' She had turned her face away and hissed out the words, 'with a scarlet woman. Even her name reeks of it. Olympe. You have to save him, James. Only you can do it. Bring him back. Bring them both back. He's hideously enmeshed. I can't speak all of it. Can't. The shame.'

She had wrung her hands. Her contorted expression moved from disgust to abject fear. In her spiralling imagination of disaster, her grown son had been transformed into a hapless babe snatched from her by a Paris of harlots and perfidy. If he were to be returned alive, it could only be by the intervention of some saintly knight.

James's stiff protests that Raf was an adult had no effect. His mother was impervious to reason. She was already engaged again on her trajectory round the room, her eyes fixed on some middle distance fraught with torment. From the midst of it, she hailed him once more. 'You will have to go, James. There's no choice. It's up to you. You're his only chance.'

The words came with the force of an injunction. Like some empress marking the end of an interview, she had then lowered herself slowly into a chair and given him her back.

James took a certain pleasure in duty. He had always combined an older brother's burden of responsibility with an ability to bear the freight. His early love of architecture had been abandoned to follow his father obediently into the law and he had done well-enough by it. Wooed some years ago by James Barr Ames to Harvard and to the law school's experimental teaching by the intriguing case method, he had gradually left behind the cut and thrust of active practice. He took real satsifaction in his new work, yet he had propelled himself away at his mother's behest as soon as term permitted, so that he now found himself staring out on the Place de l'Opera wondering why it was that his rebellious younger brother could stir such passions in their mother, while he, who stood by her, generally went unnoticed. He wondered, too, why it was that even though he had not yet laid eyes on Raf, his presence, like some age-old irritant, was already igniting the buried embers of old rivalries.

He didn't allow himself to wonder for long. The clerk had handed him letters which demanded attention. He settled at the carved walnut desk and noticed that the top envelope wore his sister's neat hand. The script on the second was unknown to him. Intrigued, he opened it first, aware as he did so of the subtle whiff of a foreign scent.

> *My dear Professor Norton,*
>
> *Forgive me the liberty of addressing you so soon upon your arrival in our city. Your brother and sister have made me think it would not altogether displease you and have, indeed, asked me to help look after you. I trust your journey has not proved overly fatiguing. If you feel so inclined, I would be honoured if you could join me for tea at . . .*

James skipped details and leapt to the signature. Marguerite de Landois. He played the name over in his mind as he reread the slightly stilted English of the note. No, the name meant nothing to him. Neither Raf nor Ellie had mentioned it as far as he could remember.

Hoping for an explanation, he turned to the second envelope.

'Welcome to Paris, brother dear.' Elinor's playful voice addressed him as directly as if she were standing in the room.

> *I apologize for not being there amidst the station crush to greet you. The spirit was willing, but the flesh just a little weak today. More than today, if I dare admit it. These last weeks have turned me into an appendage to a mountain of bolsters, not to mention two shawls and a pot of sturdy tea. I hope you will partake of this last with me at your earliest convenience — say tomorrow morning.*
>
> *From the palpable spaces between the lines in your last letter and the abrupt stops in your telegram, I gather our splendid mater has had more than a small hand in your expedition here. She reminds me of the great George's (Eliot, I mean) dramatization of the differences between the sexes. She sends her male champion off to fight the gods and monsters*

while she continues to live in her fears and anxieties. My only fear is that you will find no monsters (I leave the gods to you) — save, perhaps, the monster of my weakness, which I do not like to confess to anyone.

A demain, my biggest and best brother . . .

James studied the letter, wondering what it was that struck such a curious note for him. Perhaps it was that Elinor had not once mentioned Raf. Nor was there any reference to this unknown Marguerite de Landois. On top of it, Ellie claimed that she was resting at home, whereas when he had telephoned earlier, there had been no reply.

He fumbled for his pipe and filled it slowly as he took up his position by the window once more. With the first billow of smoke, it came to him that this was the first time Ellie had ever broached the subject of her condition directly to him. In the past it had been an unmentionable given, a matter reported on by their mother in hushed tones. He allowed himself a small sigh and turned his attention to the square.

A hurrying figure caught his eye. Something about the grace of the man's form, the passionate cut of the face, the agile speed, like an ancient Olympic runner weaving his way skillfully between strollers, brought to mind his brother. But this wasn't Raf, James determined as the figure grew closer. He looked at his watch again. With a wave of irritation first at his brother for his incorrigible waywardness, then at himself for rising, like a tin soldier, to the trumpet call of familial duty, he headed for the streets.

His carefully erected plans and the order of his days, James noted with passing irony, were already succumbing to the siren song of the city.

Three hours later, having wandered a little, snacked in a *terrasse* and stopped at the American bank, James was hurtling across the river in a Hackney cab. From his vantage point, both arteries, solid and fluid, seemed equally busy. Beneath him brightly painted barges moved alongside dark, heavy goods vessels and light fishing skiffs. The shores were lined with wash boats. As they turned onto the quai, he noticed a group of stout women carrying baskets loaded with linen.

When the cab reached its destination on one of the old streets of the Faubourg Saint-Germain, he hopped out no longer certain he had done the right thing in coming. The agreeable note he had received bore little relation to the grim, darkened stone and austerely formal façade of the house in front of him. Heavy doors creaked, as he considered. A carriage emerged. The horse, the vehicle, the coachman in his black cutaway, all bore a marked resemblance to those that had ferried him from the station not so very many hours ago.

He murmured his name to the uniformed footman, who ushered him through an arched passage into a courtyard. Its aspect astonished him. He was in a garden. Cherry trees in full blossom graced every corner and dappled the light. Orange shrubs grew from ornate stone urns to flank long windows with their glossy leaves. Wisteria climbed, softly purple against a wall. The unexpectedness of it all rendered it even more beautiful. He stopped for a moment to take in a bird's song and sniff the fragrant air.

'You like my greenery, Mr. Norton.'

James veered to see a woman walking towards him. He had an impression of slenderness, a graceful step, light hair intricately coiffed, a dress in the same shade as the wisteria, an outstretched hand which was so proffered as to demand a response of hand and lip.

'Madame de Landois.' He bowed, found his voice. 'Your English is very good.'

Her laugh rustled. 'I do my best.'

'And your secret garden, exquisite.'

'Ah, for that you must thank Philippe. He spent his childhood in England.'

James nodded sagely, though he had no idea to what she was referring. On closer inspection though, he noticed that her eyes were warmly brown, like milk chocolate, but streaked with yellow and as full of humour as her voice. He wondered if he cut a comical figure, standing there now, his hands hidden in his pockets like an awkward youth. He straightened himself as he felt her direct gaze.

'I am so glad you could come. We shall be quite alone.' She tilted her chin a little. 'Yes, the resemblance to your brother is clear. Not the eyes, of course. And you are — how do you say, a little more *costaud* — sturdier. But the rest . . . I hope you are not too tired. Come. Tea will restore you.'

She was already through one of the glazed doors and he followed dreamily, shaking himself once he was inside as if to throw off a mesmerist's far too pleasant pass.

The airy room that bordered the side of the garden had a grand piano at its far end. Next to it stood an easel, supporting an unfinished canvas.

James cleared his throat. 'You paint, I see.'

'That is to flatter me, Monsieur. I dabble. It helps me to see things clearly. And to pass the time.'

'You have too much of it?' It was an idea he had never really contemplated. Time, for him, was something there was never quite enough of.

She stopped to consider him. 'Sometimes there is that illusion. Yes.' Irony played over her features. 'I am a woman after all, Monsieur. A French woman of little gainful employment. But I see we shall get on.'

It came to him that he was no longer used to the company of women.

They were at the base of a grand marble staircase and she moved her skirts aside to take the steps more quickly. 'At this time of day, the light is best in the library. You will see.'

He did. The high-ceilinged room, lined with tomes he would have liked to examine at his leisure, seemed to float on a lake of pink blossom. A small round table, sparkling with silver, had been set in one of the tall window alcoves.

He pulled back a chair for her, surprised that the splendour of the house did not dictate the constant presence of servants. She seemed to read his mind.

'I thought it would be pleasant to be informal. You Americans prefer that, no? Everything is ready.' She gestured at the array of small cakes and sandwiches and poured amber liquid into thin porcelain. 'We shall help ourselves.'

James filled his plate, but he didn't eat. He was too full of questions, yet altogether uncertain where to begin.

'This is all very kind of you.' He stammered a little.

'Oh, I am kindness itself. When I choose, of course.'

He met her smile. 'I'm happy that you've chosen then. I shall thank my brother for it. Have you known him long?'

'How does one measure the length of friendship, Monsieur? Months, years, seem to have little to do with it. Let us say that I count Rafael' — she gave the name the lilt of all its syllables — 'and Elinor amongst my good friends. When they asked me to help look after you during your stay here, I was more than happy to agree.'

James was not indifferent to the stress she had put on Ellie's name.

'Rafael is so busy these days and Elinor, sadly, indisposed.'

'So she says. She preferred to see me tomorrow.' He had a sudden image of Ellie in a darkened room and he noticed that he was tugging at his collar. 'Is it very worrying?'

Madame de Landois' voice was soothing. 'I have recommended her to the best doctors. Let us hope one of them will find a cure for her.'

'Yes.'

'She has such a complexity of character. It can produce such a complexity of symptoms.'

James sat back in his chair with abrupt awkwardness. He found he didn't like this stranger speaking of Ellie with that peculiar mixture of familiarity and clinical distance, as if she knew her better than her own brother.

Madame de Landois arched a well-formed eyebrow. 'Have I overstepped myself? It is only that . . .'

James cut her off, more rudely than he wished. 'Do you know where my brother might be, Madame? He hasn't come to me yet. And I had hoped to catch up with him today.' He stopped himself and changed tack. How could this patently aristocratic woman possibly know where his brother had got to, let alone anything about the murky business that had brought James to Paris. 'I have so little time, you see.'

'Rafael is negligent.' She filled James's pause lightly. 'But I know he is "chasing a story", I think you say. And when he is chasing . . .' She held her hands up and shrugged. 'C'est comme ça. So much has been happening these last weeks. The Cour de Cassation, our supreme court's decision to look again at the Dreyfus case. Then the attack on our new President by this madman, the Comte de Dion, at the races. Such tumult. I don't know if you had the news of all this on shipboard.'

'Indeed. Nonetheless . . .'

'You would like to see your brother immediately, n'est-ce pas?'

James met the irony in her eyes and had a passing sense that she was older than he had first assumed, closer to his age, perhaps, than to Raf's. But the intervening decade only hovered over her expression without quite settling on her face. He found himself wondering about her husband. It was unthinkable that she didn't have one.

'Yes, I can see it now. You share Rafael's tenacity, but you are reticent, more secretive. Though you have cultivated a certain bluntness to hide it. Or perhaps had it thrust upon you?'

A knock at the door saved him from having to answer. Madame de Landois seemed a little taken aback as she called out a 'oui'.

A trim, balding man came in and in a low voice proceeded to pour out a hurried sequence James couldn't quite catch.

'Faites-le monter, Pierre. Apportez une autre tasse.'

It took the last phrase for James to shed his prior thoughts and realize that the man was a servant.

'Are you interested in life in France, Monsieur Norton?' Madame de Landois' next question caught him off guard.

'I . . . I hope so. Do I strike you as too enmeshed in my own affairs?'

'No, no. It's understandable.' She studied him, then rose to pace a little. It gave him the full benefit of her fine figure. She was, he decided, remarkably pretty, rather tall, too, for a French woman.

'You may, however, be interested in my visitor.' She carried on with her previous thought. 'I doubt that you have ever met quite his kind before.'

Her expression bore the glimmer of a challenge. James was more than prepared to rise to it.

A thin, stoop-shouldered man shifted from foot to foot at the open door, as if to cross its threshold marked a transgression.

Despite the warmth of the weather, he was all but muffled in a shabby black coat. His streaked, ragged beard half covered his gaunt face. Dark eyes blazed from between jagged cheekbones. His prominent forehead was moist with perspiration, the ungroomed hair above an untidy grizzle. A sizeable black felt hat sat in his hands. He played nervously with its brim as he bowed and bowed again.

'Thank you for seeing me, Madame. Thank you.' He spoke in a deep baritone of a voice, his tones hesitant, accented.

The slowness permitted James to understand him clearly. He also understood that the man was unmistakeably a Jew — a Jew of the kind he had only ever glimpsed before in the nether reaches of New York.

'Come in, Monsieur Arnhem. Please sit down. Take a cup of tea with us.'

'No, no.' The man stretched out a staying hand. 'I don't wish to disturb. I would not have bothered you, except for my worry. My great worry.'

'Please, Monsieur Arnhem.' Madame de Landois insisted. 'And let me introduce you to Monsieur James Norton. I believe you have met his brother.'

A shadow crossed the man's face, but he bowed again, deeply. 'Honoured, Monsieur. I am honoured. He quickly turned his attention back to Madame de Landois. 'Rachel . . . ,' he faltered, 'I mean Olympe. Olympe would not be pleased if she knew I were here.'

James edged forward on his chair. Olympe was the name of the woman his mother had called a harlot, the woman with whom Raf was purportedly enmeshed.

The man continued. 'Olympe has always named you as a great friend, a benefactress. And I didn't know where else to turn. Forgive me. Forgive.' His fingers fretted with his hat, edging it into circular motion.

'Do please sit down, Monsieur Arnhem.' Madame de Landois took the hat a little impatiently from his hands and placed it on a side table. 'Now, tell me what the problem is.'

'Rachel. We were due to meet for lunch on Monday. Two days ago. Rachel never lets me down. She is a really good daughter, you must know that, whatever our disagreements.'

James's cup rattled in its saucer as he placed it roughly on the table. Olympe was this man's daughter. This man's. That could only mean . . . He swallowed hard. No wonder his mother had insisted on his mission. Olympe was the daughter of a Jew. He tested his own reaction, but the man's narrative gave him no time for reflection.

'Olympe didn't come. I waited, waited well beyond the time. There was no message from her at home either. I went to her rooms. I am barred from them, but I went. No sign of her. Nor at the theatre the next day. They had not seen her since last Thursday. They are angry. It isn't like her. No word. Nothing.'

Like a wiry mongrel contained for too long, he seemed about to leap from his chair, but the chains of decorum kept him in place. He looked round the room distractedly. 'I have this premonition.' His voice had become a hoarse plea. 'Please, have you heard anything from her? Do you know where she might have gone?'

Madame de Landois shook her head slowly. 'When did you last see her?'

'Two weeks ago. A little more now.'

'Is your premonition . . . your fear . . . that she may have . . . taken off?'

The man lowered his burning gaze. He wrung his hands. The ability to speak had left him. Instead, he took a large handkerchief from his pocket and wiped his brow.

Madame de Landois turned to James and murmured in English. 'Some years back, Olympe had a spate — I don't quite know how you describe this in America — of, well, walking. Walking, in something like a trance, and disappearing for days on end. Not quite knowing where she'd gone and then waking up in a strange, sometimes precarious place.'

Had his mother been privy to this biographical item, too? No wonder she had wrung her hands.

'No, no.' The man spoke at last. 'I don't believe so. All that is in the past. She has been much, much better. Her work was going well. She . . .' He leapt up suddenly like a spring that had to be released. 'I mustn't trouble you any further. But if you hear anything, please let me know. I have given myself another twenty-four hours. And then I go to . . . to the police.'

The last word was a scraped breath. He rubbed his throat, then bowed again before reaching for his hat.

'If you wish, I shall accompany you there, Monsieur.'

An angel seemed to have alighted on Arnhem's shoulder to lift him from his abject state. His face was transformed. 'Ah, if you really would Madame, my gratitude would be limitless.'

'Of course, I will.' She rose.

James watched her escort Arnhem to the door and murmur a few more words. He was thunderstruck by her liberality.

His feelings must have made their way to his face, for when she sat down again her expression was wry. 'I think, Monsieur Norton, that you disapprove of the company I keep.'

'I . . .'

Her laugh trilled. 'You remind me of my husband.'

'Oh.'

'Fortunately, for my freedom, we have lived our separate lives for some years now.'

'I see.'

'I'm not sure that you do.'

'I . . . I was only somewhat surprised . . . at Monsieur Arnhem.'

'Yes.' She examined him forthrightly. 'Our situation in France these last years demands that we show kindness to these people. They have suffered through no fault of their own. Captain Dreyfus, as you must agree, was wrongly indicted — set up as a spy, indeed, because his origins made him easy prey to prejudice. Then, too, Monsieur Arnhem's daughter is a true artiste, a talented musician and dancer — and now an actress. She has even performed here on occasion for small gatherings of my friends . . .'

James felt like a small boy chastised by a stern governess. He wouldn't have expected this regal woman to so value a figure his mother despised. Perhaps she didn't know of this artiste's relations with Raf. There might even be more than one Olympe.

'Olympe is also a friend of Rafael's.'

Madame de Landois responded to his scurrying thoughts.

'A special friend?' James stammered.

'So you know?'

'I know very little.'

'You know that.' She smoothed her dress and turned an innocent face on him, but the eyes glinted with something like humour. 'Rafael warned me that I might find you a little cold, a little distant. But no, I do not altogether think so. The perceptions of brothers are often askew.'

'He said that to you, that I was cold?'

'Perhaps I should not have repeated it. You will think me interfering.' She smiled a smile which made interference the best possible characteristic in the world.

Before he could find an appropriate response, a bell sounded and she leapt up.

'Excuse me a moment.'

Her expression was one of open relief as if she'd been waiting too long for the call. She walked lightly to the far corner of the room where she picked up the telephone.

An odd sensation flickered at the edge of James's mind as he surreptitiously watched her movements, some inchoate sense of familiarity.

He set it aside to distill his admiration, for that was what he principally felt. Madame de Landois was a thoroughly modern woman, not at all what he had anticipated when he stood in front of the cold, formal stone of her *hôtel particulier* so little time before.

Her profile was alight now. The voice at the other end of the line was distinctly in favour. Then he heard a sharp intake of breath.

'Non, ce n'est pas possible.'

He turned away in embarrassment and focused his attention on the garden. He didn't want to be caught eavesdropping. The new technology engaged people in audible, yet private conversations. No set of manners existed for the excluded party. The situation always made him ill-at-ease.

A few minutes later Madame de Landois, her face distraught, was beside him. 'My apologies, Monsieur Norton. I shall have to cut our meeting short. Feel free to finish your tea. Pierre will see you out.'

She was already halfway through the door when she turned back. 'No, no. It's best if you come with me. Yes. Far better. If you're free, that is.'

James rose with alacrity. He was about to ask her what was amiss, when she held up a staying hand.

'No, please. No questions. Just come quietly. Things are bad. I need to think.'

TWO

The road which wound along the Seine was a clamour of construction sites. Everywhere ragged fencing squeezed traffic into ungainly rows. Men carrying planks clambered waist deep through mud or hung from ladders. Shouts vied with hammering. A new railway station rose from the ground like the partial skeleton of some prehistoric dinosaur and abutted in jagged spikes where a roof might be. Along the Quai d'Orsay, scaffolding arced precariously across the river, a giant cobweb glistening in the amber rays of the low sun. Tiny figures clung to its many levels like so many marooned insects.

Farther west, traffic ground to a halt as the road gave way to a pitted track.

'We'll get out here and walk,' Madame de Landois announced.

These were the first words she had uttered since they had started out and they were stiff with an emotion James couldn't name. She waved her arm in a wide circle which encompassed both sides of the river.

'You see all this, this mammoth effort of building work. We are poised to welcome in the new century with an Exposition Universelle. For one year, a fairy tale of a city will take shape. The elaborate structure you see here is the Italian Pavilion. Next to it the Turkish. And then your own country. And so on. And so on. A great spectacle waiting to be born. A hymn to brotherhood and progress. To industry and invention. All the nations working side by side — African, Asian, American, European. And then,' she snapped her fingers. 'Then nothing. It will all be torn down. All this effort will have been like a café-concert ditty to impermanence.'

She laughed oddly, her face hidden from him by the wide brim of her intricate hat.

Passers-by turned to stare. She was the only woman amongst scores of working-men, their faces worn from the day's labours. James wondered again where she was taking him. This was no place for a woman. The ground was heavy with mud. Slippery planks covered it here and there to provide a passage. He offered her his arm and she accepted it without meeting his eyes.

'But perhaps that, too, is fitting.'

He didn't know quite what she meant. He was busy trying to navigate them through the gathering human tide that poured from gaping pits and half-erect structures. In the distance he spied the towering steeple of the iron structure which had not yet been completed on his last visit to the city, almost twelve years ago now. Maisie had clung to his arm then and cried out at its brute ugliness.

As he looked at the finished tower now, he marvelled at Eiffel's feat of engineering, a challenge to the visionaries of the new century. That hadn't been torn down. He should mention that to reassure Madame de Landois. But she was pointing, tugging them to the right.

'There. We go down those steps over there.'

She paused midway down the steep incline. 'I trust you won't hold this against me, Monsieur. I trust too, that you have a strong stomach.' She held his eyes for a moment before moving forward once more.

A cobbled width of quay stretched before them. At its edge old horses lapped water and an assortment of barges swayed, two of them still part loaded with building materials. A lone houseboat bobbed amongst them, half-hidden by a strip of washing. It was towards this that Madame de Landois headed with a newly determined step.

A narrow gangplank creaked beneath their feet. From the deck a rank odour of vegetation and sewage rose like a miasma. For a brief second, James wondered whether this was what Madame de Landois had meant by her warning comment. But then, as she called out a loud greeting, there was no more time to wonder.

A burly man with a pugilist's threatening features appeared from the prow of the boat. He paused as he took in Madame de Landois. She uttered something James didn't catch. A moment later they were round the other side of the deck and through a narrow door into a cluttered room.

The air was fetid. Smoke curled round the low ceiling. In the dusky light, it was difficult to distinguish people from looming barrels and ramshackle furniture. Everyone seemed to be speaking at once. As his eyes adjusted to the gloom, James made out two kneeling men, between them a prone figure stretched beneath a rumpled blanket. One of the kneeling men wore a police uniform. A few more leaden seconds passed before he realized that the other one, with his back to him, was his brother.

'Raf.' The single syllable fell into the taut silence which Madame de Landois' entrance had precipitated.

His brother turned and leapt up, his head narrowly missing the ceiling. His eyes were glazed. He hardly seemed to recognize him. Finally with an erratic gesture he raised his hand to grasp James's. 'Bad day, Jim. Bad timing.' His attention flew to Madame de Landois. 'C'est vraiement elle,' he mumbled. 'Her.'

She nodded once abruptly, then clutched Raf's arm with an intimacy from which James averted his gaze.

It was only now, as Raf introduced Madame de Landois to someone called Durand, a small, dapper, but distinctly stout man who bowed with the exaggerated deference of a perfect functionary, that James realized the figure on the floor was dead. He took a step backwards, wishing there was an unencumbered wall to lean on.

The body was a woman's. A long lock of dark hair fell across her shoulder. One arm, bare but for the lace of a chemise, lay arched in an abrupt V at her side, as if the elbow had been cracked. The face was puffy, blotched, bloated with water. But the lashes were thick, the brow high, the bone structure fine. She was young and all-too-recently beautiful.

A blinding flash lit up the room. For a split second it transformed the reclining body into alabaster. The blanket had been pushed aside. Limbs glowed with a pale fire. The odour of burned sulphur hung in the air.

James took in a tripod, the hooded head of a photographer. He stepped outside unsteadily and filled his lungs with air. Through the leap and bounce of associations and half-heard words, it came to him that the dead woman must be the Rachel about whom Monsieur Arnhem had been so worried. The very Olympe he had come to extricate his brother from. Well, he was extricated now, but not in a manner even his mother might have wished. No. Then, too, death was not always a form of disentanglement, as he, himself, knew too well.

To still his racing senses, he hurried to the far end of the boat. A young, blonde woman emerged from the shadows at the corner like a hallucination. She was sitting on a bench and nursing a baby, crooning to it.

He averted his gaze, but her voice stopped him. 'Vous êtes aussi du Commissariat?'

No, no, he wasn't from the police. James shook his head and cast his eyes to the ground. The woman's boots protruded from the flounce of her skirt. They were black and shiny.

He reached for his pipe, then thought better of it and turned to retrace his steps. He should go back to that room to see how Raf was doing. Yet he couldn't quite face the sight of that body lying there so still amidst the onlookers. Maisie had had that stillness about her. Her cheeks, too, had a puffiness, but she had lain on sheets of the softest white. Yes. Maisie.

He realized that his nails were biting into his palms. His stomach churned. He leaned against the boat's rail and gazed into the waters, willing the turmoil of those old emotions away. He wished for a habitual task to escape to, some responsibility which would whisk him away from the clotted hold of that past ordeal.

The man who now approached him and offered cigarettes from a silver case had the glow of a saviour, despite his appearance. He was of middle height, bearded, slightly built. His shirt protruded from his open jacket as if he had forgotten to tuck it in. His tie was askew. Lank hair fell over his brow. There was an unsavoury air about him as he took a long puff of his cigarette.

'The second Mr. Norton, je crois. I am Gilles Touquet. Journalist,

Anglophile, and a friend, a collègue of the first Mr. Norton.' His laugh was hollow as he tipped his bowler. 'Bad business, this. Very bad business. La Tristesse d'Olympe. You know, Olympe Fabre once did a dance to which she gave that name.'

'What happened to her?' James asked.

Touquet shrugged. 'Who knows! But I found her. Well, not exactement found. I do the crime,' he pronounced the word in the French way, 'for my paper. *Le Journal.* You know it?'

James encouraged him with a nod.

'I heard from one of my contacts at the Préfecture that a body had been fished out of the Seine. I rushed over. Recognized Olympe Fabre immediately, but I pretended not to. I wanted to get your brother here. I knew he was looking for her.' He threw James a swift sidelong glance.

'And he came quickly, made a big brouhaha. Insisted that the police get Durand on the scene.'

'Durand?'

'Yes, Chief Inspector Emile Durand, you saw him perhaps. The stout little dapper man with the heavy brows and the big broom of a moustache.'

He gestured down the deck and moulded his body into a perfect parody of the man James had noted. 'Durand is high up in the Judiciaire and a reputable detective. One of the force's all too rare upholders of justice and scientific investigation. If you had come a few moments earlier, you would have heard him chastising the boatman for dragging Olympe's body along the deck, perhaps breaking her arm, obliterating useful clues. He was fierce.'

Touquet chuckled, then stopped himself abruptly. He puffed at his cigarette. 'It's a good thing, too, that Rafael brought Madame de Landois here. Her association with the case will mean that our police take the matter seriously. Otherwise you know, they can be a little lazy. Another lovelorn grisette in the Seine. Another suicide. What difference can it make, eh?' He shrugged in exaggerated fashion.

A half-empty bateau mouche passed them. One of the passengers waved. Touquet beckoned back in hearty fashion. Waves rocked the boat. James clung to the rail. His stomach was churning.

'And is it suicide?'

Touquet peered at him from his bulging eyes. 'Your brother does not think so.'

'No?'

'No. And now that Madame de Landois is here to cast her — how do you say — influence, there will be a proper investigation. An autopsy, too.' He flicked his burning cigarette into the water. 'So we shall know.'

Heavy steps echoed over the length of the deck. Two uniformed men bearing a stretcher appeared. They paused at the door of the cabin. James saw Madame de Landois come out, followed by Raf, Chief Inspector Durand and the surly thickset man they had first seen, who was evidently the boat's owner.

James walked towards the group. Touquet followed.

'He found her,' Touquet gestured. 'Quite a raconteur he is, when he's got a few glasses in him. Fished her out. Thought he'd fished himself a sirène, at first. You'll read all about it in the paper.'

The prospect took James aback. He gave the man a sharp look. The latter was oblivious to it.

They had reached the others. Durand was gesticulating, his demeanour Napoleonic. 'You can rest secure, Madame. My men and I will take care of everything. Everything.' He bowed to Madame de Landois with the magisterial panache of some defender of the grandeur of the French state and ushered them away.

Raf held back and looked once more into the room where a single light had now been lit. By its yellow glow, the body of Olympe was being raised onto the stretcher.

James was struck by the longing in his gaze, Orpheus losing Eurydice to eternal darkness. Everything was clear in that shivering look. His mother had been right. Raf loved this woman more than he ought. Loved her with a terrible passion which made James recoil. He held himself rigid against a sudden tide of nausea.

Madame de Landois urged Raf into motion. Two-by-two, like a funeral cortège, they made their way slowly off the boat and onto solid ground, trudging up the steps and along what was now deserted terrain. The spectral frames of the twilit pavilions hovered like some ghost town to their side.

Madame de Landois' carriage waited at a short distance from where the paved road began. She and Raf were engaged in a murmured conversation. James would have liked to overhear, but he kept his distance. In the flickering light the carriage lamps cast, her face was sombre. She turned to James as the coachman held open the door.

'Our first meeting may not have been propitious, Monsieur Norton, but I hope for all that we shall meet again soon.'

James bowed. He only realized as the carriage pulled away that he had half-expected Raf to accompany her. Instead, the three men were left on the darkened street. They walked along it in desultory fashion, his brother firing off short bursts of sentences to Touquet until the man tipped his hat and disappeared round the first turning.

'I badly need a drink, Jim. What about you?'

James nodded.

Raf hailed a passing cab, gave directions to the driver, then sat back in his seat. His handsome face, so often a witness to fleeting passions, was stonier than those of the statues which flanked their passage to the right bank. James, himself, felt seized by a torpor which made both mind and tongue too heavy for use.

At last, after what seemed an interminable rat-run over cobbles, the cab stopped.

'You should feel right at home here, Jim.' Raf spoke at last. 'It's one of my regular haunts.'

He led him into a long dim tavern tucked between unremarkable buildings on an unremarkable sidestreet. A few lone drinkers sat at its highly polished zinc counter. The wall behind it, covered in mirror, reflected a string of booths and trebled their number.

'This is Bill. From Minneapolis.' Raf introduced the shirt-sleeved barman. 'A whisky for me, Bill, a large one. And for Jim here . . . what'll it be Jim?'

'The same.'

'And get Armand to bring us a plate of whatever's best.'

They settled in a booth towards the rear of the bar. Raf swallowed a large mouthful of his whisky and met his brother's eyes. 'To paraphrase our grand friend, you've chosen one helluva time for your Parisian holiday, Jim.'

James studied him. Raf had changed. He couldn't quite put his finger on what it was, but there was a quickness to his movements, a kind of contained determination, where before there had been cocky languour. He had always had an abundance of charm, been almost excessively handsome, but his features now seemed sharper, more defined, edged with drama. The dark eyes, once sleepy, darted with an intelligence he had failed previously to notice in them. They made him feel big and slow and somehow inert in comparison. The longer fall of hair, the sweep of moustache were incidentals. It was more that Raf seemed to have been put into a firm and foreign mould and had turned out successfully — had turned into a man. He wondered what, aside from time itself, had wrought the change.

'I hadn't intended exactly a holiday.'

'No, of course. You're here to urge the return of the prodigal. And his hapless sister. We mustn't forget her. Have her letters been complaining about me?'

'Not in the least.'

'Well, that's something. Not that I believe you.'

The hostility in Raf's voice was a surprise. His younger siblings had always been so close. A mere woman couldn't have produced this animosity. There had been women in Raf's life before. Plenty of women.

'It's just that mother . . .' James began again.

'Wants me back.' Raf finished for him.

'Yes.'

Plates had arrived brimming with fries and slabs of steak. Raf dug into his meat. 'Her letters have hardly been unclear on that point. They make my own virtually impossible.'

'She's ailing.'

'Aren't we all!' His voice had grown grim. 'Look Jim, to be perfectly blunt, I can't think about all that now. I've got rather more pressing business.' He looked at his plate and pushed it abruptly aside.

'The dead girl . . . now that . . . that she's gone, why is she your business?'

Raf didn't answer. He was staring into the distance, his knife and fork forgotten.

'I met her father earlier,' James continued. 'Not altogether a prepossessing figure.'

'What do you know about it, Jim?' Raf stabbed the air with his fork. 'You think the man's had the advantages of our alma mater. Not to mention the grandparental millions.'

James persisted with a kind of perverse stubbornness. 'Mother has been worrying about the company you keep.'

'So that's it, is it? The gossips have been at it. Worrying her about the fact that Olympe is Jewish. Well, the dear woman must worry about something.'

'She thinks,' James invented brashly, 'that this whole Dreyfus matter you've been so immersed in also influenced your choice of . . . of women.'

Raf glared at him. 'Let her think what she will. It hardly matters now.'

'So you'll come home?'

'Don't be ridiculous, Jim.'

Silence covered them, edged with animosities, old and new. At least he had got it out, James thought. He had hardly presumed, whatever the circumstances, that Raf would be instantly amenable. But what next? He hailed the waiter and asked for another round, just to cut through the thickness of the atmosphere.

Raf fixed him with an intractable gaze indicating that he was willing to talk, but not about coming home.

'How did you happen on Monsieur Arnhem?'

'He came to Madame de Landois' home. She was excessively kind.'

'Hardly surprising. Narrowness is not one of Marguerite's characteristics.' He paused, waiting for James to take in the comparison, then asked softly, 'What did he say?'

'He was hoping to have some news of his daughter. He was worried. Rightly as it turns out.'

'Some forms of parental worry are more justified than others.'

James nodded equably enough, despite Raf's ready provocation. 'How did you come to be . . . to be involved with the girl?'

Raf didn't seem to have heard him. He looked tormented, as if Olympe's lifeless body were once again before him. 'I thought I'd prepared myself for the worst, but I hadn't. I hadn't. I shall have to go to him.' He downed his whisky in a single gulp and reached for his hat.

'Now? He's hardly your concern. Surely the police . . .'

'Don't be such a pompous ass, brother dear. And don't forget you're not my father — even though you've taken on the paternal role for so very long I imagine it's hard to shed.'

James was astonished at the bitterness in Raf's voice.

'None of this need implicate you. I've hardly asked you to come along and besmirch yourself.'

'But I am coming, Raf.'

James was already on his feet. Now that he'd found him, he had no intention of letting his brother out of his sight.

A light drizzle had started to fall. It coated the narrow street in a slippery sheen. There were no cabs to be had. Raf didn't seem to mind. He mumbled something about a walk doing them good and proceeded at a rapid pace. He shunned James's minimal attempts at conversation. Only their footsteps sounded, setting up a hollow echo between the canyons of houses. These grew dingier as they wound their way through a labyrinth of alleys. Festering garbage appeared at doorways. A rat scuttled across their path. From a corner a mangy dog howled like some demented coyote.

And then suddenly, they were on a wider street alight with cafés and thick with human traffic. A few minutes passed before James took in his fellow strollers. The men seemed to be of all kinds and classes, quietly suited, walking sticks in hand or raggedly clothed, bandanas round their necks. The women's lips were as bright as the shawls they draped loosely over an expanse of naked shoulder. They were bare-headed. Their eyes clung to him, as they leered and gestured their availability.

'Do we turn off here?' he growled at Raf.

'No, farther down. Don't fret. They won't bite. They're only earning their keep.' As if to taunt him, he waved at a woman who seemed barely old enough to be in long skirts. The girl waved back with a frank, open smile.

'Ça va, monsieur l'Americain?'

'Oui, Poupette. Et toi?'

'Viens demain. J'ai a te parler.'

'What does she want?' James asked, his curiosity overcoming his distaste.

'To talk. She's a useful source. Clever. She's got her wits about her and she tells me things. Did I mention that I was doing a bit of writing for the French papers? Anonymous, of course. Touquet helps. We're running a little joint investigation.'

'On what?'

'This and that. I'll tell you another day. It's a long story. This way.'

Another dank, narrow alleyway. No gaslight here, only the occasional flicker of candles from curtainless windows. Shapes emerged from the shadows, a man tugging a woman into a doorway. A brazen laugh sounded.

'It would have been better to come tomorrow,' James murmured.

Raf didn't seem to have heard him. His pace had picked up.

As they turned a corner, a streetlamp suddenly illuminated his profile. The bleakness in it tore at him. A long-forgotten scene crystallized. Raf could only have been about four to his thirteen. Their dog had been run over by a passing cart. It lay there shuddering on the ground, its helpless whimpers heart-rending. 'Will he die?' Raf asked, his hand clutching at his brother's. James nodded with an elder sibling's casual brutality. He waited for Raf's inevitable howl, the stream of tears. They didn't come. Instead a look of utter bleakness settled on his little brother's face, hollowing out the childhood pudge, instilling his eyes with a grim horror, transforming him in a matter of seconds into an old man.

James wanted to do what he had rushed to do then — speak soft words of comfort, proffer hot chocolate, talk of new pets, anything to turn his brother back into his usual rambunctious, rather pesky self.

Those avenues of consolation were now closed to him. Instead he said, 'Poor Monsieur Arnhem. He'll be heartbroken.'

Raf shot him a darting look. 'We're here.' He pushed open a dilapidated door. 'Watch your step. It's one floor up.'

The stairwell was as narrow as a ladder and in the dark felt more rickety. The walls peeled beneath his hands. They gave off the musty, sour smell of cabbage and poverty. But from above came a sound which made him pause in wonder — the soft, haunting music of a perfectly pitched violin. Like children under the sway of a piper, they followed it to its source at the end of a corridor.

Raf knocked and the music stopped. 'Oui,' a gruff voice called out.

'Monsieur Arnhem? C'est Rafael Norton.'

The door creaked open. The man looked up at them, his features tense, and then with a glance behind him stepped towards them into the hall. 'The little ones are asleep,' he murmured. Through the half-open door, James made out a cramped, denlike room. A single tallow candle sat on a small corner table. Beside it, a violin. Much of the rest of the space was taken up by a bed on which two tousle-headed children lay.

Stumbling over his sentences, Raf conveyed the terrible news. A moan came to Arnhem's lips. He crushed his hand over his mouth to stifle it and swayed slightly, moving back against the wall for support. 'Not Rachel. Not Rachel.' He repeated the words over and over again.

In the wavering candlelight he looked like a biblical prophet painted by an old Dutch master.

Raf talked. But for the odd word — police, Madame de Landois, the Seine — James wasn't following. He couldn't transfer his attention from the man's face. His eyes had become two bottomless pits of misery. All the world's pain seemed to have taken up residence there.

Then, as if jolted by an electric current, a fierceness came over him. He pressed Raf's hand. 'I do not trust the police. They are not concerned with my kind. I will not rest. I will not rest until I have found who has done this to her. You must help me.'

'Depend on it. I will.'

James found himself nodding in acquiescence, as if he, too, were party to the pledge. The act took him by surprise.

THREE

The Boulevard Malesherbes stretched from behind the Madeleine in a double rank of stately buildings which bore the unmistakable imprint of the Baron Haussmann's refashioning of the city. The broad avenue was flanked by the green of chestnut trees, still fresh from their dawn shower. Nineteen had its number inscribed on a carved stone shield framed in oak leaves above a fine wooden door.

The dappled beauty of the morning helped to disperse the tempest of graveyard prophets and waxy corpses which had invaded James's dreams. But a cloud of disquiet remained with him. He tried to prod it away by standing back to examine the façade of the handsome building with its long rows of iron balustrades, one each for six of the seven storeys.

From behind a window on the second floor, he thought he saw a curtain move and then quickly find its place again. He shunned the boxlike elevator and went up the stairs to the apartment.

A young, aproned woman with protruding eyes and a frizz of pale hair opened the door to him. She took his hat and murmured him along a dim corridor towards a room in which voices already played.

'Jimmy, how wonderful!' he heard his sister's voice even before he entered the long rectangular salon with twin marble fireplaces. The curtains were partially drawn, inducing a gloom in which objects and people seemed to float.

At the far side of the room, Elinor reclined on a cushion-strewn divan with all the grandeur of a hostess in ancient Rome. She was wearing a starched white blouse and round her shoulders an aquamarine shawl which matched her smile for brightness. Seated round her were three women. With an inward groan, James recognized two of them at once.

'Jimmy, how very handsome you look.' Ellie's tone was excited. 'Decidedly, the groves of academe become you. You flourish in them. Even your hair bristles. Like newly mown grass.'

He bent to brush her forehead with his lips, felt a sensation of dry heat. He stood back to examine her.

'You're not looking so bad yourself, little sister. Your letter yesterday had me half expecting a ghost.'

As he said it, he realized that the colour in her cheeks could easily be the result of fever, so brightly did the two spots of pink stand out against her more general pallor. Beneath the high forehead, her dark eyes, too, had a hectic glow, giving her sharp foxy features the operatic quality he always forgot in her. In his mind she was so often simply his sister that the category induced a blur which was feeling rather than sight.

'Not quite a ghost yet, Jimmy, though I can't go out to the world.' She laughed archly. 'But you see the world comes to me. It's an adequate solution. Let me introduce you.'

'Oh we've met your brother, Miss Norton. We had the pleasure of sailing together.' Mrs. Elliott gave James the benefit of her steel-grey eyes and her determined beam. 'We were hoping to see him again, weren't we Charlotte?'

Charlotte nodded and put down her cup with an awkward clatter. 'Are you enjoying Paris, Mr. Norton?'

James smiled politely and made an inane comment about the weather. He itched to pull open the curtains.

'And this, Jimmy, is my dear friend, Harriet Knowles. You may remember her. She was part of our little women's circle all those years ago in Boston. She's been travelling in Italy for the last three or is it four months. I've missed her. But she's back now which pleases me immensely. Harriet is a brick.'

Elinor smiled serenely at a sturdy, grey-suited woman whose intelligent eyes made up for the scrubbed plainness of her face. She greeted James with a marked directness of manner.

For a few minutes they all chatted about what it was essential to see in Paris and which couturiers and hatters it was worth visiting. Then Harriet rose. 'We don't want to tire Elinor out, ladies. We should leave her to Mr. Norton. They have a great deal to catch up on, I'm certain.'

'A very great deal,' Elinor echoed.

With the click of the front door, Elinor lay back on her pillows and closed her eyes.

'Would you like to rest now, Ellie? I can come back later.'

'No, no, Jim. We must talk. I'm so glad you're here.' She propped herself on an elbow and tucked a stray wisp of hair into smoothness. 'Though I'm sorry it was mother who sent you. I really wish you'd come in order to see the wondrous sights of this hoary ol' capital. Or to find yourself a new wife.'

He stiffened slightly. But her tone was the bantering one they always fell into, edged with flirtation, and he allowed himself to relax.

'But not in order to fetch us home. Mother forced the information out of me, you know. Raf doesn't, does he? He doesn't think it was because of me that she sent you?' Her voice rose in something like terror.

'No, no, Ellie. Calm yourself.'

She took a deep breath. 'And, you see, it's too late. There really was no need to come on that account.'

So she knew about the death, James thought. Raf had told her. He was relieved.

She lifted a little bell from amidst the books and water pitcher on the table beside her. Its tinkle brought the maid. 'Encore du thé, Violette. Et la brioche, s'il vous plaît.'

'Your French has blossomed into perfection.'

'If only everything blossomed like that, eh Jim.'

He couldn't plumb the source of the tension on her proud face. It misaligned her eyes and mouth, etched a new line.

'And here I thought you were having a grand old time.'

'I have been. In my way.'

'Let's get some light and air in here, Ellie. It's close. Or let me take you to a restaurant. It will do you good.'

She let out a dry laugh as he heaved the curtains all the way back and opened the French doors to bright daylight. It made her shield her eyes with her hands.

'I wish I could do that.'

'Do what?'

A dreamy little smile crept over her face.

'Put one leg in front of the other. The way you're doing now. Walk.'

He was aghast. 'I don't understand. Can't you? How long has this been going on?'

'Don't sound so stern, Jimmy. It makes your face go all ugly.'

He sat down and studied her.

'How long?' he asked again, more quietly.

'Oh not so very long. Three weeks. Four. Maybe more. I've lost track. Time is better measured when you can take steps. Mother, mother, let me take a step . . .'

'How did it happen? What caused it? Whom have you seen?'

'Don't pounce on me with your attorney's vehemence, big brother. One question at a time.'

'All right. How did it happen?'

'I don't know. I really don't know, Jimmy. It just happened. My legs got heavier and heavier, too heavy for my body to move. And then they wouldn't move at all. I'm so tired.'

He stared at her. 'And you've just been lying here. All this time.'

'Oh no. I've got wheels. A chair. It's downstairs. Got a bit dusty now. At the beginning, Raf would come and take me out. Even tuck me in at night . . .' Her voice drifted off.

'What does the doctor say?'

'The doctors, Jimmy. There have been more than one. Let's see . . . which diagnostician would you like to hear from first? But it'll pass. Everything passes.'

'I want to speak to your doctors.'

'Horrible doctors. So demeaning. Tapping and prodding.' Her face grew taut with a look he could only interpret as disgust. 'I'm seeing a new one next week. Highly recommended. Raf was . . . But you can come with me. Yes. That will be good. Monday. But right now, I'd rather you helped me up, Jimmy. With you, I might be able to. I might just be able to. You bring with you a good solid whiff of that old American determination. Let's aim for the terrace.'

She slipped off the stole and edged her body round into a sitting position. Her feet touched the floor. James stared at the thick socks which protruded from her dusky skirt. They looked as if they might belong to Raf.

A sense of helplessness overcame him like a thick blanket, muffling his movements. He grappled clumsily to thrust it aside and stepped towards her.

'What have you been reading?' he asked, seeking to distract them both as he bent to wind his arm round her back. Her bones felt frail, like a newly hatched bird's, and as he hoisted her up, he was astonished at her lightness. Compassion flooded through him.

'The French. Mostly the French. Too saucy by half for you.' Her laugh was strained. She took a deep breath and held it.

He could feel the effort she was making as if instructing her feet to move. The distance between brain and limbs proved too long. He half-lifted her forward in little jerks so that she seemed to be hopping, though her toes dragged along the rug.

'Rachilde. "Monsieur Vénus". Do I shock you? You know, that woman dresses as a man. Claims it gives her the freedom of the streets.' She babbled about scribblers, giggled strangely, hiding her nervousness. He could feel that he was holding all her weight.

'Hardly sounds like the woman who left Boston clutching Emerson.'

They had reached the window. 'Let go, Jimmy,' she whispered. She was gazing down at the street with a somnambulist's unseeing stare. 'I want to try standing on my own.'

He released her slowly. First one elbow, then the next, and hovered beside her. For a split second, she stood upright. Then he felt as much as saw her legs crumple. He caught her.

'Not bad,' he lied. 'We'll try again later.' He carried her back to the divan. A stale smell came from her mouth. It threatened to envelop him.

He put her down too quickly.

'What time did Raf leave you this morning?'

'Leave me this morning?'

'Yes.'

She tightened her shawl round her. 'He didn't come this morning. I haven't . . . haven't seen him for almost a week. He's so busy these days.'

James scalded his tongue on the hot tea. 'I don't understand. Isn't he living here? The address . . .'

'Is the same, yes. But he has his own solid front door.' Elinor pointed in a direction behind her. 'Has had for over four months now. And he hasn't rung at mine today.' She laughed suddenly, a high, shrill peal, which swiftly faded into nothing.

'You've quarrelled?'

'Not exactly. No, not exactly.'

Silence threatened. She played with the fringes on the divan blanket. His eyes strayed to the mantle where a blackbird perched, eerily life-like in its glass tomb.

'So you don't know?' he cut through the thickness.

'Know what?'

'About her? About Olympe.'

'The beautiful Olympe. Has she seduced you, too, Jimmy? I wonder if she could.'

'Hush.'

'Don't make that face, Jimmy. Is it the word *seduce* or the fact that offends you?' She laughed at his expense. 'You have the look of a man whose excessive preoccupation with virtue is beginning to stunt his intellectual growth. Yes, yes, Jim, don't protest. If you carry on clinging to purity this way, you'll be more alert to smut than a bevy of demi-mondaines.'

'That's enough, Ellie.' He was angry now. 'So you don't know? Know about the death.'

'A death?' Panic hollowed out her eyes, robbed her cheeks of colour. He wished now that he had kept his counsel.

'Whose death?'

He didn't speak. He barely wanted to remember.

'Tell me, Jimmy. I'm not a little girl anymore. I'm a grown woman. Twenty-eight. Old enough to have had a half-dozen children. Old enough to . . .' She stopped herself. Ordered, 'Tell me.'

James stumbled. The image of that dead face had come back to him. 'Olympe Fabre.'

'Olympe dead! No. No, I won't have it.' A great rush of breath came from her. She fell back onto the divan.

She was so still he thought she had fainted. Then a voice issued from her which he didn't recognize, deep, croaking, like a swarm of frogs on a hot night.

'It's his fault. His. He drove her to it. I warned him. She was so in love with him. That's why I told mother. I was afraid. Afraid for her.'

'Hush, Ellie.'

'His fault. Poor Olympe.'

Her eyes flew open and she sat up. 'How did it happen?' she asked in a strained, but ordinary enough tone.

'I don't really know. You knew her too, then? I thought . . .'

Elinor nodded. 'We were friends. Such a beautiful thing. The most delicate features . . . Where? Where did she do it?'

James stared at her. So the concern about Raf and a Jewess had all been on his mother's side. He wanted to ask more questions of Ellie, but she was too overwrought. He remembered the repeated family injunction that she wasn't to be overexcited, overstimulated. He had done too much of that already. He chose his words about Olympe carefully.

'She was found in the river.'

'The river.'

Tears quivered on Elinor's cheeks. She didn't bother to wipe them. Her eyes were fixed unblinkingly on some invisible point.

She was utterly still. It was as if her body had been robbed of sensation, as if the paralysis had spread upwards.

When her lips moved, at last, he shivered.

'He must be devastated. Tell him to come to me. No one knows how to comfort him as I do. You remember that, Jimmy. It's always been thus. Always. Tell him. I'll be gentle with him. Go now. I need to rest.'

Her unblinking eyes followed him from the room. They unnerved him, so that he hesitated when he reached the landing, his hat in his hand, uncertain of whether he ought to do what he had thought to do next. It was as if she might be able to see through walls.

After another moment's pause, he knocked softly on the door opposite, then more loudly to reassure himself.

The door opened before he had finished.

A woman confronted him. Her hair tumbled in stray curls round her face. Her wide lips were painted scarlet, her blouse a striking fuschia pink. It dipped at the bosom, revealing an acreage of rosy flesh from which he averted his eyes. 'Oui?' The word interrogated him as boldly as her stance, one hand on hip.

James stepped backward. Had he misunderstood Ellie and come to the wrong place. 'Mon frère, Monsieur Norton, est-il là?'

'Non, monsieur.' The woman studied him shrewdly, as if she were sizing him up for potential custom.

'When do you expect him?'

He only half listened to her reply. He had just noticed that the bundle she held over one hip was a swaddled babe. His mind reeled. He felt an uncomfortable urge to rush into the bedrooms and explore the lay of the land. Is this what Ellie was pointing to when she said Raf was guilty of Olympe's suicide? Another woman. A child.

He grunted something and raced downstairs.

The streets gave James no repose. They were as noisy and unsettling as his reflections which pursued Raf into unseemly corners. He had an hour before he was due to meet his brother and he needed to order his thoughts.

He crossed a wide avenue swarming with traffic and almost collided with an omnibus. Its driver screeched what he imagined must be a series of expletives. As he made his escape, he narrowly missed being hit by a cyclist, only to find himself the subject of a threatening lecture by a caped gendarme. The man spouted statistics at him, one of which he instantly grasped. Twelve thousand citizens had been injured by vehicles in this last year, one hundred and fifty killed. Did he want to be one of them?

James doffed his hat, apologized in English and tried his best to induce a state of calm as he kept to the sidewalk.

From the corner of the street, a newsboy shouted his papers. James stopped to purchase one and after a quick glance at a headline blaring a crime, he thought again of his brother.

When Raf had last been in Boston, they had spent a single evening alone, talking mostly about France and the Dreyfus Affair and what appeared to be the trumped-up charge for spying which had sent the poor captain to Devil's Island way back at the beginning of '95. But there had been other things too.

He tried now to piece together what had been a fragmentary conversation, inspecting it for clues to Raf's state of mind. He recalled that Raf had talked about a strange syndrome, a series of railroad-linked illnesses which brought patients complaining of dizziness, sight disorders, neck and back pains to bemused doctors who named the condition 'railway spine'. The railways might bring fresh fruit and vegetables speeding to the city. They also disgorged a daily load of provincials in search of work or pleasure, who inflated the city's population, not to mention its horde of prostitutes, together with its crime rate. The latter fed the penny press as efficiently as the food fed its hungry readers. No day passed without the latest installment in a series of scandals and murders, including railway murders.

It came back to him that in the same context Raf had also talked about nerves, how they were affected by speed and mobility — social and class mobility, as well as the physical kind. Nerves frayed, like train tracks from too much stimulation. Collisions and disasters could ensue. Had he been thinking about himself? About Olympe? If he had known all that, why had he plunged Ellie into the midst of it all? Ellie who had always been his confidante, his principal friend within the family. Ellie who had bandaged his knees and spoken soothing words.

James slowed his steps. The vista of the Place de la Concorde had opened before him with its nymph-clad fountains, its lustrous obelisk and ranked statuary. It was one of those spots that brought dusty memories in its train. He didn't want to be deflected by them now, yet a walk through the park would do him good.

Squaring his shoulders, he crossed the first arc of the square and headed quickly into the Tuileries Gardens.

Children's voices reverberated through the gardens. A hoop passed him, closely followed by a skipping boy. Nurses chatted as they pushed large prams lazily before them. A dog leapt up onto one of the scattered benches and was promptly chastised by a small girl in a chequered pinafore.

Ellie had once been like that small girl, all unrestrained activity and certainty of opinion. Brimming with good health. Both the brothers had doted on her. Their father, too. She was the only one who could sway him from his occasional black moods.

Then everything had changed, not irreparably, no. Not even all at once, except when one examined it with hindsight — like one of his cases. He could date it precisely now. It was the summer they had all gathered in Provincetown to breathe the tangy air of the Cape. He had just graduated from Harvard and was preparing to join a firm in Philadelphia. To broaden his experience, his father had said. It was that summer, too, that he had first met Maisie. Maisie who had looked up at him from beneath the wide brim of her sun hat with innocent eyes that singled him out from the crowd and declared, 'you'.

James walked more quickly. The gravel crackled beneath his feet, coating his shoes with a grey film.

It was in the middle of that hot summer that Ellie had suffered her first episode. She had developed a blinding migraine, so intense and debilitating that their mother had her confined to the coolest room of the house. The shutters there were kept permanently closed. The boys were prohibited from visiting. Their parents took turns sitting by her side. The only outsider who was permitted to enter was Dr. Field, who maintained a stubborn silence about any prognosis. 'Patience', was the only word James ever heard him utter to their mother.

The large, bustling, clapboard house developed a troubled hush. There were fewer and fewer visits from his parents' large circle, the politicians and writers, artists and advocates whose company he had begun increasingly to enjoy that summer. There were no more parties in the spacious living room which spilled over onto the wrap-around terrace, where his friends and Raf's mingled with Ellie's, and his father, revelling in the young, engaged all and sundry in whiplash political debate. Nor were there any more of those lazy gatherings on the lawn after a day's boating or on the surf-lapped beach where cool lemonade flowed in time to conversation. Now everyone tiptoed. Speech was confined to whispers. The piano was kept permanently shut.

Only the cries which sometimes emanated from the sick room ruptured the stillness. A cascade of strange, piercing monologues, more sound than sense. Once he had heard Maisie's name in the midst of one, coupled with an epithet he didn't like to repeat and was astonished to find on Ellie's lips. He was glad then to be ousted from the house — as the boys always were when what their mother euphemistically called Ellie's 'growing pains' and their father's 'passing fits' came on. On their way out, they would see Maria, the plump Irish housekeeper, rushing towards Ellie's room with a bowl of cold water and an assortment of cloths.

After some three weeks, Ellie emerged from her sick bed to take up a position on a chair by the window of the sitting room. It gave her a view of the activity on the street and, in the distance, the ocean. She looked very pale, but rather more beautiful than when she had first been taken ill. Her smile was radiant, her wit more agile than ever as she entertained them with snippets from her reading. She never once mentioned her illness. It was almost as if she had forgotten it. And soon, she was up and about, once more party at least to their less exuberant pleasures.

That summer had marked a turning point in more ways than one. From then on, Ellie's condition, the possibility of what was always an erratic recurrence, had played an unuttered but shaping part in family life.

Poor, dear Ellie.

He had never seen her as poorly as today. He must buy her a present to cheer her. She had been so well when she left Boston with Raf late in September. And her letters to him throughout the winter had been studded with lively vignettes from what seemed an ever-amusing Paris life. True, these had been sparse of late. But he had hardly expected her health to have reached such an impasse. Raf had been seriously remiss. He would take matters in hand now. The visit to the doctor would be only the first step. Yes, only the first step.

As he walked, James had a sense that he had distanced himself from his siblings, as indeed from so much else, for perhaps too long.

FOUR

'Sorry I'm late, Jim. Couldn't be helped.' Raf raced into the lobby of the Grand and stopped short in front of him. He looked haggard, his eyes red-rimmed from lack of sleep. James's inclination to reprimand evaporated.

'I've brought you this.' He waved a black leather satchel in the air. 'We can leave it at the desk until later. I want your opinion, once you've read the contents.'

Without waiting for James to reply, he had a quick word with the clerk.

Moments later their carriage had merged with the traffic on the boulevard. Raf was rubbing his forehead with his hand, like a man trying to efface an indelible image.

'What have you been up to?' James asked gently.

'The morgue. I've been to the morgue.'

'I see.'

'Do you? I wish I did.' Raf rubbed his brow again. 'They haven't examined the blood for poisons yet.' His voice grew cold, detached. 'Her left arm was broken. There was some bruising. Across the thighs. Across the shoulders and chest. Two bands. Both could have occurred either before or after she was in the water. There are conflicting opinions on the timing. It could have happened over a week ago. It could be far less.'

The horse had taken on a brisk pace. The sound of iron on cobbles reverberated in the carriage.

'So it could have been . . .' James didn't quite know how to put the question. 'She might have done it . . .'

'Herself. No.' Raf's fingers were clenched into tight bloodless fists. 'No. Not Olympe. Not now.'

'Why are you so certain? Ellie says . . .'

'Ellie is full of fantasies.' His voice was harsh. He modulated it. 'This last while, since she's been so weak, her imagination has grown even more florid than usual. You saw her then. You told her?'

James nodded.

Raf was staring out the window. There seemed to be little to look at except a row of uniform grey façades.

James waited, then took a deep breath and put the matter that had been troubling him. 'Her father, no, no, it was Madame de Landois, said that Olympe had once suffered from a condition which I think William James describes as ambulatory automatism. Did you know that about her?'

Raf didn't respond.

James pressed on. 'I attended a series of lectures he gave some years back. On exceptional mental states. He talked about physical or mental activity performed without the awareness of the conscious self. It happens that a hidden or secondary self can take over from the person and spontaneously perform various acts — including walking. So it's possible that if Olympe was prone to such trances that . . .'

'No. That kind of automatism is epileptic in origin. Often hereditary. Or it's brought on by some kind of trauma. A shock to the whole system. That's what the best of the French neurologists say. I've learned something over the years, too. There's no history of epilepsy in Olympe's family.' He paused, his face a battleground of conflicting feelings. 'And at the time of the incidents Marguerite was referring to, there was . . . well, let's call it a shock. Olympe's mother died. In terrible circumstances. But all that's in the past. I'm certain of it. Absolutely certain.'

'How can you be?'

'She was happy,' he said simply, then rushed on to override James's doubts. 'All right, more important that that, she was earning her keep. She was helping to support her little brother and sister. She was devoted to them. Utterly devoted. She would never have . . .' He let the sentence hang. 'If you'd met her, you'd understand.'

James didn't pursue it. He considered what Raf had revealed. From his practice, he knew that the instincts of near ones were worth trusting. Though he also knew that they were often neither as near, nor as infallible as they surmised.

'How . . . how did you come to meet her father?'

'I insisted. It was only recently that she allowed it.' He paused. 'I guess there was an element of curiosity, too, on my part. Here I am writing about all this Dreyfus stuff, all the hatred the affair has unleashed, and . . . well, you understand. Olympe watched me like a hawk that first time — to see what prejudices I'd let slip.'

'What's the father's story?'

'Common enough. The family comes from Russia. They left in the early eighties, fleeing the pogroms, myths of ritual slaughter, poverty. Only to find it in a new guise.' His tone was bitter, angry.

'Hardly the same.'

'Easy for you to say that. You and me. What do we know about it? Take just the getting here. You and I we travel, we board a luxury liner, land in first-class hotels, get by in one language or another. And have the security of a home to go back to. They . . . Olympe's family, they walk, beg rides in carts, scramble into crowded third-class compartments when they can raise the fare. When they arrive, there's no welcoming committee. They . . .'

'That's enough, Raf. I get the picture. What does Olympe's father do?'

'He works for a tailoring establishment.'

'I see.'

They lapsed into silence. Raf broke it after a few minutes had passed. 'We're not far now.'

'Are we going to the theatre where Olympe was working?'

'No.'

'But surely that should be our first point of call.'

Raf gave him a scathing look. 'Trust me, Jim. Don't you think I've already interrogated everyone at the theatre? I talked to them before . . .

before Olympe was found. They were as mystified by her disappearance as I was. In any case, that will be Durand's first point of call. You think like a policeman, Jim.'

'I'll take that as a compliment in the present circumstances,' James muttered. 'So where are we going?'

'You'll see. My friend the journalist, Touquet, is joining us. And I've asked Antoine to come along. He can be useful.'

'The boy you sent for me?'

Raf nodded.

'Good. I didn't get a chance to thank him. You should get him some cleaner clothes.'

Raf grinned his old grin for the first time. 'He refuses. Says he's got better things to do with his money.'

'And Touquet?'

'I didn't altogether explain, did I, about the work we've been doing together? There's been a series of strange deaths here over the last months. We're not altogether sure how many, four certainly. Maybe five or six. Young women. Two of them identified as prostitutes. The others . . . well, they might have been. They weren't on the official police lists. They could have been what they call *insoumises* — clandestines. So many of the women lose their identity cards just to get off the lists. And to get the police off their backs. Harassment is prevalent to put it mildly. There are some hundred thousand whores in this city, Jim, servicing a population of only three million.'

'Really!'

'Takes one aback doesn't it. Tells you about levels of poverty. And the good citizens of Paris simultaneously want their streets orderly and clean and want their vice squad to behave like gentlemen to the whores they both loathe and desire. Publicly, they want the first a little more, of course. Anyhow, Touquet started off with a press campaign against the behaviour of the vice squads — harassment, arbitrary arrests, but also, of course, profiteering. A poor cop's gotta earn a buck, let alone enjoy the more fleshly pleasures. The way Touquet puts it is that any given policeman acts not only as judge and executioner, but also as pimp and sometimes drug dealer.'

'Hold it.' James cut off the lecture. 'Let's go back a bit. You think there's a Jack the Ripper on the loose?'

'If only it were that clear.'

The cab had stopped and they both leapt out. They were on a broad street which abutted on a square in a part of the city James didn't recognize. From the dilapidated exterior of the buildings, it looked working class. A market seemed just to have run to its closing time. The stalls were empty, the ground covered with broken crates, bits of greens, and squashed fruit. Hunched, grizzled men and ragamuffins sifted the remains, while flies buzzed, gorged on entrails. Here and there, sturdier figures with muscled arms heaved panniers onto wagons.

'No,' Raf was still immersed in his train of thought. 'The difficulty here is that the girls aren't mangled in any way. Their deaths could just as easily have been self-willed. All neat and tidy, mimicking suicide.'

He waved suddenly. 'Touquet's already there. Let's go. He's pursuing all this because he has a real passion for justice . . . and the police don't conform to it. I've put some of his articles into the satchel I left for you. They'll add some colour to your French.'

By the time they had reached the sallow journalist, Antoine had appeared from another side of the square. He nodded at James who returned his greeting. The youth was still in his grubby clothes, his face even dirtier than the last time he had seen him. Perhaps he had been working in the market.

'Good afternoon, Monsieur Norton.' Touquet doffed his hat, then looked to Raf. 'In English, yes? We don't want to give the boy idées. So . . .' He was holding what looked like a miner's lamp in his hand and he waved it in front of him. 'The last time I was here, just after it happened, there was a high fence just there.' He swept his arm to the right. 'And a big hole. Covered now. Maybe the Vincennes-Porte Maillot line of the Metropolitain really will be ready in time. Our construction system is far in advance of the English.' His grin was jubilant. 'Progress, eh! Soon all Paris will be accessible in minutes. Speed. The wonders of speed.'

Seeing his excited pride, James didn't mention how much he hated the Boston subway which had opened to civic fanfare some two years back.

'Have you arranged everything?' Raf asked.

Touquet nodded. 'My contact should be here now.'

He had barely had time to turn round before they saw a man emerging from the ground, like some bleary erect mole clad in dusky blue. Touquet waved to him and hurried their group over. After brief greetings, the man handed them each a long, heavy smock, pausing at Antoine, who shook his head in refusal.

A first set of stairs led them into a square chamber and then a little deeper, a gloomy tunnel, its roof arch covered in wooden shuttering. Cold wind whistled through the dank air. A fine grit clawed at eyes and nostrils. From somewhere came the echo of hammers and voices. They could see only a few feet ahead. Two dim beams lit their way, creating a vertiginous criss-cross of tunnels within the larger one. Suddenly their guide stopped and pointed upward.

'Here,' Touquet translated for James's benefit. 'This is where the vertical shaft was originally sunk.

From the flurry of excited conversation that followed, James learned that some five weeks ago the body of a young woman had been found in the area where they stood. Her neck and one leg were broken by her plunge from the street-level excavation. She lay there, her arms splayed, her head bent, her face pure, like some angel who had fallen from the heavens into infernal depths, the workmen who found her reported. There was no identification on the body and for ten days her absence went unnoticed by any of her familiars. Then one of the plainclothes men in what Touquet called 'the morality police' discovered from the Madame of a brothel on his beat that one of her girls was missing. The description matched that of the dead girl, who was a tiny brunette, with a coil of hair that reached to her waist.

She had no relatives anyone knew of. She had been in the brothel for about six months and had arrived there through some intermediary who had either since vanished or whom the Madame found it best not to disclose. Just another of the thousands of vagabonds, the Madame said with a sniff that would have sat better on the face of a good bourgeoise.

Touquet suspected the dead girl was a victim of the white slave trade from one of those confounded countries in the east whose borders were as shifting as their populations were shifty. She had no possessions that she didn't already owe to the brothel. The police put her death down to suicide. Wouldn't you? — was the general feeling.

No one seemed bothered except Touquet. As he said to Raf, he could imagine him with his height and strength somehow clambering in the dark over some two metres of fencing, not to mention struts and planks and rubble to find the opening to the shaft, but some waif of a girl? Never. Either someone who had access to the entry point had led her there for nefarious purposes which had resulted in death; or she had been lured by some client or secret lover, who had helped her scale the barrier and had finished her off when he had finished with her. There was no question of suicide.

Raf had already taken the lamp from his friend and was directing its beam, like some luminous sniffer dog, inch by inch along the ground. The dank rubble shifted with shadows. Antoine handed him a small garden fork and Raf crouched, raking the earth.

'What are you hoping to find?' James asked, his voice shakier than he liked. He had a vision of skeletal remains lurching from excavated soil, like the bones of early Christians from Roman catacombs.

'Anything. Nothing. You never know. No one has really looked.'

Antoine too was now on his knees, scrabbling round wherever the earth was loose, straying farther afield.

Their guide shook his head, muttered something.

'My friend says there's been so much activity here that Bertillon, himself, would be hard put to find anything. Bertillon is our master of scientific policing.' Touquet let out a sceptical snort. 'Not altogether a great graphologist, though, judging by his examination of Dreyfus's supposed handwriting.'

'Graphology is hardly an exact science,' James murmured.

'Neither is policing, my friend.'

They watched Raf now as he scrutinized the wooden slats along the walls. After a few moments, he approached their guide and engaged him in a low-voiced exchange, followed by a 'Let's go' of marked impatience.

The crowded omnibus rattled and bumped through the streets. James and

Raf had hopped on it for lack of a cab. They sat on its top level, glad of open air after their time in the bleak underground tunnel.

Raf was enclosed in his own capsule of silence. The frown had become a permanent fixture on his handsome face. James, having thrown a second cursory glance at him, decided to speak his mind none the less.

'There's so much I don't understand,' he began hesitantly, then blundered on. 'Olympe wasn't . . . wasn't one of those girls, was she? A prostitute?'

'Of course not.'

'Then why . . . ? What does what we've just seen have to do with her?'

'I don't know. I'm just tracking possibilities . . . It could be that . . . Read those articles. It'll be clearer to you then. There were previous drownings, too.'

The omnibus stopped and James waited for the passengers to settle and the return of noise to pose his next question. 'With my lawyer's hat on, it's still not clear to me why you're so certain it couldn't have been suicide. Sometimes one doesn't know people as well as one presumes.'

Raf turned on him. 'All right. Let's forget what your little brother thinks. Let's just look at the facts. You've got a beautiful young woman, gripped by her vocation, doing well at it. Let's presume she's had a bad day, a pitch black one, and determines to throw herself into the Seine. Does she bother to strip down to her undergarments first and risk being seen by a passer-by or picked up by a cop and taken to the Quai de l'Horloge? Doesn't she just plunge, shoes and all?'

'You're telling me that . . .'

'Yes. That's just what I'm telling you. Didn't you know? Olympe didn't have a dress on when she was found. So someone must have been with her. Someone must have undressed her, brought her to the water's edge like that.'

'I see.' James considered. 'On the other hand, she might have been a parsimonious soul and left her clothes on the river bank. Maybe on the outskirts of town somewhere. She might even just been wanting a swim and accidentally . . .

Raf let out a laugh which was more of a bark. People turned to look at him. He lowered his voice. 'We're hardly in Mark Twain country here, Jim. No clothes left on river banks. Still less by women on their own. And Olympe wasn't a swimmer.'

'No. I didn't really imagine so. I was just trying it on. I know so little about her, it's hard to be of help. Have you tracked her last days? When did you last see her?'

'That's the pig of it. I last saw her a week ago. On Thursday afternoon. I couldn't meet her after the theatre. That Deputy, Déroulède, who heads the League of Patriots had just been acquitted for fomenting a conspiracy to unseat the government after President Faure's death. I wrote about that last month for the *New York Times.* Did you see it? Anyhow there was a large demo in the Saint-Antoine area. I was covering it. Friday I was busy writing it all up when I heard that Paty de Clam was being arrested — one of the officers who'd conspired against Dreyfus, way back in '94. And Saturday, the Supreme Court decision about the re-trial came through. More protests from the anti-Semites and riots and calls to action. I went to Rennes to check out the reaction of its good citizens to the Court's decision to hold the new Dreyfus trial there. So I'd been working like a coolie. I was due to see Olympe on Sunday. I went round to her rooms. She wasn't in. No note for me with the landlady — which is where she usually leaves one. And no sign of her anywhere. The neighbours hadn't seen her. She didn't turn up at the theatre either. You know the rest . . .'

'Have you been into her rooms?'

He nodded once sharply.

James could see that imagining it cost him an effort. He asked softly, 'Any clues? Any notes? Could you tell what dress she might have been wearing?'

'Nothing.' He rubbed his eyes.

'I'd like to have a look at her place sometime. To get a sense of her.'

Raf studied him. 'All right. But I can't take you there now. The next stop is yours by the way.'

They were on the Grands Boulevards. Theatres dotted the avenue, their façades bright with posters.

'Where are you going?'

'I remembered last night as I was trying to reconstruct our last few meetings that Olympe had said something about visiting an old friend of hers. A milliner. She hadn't seen the girl for some time and a visit was overdue. I didn't have any details, not even a name, so I dropped in on Arnhem this morning.' He paused for too long as if he had lost the thread.

'And her father knew.'

'He came up with a possibility. I'm going to see the girl now.'

'I'll come with you.'

Raf grimaced. 'You think that if you don't let me out of your sight, I won't get into any more trouble, Jim. Is that it? And you can get me home quicker.'

James smiled ruefully. 'Maybe. Maybe something like that.'

At the church of Saint-Germain, they hopped off the omnibus and made their way south along the Rue du Cherche Midi. Raf kept up a rapid pace. James had a feeling it would have been a run if he weren't at his side.

As they neared the Boulevard Montparnasse, a shouting crowd ruptured the quiet of the narrow street and halted their passage. There were banners again, this time announcing the League for the Rights of Man and demanding justice for Dreyfus in bold letters. The alliance between the sabre and the holy water sprinkler, the military and the church, was condemned in scrawled placards.

The protesters looked young. They were facing a set of heavy wooden doors in front of which stood a rank of soldiers in resplendent uniform, so theatrical that they could have been part of the chorus in an opera.

'I'd forgotten,' Raf tugged at James's arm and simultaneously waved at a bearded youth. 'There was a demonstration scheduled for today. Students and the League. For Dreyfus and against the officers who set him up on the spying charge. I was thinking of covering it, but there's no time now. Let's go round.'

They squeezed towards the edge of the crowd and had just about managed to make their way to a side street when, from somewhere above, a projectile landed on James's hat, whisking it off his head. He saw it there on the ground, tomato-splattered, then trampled by innumerable feet. Raf was screaming, his fist raised towards a balcony where an elderly man stood scowling.

The crowd pressed at them. Someone handed him his hat with a laughing exhortation of 'C'est la guerre'. War indeed, James thought, and with a sense of exhilaration threw the battered boater at the man who had launched the missile. It hit the terrace rails and leapt off in the opposite direction.

Raf was grinning. 'Careful there, Jim. You risk becoming a paid-up member of the Dreyfus squad.'

'Could be worse, I guess,' James grunted.

At last they reached the far end of the fray. Behind them the crowd had burst into song, a rousing chorus of 'Ca ira.'

'I'll get you a new hat, Jim.' Raf was still grinning as they crossed the Boulevard Montparnasse.

'Why were they demonstrating there? Is it a barracks?'

'No. It's the military prison where Dreyfus was held before they shipped him off to Devil's Island. And Paty de Clam, one of his chief accusers, has been in there under arrest since last Friday.'

They walked, more quickly again now, while James told Raf about the demonstration that had greeted him on his arrival at the Gare Saint-Lazare and his sense that the policemen were only playing at maintaining order.

The frown returned to Raf's face. 'Yes, I can imagine. They're hardly Dreyfusards.' He seemed about to embark on an explanation, then stopped and pointed to a storefront which formed a triangle where two streets merged. It bore the name Odette.

'We're here.'

A few hats with lavish plumes sat in the store window. A bell tinkled as they pushed open the door.

It brought a woman from a back room. She was stout, her hair carefully coiffed, her blouse ruffled over her bosom. She smiled a gracious greeting and swept her arm around the small premises as if it contained the entire wealth of the Bon Marché.

Raf explained in his charming way that they wanted to see a Mademoiselle Louise Boussel who worked there.

The woman's demeanour changed. 'No. No. I'm sorry,' she said stiffly. 'She's no longer with us.'

'Oh, that's too bad. We wanted particularly to find her. Have you an address for her?'

'No. If that'll be all . . .' She seemed about to whisk them from the shop.

'It's only that . . .' Raf lowered his voice. 'She's come in for a small inheritance. From a cousin in America.' His eyes fell to the gleaming mahogany counter. 'Look, Jim. Some fine gloves. Ellie would like a pair, don't you think? These white ones, for summer.' He met the woman's face again, his smile seductive. 'Would any of your other girls perhaps have an address for Louise?'

Avidity vied with disapproval in the woman's face and triumphed. 'Do have a look around. I'll ask for you.'

A puff of steam together with the sound of chattering voices came from the door as she disappeared behind it. Raf winked at James.

She was back a moment later with a young woman who curtsied prettily, all the while examining them with a shy sauciness in her look. A lemon scent rose from her skin. Her cheeks were slightly moist.

James shivered and forced his attention to the older woman, who was now eager for a sale. He took his time, finally choosing a pair of cream-coloured gloves. He asked for them to be wrapped. To his side, he could hear Raf eliciting the necessary information. He didn't dare look back at the girl. She was so like the other one. He hadn't realized he remembered so well.

As the door of the shop closed behind them, he let out a sigh of relief.

'It's quite a trek, Jim. And probably not pretty. Are you sure you're up to this?' Raf quizzed him while they walked briskly towards Montparnasse. 'You're looking a little the worse for wear.'

James shrugged. 'In for a penny . . .'

'The girl offered to take us there after she'd finished. But I thought that would prove too much of a delay.' He studied the piece of paper on which he had noted an address and hailed a cab.

'It's not a neck of the woods I know. Apparently, after she lost her job Louise moved in with her sister.'

'Why did she lose it?'

'She didn't say. I imagine some story that involves a man — from the look of Madame, in any event. These milliners are only a step away from prostitution. It's a big enough step, mind, but a shifting one.'

They rode in troubled silence. The wide boulevard, glittering in its newness, gradually gave way to a maze of smaller, older streets and then fields of detritus. Shacks, their roofs covered in card and rag, dilapidated coaches converted into hovels, sprawled across the wasteland. Children, with the thin limbs and vast urchin eyes of poverty, watched their passage. To their left behind a derelict wall stretched a crumbling two-storey edifice, its stucco long forgotten, its façade a series of rickety doors and peeling shutters.

The driver pulled up and waved vaguely towards a lane. Raf asked him to wait, insisted despite his protests.

They walked, Raf counting houses, and knocked at a ramshackle door. From within came the sound of crying, but no other response. James tried the door next to it and a wrinkled, white-haired woman poked her head from the window. 'I'm looking for Louise Boussel,' James said in his best French.

The woman screwed up her eyes and stared at him. Suddenly she started to shriek and rattle her shutters. 'Laure. C'est la police. La police.'

Neither James's attempt to deny her statement nor pacify her served any purpose. The screaming continued even after the door at which they had first knocked creaked open. A painfully thin woman with dark, ragged hair emerged from it and shut it swiftly behind her.

'Arretez. Stop,' she screeched back at the old woman and only then looked up at Raf and James. She wiped her hands on her apron, smoothed it a little and shot them a regal glance. Behind them, three men had gathered, their stance exuding menace. Two small children threw stones desultorily against a wall.

'May we come in?' Raf asked softly. 'We're friends of Louise.'

The woman pushed back a strand of hair and stood her ground. 'Louise isn't here,' she said firmly.

'Are you sure? We really are friends. Friends of Olympe . . . of Rachel

Arnhem, too. That was why we wanted to speak to Louise.'

The woman stared at them. 'You're not French?' she asked.

'Americans.'

Her gaze softened. 'You're friends of Rachel,' she repeated as if to herself. She looked round quickly, took in the presence of the men who were now eyeing them curiously, and with a shrug opened the door.

They stood in a dark, cramped space. A table, two rickety chairs, a wicker basket stuffed with what could be clothes or rags and a mattress made up its furniture. On the mattress, a baby lay, kicking its bare legs in the air and cooing softly.

'Louise . . . Louise doesn't live here.' The woman's eyes filled with tears. 'She was only staying for a few weeks. Between jobs.'

'Do you know where we can find her?'

The woman turned her back to them.

'Please. We don't mean her any harm.'

'Louise . . . she was picked up. Four days ago.' She swung back to face them with a savage gesture. 'She wasn't doing anything wrong. Nothing. Just walking home. She was near the Jardin des Plantes. And they took her in. In their black coach. Bastards. As if she was a whore. Straight to the Palais de Justice. She spent all night there.' She suddenly clutched at James's lapel. 'You can help her. I'm sure. They put her in the infirmary. The prison infirmary. I saw here there yesterday.' The tears were rolling down her cheeks now. 'It's horrible. Please. Get her out.'

'They'll release her after the cure,' Raf said softly.

'Will they? Will they?' Her voice rose. 'Don't believe it. There's no justice for us. None. And she's so ashamed.'

She wiped her eyes fiercely with the back of her hand, then unfolded a cloth that was on the table. There was a slab of cheese in it. She cut it in half, wrapped the larger section and handed it to James. 'Yes, go and see her. Give her this from me. And tell Rachel. Please. I couldn't get to her. Rachel will help her. Please.'

Raf's face was a mask. He didn't gainsay the woman. There was already too much misery here. Instead he offered words of comfort and politely refused the cheese, saying they would bring Louise a treat of their own.

Meanwhile, James looked at the child. Surreptitiously, he took a note from his wallet and with a pretence of bending to touch its small hand, he placed the money in the fold of the blanket.

Dusk had fallen on the lampless streets. Only their driver, in an attempt to ward off the grimness of the area, had lit his lanterns. He took off impatiently, whipping his horse into action. When they reached the glittering streets of a more familiar Paris, with its bustle of top-hatted men and silk-clad women, James felt they had entered a fairy tale. But these streets, he now knew, led to ones of which he had never been properly aware.

'What is this infirmary Louise's sister was referring to?'

'When the police pick up their suspected streetwalkers, the women are subjected to a medical examination.' Raf's speech was terse. 'A rather brutal one, I suspect. No bedside manners. If they have any kind of venereal disease they're taken straight to the infirmary for treatment. It's the Saint-Lazare prison infirmary. They never, of course, pick up the men. It's as if men were too pure to spread anything. You can come there tomorrow with me, if you like. It's too late now.'

He put up a staying hand to James's next question. 'Just read those articles Jim. And think. Think about Olympe.'

'When did you first meet her?'

Raf didn't answer immediately. His face took on a dreamy look. 'Just after Christmas. On stage. At the Minema. She danced . . . She stole the show.'

James's mind sped, counting months, thinking of Raf's near acquaintance with a world he had barely imagined. He had always been so hungry for life in all its beauty and all its sordidness. His next words came haltingly. 'And the woman in your apartment . . . the woman with the infant?'

'What woman?' Raf stared at him, then burst into raucous laughter. 'Jim, you didn't . . . You didn't really think that Arlette and I . . . No, no. You're too eager to add to the quantity of my sins. I've just been helping Arlette out. I've given her my *chambre de bonne* at the top of the house. She's a friend of Touquet's. He's saved her, so to speak. And she does for me. But only in the housekeeping way. Jim, you're as bad as the neighbours.'

They had reached his hotel and James stepped out with an audible sigh.

'I won't join you for dinner, Jim. Sorry. I've got a piece to catch up on.' Raf held his eyes for a moment, then stretched out an awkward hand. 'But I'm glad you're here. Glad of your help,' he mumbled.

James held on to his hand. 'You'll see Ellie, won't you? She wants to see you. You'll give her the gloves.'

'Yes. Yes, of course.'

As the cab moved away, James saw him rubbing his temples again as if the weight of the world pressed on them and Olympe's dead body had once more usurped his entire field of vision. It came to him that he, too, must once have looked like that, felt like that. This was hardly the fraternal common ground for which he might have wished.

FIVE

The satchel Raf had left for his brother contained a welter of newspaper articles. There were clippings, whole pages or entire issues of a paper. They seemed to be in no particular order and after a quick rummage, James grew impatient and determined that he had to classify the material in some way if he was to begin to make sense of its content, let alone sniff out any clues to Olympe Fabre's death.

He cleared the top of the hotel desk of any extraneous matter, turned on all the lights and with his spectacles on his nose and a sheet of writing paper in hand, he proceeded to organize the articles into rough piles, guided in the first instance by headlines. The piles spilled over onto the floor. Wishing for a dictionary, he began to read with a laborious slowness, which only gradually acquired momentum. He took meticulous notes. If nothing else, this was the French refresher course he needed.

He started with the scattering of reviews which mentioned Olympe Fabre. She was variously characterized as the most talented dancer to burst on the Parisian stage in recent months or as a dramatic actress of great promise. Epithets such as 'mesmerizing', 'beautiful', 'of astonishing grace' were in plentiful supply. There was a drawing showing her in the midst of a leap, some gauzy stream of fabric flowing with her, her arms raised, her hands buried in a welter of hair above her clear profile. James stared at this for a moment and tried to imagine the living woman. She was all of twenty-three he learned, far too young to die.

Three of the articles mentioned her Israelite origins. One of them spoke of the artistic heights we have come to expect from this talented race. Another talked of the plight of the Parisian theatre, when the highlights of an evening have to depend on the seductive skills of an upstart foreigner.

James made a note of these. He rued the fact that Raf had too often clipped away the names of papers and more importantly, the dates of the articles.

He turned next to a series of notices reporting on mysterious deaths. He sniffed Touquet's hand in the first of these, though the article was unsigned. Highly rhetorical, it evoked the death by murder or suicide of the woman who had plunged to her end in the underground, the first death in the great transport system which would transform Parisian life. What was it in the tumultuous hub of modernity that Paris was which drove hapless young women to confront their maker in such violent ways? Was the life of these women worth so little that they could fling it away? Or were there foul forces at play which condemned them to a terrible end? It was the duty of the police to answer these all-important questions, before life for any and all women grew even more treacherous.

Other articles on the same case took up different positions. One contended that the death pointed to a moral for all women: to fall into the morass of prostitution was to invite a violent end. Girls beware. Their proper place in life was in the safety of the family. Another chastised the police for failing to clear the vice-infested streets in preparation for the centennial year.

Wishing for more fact and less rhetoric, James took notes.

Three other deaths were the subject of the clippings. All were reported in the same vein of moralizing hyperbole. But the deaths were terrible enough. One young woman, the daughter of a reputable Jewish shopkeeper, had been found in the Seine near Passy. She had been missing for ten days and her disappearance had been reported by her parents. The neighbours talked of elopement. They had seen her in the streets with a young man in military uniform. Police experts debated whether the marks and bruises on her neck were signs of strangling or the effects of clothes and jewellery. Despite the number of column inches devoted to speculation, no suspects had been found. Nor had the man in military uniform been located. The right-wing press characterized him as a fabrication by socialist neighbours, invented to cast aspersion on a sacred French institution.

Another woman had been found in the canal north of the République. Eventually discovered to be a listed prostitute, her death was quickly attributed to suicide and seemed to have generated little coverage.

Finally, a woman's body had been found hidden in shrubbery not far from a waterside inn on the banks of the Seine in one of those outlying areas of Paris frequented by weekend countryside seekers. The woman had either fallen on a rock or been hit on the head with a heavy object. She was unidentified and there were no witnesses to her death. Because of the lack of identification, the police claimed she was one of the thousands of vagabonds who flocked to the city in search of work. Inquiries were still in progress.

James sighed. The cases seemed to him to be random. Apart from the fact that they were young and female, no thread tied the women together — not even the one of abject poverty. He put the clippings aside and turned to the next pile.

It was large and seemed mostly to contain articles from two papers, *La Libre Parole* and *l'Intransigeant*. Their content consisted of fanatical diatribes against the Jews. The words spewed venom, characterizing the Jews in one long, foul breath as traitors without national allegiance, rich, powerful and secret enemies of the state who despoiled it of its wealth, who were an ugly canker within, draining the blood of the nation, filling the streets with their dangerous, degenerate spawn, fomenting unrest and rebellion.

Feeling sullied, James shuffled the sheets to one side and pulled out his pipe. He didn't altogether understand why Raf had given him all this — except perhaps to emphasize the sheer scale of irrational hatred which attended Olympe's people. But he knew that already.

He suddenly thought of his mother and the telegram that had gone unanswered. He paced for a moment, and then opened the window to take a breath of the cool evening air. The square was crowded with revellers. Massenet's *La Navarraise* was playing at the opera. Not for him this world of pleasure. He returned to his desk and started on the next pile of clippings.

At its top lay a long article signed by Touquet. The piece and its fellows told the complicated story of a Republican deputy who had been involved in a heated scandal. The man had been arrested in the Palais Royal for making advances to a child. He had vigorously denied the charges. Asking to be freed from his parliamentary immunity, he had sued to clear his name, attesting that he was the victim of a police frame-up. Their one witness, it transpired,was a paid homosexual informer for the vice squad, which had fabricated the whole scheme because the deputy was a staunch Republican, a spokesman for reform — and a pro-Dreyfusard. The scandal, first surrounding the calumnied Member of Parliament, then the police, had enmeshed the country for months.

There followed a swathe of articles about the workings of the police force.

Two upper-class women had been picked up around midnight by a drunken police officer and charged with clandestine prostitution. They had been kept overnight in a squalid cell and subjected to a shaming medical examination the next day. Both were virgins. The brother of one of the women, a journalist, had launched a furious campaign against the excessive powers of the morality police which allowed them arbitrarily to victimize innocent women. The chief of police defended his officers. No apology was given.

In another case, a working woman had gone out in the middle of the night to try and find medication for her sick child. She too had been picked up and despite her protests, incarcerated. During the night, her child had died alone in bed. Threatened by police should she make the unjust arrest public, the woman had succumbed to delirium and been packed off to the Salpêtrière asylum where she died six months later.

In yet another story which covered hundreds of column inches and sparked contending editorials, a girl of thirteen and a slightly older woman were picked up late at night on the Champs Élysées and arrested by the vice squad for unlicensed prostitution. The girl, it transpired, was the granddaughter of the head of the League for Human Rights. The older woman, her governess. The two had been to the theatre, and unable to find a carriage to take them home, had decided to walk. The Head of the League lodged a complaint, but withdrew it after a personal apology from the Chief of Police.

Editorials fulminated. This case was simply the tip of an iceberg. If women of this class could be arrested and subjected to such scabrous treatment, what about the thousands of unreported cases of poor, working women? Their treatment at the hands of the police was scandalous, yet no scandal made the headlines. Harassed, humiliated, subject to arbitrary arrest by men who handed out sentences without investigation or a call for witnesses, placed on the register of prostitutes against their will, these women had been robbed of their rights as citizens. It was as if, for a whole sector of society, the *ancien régime* with its secret powers of arrest had never been transformed into a free Republic. Police powers had to be curbed. Such discrimination was scandalous.

'The mark of the civilization of a people lies in the guarantees it gives to each individual's liberty and the respect it accords to women,' one writer stated in the crisp, clear prose James approved. Maybe this particular article was by Raf. He had no way of determining anything by style in French.

Other editorials exonerated the police and put forward public health and order arguments. Prostitution might be legal, but it had to be kept severely in check. Crime always came in its train. Syphilis was rampant, corrupting the blood of the nation, robbing it of manliness, so that the French would never be able to stand up to their long-term German enemy. A few random instances of police misconduct were worth the price of safe and decent streets and the health of the populace.

The police themselves defended their role as guardians of public order. The challenge they were set was a monumental one. They might make the occasional mistake, but if their powers were curbed, no citizen would be safe from assaults on their person or dignity in the streets of Paris.

James rubbed his eyes and leaned back in his chair. He was tired. The effort of reading in a foreign language didn't help. Arguments which pitted the demands of public order against individual rights and liberties may not have been new to him, but the particular French situation, which brought them into play over the question of prostitution, was.

Why had Raf given him this particular set of clippings? Was he simply trying to fill James in on a set of concerns which had preoccupied him in this last while? Or did he think that the whole prostitution question really was somehow linked to Olympe's death. He tried to ease himself into his brother's mind. He had to acknowledge it was now quite foreign to him.

The most obvious relation between Olympe's death and these articles was that she had been picked up by the police and following the shame of the event had taken her own life. But even with his small knowledge, he didn't think Olympe was a character to be so easily cowed.

Perhaps Raf suspected, without quite admitting it to himself, that Olympe had — when she was still Rachel — been somehow linked to the prostitute's underworld, that some figure from the past had come back to haunt her, even perhaps some crooked policeman who threatened her with exposure in her newfound fame. A struggle had ensued and Olympe had met her death. To build up such a case, to locate a possible suspect, would mean tracking back through Olympe's life. The girl, Louise Boussel, would be a help in that, which was probably why Raf was so keen to interview her.

James returned to his reading. There were more stories of police harassment. Beside one which detailed an actress's complaint about summary arrest by the vice squad while returning late one night from the theatre, he found a row of asterisks, so savagely scratched into the page, that the paper had been torn. In that tear, he felt Raf's emotion, as surely as if the marks had been ripped into his skin.

The ache still with him, he leafed through more pages, hurriedly now, stopping only when a headline about a shopgirl caught his eye. As he read the poignant story of this young woman, she took on the form and face of the shy little milliner they had interviewed that afternoon. He could see her walking home in the rain after a long day's work, could feel the edge of tiredness which made her slow her steps, pause, only to find herself approached by an ordinary man, suited, soft-spoken, who offered to accompany her in the darkness. In her sweet, naïve way, the girl accepted. Better the protection of company, than this solitary trek through the night streets.

Some ten minutes along the way, she finds herself charged with soliciting out-of-bounds and without the necessary licence by this policeman in plain clothes. She protests her innocence, but is nonetheless manhandled and arrested, subjected to some thirty-six hours in the company of lewd women who rail against her for taking away their legitimate trade, who tell her she is worse than a whore. The next day, she suffers the mortification of a sanitary examination which she experiences as tantamount to rape. She cannot forget the indignity of this even when she is released with a clean bill of health. When she tells her boyfriend the story, he flays her with suspicion, takes on all the punishing ferocity of the police. Two days later, her body is fished out of the canal.

His mind reeling, James went to lie on the bed. His hands were clammy. His thoughts moved into prohibited realms of their own volition. He didn't want to remember that shameful episode, nor its dire aftermath. But the scenes burst upon him with all their original force, like storm clouds that had hovered too long.

He was on his honeymoon. So long ago. Over a decade. Had been on his honeymoon for some two weeks already. With Maisie. Maisie with her blonde delicacy and those long-lashed gentle eyes which looked up at him with innocent admiration. Fourteen days, the last four of which had been here in Paris. He had so wanted to introduce Maisie to the city he remembered so fondly. The family had spent part of his sixteenth year here, a protracted holiday his father had long promised himself and them. James had adored the city, had woken to manhood amidst its sights and smells, its dense history and bizarre particularities. His French had been laid down in those months, together with a host of impressions he now wanted to share with Maisie.

They were staying in a hotel on the Place Vendôme. Maisie loved the hotel, liked Paris, too, in a way, liked it with a girlish excitement which animated her features. She chattered enthusiastically, clinging to his arm with something like fervour as they promenaded through the bustle of the boulevards and took in the sights. Yet, she was also uncomfortable, dismayed by the unfamiliarity of it all, the thick texture of this alien environment.

Like a heavy grid, her responses had overlain his own earlier ones, so that his youthful devotion to the city grew shrouded, could no longer be recaptured. It was almost as if the Paris he remembered so vividly had disappeared into some subterranean vault to which he could no longer find the key.

But to be altogether exact, the problem hadn't been with the city. It lay elsewhere, in more intimate, more elusive spheres. Everytime he tried to approach Maisie at night, she would tremble with animal fear, her face a mute plea, so that any performance of conjugal rites became an impossibility. He minded more than he liked to admit and as the days passed he sensed that Maisie minded too, but differently. She would rather he never approached her again.

Her cheeks lost their brightness. She would shudder slightly if he walked into her room and caught her unawares. At last he determined that he would somehow make it plain that they need not think of all that, not yet, not now. One afternoon when Maisie was resting, having pleaded one of the headaches which had begun to plague her, he had gone for a walk and come upon a milliner's where she had admired a hat seen in the window. He stepped in. He would surprise Maisie with a present which would bring a light into her face.

Inside, a young woman greeted him. She had wide eyes, not unlike Maisie's, and she smiled at him shyly when he asked if she might try the hat for him. It looked fetching atop her high-piled curls. She offered to try some others for him, turning this way and that with light movements, so that he could see the different models from various perspectives. Each time she cast him demure, lingering looks, which sought his confirmation. Each time he gave it openly, increasingly aware of the freshness of her skin, the nimble motion of her quick hands as she edged a hat just so, the light scent of lemon that came from her. At the end he couldn't make up his mind. The hats had become like so many images in a kaleidoscope, their shapes and colours fragmented, merging, though her eyes and the fine line of her cheek remained clear. Finally he opted for the first one, dimly remembering that it was the one Maisie had liked.

When she handed him the box, she looked at him directly and asked whether perhaps he might like her to show him a little of Paris. She finished at eight. There was a ball at the Moulin de la Galette he might enjoy. It was all the fashion.

James left with a flush in his cheeks and with no intention of returning. But two evenings later, after Maisie had pleaded headache and fatigue and urged him out, he had somehow strayed in the direction of the shop. The young woman was just leaving. She had remembered him and with a delicious smile, had walked with him and accepted his stumbling offer of a drink.

One thing had led to another and after the bonhomie of the café concert, he had found himself in her tiny room in the Marais. He could still visualize its impeccable neatness, the bouquet of white blossom he had bought her bright on the blue-covered table with its two chairs, the divan which had shuddered slightly beneath their joint weight, the smooth arch of her neck on the striped bolster. She had made it all so easy. Yet he was ravaged by guilt.

He had left money hidden behind the lamp on the mantlepiece and told himself he would never return. Despite himself, he did.

It was as if Maisie was colluding with his worst instincts. Her vacillating health seemed to propel him out into the seductions of the Paris evenings where the summer air buffeted him like a pillow, warm with a sleepy sensuousness which lulled his conscience. Time and again, like a dreamer, he found himself in front of the millinery shop, where a softly smiling Yvette slipped her arm through his and led him off into a world where he was himself and not quite himself. It had gone on for the four remaining weeks of the Paris stay. And as the train which would take Maisie and him to London for another stage of their honeymoon pulled out of the station, he had waved a goodbye of mingled regret and relief to the city which held a part of him he never wished to meet again.

On their return to Boston, he looked back on the episode with a shuddering horror and buried it deep inside himself. If sometimes the traces of its fragrance caught him unaware on a lingering summer's evening, he forced his mind onto other paths. He and Maisie had all their lives to build and he loved her. Loved her with a kind of fraternal protectiveness which waited for her to blossom into a woman. Five years passed before she did and the consequences made him wish she hadn't. Passion was dangerous. His uncontrolled manhood was dangerous.

James leapt off the bed and found himself in the bathroom scrubbing his face and hands as if he wanted to peel off a layer of skin to find the pristine man within. He looked in the small mirror and saw a mask of unflappable health which seemed to bear no relation to him. There was an injustice in that which no laws could temper.

Maisie had conceived. He sometimes thought the act had more to do with their respective mothers' constant veiled queries about grandchildren than with any shared desire on his and Maisie's part. Nonetheless, the conjugal rites had been performed and soon Maisie was with child.

She had been happy during the pregnancy. The strain had fallen away from her face to be replaced by a musing contentment. She played the piano for hours, her fingers flitting over the keys in the dance her bulging form could no longer perform. Or she sat contentedly by the fire and stared into the flames, her knitting needles clicking out an unstoppable rhythm. Then in the seventh month of her pregnancy, she had tripped and tumbled down the long row of stairs in the Beacon Hill house.

James had come home from the office to find a grave Dr. Bradley waiting for him. He reported the accident, told him Maisie was well. There was a broken leg, which he had set and which would mend. He had given Maisie something calming. He averted his eyes. Tragically the baby had been born too soon. Born dead.

He tried to keep James from the bedroom, but James had rushed up past him. Maisie was lying there ashen-faced. She was staring at a tiny cocooned form at her side, its eyes closed, never to open. James took her hand.

'I wanted to keep her. Just for a little while,' she stammered.

They were the only words she spoke to him for the next weeks. No matter how much he tried to hide his own sadness, to distract her with stories of his doings or the gossip about friends she normally loved, she merely lay there, enveloped in a profound muteness. When she emerged from silence, it was to cry, great heaving tears in the midst of which she asked him to forgive her. It tore at his heart.

It was then that Yvette suddenly, abruptly, randomly leapt into his mind. He knew this was his punishment.

He took time off from his legal practice to spend it with Maisie. She chatted to him now, lightly, evenly, about nothing in particular, a distracted gaiety in her voice. It was clear she was trying to please him and he gave her his pleasure and his attention, as well as little daily gifts, chocolates, trinkets, even a puppy, though he was all too aware that nothing could make up for the loss. And all through those weeks, he knew. He knew she was dying. He also realized he had never loved her so much.

Two months later, she was dead, her face still a mere girl's, a sculptured paleness against the deep gold of her hair. Just before the end, she had looked him in the eyes and said, 'I don't mind, Jim. You see, I was never really meant to . . . meant to grow up.'

He had grasped her hand and felt like a murderer.

With an angry, abrupt gesture, James collected all the articles he had scattered and heaped them back into a single pile. He stared out into what was now an empty square. Against his will, he populated it with thoughts of those distant years. Wisps of memory like gossamer, trailing shadows wherever they flew. He had refused himself such reminiscences for so long now, that their repressed emotion leapt out at him with the force of cannon fire. It left its imprint on the calloused skin he had grown to defend himself.

Through the blur his moist eyes made of the square, it came to him that his widower's weeds had become like one of those suits of armour worn by knights of yore, so cumbersome that even his sense of himself had begun to disappear beneath its weight. Yes, he had buried a part of himself with Maisie, who had died for him, while the rest determinedly went off to lose itself in the details of work and responsibility.

His shoulders heaved with the sadness and guilt of it. As he finally stretched out on the bed, it occurred to him that even if it paled beside what was due to Maisie, he owed a debt to Yvette, too. He had no knowledge of her fate, though Raf's clippings had given him a greater sense of the dangers of the world she inhabited.

His eyes played over the shadowy ceiling. Throughout those months of Maisie's dying, he remembered, Ellie had been a brick. She had sat by Maisie's bedside, had chatted, cajoled, or been silent as need demanded.

She had fetched drinks and library books. She had read aloud for hours. She had never before been so close to Maisie, nor indeed, for a long time to him.

Elinor understood about pain. He hoped Raf was with her now.

SIX

Except for the bars on its ground-floor windows and its dilapidated façade, Saint-Lazare had the aspect of a convent or, at worst, of an old and stately, civic building. Its name, too, was misleading. The prison stood on the Faubourg Saint-Denis far closer to the Gare de l'Est than to the station which bore its saint's name. It housed some 12,000 women — many of them as Raf sardonically put it, women of easy virtue.

The harsh irony stayed in his face as he pointed to the words inscribed above the arched entrance: Liberté, Egalité, Fraternité.

'Not much of that for the ladies incarcerated here, eh Jim?'

'No, but the ideal is worth upholding.'

'I dare say.' Raf shot him a querulous glance, which made James aware that his words must have come out with a pomposity he didn't feel.

It was odd how, whatever his intentions, he always ended up by wrong-footing it with Raf. This morning they had already argued over Ellie and then Olympe. James had probably put too much insistence in his voice when he had said that before they went any further, they really had to get a clear picture of Olympe's past — her past before Raf had met her. Raf had countered by saying that Jim was beginning to sound like a French investigative magistrate: get the low-down on a life and a past and you immediately know whether a person is guilty or innocent, whatever the facts of the case. Squalid beginnings, criminal ends. Bad blood, alcoholism, crime, wending their way uncontrollably down the inherited line towards the ultimate cesspit. Bye, bye, free will.

James hadn't bothered to argue. He sensed that Raf's vehement exaggeration of a position James might have taken in a measured way was partly to do with the fact that he had been thinking along the same lines, but didn't like to admit it. Or have it served up as an incontestable truth by his older brother. In any case, by then they had arrived, and had to confront guards, fill in forms, shamble down corridors.

The infirmary took up a wing of the building and housed both sick prison inmates and prostitutes who had been sent here for a cure after their enforced sanitary examination. As well as hapless girls picked off the street.

James had an impression of a sea of filthy beds stretching towards an infinite horizon. A billowing nun surfaced from amongst them like a storm cloud to block their passage. The weight of her wimple seemed to have turned all her features downward so that they took on a punishing severity. With thin-lipped terseness, she asked them their business. James let Raf work his charm and surveyed the women.

Some lay on their beds, their expressions cowed, their eyes half-closed, somehow slumbering in what was an echoing din of sound. Others perched in little groups on the beds' edges, their mouths moving, their faces sharp, combative. In their dirty, shapeless smocks, it was hard to distinguish them from one another.

A hundred eyes watched Raf and James as they trailed behind the nun. An occasional hiss or a raucous laugh accompanied their passage. One woman, perhaps emboldened by the massed presence of her mates, tugged at James's sleeve. Mistaking them for doctors, several shouted for attention only to be harshly silenced by the matron.

'Louise Boussel,' she suddenly called out in a stentorian voice. There was a rustle in a bed James had thought empty and a thin, pallid face peered out from beneath a blanket.

'Oui.' The word was barely audible.

'De la visite,' the nun declaimed in disapproval.

Louise stared at them with visible incomprehension.

Raf smiled and presented her with the box of pastries they had brought. As she opened it timidly, her eyes grew wide. A hand reached up to put some order into lank, dark locks. All the while, voices beckoned from other beds and exhorted her to keep some patisserie for them.

Raf encouraged the girl to eat, saying it would make a change from infirmary gruel. Only then did he mention Rachel Arnhem.

The girl sat up straighter in her bed. Her cheeks took on a tinge of excited colour. 'Oh, it's so kind of Rachel to send you to see me. I didn't know anyone had told her I was . . . well, I was here.' A look of shame flitted across her face. 'We had such a nice lunch together last week. Only last week. It feels so long ago now. Are you . . . ?' She looked directly at Raf. 'Are you the man Rachel . . . ? I should really call her Olympe, shouldn't I? Are you the agent she said might be able to find me work in the theatre? I can sew anything, you know. Anything. Any kind of costume. I used to make Rachel's. In the early days when . . .' She stopped herself.

Like a wolf, a woman from a neighbouring bed had loped behind them and was rooting in the pastry box, stuffing a cake into her mouth. A chorus of mingled boos and cheers attended her act.

James met Raf's eyes. If they were to tell Louise about Olympe, they couldn't do so here.

Spying a white-coated man cross the room, James rushed over. He introduced himself with his full credentials, Professor J.A. Norton from Harvard. He insisted that they really must have a quieter space in which to speak to Louise Boussel. It was important.

The man examined him with a slow, speculative gaze. He had a round, fleshy face, not uncongenial, except for the florid pucker at his brow.

'Dr. Henri Comte.' He bowed slightly. 'I'll see what I can do.' He waved to a passing lay nurse, who smoothed her white apron as she approached. 'Show this gentleman and Louise Boussel to the second cubicle, Mademoiselle,' he said authoritatively, and then turned back to James. 'What exactly is your relationship to Louise Boussel, Monsieur Norton?'

It sounded like an accusation and James heard himself saying, 'Cousins. We are cousins.'

Comte nodded a little dubiously. 'So she has been keeping secrets from her family and now they are out in the open . . . You might give her a little lesson in morality, Monsieur. Though perhaps leaving her here' — he waved his arm in an expansive arc — 'rather than taking her to a, shall we say, more genteel cure may be lesson enough. Good morning, Monsieur.'

The man clearly suspected him of having relations with Louise. Despite a shudder of guilt mingled with distaste, James hurried after him. 'How much longer will Louise's treatment take, Dr. Comte?'

'Point her out to me. Oh, yes. That section over there have another five days. If she can take the nervous strain and is strong enough to resist secondary infection, there is really no good reason to move her now. It would entail not a little negotiation with the police.' He gave James a meaningful look, then rushed off, brisk despite the shortness of his legs.

The cubicle was airless, but at least the noise had receded to a background hum. Louise sat on the shaky stool, her thin shoulders hunched. She gasped as she heard Raf's stammering announcement of Olympe's death and the reason for their visit.

'I can't believe it, Monsieur. I can't take it in. Not Rachel.' Sobbing took her over.

'How was she when you last saw her?' Raf asked softly.

'She was well. She was happy. Full of plans,' she stifled a moan. 'For me, too.'

'And that was on what day?' James interjected.

'Monday. Yes, a week ago Monday.'

Before she could begin crying again, James asked, 'Did she say anything at all to you which might indicate that something was troubling her? Think carefully now.'

The girl looked up at him with tear-laden eyes. She shook her head. 'We just caught up. Caught up on news. We hadn't met for a while. She told me about the little ones. Juliette is doing well, very well. Rachel is so proud of her. She wants her to train for a . . . well, a proper job. You know, Rachel and I, we went to school together. We go back a long way. I know her family.'

'So there was nothing at all that was upsetting her?' James persisted, only to feel Raf poke him in the ribs for his leading questions.

A frown creased the girl's forehead. 'Well, I'm not sure. There was something, though Rachel laughed about it. It was just a . . . a sensation.'

'About what?' James urged her on gently.

Her hands played with the coarse smock, folding its material into tiny pleats. She glanced up at Raf and in that look James was suddenly aware that she now knew who Raf was, that Rachel must have mentioned him to her friend, perhaps done more than merely mention.

James repeated his query.

'There was this man. So long ago, I can barely remember him. We were only sixteen. Maybe seventeen. It was soon after Rachel's mother died. He was much older. He wanted to marry her.'

'What was his name?' Raf's voice was a hiss. James threw him a stern look.

Louise shook her head. She looked frightened. 'I . . . I don't remember.'

'It doesn't matter,' James said. 'He wanted to marry Rachel?'

'Yes. He wanted to look after her, I think. He was . . . well . . . older. I only met him once or twice. He didn't speak much. He had big features and his skin was all pock-marked. Anyhow Rachel didn't want to get married. She refused him.'

'And then?'

'Nothing really. Well, they moved soon after that. We didn't see each other so much.'

'But this man had come back into her life?'

'Oh no, Monsieur,' she threw Raf a sidelong glance. 'No, no. Not like that. She'd had a letter from him. That's all. Or maybe he'd come once to the theatre. I had the impression she wasn't altogether pleased to see him. She gave me a ticket, too, you know. To come and see her. And then this happened . . . they put me in here.' A look of disgust covered her face. She crumpled the smock material into a tight ball.

'But you'll be cured soon,' James offered softly.

'Yes, yes.' Her eyes filled with tears again. 'Poor Rachel. She can't be cured. There is no justice in the world, is there, Messieurs!'

James waited for a moment. 'When did Rachel change her name?'

Louise looked beyond them, as if a window had been cut into the bare wall. 'I'm not sure exactly. I think someone, a friend, told her a different name would sound better on the stage. When we met up again, after they'd moved. It was a good year later, maybe more. Anyhow, she'd already invented it then. Olympe . . . it comes from a picture someone said she looked like.' The girl paused. 'Isak . . . that was the man's name. I remember now.'

She suddenly looked like a girl of no more than sixteen, all triumph and grief and wide-eyed perplexity bundled up together in a slight form.

'Isak. You don't remember a second name?'

She shook her head. 'I don't think I knew it.'

'But Olympe's father would know.' Raf muttered. He was already reaching for his hat.

'Oh, yes. Of course. It was an offer of marriage,' Louise said gravely.

They walked her back to her bed. The box lay on it spread-eagled, a lone pastry left in its depths like a superstitious offering.

After the rank closeness of the infirmary, the sky had a wondrous height. Without needing to consult, they strolled, breathing in the welcome air, each of them reflecting separately on what they had learned. When they passed a patisserie, Raf wanted to go in to have more cakes delivered to Louise. James dissuaded him. It seemed more sensible to wait until she got home, when at least she could share them with dear ones, rather than provoking the jealous hostility of the other inmates. For once, Raf acceded. He was suddenly in a hurry.

'We must go and see Arnhem.'

'Not now, Raf. It'll wait.'

'What do you mean, it'll wait. This Isak, if he's had anything to do with Olympe's death, won't wait.'

'We don't know that Arnhem will have any inkling of where to find him.'

'More than we have.'

James hesitated. 'It's the Sabbath.'

'Olympe never . . .'

'But her father may. And we must go and see Ellie. You didn't last night. Where were you anyway?'

Raf waved his arm vaguely and then more purposefully to hail a passing cab. 'I'm a working man, you know. I had some matters to attend to. Look, we'll go via Arnhem's. I'll just pop up for a moment, ask him, and then we'll carry on.' He instructed the driver before James could stop him.

James lowered his voice. 'I want to go through some things with you — having read all the material you left for me yesterday.'

'Shoot.'

'If I'm following your thinking correctly, you're definitely ruling out suicide and imagining that Olympe was murdered in one of four ways.'

'Four? Did I enumerate them?

'No, but I did.' James counted the possibilities on his fingers. 'One. There's a killer on the loose who targets solitary women. Women he probably thinks are prostitutes. Two. This killer is somehow linked to or is a member of the morality police. Three, the killer not only targets women alone — but Jewish women alone. Therefore the killings aren't random. The man knows who they are, knows their origins. He's a racist, either with a direct gripe or a political one, if the two are separable. Four. There is no link whatsoever between any of the deaths cited in the papers and Olympe's. Any or each of them was a separate unrelated affair.'

Raf was staring at him with a bemused expression.

James carried on. 'And now we have five: Olympe's death may be the result of a crime of passion, committed by a rejected suitor. So which of these possibilities do we pursue first?'

'Your implacable logic does me in, Jim. We pursue all the possibilities, of course.' His voice rose. 'Olympe isn't a case, for me. Some cipher subject to law 400 or 2002. She's Olympe. Wonderful, irreplaceable Olympe. You must understand that. You've been there, after all. In your own way.'

James didn't answer immediately. He stared out the window. They were driving along the street they had walked just two nights ago. In the sunlight, it looked tawdrier, but less frightening. The bars had a fatigue about them, their energies spent in the night. Rubbish lay scattered in the unkempt streets. Children kicked bits of it in desultory games. A woman with a plain, unpainted face and broad hips smacked a little boy on the bottom. He burst into a howl.

James sighed. 'I'm sorry if my logic offends you, Raf. But if we're going to get anywhere, be any more useful than Durand — whom you've probably been too hard on — I suggest we split up the territory. Rationalize our efforts. Touquet is evidently an expert on the vice police. Get him to sniff around there. See if any of them knew Olympe, for whatever reason. And so on. You — well, judging from your Dreyfus articles, you must have contacts aplenty amongst the patriotic and anti-Semitic leagues . . .'

Raf nodded.

'Hang out with them a bit. See if anything smells like a lead. You remember you said there were demos, rioting on the day that deputy was acquitted. That was a Thursday, wasn't it — the last time Olympe was seen. Maybe, just maybe, she got caught up in something unpleasant.'

Raf shivered. 'All right. What about you?'

'Well, I guess that leaves me to probe Olympe's past and present.' He put out a hand to stay Raf's protests. 'In a way, it makes more sense, Raf. I'm not involved. Also my French is better in one-on-ones.'

'I'll work with you.' Raf's flare of jealousy was unguarded.

'Fine. The first thing you can do is take me to her rooms. I need to get a sense of her.'

Arnhem wasn't in. After leaving a note, they carried on towards the Boulevard Malesherbes. James wondered at his own surge of relief as their vehicle moved into more decorous streets. Here was the Paris of dream and history, with its spacious boulevards, its elegant women and dapper men, its majestic buildings a stage set for the theatre of everyday life. This was the Paris the newspapers lauded in their evocation of the *belle époque*. But there was nothing beautiful about the underbelly of the city. It festered in poverty and gave off a distinct aroma of menace.

He let his eyes play over the fresh green of the plane trees, their dappled bark, and for a moment he was overcome by a nostalgia for the gentle roll of the Massachusetts countryside with its dense colour, the simplicity of the pursuits it fostered. Yet he had to admit to himself that he had woken this morning with a sense of new energy, a kind of lucidity which had too often eluded him in these last years.

A woman stepped gracefully from a stationary carriage. Long, gloved fingers rose to adjust a hat. Madame de Landois came into his mind. He must arrange to see her soon. There were things she would be able to tell him about Olympe that would almost certainly have eluded his brother-in-love.

For once the curtains were wide open in Ellie's apartment. So too were the doors to the terrace. Motes of dust paraded in the sunlight as if relieved to be allowed to fly. Harriet Knowles ushered them in with her direct gaze. 'Elinor will be so pleased. You'll join us for lunch, of course.'

James nodded, aware that Raf might demure.

'I'll alert Violette. You'll find Elinor on the terrace.' She met Raf's eyes for a moment, then looking away with the swiftness of veiled disapproval, she strode towards the kitchen.

'Is that my dear elder brother I hear?' Ellie's melodious voice reached them as they made their way through the room.

'You do.'

'And my oh so remiss younger one. Well Raf, it has been an age. You'd think we were divided by an ocean rather than a corridor.' She fixed Raf with her dark eyes. James could feel him wriggling like a butterfly about to be pinned in a collector's cabinet.

'I've been busy, Ellie. Preoccupied.' He patted her on the shoulder.

Poised in her wheelchair, so that she could take in the trees and the placid activity of the street, Ellie looked for all the world as if she were at the seaside. She was wearing a fresh blue-striped dress with a row of tiny buttons at the bodice. Beneath the straw hat, which protected her from the terrace sunshine, her hair was newly coiffed. Her fine aquiline nose trembled a little in response to Raf's comment.

Sensing danger, James interceded. 'You're feeling better, Ellie. I'm so pleased.'

'Yes Jimmy, as you can see.' She gestured grandly towards the cumbrous mass of the chair. 'I'm about, if not altogether up. Harriet has been a veritable ministering angel. She's cheered me no end.'

The woman had come up silently beside them. Her face was grave.

'But it isn't time for cheer, is it Raf?' Ellie's tone grew soft. 'I'm so sorry. So very sorry. Olympe was such a rare being. I can't bring myself to accept it.' Tears moistened her eyes. She pulled a handkerchief from her sleeve. 'She shouldn't have done it. If anyone . . . it should have been me.'

'Stop it, Ellie.' Raf was brusque. He turned away abruptly.

James saw Harriet cast a bitter look at his back.

'There's no crime in suicide, whatever the clerics say.' Ellie's voice rang a challenge after him, 'I've thought about it a great deal. After all, we're born without being consulted. Why consult at the other end?'

'Hush, Ellie.'

'Help me in, Harriet. I can't get used to manoeuvering this blasted contraption.' She crushed the chair's weight against a rail as she tried to turn it round, then waved her hand in irritation.

'We should have the men move some of the furniture back against the walls. It would give you more space,' Harriet soothed.

'That's a splendid idea.' James was already through the door, repositioning one armchair, then a second, creating an aisle. The encased bird met his eye. 'What if we clear the surface of this table, as well, Ellie?'

She wasn't listening. She was calling after Raf who had preceded them. There was a glimmer of fear on her face. The front door slammed.

James had the impression he had walked in on a relationship he no longer understood. What was it that had set his younger siblings at odds? He caught Harriet's gaze. She seemed to be signalling something he couldn't make out.

He remembered the present he had left on the hall table and rushed to fetch it. 'A little token, Ellie. I thought you might like it.'

Her eyes fell on him from a distance of miles. 'You are a dear one, Jim.' Her fingers pulled ineptly at string until at last the box he had purchased for her in the Arcades lay revealed. 'Oh, it's lovely. Look, Harriet. All these secret drawers. What shall I hide away in them?'

They watched her, like parents wary of an unpredictable child.

As suddenly as he had left, Raf reappeared. He held a bottle of wine in one hand, a package in the other. 'And here's something else, sister mine. For our days out in the Bois de Boulogne.'

Ellie looked up at him. 'Oh, I hope we will go, Raf. I do hope so.' Her voice fluttered, hiding a tremor.

'We will. Never fear.' Raf was making a great show of uncorking the bottle. 'And meanwhile, a little of this red in our veins won't do any harm. What do you say, Harriet?'

Harriet smiled for the first time, revealing a row of strong teeth. 'I say we can go in to lunch.'

Elinor was pulling on the gloves. 'Perfect. So clever of you to get the right size.'

'Thank Jim, Ellie. He seems to have become an expert.'

James saw Ellie's face tighten, but she was gracious. 'Yes, perfect. Thank you, Jim. All I need now is a parasol. And a new pair of legs.' Her laugh teetered, reminiscent of a sob.

The dining room gave out onto the gloom of a narrow courtyard. Burgundy curtains arched the windows. A stiff white cloth covered the mahogany of an overlarge rectangular table set with gold-rimmed china. On an expanse of sideboard, which reminded James of the Boston family home, Violette had spread an assortment of cold meats, cheeses, breads and condiments. A small bowl of pinks and lily-of-the-valley sat like a breath of fresh hope in the midst of the dark stolidity. James sniffed Harriet's hand in their choice.

He wondered at the change the woman had wrought in Ellie in so short a span and he smiled at her in gratitude. He would have to take her aside and speak to her about his sister's condition. She would, he was certain, be full of the good sense his siblings seemed to have left behind like forgotten tools, so that the construction of their daily lives had gone seriously awry. That reminded him that he must write to his mother as soon as he got back to the hotel.

Violette served them, James first, then Raf, then Ellie, and finally Harriet, as if she had intuited her place in an unspoken hierarchy. James tried to remember what he knew about the Knowles family, but came up with a blank. Ellie's animated voice overrode his thinking. Her cheeks had grown flushed with the effort or pleasure of gaiety. She was in control again, entertaining them as she was wont to do in Boston when friends and family gathered.

'Harriet's been reading to me, you know. She's afraid I may grow stupid and cease to be good company for her.'

'That's not true, Elinor,' Harriet demurred.

'True enough. When you arrived, she was reading to me from *Le Figaro.* President Loubet is apparently recovering well from his attack at the races by that demented aristocrat. Canes aren't killing implements, it seems. Only a passing injury for "the synagogues' candidate" — did you know that's what they call him, Jim? Bet Raf never put that into one of his articles.' She laughed. 'I wonder whether the attack will make Loubet a fiercer Republican or still his ardour. He really shouldn't have chosen the day of Zola's return from exile to go to the races. You know he was never elected by the populace, Jim? The senate and the assembly stitched it together, after old Faure croaked in the arms of his mistress. Quite a country, isn't it? Rather more eventful than our staid Mr. McKinley. They've had more governments here in the last years than I think I've known in my entire lifetime at home.'

'Don't exaggerate, Ellie.' Raf emptied his glass.

'I know. All this heated democracy is rather more exciting for you journalists. Everyone takes you so seriously, too. Almost as seriously as the politicians themselves.'

'That may not be so different,' James said. 'Mr. Hearst managed to engineer quite a fuss over the Cuban war. Anyhow, you'll be home in quieter spheres soon enough, Ellie.'

'Are you going to bundle us all up, Jim? Put us in your cabin trunk? Better, I guess, than a coffin.' She stopped herself, stole a glance at Raf.

'Do have some more of this beef, Mr. Norton.' Harriet covered over for her.

'I will, thank you.' James helped himself.

'There was an article about Olympe, too. A very nice piece. Heartfelt. About the tragedy of her suicide.' Ellie seemed unable to stop herself.

'Where?' Raf leapt up from the table.

'Don't be rude, Raf,' Ellie snapped. 'It'll wait for coffee. There's nothing there you don't know already.' She calmed herself. 'It was about her career, her wonderful talent. She was wonderful, Jim. I wish you had been able to see her on the stage. And she sang . . . she sang like an angel. An Italian angel — the very best contralto. It was astonishing. She was quite delicate.'

'I wish I had known her.'

Raf had stopped eating. *'Le Figaro* said suicide?'

Ellie nodded. 'I think so too, Raf. You didn't know her as I did.'

'Didn't I?' Raf's lips were so stiff, the words seemed to come from somewhere else.

'She had a deep melancholy about her. A kind of inner pessimism. We women talk to each other about things. And I did know her well — and well before you.'

Raf sprang from his seat with the speed of an arrow propelled from its bow. As he raced towards the front room, he cast Ellie a look of bitter hostility.

'You do goad him, Elinor. There's no need,' Harriet murmured.

'But he's partly to blame. And he won't face it.'

'Why is he to blame?' James asked.

Ellie looked at him as if he were a stranger who had asked an impertinent question.

'He shouldn't have led her to think of marriage. It was altogether impossible. She wasn't one of us. It confused her.' She was staring out the window, seeing things that were invisible to him.

'And you know he did?' The notion troubled him. He hadn't gone that far in his thoughts.

Ellie nodded once, almost imperceptibly, then slumped suddenly into her chair as if all her musculature had given out.

'I'm tired, Harriet. I think, I really think I should lie down.' She smiled sweetly at James. 'You'll forgive me, Jim. Violette will serve you dessert. And do tell Raf, when he calms down, to come and see me later.'

Harriet wheeled her from the room, while James sat and took in the wreckage of their meal. The destruction seemed to have gone deeper than that. Ellie and Raf were at war and it was evidently a battle that preceded recent events. Was it her standing out against him on the question of marriage to Olympe that had made Raf so irascible? Yet he must see her side, the family's side. And he had always been so patient with Ellie, so solicitous of her needs, far more generous than James himself towards her eccentricities and her directness. He remembered when they all still lived at home, that Raf's first point of call on returning from school was always Ellie. They would read books together, pass them between each other, talk or sit silently in each other's company, play complicated word games. And later too, when Raf was at Harvard, he would bring his friends home to meet the sister he so patently admired, depended on, almost as if she were a twinned soul in a body of the opposite sex.

A knock at the front door intruded on his thoughts. He heard women's voices, Violette's and another, speaking French, and then Violette's quick step. 'Monsieur Rafael?' her voice sounded.

James got up, saw the blowsy form of Raf's housekeeper at the entrance and Raf himself following her across the corridor. With a guilty look at the table behind him and a sense of his own bad manners, he quickly went after them.

Raf's apartment was the mirror image of Elinor's, yet James felt he might have travelled to a different planet. Where Ellie's was a dense hive of curios and bric-a-brac, patterned rugs, brocades and velvets, here light and air poured from curtainless windows onto gleaming parquet and the barest essentials of furniture. A single large painting in dabs of almost garish colour dominated the space, though for the moment its drama was shrouded by Monsieur Arnhem.

He was pacing the bright emptiness of the room as if it were Lear's blasted heath. His eyes were haunted, darting this way and that in search of invisible objects. His shaggy eyebrows moved dramatically, accompanying unspoken speech. When they greeted him, he stopped with the abruptness of a man caught out in perfidious thoughts.

He bowed in their direction. 'So sorry to intrude like this.'

Raf waved aside his apologies. 'You had my note?'

'Note?' Incomprehension played over Arnhem's gaunt face. He shook his grizzled head. 'I . . . I came because . . . what was in your note?'

'Let's sit down Monsieur Arnhem. Arlette, bring some coffee for everyone.' Raf addressed the woman whose eyes James had still not been able to meet. At least she wasn't holding the babe today.

Arnhem perched at the edge of the proffered chair and eyed them warily. 'Has there been some news from Chief Inspector Durand? One of his men came to see me yesterday. His questions were perfunctory. It seemed to me they wanted to draw a line under Rachel's death.'

'No, no.' Raf was adamant. He met James's eyes for a moment as if to signal an 'I told you so'. 'We won't let that happen. I wanted to see you because in speaking to an old friend of Olympe's . . . of Rachel's, she mentioned that a man called Isak had suddenly turned up in Rachel's life again after many years. Rachel wasn't pleased. She felt threatened.'

James stopped himself from intervening. Raf was putting words into Louise's mouth. This time he was leading the witness.

'Isak?' Arnhem looked into the distance. He met his own face in the mirror over the mantle and as if he had confronted an unwanted double, he swerved away. 'You mean Isak Bernfeld. No, no.' The man eyed them in visible confusion and then like a tortoise withdrew into the shelter of his jacket collar.

'Yes, Isak Bernfeld. Isak Bernfeld,' Raf repeated to etch the name in his mind.

'Isak moved to Toulouse many years ago.' It was a mumble.

'Well, it seems he's back. Rachel wasn't happy about it.'

'You say she felt threatened by him . . . Who told you this?' There was a sudden edge of anger in Arnhem's voice. 'Are these her new friends casting doubts, vilifying an old friend of the family? Is that it?'

Arnhem moderated the shrill rise of his tone. 'What I mean to say is that Rachel may not have wanted to . . . to link her future to Isak's, but she agreed that he was a good man. Isak is . . . how do you say . . . a traditional man. He wished to protect her, to look after her. But to feel threatened by him . . . that is not in his nature. Nor hers.'

'His nature to you may not be what it appeared to Olympe.' Raf grunted.

Arnhem stood up and started to pace again. James could almost follow his thoughts from the dramatic turns of his expression, the suspicious glances he cast at them. The man was astute. He had recognized as soon as Raf had mooted the word *threat* that they assumed Isak Bernfeld was somehow mixed up with Olympe's death. Which would mean that they would blame her murder on one of his own. He couldn't allow that and not only because it couldn't, in his eyes, be true. It would compound the tragedy. It would throw an even more hostile light on his community. The police would jump on it as a way of forestalling any hunt for the real criminal.

'Monsieur Arnhem,' James began in his slow, careful French. 'No one is saying that Monsieur Bernfeld is involved in Olympe's death. It is simply that he was mentioned as one of the people who had seen her, had also written to her, in recent weeks. We need to trace anyone who can give us a hint about her last days. Louise Boussel mentioned Monsieur Bernfeld and it would be useful simply to talk to him. If you have an address, we would be grateful for it.'

'You saw Louise?' Arnhem's features were still tinged with mistrust.

James nodded. 'A sweet young woman. She said Olympe had been very kind to her. She was trying to find her a new job.'

Arnhem nodded, as if that were altogether a generosity that could be expected of his daughter.

Arlette had brought in a tray with coffee. She poured it slowly, her face avid with curiosity.

'Thank you, Arlette.' Raf dismissed her and as if his own impressions had tracked those of his brother, he said in a gentler tone, 'Yes, Monsieur Arnhem, we only want to ask this Bernfeld a few simple questions about Olympe.'

'I do not have an address for him. We lost touch over the years.'

'Perhaps you have mutual contacts. Perhaps you could trace him,' James suggested. 'Everything helps, particularly if — as you imply — the police are not being overvigorous in their investigations.'

Arnhem studied them. 'I will try to locate him,' he said at last. 'I will try.' He emptied his coffee in a single gulp, seemed about to rise, and then changed his mind. A prickly silence fell over them. In it, James could feel a gulf growing to what would soon be an unbreachable expanse. He cleared his throat.

'Do, Monsieur Arnhem. Please. I know my brother did not mean to offend Monsieur Bernfeld in any way. It's only that he feels so passionately about the tragedy your daughter has suffered that his emotion seeps into impatience.

Arnhem gave him the glimmer of a yellow-toothed smile. 'This is something I understand.'

'You came here, you said, not because of the note Rafael had left you, but for another reason . . .'

Arnhem fidgeted. He seemed to be weighing something up. 'Perhaps it is not so important. Like you,' he gestured towards Raf, 'I allow myself to get carried away with suspicions. Everything, everyone becomes suspicious. When one is in a situation of weakness, of a lack of knowledge, it is perhaps inevitable.'

'So tell us your suspicions,' Raf said.

'No, no. It is nothing.'

'It was enough to make you come here, damn it. It must be something.' Raf suddenly banged his fist on the table. 'Look, Arnhem. We're on your side. All this shilly-shallying is just a waste of time. If you can't trust me and my brother here, forget it. There's no-one you can trust. I'm not even a bloody Frenchman. Olympe trusted me. She introduced me to you. If your own daughter's not enough of a recommendation, I don't know what is.'

A twinkle appeared in Arnhem's eye only to disappear as quickly, as if for a moment in Raf's heated declaration, he had forgotten the situation.

'All right. I will tell you. But now as I think about it here' — he looked round the large, bright room with its polished floors, its sparsity of furniture — 'I have the feeling it is just ramblings. It is something my daughter said.'

'You mean little Juliette?' Raf intervened.

'No, no. Not Juliette. Judith.'

'Judith?' Perplexity settled on Raf's face.

'Yes, Judith. My eldest daughter. You have not met her, I imagine.'

It was clear from Raf's expression that he had also never known of the existence of a Judith.

'I see.' Arnhem frowned. 'It is probably best to forget I ever mentioned any of this.'

'No, go on. Go on.' Raf leapt from his chair and walked towards the fireplace, coming back a moment later with a silver box. He offered them cigarettes, lit one quickly himself and inhaled deeply. 'Go on.'

Arnhem's frown still furrowed his brow. Pain shadowed his features. 'Yes, Judith is my eldest. She . . . she is in a hospital. The Salpêtrière.' He let the name hang as if nothing more needed to be said.

'The Salpêtrière?' James echoed, after too long a pause.

Raf crushed his barely smoked cigarette into the ashtray. 'That's an asylum, Jim. Few leave it.'

Arnhem was studying them, clearly wondering whether to say any more.

'I'm listening, Arnhem.' As if to contradict his words, Raf got up again, his long limbs visibly restless. 'Go on. I just need to move. To take this in.'

'Yes, Judith has been there for many years. Too many. I can understand that Rachel would not want to mention her to . . . to her new friends. But she was loyal to her sister. She visited her not infrequently. Judith is sometimes lucid. Often, I regret that I took her there. But at the time there seemed no other solution. I wanted to . . . to protect her. And I thought they could help her. That it would pass.'

'She tried to . . . to kill herself?' James asked.

Arnhem nodded once, abruptly. 'Several times. But don't think that Rachel . . . no . . . no, in that they are very different, whatever those doctors' theories. They are completely different. Suicide is not in the blood.'

James wanted to argue with him, but the moment was wrong. Instead he asked, 'What did Judith say to you?'

'I needed to tell her about Rachel. When I did, to put it very briefly, she said, "So they got her. They're going to get me, too. So many of our people gone." She went on in the same vein.'

'Do you know who she means by "they"?' Raf's eyes glinted like fiery coals.

Arnhem shook his head. 'No. But the only people she sees are hospital staff. Doctors, nurses . . . Or perhaps Rachel said something to her.'

'Didn't you question her more precisely?'

'It is not easy to question Judith. One just has to listen.' He shrugged. 'But as she was speaking, I believed her. I believed that her fear was real, not an imaginary one.' He rubbed his eyes as if it might help him to see better.

'Shall we go and visit her now?' James pulled his watch out of his waistcoat pocket. 'It isn't too late.'

'No, she has had enough visits for one day. She wasn't . . . what I mean is that when I left her . . . she had scuttled back into her shell of silence. It takes her by turns. We should give her a day or two. But it would be useful to interview some others. Some of the doctors, too . . . Vaillant, maybe. Monday would be best for that.' He looked beseechingly at Raf. 'They will not talk to me in the same way.'

'I don't understand how this has anything to do with Olympe's death.'

'If you'll permit me to say, Monsieur Norton . . .' Arnhem squared his shoulders and stood to his not inconsiderable height. His face took on the severity of an ancient patriarch. 'I don't understand how Isak Bernfeld has anything to do with my daughter's death either. Yet I shall try my best to discover his whereabouts for you.'

SEVEN

The house where Olympe Fabre rented a small apartment stood on one of the steeply winding streets of Montmartre which abutted on the unfinished flank of the Sacré Coeur. Remote from the hub of Paris, some of the streets of this mount of martyrs were still unpaved. Gaps between houses showed vineyards, the rise and dip of countryside and patchy waste-ground. Stout women in black hauled buckets from neighbouring wells. An occasional chicken clucked and scrambled through dust at the passage of thick-booted feet or donkey's hoofs. Young men with unsavoury expressions and large hats lounged against door jambs and smoked, at once indolent and poised for action like so many cowhands. From the late afternoon gloom of a tavern came the sound of a guitar and a baritone drawling a slang of insolent inflection.

Olympe's building stood a little apart from the poverty of its neighbours. A plaque bolted into the pale stucco boasted 'eau et gaz' — water and gas. Flower-filled boxes adorned the first-floor windows, their colour spilling out into the grime of the street.

Before they could cross the threshold, Raf pushed James back and gestured him towards the corner. 'Durand is in there. He's talking to Madame Ribot. Better to wait.'

'Why?'

James was about to object at greater length, but Raf's arm was a barricade, pinioning him into the shadows.

'He may not like us coming here,' Raf mumbled.

A moment later, they saw the policeman emerge. He walked briskly past them, his short quick steps clacking with officious determination on the cobbles. As soon as he was out of sight, they hurried back to the front door.

A heavy, gap-toothed woman in an ancient bonnet stood on the step. When she saw Raf, she shrugged and shook her equine head in consternation. 'Ah, Monsieur Norton. Quelle histoire. Voilà encore la police.' She proceeded to explain to Raf in an agitated manner, that the police had already been twice and now this man, claiming he was their chief and what did they expect to find in any case in poor Olympe's rooms. There was little enough there to begin with.

Raf consoled her, introduced James and said they'd like to go up too.

Swirling her capacious skirts, she barred their way and exclaimed that she had just been told not to let anyone up, no-one at all.

'But that could hardly include us,' Raf protested. He dug into his pocket and brought out a note which he tucked discreetly into Madame Ribot's apron. 'We're working with the Chief Inspector. And I must bid Olympe's rooms adieu, Madame Ribot.' His face took on a stricken look as his tone fell. 'You understand.'

The woman looked into Raf's handsome features and softened visibly. With a superstitious glance down the street, she nodded and whisked them towards the stairs. She breathed audibly as they climbed to the top floor and unlocked the far door. 'You won't touch anything. And no souvenirs,' she admonished Raf. 'Not because of me, mind. But the Chief Inspector . . .'

James took in the long narrow room, partitioned by a flowing muslin curtain, half drawn. One end served as a dining and sitting area, complete with a sink and a small gas ring, the other as a bedroom. The walls were unpapered. Their white-washed purity gave the space the aura of a convent, which the images they held belied. There were some garish playbills and drawings, studded here and there with a wash of blues and reds. He examined these more closely and saw that they depicted a young woman in various poses. They were executed in the modern style, almost but not quite caricatures. In all of them, whether a gloved hand arced the air or the figure lay curled on a divan, the face had a sweet serenity, a pensive seriousness which both captivated and took him aback. He hadn't imagined Olympe like this, had conjured up a more open, a more actressy appeal. The dead body had given no clues as to expression or stance or character.

'Yes, that's her.' Raf had come up behind him. His voice held a tremor. 'Come next door.'

On a mantle stood a photograph in a curving frame. The image was of a young woman, almost a girl. Her wide-set eyes were cast downward in a look of shy gravity. Lips and nose and cheekbones and hair arced in fluid harmony above the cup of her hands. Sadness haunted beauty.

His eyes strayed to the mantlepiece. It was covered in a fine grey powder. Not dust, no. He looked round. The powder clung to all flat surfaces. His mind raced. Dactyloscopy. Emile Durand was indeed versed in the latest scientific methods.

Raf had sat down on the bed's edge. His hands covered his face.

As James murmured that Durand was being thorough, he sprang up. 'Look Jim, I don't really want to be here.' His eyes were moist, his expression brooding. 'No. You stay. I've got things to do. Too many things. I've got to check out the Patriot's League. Did I tell you about Antoine. That sharp-eyed scoundrel found a charm on the ground of the metro site. It had a Hebrew character on it. Which means the girl must have been a Jewess.'

As if he still hadn't heard James, he fingered the jewellery in a small open case on the bedside table, holding up earrings to the light, rubbing a ring.

'You're not paying attention, Raf. I said Durand has had the place dusted for fingerprints. You shouldn't touch anything. Not with bare hands. Or he'll know we've been here.'

'What?' Raf clamped the box shut. 'Oh, I see. Yes, well, I'm off. Can't stomach this place now. Can't bear it without her.' He looked round him in panic, swallowed what seemed to be a sob. 'We'll meet up tomorrow some time. Or the next day.' Before James could say anything, he was out the door.

James had a sudden memory of his father admonishing him. 'You really have to look out for your little brother, James. He's spending too much time with his sister. She's stuffing his head full of poetry, silly emotional stuff. Women's stuff. Get him out into the open air. Toughen him up.'

James had patently not succeeded, despite the reputedly cold and paternal role into which he had been cast. Raf was as mercurial as ever. A disquieting sensation crept up on him, like a longing, but one that churned his stomach. It was almost as if he envied his brother his ability to feel — to feel deeply, to be swept beyond the bounds of propriety.

But there was something else about Raf's behaviour in these last days which niggled at him. He put it into words for the first time. Raf might want with all his heart to uncover the particulars of Olympe's death and to avenge it. Yet at the same time, he seemed averse to discovering anything about Olympe he didn't already know. It was unthinkable to him that a woman who possessed the good fortune of his attention, should wish to do away with herself.

Then, too, the luminous portrait he had painted in his mind mustn't be altered by fresh brush strokes. He had responded badly to Louise Boussel's mention of a past suitor. Arnhem's revelation of a second sister had been even worse. It had irritated Raf to the point that he hadn't been able to think about anything else, as if Olympe's omission constituted a veritable betrayal — not simply, in the circumstances, an understandable family secret. And now, he had fled, only to leave James alone amidst the material possessions of a mistress he had never met. But perhaps the dead urged on one a necessary blindness. The ideal had to be kept intact, now more than ever. If he understood little else about his brother, he understood that particular need. He shared it.

With a shiver of apprehension, James took a handkerchief from his pocket and carefully opened a wardrobe. A rustle of silk and cool, smooth satin met his exploring fingers. He withdrew them abruptly, as if the material burnt. He forced himself to concentrate on the base of the cupboard, edged aside shoes. No, there were no boxes hidden amongst them. With relief, he wedged the door shut. Whatever his good intentions, he felt like a peeping Tom, an interloper transgressing the limits of another's intimacy.

He looked at the portrait of Olympe and heard himself whisper an apology. Then steeling himself, he pulled open the drawers of the small dresser and finding nothing but lace and whites and a whiff of rose petals, closed them as quickly. He turned gratefully to the bedside table. Books were stacked on it. He examined their more familiar solidity one by one. There was Zola's *Bête Humaine,* a novel by Anatole France and another by a writer he didn't recognize, a few playscripts and volumes of poetry. Right at the base of the pile was a handsome leather-bound volume with gold-etched script. Shakespeare. Olympe's tastes were serious. Curious about the translation, he moved the top dusted volume aside and lifted out the bottom tome. A drawer slid out spilling letters onto the floor, some loose, some tied with blue ribbon.

This was more like it. He picked up the letters carefully. Amongst them he noticed a small notebook. He spread the lot on the bed, apologized to Olympe's captive image and perched to read.

As luck would have it, the first letters were from Raf. He scurried over their lover's heat and feeling his own face grow hot, put them to one side. He had a sudden sense of his mother, hovering at his shoulder, that look of pure Bostonian disapproval straining her haughty features. To chase her presence away, he paused to take in the atmosphere of the room again. There was a kind of peace to the place, he suddenly thought, like a nest above the fray of the streets, safe. He remembered the cramped, musty quarters the rest of her family inhabited and had an acute sense of the distance Olympe had travelled. In a way, a little like his brother, he didn't altogether want to know how she had got here, what breaches of dignity had marred her passage. It was enough to know that she had arrived.

Only to be cut off, he reminded himself. Who could have wanted to do away with this brave girl? For a moment, he was filled with the sense of a malignant presence envying Olympe her newfound height. With a shudder, he returned to the letters. He assumed that the ribbon-bound letters were sentimental in content. Lovers that preceded his brother? Perhaps. With sudden compassion, he had the urge to burn these traces before Raf could come across them. He pushed them to one side and concentrated on the loose pages — perhaps more recent since they hadn't found their place yet within a set. He noticed a leaf in strange scrawling script and pulled it to the surface. Hebrew, he decided. Perhaps from her father.

A knock at the door made him jump. Quickly, like a criminal caught in the act, he crammed what letters he could into the satchel he had used to carry Ellie's present. He smuggled the all-but-empty Shakespeare box onto the bedside table, and had almost replaced the remaining volumes when Madame Ribot bustled in.

She looked first at him, then round the room incomprehendingly. 'Where is Monsieur Norton?' she asked with a trace of anger.

'He had to go. He asked me to thank you if he didn't catch you downstairs.' James was at his most gracious.

Her face was all narrow-eyed suspicion. 'Well, you can't stay here. I don't know you.'

'I was just going.' James bowed politely.

She grumbled something, then walked heavily across the room. James saw her remove the photograph of Olympe from its frame.

'You're still standing there?' she turned on him. 'It's for the police not for me. They've sent somebody back. They want the photo, don't they? They're going to check it against their records. Measure it. Ears, eyes, nose, everything.' A sly look came over her face. 'He's waiting downstairs. Now get out of here, before I tell them you've been snooping.'

James wished her a polite good-bye. He was fairly certain she would say nothing, if only so as not to implicate herself.

At the next landing, a door creaked open. A dark sullen face peered out at him, furtively sizing him up. He could feel the eyes on his back as he continued down the stairs. They made his skin prickle. He nodded briefly to the uniformed policeman at Madame Ribot's front door and rushed away.

With the approach of evening, the streets had grown more crowded. Music poured from the open doors of bistros and bars. Unkempt youths with feverish eyes jostled with men in frock-coats, laughing women on their arms, their skirts raised against uneven cobbles to show a flash of ankle. The narrow lanes of the quarter, still almost a village unto itself, had gained a reputation for pleasure and danger, the second spicing the first.

Uncertain of his destination, James followed the wind of the streets. At a juncture, he came across the old wooden windmill which served as a beacon for the dance hall he had gone to with Yvette, all those years ago. He paused to watch the smiling couples in their summer finery parade through the doors, was almost tempted to track that mingled scent of lemon and perspiration to its source. He didn't. He hurried on, remembering that he still hadn't replied to his mother's letter.

It came to him that his ambassadorial zeal was fading with an astonishing rapidity. It had been so strong on his arrival a few short days ago. He had been prepared to overcome any and all of Raf and Ellie's resistance and coerce or persuade them home immediately, so that he could wrap himself in the soft blanket of habit once more. And now?

They hadn't been short days, he corrected himself. Long days, so replete with events and sensations they had transformed Boston into a faint murmur somewhere at the far edge of his consciousness.

It came to him, too, with a louder surge, like a wave breaking on the shore, that he had spent much of his life as an intermediary — arguing on behalf of others whom he believed more or less, negotiating the finer points of contracts that touched him in no particular way, a shuffling go-between. So he should have been well cut out for his present mission. But the firmness of its initial outlines had grown blurred. He could no more see the imperative of shepherding his siblings back to Boston, than he could of returning himself. Olympe's death had taken him over, as if she had been one of his own, as densely present to him as Maisie had once been — though there was no justice to be found in the first case unless he locked himself up. Which he had done in a manner of speaking, James acknowledged with restless irony.

His thoughts faltered, dispersed by an uncanny sensation of eyes on his back. He turned, half expecting to see the sullen face that had peered out at him on his way down from Olympe's apartment. Under less tense circumstances, he would have stopped to interview the neighbour. But the policeman had been there. He was here again now.

James clutched the satchel in his hand more tightly. With a show of casualness, he stepped past a braying donkey. The open door of a tavern beckoned. The large painted sign above it showed a hare leaping out of a casserole and James leapt across the threshold with the same alacrity, half-turning to see if the policeman would pass him by or follow him. The man paused to give him a steely glance, but then walked on. James calmed himself. His own guilt at pinching Olympe's letters was affecting his nerves.

The stares of the motley crew assembled in the tavern didn't help. They eyed him with the morose curiosity of regulars. He hastened to a table in a dim corner of the ramshackle room. As his eyes grew accustomed to the smoky half-light, he was struck by the oddity of his surroundings. At a long wooden refectory table at the centre of the room, a hirsute man with the look of an ancient mariner picked a desolate tune from his guitar and sang a plaintive ballad. Around him sat a heterogeneous assortment of men and women. Bohemians, James thought, and then taking in the wild assortment of paintings and sculptures which hung from the dark walls or were poised on tables and chairs, altered his thought to conclude that he was in some kind of artists' den. On the bench not far from him, one man was stretched in sleep or perhaps drunken stupor. A couple looked dreamily into each other's eyes over glasses of absinthe.

James ordered one for himself and examined the art more closely. There was a strange, gnarled Christ half reclining against the wall, a view of jagged roofs from a disorienting perspective, a series of circus performers. An odd prickling started at the base of his spine. The tightrope walker with her striated skirt and bodice, her direct, musing gaze looked remarkably like the Olympe Fabre he had seen in the photograph so short a time ago.

'Ça vous plaît, Monsieur?' The young, raven-haired waiter deposited James's drink on the table and followed his gaze.

James nodded his approval of the picture and then asked if he knew the model.

'Oh yes, monsieur. She lives nearby. She comes in often.' His face took on a grimness and he lowered his voice. 'Used to come in, I mean. She's dead now.'

He was about to move away, but James held him back. 'And the artist. Do you know the artist?'

'Max Henry.' He looked swiftly round the room. 'No, he's not here today. You're interested in buying the picture?'

'Yes,' James said with sudden decision. 'And in meeting Monsieur Henry.'

The youth gestured to the guitarist who strummed a few more chords and lumbered over. 'This is my father. He can advise you.'

Some half-hour later James left the cabaret with the picture under his arm. He had paid too much, he reckoned, but the bearded owner had turned out to have more than a talent for the guitar and mournful ballads of the city streets. He was a fine salesman. He had told him that Max Henry might be a mere stripling now, but would go far. He had also told him all about the talented Olympe Fabre and her tragic demise. Why, he could see her clearly sitting right there in the far corner of the room nursing a drink with her friends and yes, sometimes entertaining them with a ditty of her own in the late hours, after the theatre was closed. Her beauty pierced, almost like a pain. He brought a gnarled fist to his heart.

With a newfound directness, James had asked him whether she was more than a model to Max Henry and the man had winked and draped an arm across his shoulder and murmured, 'Ah, these young ones. They have hot blood, Monsieur. But I couldn't say for certain. No, not for certain.' Perhaps he had taken in the inadvertent look of disapproval on James's face, for he had then added, 'But it is some time back now. Max painted this series last year, maybe eighteen months ago. You must come back one night and ask him yourself. He is often here, later on though. After ten.' No, the man didn't have a recent address for Max.

James pondered all this as he followed the downhill course of the winding streets. Should he question Raf about Max Henry? He would have to test the temperature of his brother's emotions carefully. On the other hand, Raf must be far more aware than he was of Olympe's bohemian connections.

He clutched the small canvas to his chest and felt oddly happy with his purchase, as if he had brought a little of the dead girl to life. These were her streets he reminded himself and looked around him carefully, as if each cobble, each street vendor or brightly dressed juggler, might give up a clue to her untimely death.

He had almost reached the bottom of the Butte now. The clatter of coaches and hoofs rose from the busy intersection. A policeman stood at its edge, and for a moment, James froze, as if the man were lying in wait for the stolen letters in his satchel. He squared his shoulders and put on his most authoritative mien, the one he wore for judge and jury.

But it was a different officer and the man's attention was elsewhere. Parked in front of him stood one of those gleaming new motor cars with large spoked tires and headlamps as brazen as a lighthouse beam. A tall, weedy man in tattered clothes, cap askew over a lank abundance of hair, was running his hand over the car's shining surface as he might over a prize-winning thoroughbred. He had a rapt look on his bony face.

In the blink of an eye, the officer stayed the man's arm. 'Papiers,' he demanded in a bellowing voice. Passers-by scurried quickly away. Others stopped to watch, James amongst them.

The man looked dazed, as if he couldn't quite emerge from his dream. Then fear contorted his features. He tried to shake off the staying hand 'Your papers,' the officer repeated.

The man made a run for it. But the policeman was quicker and stronger. He caught up to him, and grabbing him by the collar of his shapeless jacket, shook him severely. 'Your name?' he said in the loud voice of one speaking to an imbecile. 'Your address?'

'A vagabond,' the man who was standing next to James muttered with distaste. 'A degenerate. Off to the Dépot with him.'

'Send him back where he came from,' another man shouted, cursing beneath his breath. 'Too many of his kind here. Dirt.'

The officer seemed altogether prepared to follow the popular will. He was propelling his captive forward in a frog-march.

Suddenly a woman appeared in front of them. She clutched at the policeman's arm. 'That's my brother. Leave him alone.'

The officer sized her up. She had a frowsy, painted face and an expanse of cleavage that didn't bode well. 'Prove it,' he sniggered. 'Or join him at the Dépot.'

The woman's face fell. With a single backward glance, she vanished into the crowd.

James moved on. Had he read it in one of those newspaper clippings or was it Raf who had told him about the stringent vagrancy laws which prevailed in the city? Tramps, vagabonds, wanderers, whose numbers had proliferated ever since the war with Germany, were seen to be a noxious social problem. They swelled the size of unruly mobs, could be used by any faction in need of numbers. Mad, alcoholic or simply travellers without the necessary identity cards, they were deemed also to be racial degenerates — dangerous microbes to be eliminated from the social stew lest they spawn and poison it utterly. Repeat offenders were bundled off to asylums or in the worst cases transported to penal colonies.

James hoped that the man he had seen transfixed by the motor car would be treated leniently and pardoned. He had probably only been dreaming about escape, a speedy escape, the kind that James could afford by simply raising an arm and hailing a carriage. A rigorous solution to social problems always seemed more attractive in the abstract, than when one saw its wounded, living face. Yet the problem remained.

A nearer problem hadn't disappeared either, he reminded himself. He would go back to the hotel now and study the bag's contents. After he had written to his mother, he promised himself.

He looked up to see if a cab was in sight and noticed a cluster of people on the opposite pavement. It took him a moment to realize that they were standing at the entrance of a theatre. The Vaudeville, curving letters on the iron-columned portico announced. It was the theatre at which Olympe had last played.

Without pausing to think, he quickened his step and joined the queue. Fifteen minutes later he watched the curtain rise on a play that bordered on melodrama. It told the risqué story of a triangle — a respectable older man married to a young woman who falls in love with the equally young man who comes to paint their portrait. Enraptured by the artist, their joint passion fed by romantic poetry, the two sin against her bonds and engage in an adulterous love which ends in a joint suicide pact. Only the woman dies. At the play's end, the husband stands alone on stage, stroking his small son's head and decrying the manipulability of women, the bitter tragedy of crimes of passion.

James watched on tenterhooks and tried to imagine Olympe in the role of the young woman, Olympe as he had seen her in the photograph, a haunting sadness accentuating the charm of her features. With an aching sense, it came to him that Olympe had been rehearsing death before meeting a real one.

He sat reflecting on this in his corner box until almost everyone had left the theatre and then, with sudden decision and a glance at the actress's name on his program, rushed to find the stage door.

A uniformed man barred his entrance. James reached for his wallet, all the time explaining that he was a friend of Oriane Martine, of Olympe Fabre, too, and needed to speak to Mademoiselle Martine. The size of the bill earned a nod and a grunt of 'First door on your right on the second floor.'

The back-stage area was an airless warren of dusky corridors. A smell of must and tired heat rose from the walls. The floorboards creaked. A man ran past him as he climbed the stairs. With a start James recognized the handsome actor who had played the young lover, but he looked faceless now, tired. When he reached the second floor, the sound of laughing voices dispelled the gloom. Two women walked down the hall, arm in arm. They pointed him to Mlle Martine's door, then giggled, as if sharing a secret.

James hesitated before the door. There were raised voices coming from the room, arguing over something. At last he knocked.

'Who is it?' A ringing voice called out.

Not knowing quite how to answer, James identified himself as a friend of Olympe Fabre. It took a moment, but the door opened a fraction to reveal the disgruntled face of a young woman, not, he was almost certain, Oriane Martine. 'Vous êtes qui?' she demanded in a surly tone.

James identified himself and heard another voice. 'Oh let him in, Marianne. What does it matter!'

He walked into the small, cluttered dressing room. Clothes hung from a rack. Bouquets of flowers gave off a dense, sultry scent. A woman sat in front of a large, yellowing mirror. Her hair was tied back and she was rubbing paint from her face with some white cream. Her features were pointed in a foxy prettiness. Beside her stood a portly man in a frock coat.

'Leave us, mon ami. Wait for me downstairs.' Oriane Martine smiled into the mirror, her cheek dimpling.

The man seemed about to argue, then giving James a slightly sullen look, left with a bow.

Dark-lashed blue eyes studied James from the mirror and measured his worth. He seemed to have passed some test, for the hair was quickly released and shaken out and Oriane turned to give him her non-reflected face. 'So you were a friend of Olympe's?'

James shifted his weight. 'Not exactly. My brother Rafael Norton . . .'

'Oh, of course, Monsieur Norton,' Oriane laughed infectiously, then put a staying hand over her mouth. In a moment, the face had grown into a tragic mask. 'How heartless of me. I really was very very sorry to hear of Olympe's death. I don't know what kind of black mood could have gripped her.'

'Do you think playing the part — your part — might have affected her, influenced her in some way?

Oriane looked at him with visible incomprehension, then as it dawned, crossed herself swiftly. 'You mean the nightly dying? No, no. We're professionals. And Olympe was well. Seemed to me to be very well. We used to be good friends you know. Years back. It's dismal that . . . how shall I put it, her terrible misfortune was my gain.' She pouted sweetly. 'Yes, I suddenly found myself in a lead part. We didn't know, of course, last week, when she disappeared that she was . . .' She stood up and paced the tiny room for a moment, picking a shawl off the floor, admonishing the girl who had opened the door to him.

James found himself liking her directness. 'Of course not,' he murmured.

'I'm very sad for her. Can I offer you a glass of wine, Monsieur?'

James nodded and accepted an inch of red in a glass which wasn't altogether clean.

'Yes, three years back, maybe four, when we were both mere girls, Olympe and I travelled together. There's nothing quite like it for making or breaking a friendship. Twenty-five towns in thirty days. Tours, Nantes, Nîmes, I can' t even name them all. You can imagine. It produces railway fever. Sometimes you don't even remember what town you're playing in. Olympe and I, we enjoyed the movement. We shared our centimes. Often, even our beds. You save money that way.' She shook her head in fleeting nostalgia, then met his eyes. 'She was a real trouper.'

James cleared his throat. 'And you were still friends. In Paris?'

'Oh yes. A little less, though, with the years. Olympe's star was rising. She was very busy. Mine wasn't . . . well, all that's changing.' She gave him a radiant smile, which crinkled her eyes in wry intelligence, so different from the demented passion of her role that he began to wonder at her performing power.

'Did Olympe leave the theatre with anyone last Thursday — after the performance?'

Oriane shrugged, made a throwaway sound. 'I didn't see her. My part was small, over by the interval and I left early.'

James nodded.

'But Antoine, that's our director, he told the police that she had left alone.'

'I see.'

'She arrived with someone though.' Oriane chuckled. 'A real toff.' She screwed up her eye to mimic a twitching monocle. 'Don't know where Olympe finds them.'

'Do you know the man's name? Did she introduce you?'

'No. He was just helping her out of a carriage. They were bantering. They felt like friends. He was quite unlike your brother. Quite unlike Monsieur Rafael. She always spoke of him. We all spoke of him. L'Americain.'

'Did you tell the police about this other man?'

'No, why should I?' She frowned.

It was James's turn to shrug.

'Olympe didn't like the police. Anyhow, the toff wasn't important. I was going to mention him to Monsieur Rafael when he came to talk to me, but then I thought, why plant ideas where they're not needed. Olympe wasn't, how shall I put it, like the rest of us.' She fluttered thick eyelashes, perused him with a coquettish smile. 'You know what I mean. She didn't indulge in ever-changing patrons.'

'Why didn't Olympe like the police?'

The woman stared at him in incredulity. 'Does anyone? Anyone like us, I mean.' She swept her arm round the small space in a grand gesture, then looked sharply at Martine who was listening with a fixed intensity. 'Go and tell Monsieur Cailleboux, I'll only be another five minutes.'

Oriane disappeared behind a painted room divider. James heard the rustle of silk and petticoats and wondered whether he should leave. But she was out again a few moments later in a pale blue ruffled gown. She did up the last few hooks on the bodice in front of him, as if to do so were the most natural act in the world. James watched her in the mirror.

'Did Olympe have any more particular reason for not liking the police?'

Oriane's eyes narrowed in suspicion.

'I only ask for the best of reasons. We, my brother and I, want to be certain that anyone involved in . . . well involved in her death, comes to justice.'

She didn't answer immediately. When she did, her voice took on a hoarseness. 'Are you suggesting that someone else was involved in Olympe's death?'

James nodded. 'Perhaps.'

She shivered. Her glance scurried round the room, darting into corners.

'There was something you wanted to say . . . about Olympe and the police,' James prompted.

'Oh, that. I think they tried to accuse her of blackmail once. It was a long time ago. And a complete lie. Nothing came of it. Olympe wouldn't. Never. She was an honourable soul.'

'Who was she meant to be blackmailing?'

'I don't know. A count somebody or other. It was before we toured together. Just malicious gossip. Not everyone in our world loves everyone else.' She shivered again.

James chose his words carefully. 'You mean this count wrongly accused her of blackmailing him because he thought she was threatening to expose an affair they'd had. Whereas, in fact, the threat came from someone else?'

Oriane's sudden burst of laughter took him aback. 'You must come from another planet, Monsieur, if you think that is cause for blackmail in Paris.' She looked into the mirror with a kittenish moue to hide her nervousness and pinned her hair up. 'Your French is nonetheless delicious.'

'But the wife of a respectable man or his parents might feel threatened . . .' James persisted. She cut him off.

'We are actresses, Monsieur,' she said, her head thrown back in defiance. 'Olympe was a particularly fine one. Any man would have counted himself honoured to gain her favour, his reputation heightened.' She paused and turned to meet his eyes. 'But I think you should forget everything I have just said. It is all utterly irrelevant now.'

She placed her hand on his arm, her expression suddenly beseeching, her voice urgent. 'I have been foolish, have let my tongue run away with me. It's always like that after a performance. Don't say anything about this . . . this nonsense. Not to anyone. Especially not to your brother, Monsieur. He is a fine young man. Olympe would have wanted his memories of her to be untarnished by suspicion.'

EIGHT

James woke to bright light streaming through the shutters and making a jagged pattern of his bed. The streaks hurt his eyes. He had been traipsing through a world of shadows who summoned him with demure glances. They murmured in foreign voices always slightly outside his comprehension only to disperse as he approached.

He raised his head slowly. The bed was an untidy heap of papers. Olympe's letters. He had fallen asleep with them around him. And yes, he acknowledged with a sudden constriction of the heart, hers was the shape-shifting presence he had pursued in his dreams. A new face rising to beckon him at every turn — a face of utter girlish innocence, a face of vulgar lascivious intent, a face of piercing melancholy, haunted by tragedy. How could this unknown woman have taken such a hold on him?

He rubbed his eyes and shunted himself into daylight practicality.

Had he really garnered anything useful from Olympe's letters except that the girl liked to keep amorous or flattering notes from admirers? Which was hardly surprising and hardly a crime. One of the more persistent correspondents signed himself Marcel and it was from these evocative letters that James's sense of Olympe's presence on stage had grown. Praise aside, the letters were full of instruction — about Olympe's singing, her movement, her phrasing. Perhaps the author was a director or critic or some kind of acting coach. It should prove easy enough to find out. He could always go back to the theatre and ask Oriane. Unless Raf knew, though James was again in two minds as to what to reveal to him about the letters.

Other writers fell into the category of star-struck lovers. Their heat, he had to admit, was contagious. But they didn't seem to persevere for any length of time. Perhaps Olympe had admonished or rejected them, or simply failed to answer. It would have been useful to have Olympe's side of all these correspondences. That would have revealed far more of her character. More consistent dating would also have been useful. He was irritated by the fact that most of the letters signalled only a day or a month, rarely a year, so apart from Raf's, he had no clear idea to which part of Olympe's life they belonged.

Indeed, James reflected with a rueful grimace as he made his way to the bathroom, what Olympe chose to throw away rather than keep, might have been of the greatest interest.

He shaved as he thought about the notebook. It had turned out to be an appointments diary, rather than as he had hoped, some kind of journal. And Olympe was not a diarist of exuberance. Initials and a time, largely served her purpose. In comparison, the terse record of his activities that James kept in Boston, provided a veritable flood of information.

Still, he now knew the initials of the people she had seen in her last days. Perhaps more importantly, the diary charted meetings and performances well beyond the date on which her body was found. Given the lack of any suicide note, this seemed to tip the balance in favour of a death which had nothing to do with her own will. On that score, Raf had been right.

Once dressed, James quickly gathered up the letters and placed them in his desk drawer. He paused to look at the painting of Olympe as a tightrope walker. In the bright morning light, it added a slightly garish note to the propriety of his hotel room, but he was already more fond of it than he had imagined he could be.

Slipping Olympe's notebook into his pocket, he hurried down to the Café de la Paix. The sun was warm on the *terrasse*, the spectacle of strollers in their summer finery a pleasure, and he would have liked to linger over his breakfast of café-au-lait and croissants, but his watch told him he didn't have all that much time. He had slept too late and he had still to buy himself a hat to replace the one lost in the demonstration, before attending to his next commitment.

Three letters had awaited him on his return to the hotel the night before. The first was the reason for his hurry. It was from Harriet Knowles and it enjoined him in a small neat hand to meet today at eleven for a walk with his sister, should the weather continue fine. It also begged, in what seemed to be a hastily added postscript, not to mention Harriet's note to Ellie. James allowed himself to reflect, but only for a quick moment, on the path of white lies and well-intentioned deviousness his sister's condition forced on people even as upright as Harriet Knowles.

He preferred to think of the second letter which was from Marguerite de Landois and invited him to a supper party at her home this very evening. She was always at home, she pointed out, on the second Saturday of the month and tonight marked her last of the season, so she hoped he would be able to attend. What James hoped, was that he could somehow steer her into a quiet corner. He had a sense that Madame de Landois' perspective on Olympe and her death would provide him with a far fuller picture than he had yet had from his brother. Indeed, had the grand lady's letter not arrived last night, he would have rung her this morning to try and arrange a meeting.

James signalled to the waiter, paid the bill and made his way briskly towards the hatter's he had noticed on the other side of the boulevard. He chose the first boater that sat snugly on his head and by 10:45 p.m. stood in front of his siblings' building, a bouquet of flowers in his hand. He tried his brother's door first, eager for any news Raf might have. But there was no response.

Ellie's bell was promptly answered by Harriet Knowles who welcomed him with a grateful smile. It reached all the way up to her grey eyes and warmed them.

'Elinor will be so pleased.'

'Who is that?' Ellie's voice reached them from the next room. 'Oh Jimmy, how beautiful, you spoil me. I don't deserve it.' She looked up at him from her divan, her face a mask of pallor in which the dark eyes glowed like coals. 'Bring the blue vase in from the dining room, Harriet. These snapdragons will look so pretty against blue.'

'How are you, Ellie?'

'Pretty well.' She gave him a nervous smile. 'I've been reading. *Paradise Lost.* Listen to this, Jimmy.' She scrambled through the pages of the book in her hand, sat up a little straighter, and with a dramatic look, intoned:

Why stand we longer shivering under fears
That show no end but death, and have the power,
Of many ways to die the shortest choosing,
Destruction with destruction to destroy?

'You hear that Jimmy?' She laughed. 'The very first of my kind. The first woman. Eve. An oracle. It's already there. On her lips.'

James shot her a stern look. 'You shouldn't be reading such gloomy matter, Ellie.' He took the book from her hand and placed it out of her reach on the mantlepiece.

'Shouldn't . . . mustn't . . . Same old James. At least Raf does me the honour of arguing with me.'

'All right. I'll argue. If you read on, Milton doesn't seem to think Eve's notion of suicide is such a good idea.'

'That's because he's a man.' Ellie's eyes sparkled. 'He's got a role in the world, things to do. Whereas I . . .'

'You,' James cut her off. 'You are coming out. You've been indoors for too long. It makes you melancholy.'

'There's plenty to be melancholy about, isn't there, Jim?' A sly, girlish expression flitted across her face. 'Olympe seemed to think so and she had no reason . . .'

'Did I hear you say something about going out?' Harriet intervened. She had been arranging the flowers in the vase and she now positioned them on the table near the divan.

'I can't go out like this,' Ellie said with a stubbornness which spoke of an earlier argument.

'Yes, you can Ellie,' James intervened. 'Harriet will get your hat and I'll roll up that chair. It's a beautiful day. The sights will put happier thoughts in your mind.'

'You think it's that easy,' Ellie grumbled, but she allowed herself to be lifted into the chair with a murmur of only, 'All right. Because you both want to. And it's Violette's day off.'

A parasol was duly found, the elevator called, which had room only for the two women and some fifteen minutes later they found themselves in the bright light of the June day. Ellie pulled her hat down more closely over her eyes and hunched into her chair with the look of someone for whom the outdoors had become a fearful place, too large to manoeuvre.

Harriet met James's eyes in apprehensive complicity. 'You'll soon get used to it,' she murmured to Ellie with the determined cheerfulness of a trained nurse. 'And I've just remembered. There's a concert in the park. The music will be a boon. It will relax you wonderfully.'

'If I relax any more, I'll forget how to lift my little finger,' Ellie commented dryly. 'And then how will I turn the pages?'

'I suspect you've had quite enough turning of pages,' James intervened. 'What you want is to turn over a new leaf. Monday. I'm starting to look forward to the visit to that doctor.'

'You begin to sound more and more like mother, do you know, Jim?' Ellie threw a mischievous look at him over her shoulder. 'Such confidence in the medical profession.'

'We'll have you back with her in no time.' James took it equably enough. 'And with all your old friends.'

'All my old friends who've been popping out babies with feline speed.'

Ellie's language startled him, as did the bitterness in her humourless chuckle.

'I had a letter from Lizzie yesterday, asking me if I'd like to be godmother to her next one. I'm about to write back and tell her I don't know enough about godly ways.'

'Elinor!' Harriet's rebuke was sharp.

They had reached the bustle of the Madeleine. The market was at its height and they made a small detour to Fauchon's to take in the double spectacle of gourmet foods and a lavish array of flowers.

'You remember that the Madeleine was Father's favourite church, don't you, James?' Ellie suddenly asked. 'He liked its grandeur without fuss. Render God his due importance but keep him out of the way.'

Harriet looked a little taken aback and James wondered whether the comment had been for her benefit. 'I didn't know it was Father's favourite,' he said in an even tone.

'Didn't you? Of course not. I'd forgotten. It was only Raf and myself who travelled with him that summer. The holiday was meant to take me out of myself.' She laughed briefly. 'It served its purpose, I guess. We had a high old time. And Raf took up with the son of some expat and was babbling away in French within weeks. He's always had a facility. For languages . . . for friendships . . .' She paused as they manoeuvred her across the busy boulevard and down, past Maxim's, towards the Concorde. 'I miss Father, you know Jim. Sometimes I miss him terribly. We grew so close in that last year.'

James now recalled that Ellie had indeed taken over the nursing of their father in his last illness. Both he and Raf were well away from home by then. It was she who had read to him and played the piano and done the crosswords and sat continuously by his side. It was she who had been with him in those final moments when the cancer had eaten away his breath. Their mother had stood aside, willingly giving over this most arduous of tasks to her daughter. And Ellie had been strong in those six months. Never once had there been any sign or suggestion of her suffering from her unnameable condition. James wondered at this, then remembered that soon after their father's death, Ellie had gone off for some months for a rest cure. He had never put the sequence together quite in this light and now he said, 'You took good care of him, Ellie. You were brave.'

She laughed, a single shrill note. 'And you were busy with Maisie. Sweet little Maisie. And your work, of course.'

James let the edge of reprimand pass over him. He had been busy at the time. Too busy. Stepping into his father's shoes at the firm, acting as executor on a particularly pernicious will which had left a large family terminally at odds. The savagery of their behaviour had dismayed him.

'Did Maisie enjoy Paris?' Ellie's query brought him back sharply. He felt Harriet's eyes on him and looked away.

'Yes, yes, she did.' He paused in his wheeling and waved an arc from the Concorde to the Tuileries. 'She particularly liked it here.'

'Sweet Maisie,' Elinor breathed. 'You knew her, didn't you, Harriet?

She used to come to Mrs. Maple's gatherings from time to time. Way back.'

Harriet murmured something vague, then asked, 'Would you like me to take over for a while, Mr. Norton? Now that we're in the park . . .'

'No, no. That's fine.' He gripped Elinor's chair harder to balance it against the incline. The fountain at its base was surrounded by children watching their tiny boats weave erratic paths through the fluttering water. They watched with them for a few minutes, saw the wind dip the tiny sails and propel a drunken circuit.

'Do you have any brothers or sisters, Miss Knowles?'

Before Harriet could respond, Ellie intervened. 'Harriet is an orphan, Jimmy. Hasn't had any real family since she was fourteen. Maybe she's the stronger for it. She writes, you know. Sends home letters from abroad to all kinds of papers. And now I've determined that we should become her family.'

Harriet had averted her eyes. 'Listen,' she said. 'The music has started. We should get on.'

They strolled down the park's central artery, its white gravel stark in the sun, and turned off into the canopy the rigorously pruned trees provided. The dappled light was a relief to the eyes.

'This is nice, isn't it, Elinor?' Harriet murmured.

'And I dare say, it will do me good.' Ellie cast her a smile. 'You were right. Harriet is always right, James. That's what I love about her.'

Around the covered bandstand, rows of chairs had been set up, all of them now filled. A military band played, the soldiers' gold braid and buttons glittering along with the trumpets and tubas. A banner announced the '117 Infantry'. Their marches were so rousing that James felt Ellie would soon be forced to get up, if only to keep time.

They listened for a while, then Harriet pointed to a free bench beneath a tree at a little distance. It had the advantage of being in the shade and still permitting them to hear.

No sooner had they sat down, than a soldier appeared and placed a leaflet in James's hand. 'Benefit performance for the League of Patriots at the Saint-Paul Riding School,' James read. 'Long Live the Army.'

'Show me that.' Ellie took the leaflet from his hands and surveyed it quickly. She coughed. 'You don't want to hang out with that crowd, Jimmy.

Though our darling brother sometimes does. Says it gives him background material.' Her voice rose. 'Long boring speeches full of pompous gobbledygook lightly veiling hatred, not to mention fear that certain privileges may disappear.'

'Don't excite yourself, Ellie. I'm not planning to participate.'

'Where is Raf, by the way?'

'I'm not altogether sure. Working, I think,' James prevaricated.

'I hope so. At last.' Ellie gave him one of her sharp looks. 'The papers this morning were certainly full of material he should be handling. It looks like the government is going to fall. Doesn't it, Harriet?'

Harriet nodded and then leapt up. 'Look, there's Charlotte and Mrs. Elliott.' She waved. 'They said they might meet us here. We thought we'd lunch together.'

James hid his irritation, not quite quickly enough for Harriet gave him an appraising stare.

'I hope you don't mind.'

'Jimmy finds too many women at once hard to bear,' Ellie teased in her old way.

'Not at all. Not at all.' James flushed as he rose to greet the women and willingly gave up his seat. 'Why don't I fetch us all something to drink from the little kiosque we passed.'

'That would be kind, Mr. Norton.' Mrs. Elliott was fanning herself with all the grace of an albatross trying to lift itself into flight. 'I think it's hotter than Boston, today.'

'It isn't, mother.' Charlotte contradicted. 'The paper distinctly said 22 degrees which is only 72 Fahrenheit.

'Let me help you with the drinks.' Harriet was at his side.

'That would be kind, Miss Knowles.'

'Do call me Harriet. It's so much simpler.'

Covertly, he studied her high, clear brow, the snub-nosed profile which spoke of determination and a candid nature. As they took a shortcut through the trees, a plan began to form in his mind.

'Tell me, Miss . . . I mean Harriet, how exactly would you assess my sister's state of health?'

The woman shrugged. 'Not wonderful. There's such a change since I saw her last. I don't really understand it.'

'No . . .' James hesitated.

'And she forgets things. Forgets the book she's been reading an hour before.' Harriet's voice held a glimmer of awe. 'It's as if she . . . well goes into a trance. I don't know what else to call it.' She threw him a shadowy glance as if to assess his reaction.

'Really.' James kept his face neutral. 'You know, I . . . I've been wondering whether she's strong enough to make the journey home. I feel she'd be so much better away from all this. I don't mean you,' James stumbled over his words. 'In fact, I was wondering whether you might make the trip with her. She's altogether different with you. Spirited. And of course, we'd . . . I'd . . .'

'Pay for my journey,' Harriet finished for him bluntly.

He met her eyes and in that brisk exchange read her wish to refuse compounded by the realization that she was in no position to do so.

'Yes. You would be doing us a great service. You see, I fear that my brother may decline to leave for some time, because of . . . because of the death of Olympe Fabre. And his work, of course. And I feel, yes I do feel that he needs my help. But Ellie . . .' James thought it through as he spoke. 'Well, the atmosphere is wrong for her. What do you say?'

'I could ask her,' Harriet spoke at last. 'I wouldn't of course do anything to try and influence her. Elinor is averse to influence.'

'I know,' James smiled. 'To my influence, in any event. But you would try . . . you would accompany her?'

She nodded once, firmly. 'I don't promise anything, though. And I sense that she'll reject the proposition out of hand. She won't leave Rafael.'

'But you'll try.'

'After you've taken her to the doctor on Monday. We'll see what he says. She decidedly wants you with her, by the way.'

'Of course.'

A companionable silence descended between them. James broke it only on their return from the kiosque. His thoughts had migrated once more to Olympe and he suddenly wanted to have this wonderfully straightforward woman's view of her. He was a little taken aback by the sharpness Harriet put into her response.

'No, I never met Olympe Fabre. She belongs to another side of Elinor's life. Our paths never crossed. Then, too, I have been away.'

'But Ellie spoke to you about her?'

'Only in passing. She admired her.'

'I see,' James said, though he didn't really and the sudden stiff set of Harriet's face told him there was no point pursuing the matter. Perhaps he had wrongly jumped to conclusions about her relationship with Ellie and assumed a chattering intimacy which didn't exist. It was possible that Harriet only engaged Ellie's more intellectual interests. Yes, that must be it. But her next comment threw his conclusion askew.

'I know she was bad for her. Was bad for her from the very beginning.'

'Oh?'

'Yes. And her death has, if anything, been worse. You've heard all Elinor's remarks about suicide. She talks of little else. She, with all her advantages. Yesterday, she made me lose my temper. I should tell you that I rarely lose my temper. I ended up by quoting a rather scurrilous German philosopher at her. Oh yes, I have German, Mr. Norton. Has Elinor not told you? For two long years I was governess to a German family. In any case I was rather caustic. I said to her that the thought of suicide is a great consolation. By means of it one can get through many a bad night. She didn't like that. She didn't like it one bit. She thought I was making light of her. She rebuked me fiercely. She told me that if one made the thought actual, like this Olympe, one didn't get through the night. And that was that.'

Harriet stopped abruptly, her face flushed from the emotion of her long speech and perhaps from the sudden sight of Ellie waving to them.

As they approached, she breathed an emphatic, 'At last. I thought you'd run off together.' She laughed. 'What have you been telling my brother, Harriet?' She studied her friend.

'Harriet has been telling me about her years in Germany.' James answered for her.

'Germany?' Mrs. Elliott sounded aghast. 'Well, we'll have no more of that.' She sipped her lemonade gratefully. 'And I've really had rather enough of this music, too. It makes one hotter. I've taken the liberty of booking a table at the Café Voltaire. It comes highly recommended, doesn't it, Charlotte?'

Charlotte smoothed her dress awkwardly and nodded.

'Do you know it, Mr. Norton?'

James shook his head.

'It's on the left bank.' Ellie's voice was tremulous.

'Yes, just across the river,' Mrs. Elliott supplied in sudden expertise. She rose with an effort to her feet.

'Oh no, I couldn't.' Ellie's eyes had grown wide with something like panic. 'No, no. Not the Voltaire. Take me home, Jim, please.'

James stared at her. Her face was white. Perspiration had gathered on her brow.

'But we were so looking forward to your company, Miss Norton.'

Ellie seemed not to have heard.

'Perhaps somewhere closer, somewhere on the way home,' Harriet soothed. 'There's that nice place just by the Palais Royal.'

'You guide us, Harriet.' James propelled Ellie's chair into motion and wondered what terrible event had taken place at the Café Voltaire.

The afternoon provided no opportunity for finding out. They had ended up at a large brasserie just behind the Palais Royal and spent far too long over a lunch in which the conversation was dictated by Mrs. Elliott. Ellie had receded into a dream state, all her energies left behind with the Infantry band. Harriet kept casting her worried looks, but was far too polite to cut off a Mrs. Elliott in full flow.

While the fans above them swirled, the woman lectured James on the law, more precisely on its teaching. Her husband, as he was supposed to know but had forgotten, had been an attorney, one whose views it seemed were fundamentally opposed to those of the great Justice Holmes, who had so influenced James's own ideas. To say that the fundamental principles of the law shaped it less than the everyday matter that went on in the courts was like saying that the ten commandments had grown less important because they were sinned against. Which was pure poppycock.

Mrs. Elliott's voice rang through the brasserie with all the fervour of an executing judge. James only finally succeeded in changing the subject by addressing Charlotte about her expedition to the Louvre Museum. He longed to escape, but there was no way he could do so, since Ellie had first to be taken home. So he sat there, taxing his resources of patience, letting his mind wander, wondering whether the police might have come up with any new information, when, as if he had been sent by a happy fate, Gilles Touquet, Raf's journalist friend, came into his field of vision.

With his quick, loping step, Touquet was making his way to the door.

James excused himself to the ladies and followed him, tapping him on the shoulder just as he stepped outside.

'Ah, Monsieur Norton.' The man's face had an unhealthy tinge in the bright sunshine. 'I saw your brother this morning.' A conspiratorial look came into his eye. 'Has he told you?'

James shook his head. 'I haven't met up with him today.'

Touquet gestured him away from the door and towards the eaves of the building. 'I have found someone. Well, I am on the trail. I spent the last two nights in the brothel where that poor creature worked — the girl in the metro shaft. And I have discovered that she had a regular. A Marcel Caro, not a salubrious sort. A big man.' He puffed up his chest and flexed his arms in gorilla motion. 'Apparement, it was through him that the girl was introduced to the brothel.'

'Did any of the women there know Olympe, know her perhaps as Rachel Arnhem?'

Touquet stared at him hard, stroked his beard for a moment. 'So you think the way I do. Your brother does not . . .'

'I know, I know.' James cut him off. 'But it's always worth making some enquiries.'

'Always . . .' Touquet winked. 'And now I must rush off to see an honest policeman. If I do not hurry, he may not be so honest by the time I arrive.'

On his way back to the ladies, James wondered whether the name Marcel Caro could have any link at all to the Marcel who signed letters to Olympe. It was, he decided, highly unlikely. The style of the letters had been too high, too subtle. But it had reminded him that he wanted, however gently, to quiz Ellie about the names and initials he had found in Olympe's papers. She claimed after all to have known the woman longer than Raf had.

But it was Ellie who interrogated him as soon as he had sat down at the table. 'Who was that odiously louche little bearded man you ran after?'

Her spirits had distinctly lifted. The food or perhaps the wine had done its work.

'A journalist.'

'You mean a friend of my absent brother's?'

James nodded.

'You see what it means to be a woman,' she addressed the ladies. 'James has been here for less than a week and he has already seen more of Paris life than I have in nine months.'

'But that is only fitting, my dear,' Mrs. Elliott's tone took on a chiding, maternal warmth. 'Our sphere is in the home. We look after our young and educate them. We bring grace and beauty into the world to complement men's more arduous tasks. We serve. Nature has made us so.' She cast a glance at Charlotte and then smiled at James. 'Don't you agree, Mr. Norton?'

James felt Ellie and Harriet's eyes on him and chose to do no more than nod briefly.

'So you would say nature has ordained Charlotte or me to serve a man, any man, even if his intelligence, his moral intelligence were a mere smattering of our own?' Ellie's voice and face were all innocence, as if she really expected an affirmative answer.

Mrs. Elliott wriggled in her chair. 'Intellect is not a feminine virtue. When Charlotte reads too much, she simply grows . . .' She stopped herself. 'You shall have to come and visit us in Boston, Mr. Norton. My cook's beef is far superior to this.'

'I dare say James is not thinking about beef. He's thinking about what Raf's friend, the one I have never met, said to him. Will you introduce him to me, James?'

'You exaggerate, Elinor.' Harriet intervened. 'You have no desire to meet that man, whom you've just called odious. You know that.'

'Maybe I do and maybe I don't. The point is I haven't been given the opportunity.' Ellie's tone suddenly changed. 'Is there any news about Olympe?'

'Olympe?' Mrs. Elliott queried.

To James's relief the waiter chose that moment to clear their table and another arrived with the dessert trolley. He didn't want to pursue this conversation. He wanted to hurry back and catch Raf, who must now be at home. Silly of him not to have asked Touquet where Raf was going.

He glanced at Ellie whose eyes hadn't left him. They were large and accusing, as if she had once more read his mind and knew that he wanted only to get away. He gave her a wide smile and reminded himself again that he was here for her, not for some woman he had never seen alive.

'Isn't it nice to be out, Ellie?' he asked softly. 'It's made you look altogether beautiful. And that brooch is wonderful on your blouse. It's the one Father gave you, isn't it?'

Ellie's lips trembled convulsively. The glass she had been holding fell from her fingers and hit the floor with an explosive clatter, splintering into a hundred pieces. Wine splattered her pale skirt and left a trail of red, dark as blood, against the white tiles.

A sob shook her. Her eyes filling with tears, she whimpered into the gathered silence like a lost child.

NINE

Gleaming carriages crowded the usually quiet street. The buttons and epaulettes of the uniformed coachmen glittered like stars on a clear night. Above, the ranked windows of Madame de Landois' *hôtel particulier* were ablaze with the light of chandeliers. As he leapt from his cab, James could see figures milling. Faces were lifted in conversation, glasses brought to lips. He was no more than twenty minutes late. Madame de Landois was evidently a stickler for punctuality.

Smoothing the lapels of his frock-coat, he raced up the stairs in the direction the footman had pointed him. He found himself in a high-ceilinged hall, its floor a chessboard of vast black-and-white tiles. His hat and gloves were duly taken and his name asked. A moment later he heard it ring through a long rectangle of a room which bore little resemblance to the ones he had previously visited.

This was a grand, formal chamber, its walls lined with portraits and gilt-framed mirrors, so that everything was reflected into a dizzying distance. In the corner nearest to him a quartet occupied a small platform, their instruments at the ready. At the far side stood a long table arrayed with food, close to it eight or nine smaller round ones, set for dining. He had an impression of some forty or fifty people in vivid, laughing groups, multiplied ad infinitum, jewels and silks shimmering, white ties stark against black.

He held back, suddenly as timid as a boy in short pants preparing to confront an assembly of towering adults. An odd scene flew into his mind. He must have been about thirteen, maybe less. His parents had asked him to look after Raf and Ellie while they held a lunch party — a special one, for James had been strictly warned that there was to be no disturbance. The children insisted on standing on the stairs and peeking in through the half-open door and suddenly Raf had made a dash, quickly followed by Ellie. James had held back at the threshold, his heart racing, his ears waiting for the blast of his father's stentorian voice, the censure first of his siblings, but then, most emphatically of himself.

Only the last had occurred. Raf had rushed into his mother's arms, Ellie into her father's. The parents had laughed and embraced the children. James had watched, unsure whether he, too, was now to come in, but the set of his father's eyes as they fell on him above Ellie's tousled head, had communicated an emphatic 'no'. Later that glance had taken on solidity, had been fleshed out in a long and severe reprimand. James had been negligent. Had failed in his duty.

'James Norton. Enchantez, Monsieur.' The sound of his name overrode James's reverie. A burly, bearded man who looked as if he might be more at home in worker's blues than in stiff shirt and frock coat was addressing him with surprising warmth. His eyes were a clear, vulpine blue. 'I am a friend of your brother's. You speak French, of course?'

James nodded, noticed that a glass had somehow found its way into his hand. Cool champagne tickled his throat. How long had he been standing here?

'I am Gustave Fromentin. You have seen my painting, I hope, in your brother's home?'

'Yes, yes, indeed. It's fine. Very fine. Altogether astonishing, in fact.'

The man bowed slightly and, like a surrogate host, drew James into the midst of the room. He introduced him to a woman of haughty mien, great clusters of emerald at her throat, and then to a count with an unpronounceable name. He was very tall, monocled, and his Adam's apple bounced up and down as he repeated James's name with a lilting slowness which rendered it as multisyllabic as his own.

'A fitting night, isn't it, Fromentin,' the woman spoke, 'for Marguerite's last gathering of the season?'

'You mean because of Dreyfus?'

'Yes, yes, of course.' Her face was a mixture of impatience and exaltation. 'At last. The poor man is on his way home from Devil's Island. He boarded the *Sfax* today. After four gruelling years.' She turned toward the count, her eyes narrowing, 'Not that my husband, here, is pleased.'

'I've told you, Françoise, and I'll tell you again and again,' the count's neck bobbed in mounting fury, 'your so-called victory for the Republic marks the end. The end of everything we believe in.'

'*You* believe in. Leave me out of this. I have no time for your friends in the general staff and the ministry of war and their atrocious conspiracies against our freedom. Our Republic.' With a savage swish of skirts, she turned on her heel.

The count shook his head in something like sadness. 'Our women are turning into men, Fromentin. La Bernhardt triumphs as Hamlet. My daughter insists on studying the law. My wife backs her up. You know, until Zola wrote his blasted article, I don't believe Françoise had ever heard of Dreyfus. Me, *j'accuse Zola!*'

'But isn't that exactly what writers are for, mon ami?' Madame de Landois was suddenly at their side. She was wearing a dress of some rich, silvery concoction which nonetheless gave an impression of warmth and lit her eyes. Her bared shoulders and arms were white and beautiful.

'Ah, Monsieur Norton,' she addressed James in French. 'I am so glad you could join us.' She gave him her hand. 'You will be at ease in no time. I promise you.' Her mouth moved in complicit laughter. 'And there are some people who might interest you.'

'Is my brother here?'

She looked round in what he felt was a feint of casualness. 'I do not believe so. But I fully expect him. His favourite musicians are here.'

As if the words were a signal, James heard strings being tuned. Voices fell away. A lingering melody began to undulate through the room, haunting the corners, turning back on itself with a rising nostalgia. James sought out a chair and let the music play through him.

The violinist was a slender young woman with the purest of profiles.

His thoughts turned inevitably to Olympe. She had performed here Madame de Landois had told him, but not in what capacity. Was it in this room that she had met the man who signed himself as Marcel? James studied the rows of faces — clean-shaven, moustachioed, bearded. Any one of them might do for the part.

His eyes fell on a familiar figure. Durand, the Chief Inspector. He had last seen him coming out of Olympe's apartment. Now his deliberately casual stance belied a certain nervousness. His square chin was an inch too high, his short, strong legs firmly planted, his arm crossed over his stomach in Napoleonic mimicry. One hand delicately teased the curl of his dark moustache. He was certainly not one of Marguerite's regulars, James thought. So she must have invited him for a purpose. He sought out her face, but her back was to him, the burnished curls piled high with an intricacy of combs. Maisie had once had her hair arranged with that kind of sophistication. He hadn't told her, but he had found it troubling as if a stranger had taken over her person and obliterated the sweet simplicity of her face.

He returned his attention to the Chief Inspector who was swaying slightly on the balls of his feet. Their eyes met and Durand nodded with evident pleasure. Surprising that the man should recognize him. They had never been properly introduced. Perhaps it was less recognition than a happy acknowledgement of familiarity in a place where few were familiar to him. He would seek him out later, James promised himself, returning the greeting. It would be useful to find out how the police enquiries were progressing.

The music had taken on an aching dissonance. He watched the young violinist, then surveyed the room in search of another figure he had to admit he was interested in — Marguerite's husband. He examined faces, settled on a tall loose-limbed man who had aristocracy written into the bridge of his nose and the indolent cast of his features. He was standing to one side of the gathering, his expression marked by boredom and reverie in equal measure.

As music gave way to applause, James found Fromentin once more at his side.

'Which one of these gentlemen is our host?' James heard himself asking before he could stop himself. Fromentin's eyebrow arched in momentary consternation. He chuckled. 'Of course. There is no reason for you to know. Our dear Marguerite and the Comte de Landois have lived their separate ways since — oh I don't know. Certainly before I met her. He has a property in the Loire, I believe.' He waved his arm as if the distance were more than one could begin to consider.

'I see. Excuse my curiosity.'

'No, no.' He seemed about to say something more on the subject when a brunette with vivid, laughing eyes put her arm through his.

'So when will you at last decide to take up this promised portrait, mon cher?'

'Tomorrow, if I could. But alas . . . Let me introduce you to Monsieur Norton.'

The woman sat down beside them at one of the round tables. A man followed. He had granite features and oddly small hands which he used to execute large, sweeping gestures. James soon learned he was a deputy though he didn't catch his party affiliation. Durand startled him by joining their group and for a moment, James had the impression that the little man's smile was less friendly than stealthy. He made his own deliberately candid.

Two women followed Durand, the first was the violinist who had entertained them. Close too, she looked barely old enough to be out so late. The second was a thin, but striking redhead with a wry curl to her lips. Finally the indolent figure he had wrongly picked out as Marguerite's husband took up a place. Fromentin introduced him as a writer.

A single chair remained empty and James looked round, assuming it was intended for his absent brother. But there was no sign of Raf. As if he had read his mind, Durand murmured, 'I, too had hoped to meet your brother here, Monsieur Norton.'

'I dare say he'll turn up in due course.'

The Chief Inspector nodded, placidly enough, but there was something in his manner that put James on edge even when he turned to speak to his neighbour.

Conversation leapt and bubbled. James surprised himself by being able to follow its course. Caught in a sea of French, he had to swim or drown, so he swam, but the effort meant that he almost failed to appreciate the excellence of the paté, the creaminess of a soup subtly tinged green, the delicate slivers of fish served with a medley of vegetables.

The deputy's voice rose above the others at the table. The flourish of his hand gestures silenced everyone.

'You'll agree with me, Monsieur l'Inspecteur. It's not a question of left or right.' He waved his wineglass dangerously. 'The press has abdicated all sense of responsibility and replaced it by a love affair with sensation. It's bad for the health of the nation.' His eyes targetted the writer. 'It's not only their daily tittle-tattle, the smut, the attack on reputations, so that not even the president is safe. It's the torrid language. Politics, the news, world affairs — everything is now conveyed to us in the sensationalist manner of the roman feuilleton. Everything has become a cheap novel.'

The writer raised a languorous hand as if to stifle a yawn.

'You can mock. But have you read the scientists on this, the doctors? Why just the other day, Bernheim was arguing that the vivid images you writers give us leave a lurid photographic imprint on the ordinary mind — without our even being aware of it. They act insidiously, suggestively. They induce a neurophysiological disinhibition which lessens responsibility. They stir, they hypnotize. Look at the way people will follow any self-styled leader. Look at the way they mass together in strikes, in protests. Your images, your language provoke . . .'

'Yes.' Durand was suddenly excited. 'And they provoke imitation. People, simple ordinary people behave as if they were in some kind of trance, on the edge of madness. They imitate violent crimes.'

'That's right,' the deputy nodded. 'Look at our recent crimes, all recounted by your consort in gross detail so that they provoke more and more imitations. Women throwing vitriol in the faces of their lovers, disfiguring them for life, taking up pistols like demented furies in a cheap drama . . .'

'Ah, really Monsieur Parmentier. Next you'll be telling us that it is only women who are suggestible. We poor women who are prone to crimes of passion. I hardly expected this of you.' The woman with the striking red hair challenged the deputy with a look James couldn't quite interpret.

The man shrank into his chair, his face sheepish, his eyes downcast. 'No, no,' he murmured.

'But that is precisely the case, Madame. The statistics prove it,' Durand intervened. 'Why just this week a woman . . .'

Madame de Landois slipped into the empty place at their table. She had, James now realized, been making the rounds of them all.

'What is precisely the case, Chief Inspector?' She smiled encouragingly at Durand.

'We were just talking, chère Madame, about how suggestible wom. . . ' he faltered, 'yes, how open to suggestion people can be. I was about to mention the tragic case of your acquaintance, Olympe Fabre.'

James sat up straighter in order not to miss a word.

'Your evidence has given you a lead?' Marguerite asked, her head tilted at an attractive angle.

Durand cleared his throat. 'I believe so. As Monsieur le Deputé has said, the factor of the vivid imprint left on the mind by strongly emotional words and images plays its part. The rational mind may be quite unaware of its intentions under the influence of such suggestion. And as we know, actresses are highly suggestible creatures.'

'Indeed.' The redhead at James's side released an exaggerated breath.

Durand puffed up his chest perceptibly and cast James what was decidedly a canny glance.

'Monsieur Norton, our advocate friend from America, will know exactly what I mean, from his own experiences of the criminal court, when I talk about the sway of irrational impulses. I glimpsed him at the Vaudeville last night.'

James leaned forward nervously. He hadn't noticed the Chief Inspector at the theatre. Nor did he know where the man had learned quite so much about him.

'Like me, he was inevitably thinking of the impact the play Olympe Fabre performed in night after night might have had on her tragic actions. As you know, Madame, in the play there is a suicide pact. The heroine commits a crime of passion. She kills herself, in the full expectation I imagine, that her lover will do the same.'

A hush had settled on the table. Everyone stared at Marguerite. Her brow was gathered in serious consideration.

'I see, Chief Inspector. I do see. With the slight difference that Olympe was neither a woman married to a man twice her age, nor had a child, it now only remains for you to find the absent party to her double suicide. Are you hoping that another body, this time a young man's, will turn up in the Seine? Do you know who this person might be?'

Marguerite's tone bordered on irony without quite toppling over into it. James was unsure of her intent and was about to intervene when the leap of emotion in Durand's face held him back. The man's features held all the marks of someone who had just suffered a savage slur on his reputation.

If Marguerite were a man, James felt certain, Durand would now challenge her to one of the city's famed duels. Instead, he fingered the edge of his knife, which lay innocently enough on the table. As if unaware of his action, he tested its sharpness on his thumb, back and forth, forth and back, until a tiny drop of blood appeared. Surprised, Durand blotted it quickly on his napkin and said with steady authority, 'Surely, this is not the moment for such speculation, Madame.'

Marguerite gave him a charming smile. It wiped away any negative interpretation he might have made of her earlier comments. 'You are altogether right, Chief Inspector. I am, as you must know, very pleased that you are putting all your skills into the matter of my young friend's death and that it haunts you as it does me. Your Commissaire speaks very highly of you.' With that, she rose from the table. 'We shall talk more in due course.'

James followed her with his eyes, saw her sinuous form move in and out of the mirrored maze until it vanished mysteriously. He had a sense that he had missed some important cue, but he wasn't certain quite what it might be.

Later, after they had all risen from their tables and he had been introduced to more people than he could hope to remember and the quartet was playing again, he caught a glimpse of the Chief Inspector and Marguerite half hidden behind a column on which a bronze dancer stood. He moved in their direction, placing himself casually in front of the pillar. He was almost certain that in the intensity of their conversation, they wouldn't see him.

'Frankly, Chief Inspector,' Marguerite was saying. 'I do not think you are on the right track. Rafael Norton is not capable of such foolishness.'

James stiffened. His mind careened. He almost abandoned his hiding place for direct confrontation, then thought better of it. Marguerite was doing his work.

'Double suicide. No. No. It is not in his style.'

'People we *admire,*' the Chief Inspector italicized the word, 'can often blind us to their less honourable, less rational parts.'

'That may be so, Chief Inspector, but I doubt this particular intrigue that you have invented. Olympe may have been capable of suicide, but not as part of such a banal plot. There was no reason.'

'Monsieur Norton could well have feared the arrival of his older brother. A Jewess, after all, a Jewess with a less than immaculate past would hardly be someone to bring into a respectable family.'

There was silence for a moment and James imagined Marguerite shaking her head emphatically.

'All the gossip at the theatre points only to him,' Durand was insistent. 'If you think that they didn't mutually persuade each other into suicide, the romantic suicide of doomed, despairing lovers, and that he was somehow interrupted in the act, then the crime becomes even more serious. We will have to suppose that he persuaded or helped her to her death in a fit of jealousy or out of a sense of dishonour because she had betrayed him with some unworthy rival. There was another man someone at the theatre mentioned. But I don't have a name. Yes. Either that, or Monsieur Norton's love had grown cold and he found an expedient way of ridding himself of a mistress who had become too persistent.'

'No, no, no, Monsieur l'Inspecteur. None of this fits at all with my knowledge of these two people. You will have to find some evidence to convince me.' Marguerite's voice had a tremor in it. 'My own sense is that you need to cast your net wider.'

'And you think that Monsieur Norton's absolute conviction that Olympe did not kill herself, is evidence of nothing at all?

'Nothing at all. Neither a momentary amnesia, nor a cover-up.'

With that, Marguerite appeared from behind the column and quickly walked towards her guests. The music was drawing to an end.

Applause filled the room.

James hurried after her.

'May we have a moment alone? Perhaps after the others have left?' He slipped automatically into English. 'I would so like to speak with you.'

She looked at him and then behind him. James turned slightly and saw Durand's vigilant gaze on them.

With a smile that had nothing of complicity in it, Marguerite held out her hand for the formality of a parting. 'Ask Pierre to show you to the library on your way out,' she murmured. 'Ah, Chief Inspector, Monsieur Norton must already leave us. But not you, I trust. I particularly wanted to introduce you to Anatole Bartholi.'

'I would be honoured, Madame,' he bowed slightly, then turned to James. 'We will meet again very soon, Monsieur Norton, I have no doubt. No doubt at all.'

In the lamplight, the library had the soft stillness of a cocoon. Ranked books watching over him like so many benevolent gods, James sat back in the striped sofa with a sense of well-being which he knew had everything to do with the magic spell of the place and nothing to do with the situation in which he now felt himself inextricably entangled. The stubborn insistence of Chief Inspector Durand's voice as it spun its web of malign speculation was at a distant remove. Far closer was the intimate waft of cherry blossom which fluttered in through the half-open window and brought with it Marguerite's presence — so appealing, so reasonable, yet so subtly mysterious.

He must have dozed off, for he suddenly heard her voice in a double register, both inner and outer. He ploughed through the haze of dream and sat up.

She was looking down at him with a whimsical smile. 'I'm so very sorry, Monsieur Norton. Sometimes my friends decide to stay for longer than they are altogether welcome. Let me get you a cognac.'

She walked to the far end of the room and poured two glasses from a decanter as James gathered his wits.

'I wanted to talk to you about the situation, about several things in fact,' James began when she had sat down in the chair opposite him.

'You overheard my conversation with the Chief Inspector?'

'Yes.'

She sighed. 'I suspect our dear Chief Inspector is more suggestible than Olympe ever was. He has been hypnotized by the very cases he purports to investigate. He sees crimes of passion everywhere. The very notion that Olympe would be taken over by her role — a part in a play that is already based on a real case . . . oh yes, Monsieur, perhaps you didn't know . . . Well that is altogether preposterous.'

'So you do not think we are dealing with a crime of passion?'

She stared at him for a moment.

'Do you think your brother is capable of such things?'

'The Rafael I know is most certainly not.'

'But you imagine a Rafael you don't know?'

James sipped his cognac thoughtfully. 'I imagine,' he said slowly, feeling the rigour of her gaze, 'I imagine that a woman could be madly, overwhelmingly in love with him. And that he might return that love.' It wasn't what he had intended to say. An imp of the perverse had taken him over and propelled him.

'Ah, as for that . . .' The sudden flush in her cheeks said more than her words. She collected herself quickly. 'But there was still no reason for suicide. There was no cause for despair. There was nothing to stop their love. Nothing.'

James suddenly had an image of his mother hovering above him, her anger palpable in the rigidity of her features, her morality, her faith affronted. He prodded her away, not without a superstitious shiver. 'No. Of course, you are right.'

'What we must absolutely do is find some evidence to point the Chief Inspector in another direction or he could make Rafael's life difficult. He is not predisposed in his favour. He does not like journalists. Nor for that matter Jews.'

'Touquet, I believe, said that Durand was an upholder of scientific detection, an honest man.'

She shrugged. 'Science can take many forms. Let's hope the juge d'instruction is better disposed.'

'Juge d'instruction?'

'Yes, the judge who will lead the legal investigation of the case. One will be named very soon I imagine or perhaps already has been . . .' she paused. 'But Touquet is right. Durand is not an altogether unreasonable man. I feel certain that if there is a track we can point him to, I can sway him onto it.'

James remembered the way the man had responded to the mildest of Marguerite's ironies and had a feeling that the Chief Inspector might not be as tractable as she assumed. It seemed likely that the Chief Inspector was in at least two minds about aristocrats as well, even the most democratic amongst them.

But he nodded. 'Yes. And it's precisely these other tracks that I wish to speak to you about.'

She looked at him expectantly.

He drew out Olympe's daybook from his pocket where it had made an unsightly bulge all evening. 'I wanted your help on this. It belongs to Olympe. It charts her appointments. My brother . . .' He paused, suddenly uncomfortable. 'My brother is not altogether easy to talk to when it comes to the poor girl. And you have known her for so many years . . .'

She laughed. It was a warm, rich sound. 'You have made Olympe's case your own. I can see that. I wonder at it. Perhaps you too have grown a little fond of her?'

'There is no cause for wonder.' He responded a little stiffly. 'You must understand. I would like to get my brother home as quickly as possible. I have a certain expertise in sifting evidence — and in this case, a necessary detachment.'

'And you have her appointment book where Durand does not . . .'

James relaxed, chuckled. 'It literally fell into my hands when I was in Olympe's apartment. Together with some letters.'

'Expertise, indeed.'

James turned the pages of the notebook until he had reached the last three weeks of Olympe's life and handed it to Marguerite. 'Perhaps you could help me with the names some of the initials she noted here stand for. It might provide some clues. There is also a Marcel who wrote to her with great regularity. Do you know who he is?'

'Marcel?' Her cheek dimpled. 'Ah yes, Marcel Bonnefoi. A fond and rather foolish young man. He adores actresses. He feels he can help them with their art.'

'Could I meet him?'

'It could be arranged. If he is still in Paris. The season as you know is coming to an end. But there is no harm in him. He wouldn't hurt a fly, let alone an adored creature like Olympe.'

'Does my brother know of his adoration?'

She laughed outright. 'You are becoming as severe as our Chief Inspector, Monsieur Norton. A woman behaves a little badly and you say, famously like Dumas, Tue-la! Kill her. I can see how your thoughts are progressing. Rafael could never be jealous of Marcel. That is another preposterous idea.'

'So he knows him?' James was stubborn.

'Of that I cannot be certain. You must ask him yourself. I am not his keeper.' She looked down at the notebook.

'There were also letters from an Armand, a Julien and an F de M. Do those names mean anything to you?'

Marguerite shook her head thoughtfully. 'I don't believe so.' She paused. 'You know, Monsieur Norton. Actresses have many admirers. Olympe was a very attractive young woman. If these men had been important to her, she would probably have mentioned them to me.'

'Did she mention a painter called Max Henry?'

'Decidedly, you have been busy, Monsieur. Yes, Olympe mentioned that she had posed for a few canvases. He is a neighbour. But nothing more, I believe.'

'Do you know how she treated her admirers?'

'You mean might one of them have harboured a passion that grew suddenly violent?'

'Exactly.'

She shivered, then rose to refill their glasses. She didn't speak again until she had sat down. 'Anything is possible, of course. But my own sense of Olympe is that she was kind. She wasn't a trifler. An *allumeuse* as we say, a deliberate kindler of men's passions. There was a sweet seriousness about her. But one never knows with admirers.'

Emotions passed over her face in swift succession and settled in regret. She looked down at the notebook. 'Here. 28 May. Di. Didi. That was her childhood nickname for her sister, Judith. Then RN, that is your brother. He figures quite often. P, I imagine is Papa, yes, he is noted on the Monday he mentioned. The others LI, IB . . . I don't recognize.

James pulled her back. 'So you know about her sister?'

'Shouldn't I?'

'Rafael didn't. Not until Monsieur Arnhem mentioned her.'

'I see. But that is understandable. There are certain things it is perhaps best to keep from men. With your experience of the world, you will know that, Monsieur Norton.'

She met his eyes and James felt his pulse beat with a sudden odd insistence. But she was already elsewhere, her expression dreamy, tinged with apprehension.

He needed to bring her back. 'How long had you known Olympe? How did you meet her?' he asked softly. 'Tell me about your friendship.'

Her gaze floated back to him. 'I will tell you. Why not? Though it is a long story.' She settled back in her chair, her dress rustling in the quiet of the room.

'It dates back to '92, no '93, just before the great Charcot's death. You know of Jean-Martin Charcot, then our foremost neurologist? A formidable man. He ran the Salpêtrière Hospital and he turned that madhouse for the poor and deranged into what he named a museum of living pathology. He gave public lectures — demonstrations, really, in what he called his clinico-anatomic method — a mixture of careful clinical observation of patients and an investigation into the phsyiological abnormalities which precipitated their condition. And they were terrible conditions — tics and strange walks and anaesthesias and paralyses and ravings.' She paused. 'Am I boring you?'

'No, not at all.' James was only astonished that a lady might be interested in such things. 'Please continue.'

'Well, Charcot held his demonstrations in a large amphitheatre at the Salpêtrière every Friday. They were open to the public. I think, everything else apart, he wanted to show us that these strange diseases were not the product of gods and demons and wicked spirits. They were not punishments or possessions or portents, but painful illnesses eventually as treatable by medical science, as any other.

'In any case, I went along to a few of his lectures. I was rivetted. He was a wonderful performer and the setting was almost like a theatre. Bright lights illuminated the stage. He would have assistants with him and patients, sometimes a man, but more usually a woman or two who were suffering from hysteria and he would hypnotize them and demonstrate the various phases their illness went through. First he would have his assistants touch the women in a particularly sensitive, what he called a hysterogenic, zone, which brought on the attack. They might foam at the mouth or immediately fall into a deep, a cataleptic sleep. He would then suggest certain things to them and under this hypnosis, it was extraordinary what they would do. I saw one woman completely convinced that a top hat was her baby. She rocked it, kissed it.

'This first stage was followed by a stage of clownisme, in which the patient went through impossible acrobatic contortions. Physical spasms, like the strange postures you see in that Breughel engraving of dancing mania. And finally came the "attitudes passionelles" in which the patient mimed scenes and spoke of her life.' She stopped. 'You are looking at me oddly, Monsieur Norton. I shock you.'

James hadn't realized he had reached for his pipe. He was somewhat taken aback by Marguerite's enthusiasm, but he was also fascinated. He knew a little of what she spoke, but he had never seen it mimed so graphically. 'No, please go on.'

Abruptly, she threw her head back and lifted her hands to the heavens as if she were addressing her lord and master. 'This is how I first saw Judith Arnhem. I'll never forget it. She seemed to be invoking God, speaking to him from the midst of her desperate passion. Then she raised her fist and shook it, like some female incarnation of Job. Her hair was flying, her face agonized. And she was speaking. It struck me as odd that Charcot didn't listen at all to what she was saying, as if what mattered most was the dramatic pose she struck. But I listened. I was near the front that day and I could hear her mumblings clearly.

'She was evoking a huge conflagration, the burning of a house, the terrible heat, a death, a horribly charred body. The details were so acute that I couldn't believe these were simply mad ravings. And she chastised God. She tore at her hair. She said she wanted to die, to burn, too, to atone for her wrongs.'

Marguerite paused again.

'Do go on, please,' James urged.

'Her pain was palpable,' Marguerite murmured. 'So I went to see her. Went the next day into the bowels of the hospital, not the new lecture theatre where I had the comfort of knowing a good number of the auditors, but into the midst of the pandemonium. It was both terrible and terrifying. And it was there I met Rachel Arnhem.'

'She was an inmate,' James breathed.

Marguerite shook her head. 'No, no, I went to see Judith. It took me some time to find her. But I refused to be deterred. I had this innocent notion that I could help her in some way. That I could alleviate her suffering. Rachel was with her. She was visiting. A frightened little girl, painfully thin with those vast tearful eyes, coming to visit her sister. My heart went out to both of them. It was only over the coming months that I was able to piece the story together.'

In a soft voice, her manner terse now as if the facts conveyed more than enough emotion, Marguerite went on to tell him about the tragedy that had struck and splintered the Arnhem household.

Like so many immigrant families, the Arnhems worked hard and all of them worked to make ends meet. After years of labouring for others, in 1890 they had amassed just enough funds to set up a small tailoring business of their own in premises outside their own lodgings. The father dealt with customers and cut the cloth and ironed, the mother and the girls sewed and looked after the younger children. They worked all hours and every day, taking in overspill from larger establishments, breaking only for the Sabbath, when this was possible.

On that Saturday late in the autumn of '92, Judith, the eldest sister by three years, was meant to go into the shop to finish off an urgent piece of work. She refused. She was only eighteen and she wanted a break from the four bleak walls. There was a young man she was seeing. The father was angry. The work had to be done. Judith persisted and to create peace in the family, her mother said she would go in her place and finish the work in no time. It was only right that Judith should see her friend. Rachel could look after the little ones.

So the mother went off on her own. It was the last any of them saw of her alive. No one ever learned how it had happened, whether it was a gas lamp or a stray coal or a candle that started the conflagration, whether the mother in her exhaustion had fallen asleep over her work or been suffocated by smoke and fumes. Or indeed, whether some madman had broken in to steal, had knocked her out and then started the fire. But it was Judith who was the first on the scene. She had seen her friend, and feeling remorseful, had decided to go to the shop and help her mother out if she hadn't yet finished the work. It was late afternoon when she reached the shop. The flames were already high, brilliant against the night, an inferno the firemen were struggling to douse. She broke past them and rushed in, only to catch a glimpse of her mother's charred body before a brave fireman dragged her out.

The family went to pieces after that. Arnhem blamed himself. He stopped working. He sat in a corner of the room beating his chest and staring interminably into space. What food there was came from the kindness of neighbours. Judith, too, was ravaged by guilt. She walked the streets in a kind of desperate trance. She was probably raped on one of these walks. In any event, she soon allowed herself to be raped for money. She brought the money home and put it on the table in front of her father. It was Rachel who picked it up and bought food for them all.

Then came Judith's first suicide attempt. She slit her wrists. It woke Arnhem into action. He rushed her to a doctor. But the attempts continued, each more desperate than the last and Judith was unreachable, raving. Finally, at his wits' end, frightened of the impact she was having on the little ones and on Rachel, he brought her to the Salpêtrière.

Madame de Landois' voice had trailed off and they sat in silence as James tried to assimilate what — even in broad brush strokes — was a terrifying story. At last, though he sensed he was outstaying his welcome, he said,

'How do you estimate the impact of all this on Rachel — on Olympe, I mean?'

Her abrupt laugh held a sob. 'When I met her, Olympe was a child, but a child that had grown old before her time. She had supped too full of horrors, as your poet says. She was very quiet, unnaturally quiet. Everything was written in her eyes, all her emotions imprisoned in her stiff little form. I thought if she spoke too much she might break. Not only into tears, but into pieces. I asked her on that first day whether she would like to come home with me to take tea, perhaps. On top of everything else she looked starved.

'I had to convince her, woo her, but she came eventually. It was spring. We took tea in the orangerie and I had all kinds of cakes and biscuits placed before her. She just sat, like a large doll and stared. Stared at everything — the garden, the trees, the piano, the food. She didn't touch anything. She was frightened of me too, I suspect. I was like a creature from a different planet.

'I noticed that her eyes kept moving back to the piano and I asked her if she played. I was babbling, you see, saying anything that came into my mind, just to try and put her at her ease. She shook her head. But then a moment later she said what were almost her first words to me, her first question in any case. She said, "Do you?"

'I nodded and for some reason I went to the piano and I started to play. A little Mozart sonatina, I think it was. And as I played, she began to move. She touched things. The table cloth, the petal of a tulip, she cupped it in her hand. She brushed the sugar from a millefeuille and brought her fingertip to her mouth. It was as if she was coming to life. I played and played and watched her and felt a kind of wonder. Felt like I had never felt before in my life. When the hint of a smile touched her lips and eyes, I had the sense that it was the first real accomplishment of my life.

'I stopped at last. I was aware that Olivier would soon be coming home. We still lived together then. And for some reason, I didn't want him intruding on us. I guess I felt he would frighten her back into her cell. I asked her if she would like something to drink now. She looked at me a little dazed as if she had forgotten my presence, but she nodded. And after we sat down, she said to me that she used to play. Play the violin, before . . .

and she stopped. I pressed her a little, very gently, and she told me it was before her mother died. I asked her whether she would like to come back the next day and play with me. I had a violin in the house. I had once played it, too. And no one here would object to our making as much music as we wanted. She said that she might.

'I left it at that. I had all the tea things wrapped and told her she could take them home. She might feel hungrier later. Then I took her back in the carriage and said I would come and fetch her the next day at about two. If she felt like coming, she could.'

Marguerite paused. There were tears in her eyes. 'And that I guess was the beginning of our friendship. It's late Monsieur Norton. We must both get some sleep.'

James gazed at her, hesitating, loath to leave. 'She was your Galatea,' he said softly.

She smiled. 'Perhaps. In a way. I certainly helped her find her new name. But that was some years later. First, she came back to make music with me. I was astonished at her talent. I didn't know of her father's then. Gradually, slowly, over the months, the story of her mother came out. One day I asked her whether she had a dream, a dream of something she would really like to do and she told me that before her death, her mother had taken her to the theatre as a birthday present and what she wanted, more than anything, though she knew it was impossible, was to be like one of those women. To act. So I set out to help her.'

Suddenly she covered her face with her hands. Her words were a stifled moan. 'I had no premonition that . . .' She rose and started to pace.

'I'm so sorry,' James heard himself saying. 'So very sorry. You . . . you behaved wonderfully.'

She said nothing. She was wrapped in her own thoughts. He got up slowly. 'May I presume to put one more question to you?'

She turned to him, a little bewildered, her eyes veiled in a sadness which only accentuated her beauty.

He looked away, suddenly uneasy with his question.

'Do go on.'

'I simply wanted to know when and how those episodes Olympe

suffered from, the ones you mentioned to Arnhem, played themselves out.'

'Decidedly you are no sentimentalist, Monsieur Norton. No, no, do not take offence. It is precisely what we need if we are to get to the bottom of this. Rachel, I call her that because she was not Olympe then, undertook, if that is the right word, most of her somnambulistic walking in the darkest months, just after her mother's death. She would leave the house for, say the market, and two days later wake up in a village on the outskirts of Paris, altogether unaware of how she had arrived there.

'Once, she went as far afield as Lyons, where she was picked up by a policeman and after long interrogation luckily transported back to Paris rather than to prison. Her shoes apparently were completely worn out. She didn't know whether she had slept in fields or auberges or taken trains or walked all the way. It is truly astonishing and fortunate that nothing terrible happened to her — a girl alone like that.

'There was only one episode after I met her. As far as I know, the ill ness then never recurred. Professeur Ponsard saw her a few times — the doctor I have recommended to Elinor.' She paused. 'When I got to know Rachel, I understood her ambulatory automatism as an altogether reasonable, though unreasoning, attempt to escape the horror that family life had become. It was one of the things her new life, her new interests helped her to overcome.'

'But when I was here, you asked Monsieur Arnhem whether it might have happened again?'

'You are truly a lawyer, Monsieur Norton. Nothing escapes you.'

'Do please call me James. The hour is a little late for *Monsieurs.*'

She smiled. 'And you will call me, Marguerite.'

'So, Marguerite,' James took a certain relish in pronouncing the name aloud. 'You thought that Olympe might have gone walking. Why?'

She shrugged. 'I always worried, perhaps superstitiously, that if anything happened to reawaken those terrible days in Olympe, she might resort to the same strategies of escape. That was why I mentioned it. She always had a horror of fires — even the crackle from behind a fire guard.'

'Had anything terrible happened of late?'

'Not that I know of. As I said to you, we weren't all that close in recent months. She had her own life. A full one.'

He wanted to explore the reasons behind their growing apart, but she was already walking towards the door. 'My coachman will ferry you to your hotel.'

'That's very kind of you.'

She raised an eyebrow. 'Of him, you mean.'

'Of both of you.' He bowed. Before he could help himself, a final question had leapt from his lips. 'How much does my brother know of all these aspects of Olympe's life?'

She was impatient now. 'I imagine he knows much of it. Judith is a special case. Perhaps Olympe never mentioned her because one can never estimate what impact a person will have on her. And Rafael would certainly have insisted on meeting her. But you must ask him, James,' she added with a lilt and laughed.

James leaned back into the leather of seats and listened to the rhythmic trot of horses' hoofs. There was so much new information to digest — about Olympe, her family, Chief Inspector Durand's suspicions.

He gazed out on the deserted street. Suddenly, a figure appeared in the glow of a lamp. He was hurrying, rushing in the direction from which James had come. It was Raf. His head was bare, his jacket akimbo.

James watched him with a fretful, dawning realization. Too late, he considered asking the driver to stop.

Here was one more matter to ponder amongst the many that had come his way in the course of this long, eventful evening.

But for a moment emotion trampled reason. He was again like the boy who had been kept from the bright room into which his brother could run at will.

PART TWO

TEN

Like a piece of cork with no will of its own, James felt himself picked up by the gathering human tide and forced along the boulevard in a direction that wasn't his own.

The mounting flow had caught him unawares as he walked away from Ellie's apartment. He had once more been fuming at Raf and wondering what on earth could have impelled his brother to squander his Sunday at the races when so much more pressing business called — when his sweetheart lay dead, his sister ill, his mother waiting for him to disentangle himself from the clutch of his Parisian affairs. Not to mention the fact that a senior police officer suspected him of a serious crime.

He had indeed begun to think that the whole tawdry nature of Raf's life in Paris had tipped him over the edge if he really presumed — as his note had specified — that James would join him at a café behind the Arc de Triomphe, so that they could go cavorting off to Longchamps.

Anger had blinded him to the life around him. The streets had taken on a frenzied momentum of their own. With a single, massed will the crowd had propelled him in its chosen direction and landed him amidst the roar and squeeze of a Champs Élysées transformed.

All around him now, the tricolour fluttered. Men in the soft hats and caps and blues of the people sprouted red flowers from their buttonholes. They shouted, cheered, screamed, 'Vive Loubet.' 'Vive le Président.'

'Vive la République.'

Stretching to his full height to catch a glimpse of the street before him, James saw a procession of carriages moving in stately rhythm up the middle of the avenue towards the Arc de Triomphe. As an open landau approached his field of vision, the cheers rose to a frenzied pitch. 'Loubet. Loubet. Vive Loubet,' the crowd chanted in rhythmic unison.

James realized he was a mere matter of yards away from the President of the Republic. He found himself joining in, shouting, 'Vive la République.' A grinning man thrust a red flower into his jacket pocket, raised his fist in a rousing salute. And then to his side, he heard a jeering chorus, 'A bas Loubet, Down with Loubet.' There was a scuffle, a flash of fisticuffs. The crowd heaved. A file of policemen broke through, pounced and the crowd closed round again, their cheers mounting into the clear blue canopy of the sky.

It was only after the procession had passed and the crowd had begun to disperse that James engaged the man who had given him the flower in conversation and learned what he had already begun to suspect. The President and his entourage were on their way to the Longchamps Races. This determined act on the President's part was a brave signal to the anti-Dreyfusistes that he would not be bullied, despite the previous week's attack on him at the Auteuil racetrack. Workers from Belleville and Montmartre, socialists and assembled pro-Dreyfus republicans had gathered in their thousands to voice their support for him. The police, too, were in heavy evidence, ordered for once to use their power in support of the President.

'You can bet your tricolour,' his informant told James, 'that no toffs are going to wield their sticks at the races today.'

As he wound his way slowly towards the river, James chastised himself for the reproaches he had mentally hurled at his brother. He ordered himself to remember from now on that Raf was neither a child nor even a rebellious, hot-headed adolescent, but a man with his fingers on the pulse of the city. Yes, a man who knew far more about life here than he did himself. He was no longer, James acknowledged ruefully, the only sensible brother.

He leaned against a stone balustrade and watched the waters of the river rushing past. An image of Olympe's body tossed by the current snaked into his mind. He shivered despite the warmth. In the course of the night, the poor lost girl had grown in his mind into a poignant, mysterious creature, as if a master painter had taken a rough, amateur sketch and added rich tinges of colour and shadowy depths to her being, far more enigmatic than the shades of his tightrope walker. It made him mourn her disappearance as well as the fact that he had never met her.

He was not far from the point at which the houseboat was moored. He peered down river towards the left bank and thought he could make out its shape. He considered going there and talking to its owner, but then decided against it. No, he would do what he had only half considered doing earlier. The passing notion had taken on substance with his realization that he had calumnied Raf. He would go if only to prove to himself and to his absent brother that he, too, could be useful. Tomorrow, after all, he would have to be wholly at Ellie's disposal.

James hailed a cab and as he named his destination saw a look of something like fear cross the coachman's gnarled face. He tapped his pocket and jumped in before the man could refuse him.

The Salpêtrière was a vast, imposing structure at the eastern extremity of the city. Its façade stretched for some two city blocks. An impressive dome rose from the building's midst like the stiff skirt of some deity of Olympian proportions whose head was lost in the clouds.

James's cab deposited him in front of an arched entrance building and whipped away so rapidly that James was left with a sense of having been abandoned in a hostile clime. He squared his shoulders and looked around him. To the corner of the arch an attendant sprawled sleepily in a chair and basked in the sunlight, as if signalling that Sunday was a day of rest, even here. James approached him and asked for directions to Dr. Vaillant's wards. The man lifted an eyelid to give him a querulous look, then pointed in a desultory manner behind him.

Beyond the gates at the remove of a flat expanse of lawn striated by paths, the bulk of the building stretched. It offered three visible entry points. A woman on crutches was hopping along one of the gravelled paths and he hurried after her, but she refused his question and hobbled on as if she hadn't seen him. A couple with downcast faces walked past without meeting his eye.

With a shrug he made his way to the central door. He pushed open its weight and followed the length of a dark drafty hall. He had a sinking feeling. Muffled sounds reached him from he didn't know quite where. Before him there was an emptiness, devoid of signposts.

He prodded open a second door. A few steps and he was in a cavernous domed space. The light was blinding. It poured through high windows to streak the marble floor. As his eyes adjusted, he made out a series of pale, life-size statues clinging to a wall. Beyond them was an alcove. A smattering of women, all in black, knelt there, heads bowed. Above them, a starkly simple wooden cross floated on a white wall. All around him, he now saw, were the chapels of a large church. The one on his right was empty, but for a solemn *Pietà* bowed under the weight of her larger son.

He proceeded on tiptoe. It struck him that this was one of the barest churches he had ever visited, as if some rigorous iconoclast had set fiercely to work to wipe out any of the excesses of idolatry. He remembered Marguerite's words about Charcot's scientific project, his desire to eradicate the notion of any links between demons and insanity. Faith seemed to have vanished in the same breath, leaving the mad to a desolate world as harsh as the one Darwin had bestowed on them all. Science might illuminate, but it was rarely kind.

James pushed aside wayward thoughts. He was putting off the moment, as if the strangely silent corridors, the sudden appearance of this vast domed space, had awoken an unanticipated fear of what he was about to confront. He plunged towards a rear door and found himself outside again, on a path which led to a courtyard. There were more buildings all around him now. These had none of the stateliness of the edifice which fronted the main street. They were run down, dilapidated. The capped figures of women peered through the windows, their foreheads pressed to glass, their faces contorted.

He walked, saw groups of old, wrinkled matrons, their backs bowed as they sat in the sun. Their glazed, blank stares forbade approach. Beside a crone in a wheelchair, he located a panel listing names of what must be wards. Vaillant's name didn't figure.

It came to him, while he strayed, that the hospital was in fact a labyrinthine complex the size of a small town. He had a sudden bleak sense of a world gone awry, as if madness stalked the streets of civilization only to pounce at ever shorter intervals, so that the confines of asylums swelled and gradually swallowed up the entire city.

At last after countless deviations, he saw a nurse making her way through a door. He raced after her only to find himself in a dispensary. A row of people queued at a counter, chatting desultorily. He was about to ask one of them the way when through an open door, he glimpsed a waxy figure — supine, deformed, dead. He jumped back and felt the colour drain from his face.

One of the nurses let out a shrill, cascading laugh. Her headdress shook, her cheeks jiggled. James wondered for a moment about her sanity.

'It's the museum. Go on. You can go in. Charcot's museum. Everyone comes to see it.'

The words bore a challenge to his manhood. James strode through the door. The long, narrow room smelled strongly of some chemical. It bit at his eyes. Through their rawness, he forced himself to confront the dead body, a poor, misshapen corpse with splayed hands and bulging feet. Only after a moment did he realize that this particular body was made of wax and that its deformities signalled a precise neurological condition. But all around him were bits of real bone and contorted joints displayed behind glass. Each had its medical description appended — locomotor ataxia, amyotrophic lateral sclerosis. Like names of exotic countries, the words required slow reading. They kept him from the skeletons which reclined on pallets or stood, somehow propped, their deformations clearly marked. There were brains, too, floating in some sulphurous liquid in large jars, and strange machines, little black boxes with wires protruding from them and numbered dials and magnets.

Photographs, prints and drawings lined one wall. Ancient, naked women leaned on sticks, knees swaying; men tottered on skewed feet, their backbones curved. There were also beautiful girls with wild eyes and seductive expressions who seemed to have little to do with this catalogue of neurological horrors. One, he noticed had her back arched in the way Marguerite had mimed to him. He realized these must be the famous hysterics. Amongst them was a portrait of a man with a strong, solid face, his gaze direct. Jean-Martin Charcot, the label announced.

Charcot, James told himself, was a far stronger man than he was. Without a backward glance, he slipped from the room. He hoped the giggling nurse would have gone. But she was still there and he smiled his thanks with what he hoped wasn't too livid a face and asked for Dr. Vaillant's service.

She directed him to the next building, telling him she was certain Vaillant wouldn't be in on a brilliant Sunday. 'He'll be at the races,' she declared with another smile.

'Isn't everyone?' James managed a rueful laugh. 'Do you by any chance know a patient called Judith Arnhem?'

She paused to consider. 'The second floor ward, if I remember. I haven't worked there for a while.'

James considered himself to be a man endowed with a requisite if not extraordinary amount of both courage and good sense. For all that, he was utterly unprepared for the pandemonium of the long, cramped ward. He felt as if all his senses were under attack. The shrieks and calls and hoots of the women on the high ranked beds fell on his ears like the mangling claws of birds of prey. Their emaciated faces and contorted limbs, their rocking and crouching forms brought to mind one of the circles of hell painted by a visionary master. There was a smell too, a high pungent reek he didn't recognize, but it made his stomach lurch painfully. It somersaulted as a woman leapt towards him and pawed at his jacket, her strange beaked face emitting a cascade of sound he couldn't begin to make out. He would gladly have retraced his steps if at that moment a nurse hadn't run to his side and with a sharp word at the creature, scowlingly confronted him and asked his business.

Before he could move his tongue into speech, a second figure stood before him, a doctor of about his own age. The fleshy, unhealthy face with its splattering of beard, the stance, at once bullish and arrogant, bore a vague familiarity. But the orderly process of his own mind seemed to have gone awry and he couldn't place the man. He stammered out his errand.

'I would like to see Judith Arnhem.'

'Judith Arnhem,' the doctor repeated with blunt suspicion. 'Mademoiselle is still resting, isn't she, nurse?'

The woman nodded and he waved her away. He placed his stout figure squarely in front of James, like a barricade with the words 'Visitors not welcome' clearly written on it. He peered up at him. 'We have met before, haven't we, Monsieur?' His brow arched into a florid pucker above the ridge of his nose, as he reached into the breast pocket of his white coat to pull out a pair of spectacles. 'Ah yes, of course.'

'Dr. Comte.' The name fell into James's mind simultaneously.

'At the Saint-Lazare Infirmary.'

'Yes, that's right. I was visiting Louise Boussel with my brother.'

'Indeed. And now you wish to visit Judith Arnhem. Another cousin, I take it.' A hint of menace came into the man's voice. His eyes behind the spectacles looked preternaturally large. 'Decidedly your cousins, Monsieur, inhabit the less salubrious sites of our city. You will permit me to say that the grip of heredity rarely allows two such specimens as your brother and yourself to emerge from the same stock as these ladies.'

James stared him down and waved his hand with as much insouciance as he could muster. 'Cousins, Dr. Comte, in a manner of speaking.'

'And what manner is that, Monsieur?' The man had moved on to the raised part of the floor where the beds stood, so that he was now at eye level with James.

'Let us say these women are cousins of friends.'

James suddenly felt something tug at his jacket. A woman kneeled behind him. Her hands pawed at his clothes. Her lips were poised in the parody of a salacious kiss. She gestured at him obscenely. He stepped back.

Comte smirked, relishing James's discomfort. 'Cousins of friends. So you are not a Jew?'

'No, doctor. Nor am I an African or a German or an Englishman.'

'I dare say it's a lucky thing you are not the first.' Comte finally ordered the woman back to her bed with a whisk of his plump hand. 'Semites have a particular affinity for a whole gamut of neurological and neuropathological conditions — chorea, ataxic tabes, epilepsy. We have a higher proportion than the general population would normally allow within the Salpêtrière. If you were really a cousin of the ladies in question, I would have felt drawn to interrogate you on your family history, your secret family history, perhaps.' His chuckle was malign. 'As for these other races you mention, my researches haven't extended to them.'

James tried to still his galloping unease. He didn't know how to interpret what the man was saying to him. He was alert though to the undertow of threat in his manner. He wished he could take the doctor into another room, away from the tumult, the leering faces, the constant movement, and focus on one discomfort at a time.

'And you carry on your researches both here and at Saint-Lazare?' he asked, puzzled at the doubling up.

'Indeed. And the research you should know is very important, Monsieur.' Dr. Comte's tone was puffed with arrogance. He took off his spectacles and like a lecturer addressing a large audience used them as a pointer. 'Both Saint-Lazare and the Salpêtrière are sites where the poorest women from the most depraved backgrounds are to be found. I am interested in the high frequency with which prostitutes, loose women if you will, move from the first to the second — or naturally to any other asylum. My hypothesis is that degeneracy, sexual disinhibition, catapults them from one to the other. But now I must ask you what it is that brings you to seek out my patient — since you are not her relative.'

James was about to invent a long-winded excuse, when the word leapt from his lips with its own counter menace. 'Murder, doctor. Murder.'

The man's glasses slipped from his hands. A capped patient whisked them from beneath his feet. All the while, she shrieked the words, 'Murder, murder.' It had the ring of an injunction.

In a moment like a freak wave, the words tore through the room, re-emerging from every mouth in a mounting torrential chorus.

Comte stamped his feet, shouted, 'Silence.' From somewhere, he found a walking stick and like a lion-tamer, beat it against the edge of one bed after another until the women cowered against their pillows and fell restively quiet.

'Nurse, take this man — your name again, Monsieur?'

James provided it.

'Take this man to see Mlle Arnhem. You will probably do no more than see, Monsieur Norton. I had to administer chloroform. If she is awake, do not mention that terrible word. You see the effect it has. You have caused quite enough of a disturbance already.' With a scowl, which made the pucker on his brow throb, he turned on his heel and marched away.

It was only when James reached the quiet of the corridor that it struck him as decidedly odd that Dr. Comte hadn't paused to ask him a single question about the nature of the murder. But this was no time for reflection.

The nurse had turned the lock on a door to reveal a minute cubicle of a room. A figure lay stretched on the bed. One frail arm protruded from the grey blanket and arched above her head. A mass of dark waving hair spread like a fan against the thin bolster.

James stared and took a step backwards. His blood ran cold. The resemblance was uncanny. The motionless figure on the bed could have been Olympe, the Olympe he had seen in pictures. The Olympe, bar the puffy discolouration of her face, he had glimpsed on the floor of the barge. Perhaps it was a trick of light or the fact that Judith, too, lay as still as a corpse.

The nurse was muttering. 'There is no point, Monsieur. There's no waking her now. She won't hear a thing.'

'Why was chloroform administered?'

The woman shrugged, her face as stolid and expressionless as a prison warder's. 'She was wild. Uncontrollable. The doctor feared she would injure herself.'

'How long had that been going on?'

'Three days. Four. Maybe a week. She was worse after her father came to visit. They're always worse after visits.' She gave him a steely look, willing him away.

He nodded and turned a feeble smile on her. It was all that he could muster. But he needed to interrogate her. He took a last look at Judith Arnhem and stepped into the hall.

'Have you ever met Judith Arnhem's sister?' he asked once she had locked the door.

'I don't believe so.' She was already walking away.

'They look very much alike.'

'If you say so, Monsieur. I must get back.'

'Are you certain? The sister would have been well dressed, of course.'

She stopped to confront him, her stout body as much of a barricade as the doctor's. Visitors to the world of the asylum were decidedly unwelcome.

'Dr. Vaillant's policy is to rotate his staff. I work here only two weeks out of every four. I have enough to do without keeping track of visitors, Monsieur. And you are the second one today to come in search of Mlle Arnhem who, as you can see, is in no state to receive anyone. Now if you'll excuse me.'

Watching her determined tread, James wondered whether Raf's impatience had paralleled his own and he had decided to make an early visit to Judith Arnhem.

He walked slowly back through the maze of courtyards and corridors, letting his feet find the way. Even when the vast façade of the Salpêtrière was behind him, his mind was still in the swirling ward with its mêlée of shrieks and strange faces. He replayed his eccentric exchange with Dr. Comte, trying to determine whether its oddness was due to the surroundings or was intrinsic to the man's words. Was it unusual that he should work both in the prison infirmary and at the asylum?

His thoughts returned again and again to the supine figure of Judith Arnhem. Had he imagined the resemblance? It was troubling and for more reasons than he could put words to.

Without realizing where his steps had taken him, he found himself in the Sunday jostle of the Jardin des Plantes. Children shouted their excitement as they pointed through the bars of a cage where a tiger prowled in taut confinement. James stared for a moment, felt the tiger's insolent gaze on him and hurried away.

On a winding street behind the zoo, he stopped in a café. Leaning against the bar, he ordered a brandy and a coffee. A well-proportioned, clear-eyed face stared out at him, radiating good health and firm intentions. It took the heat of the brandy for him to recognize himself in the mirror. He gave his returned image a sheepish, lop-sided grin and took his coffee out onto the *terrasse*.

He lit his pipe and sat there, only dimly aware of the life of the street. Like one of those hangovers he had been prone to in the months after Maisie's death, the Salpêtrière clogged his veins and his thoughts. He finished his coffee and got up restlessly, half wishing for Raf's presence or even better, he admitted to himself, Marguerite's so that he could share or argue through his impressions. He had a distant memory of one of his first cases, one which had filled him with tension because of its human rather than legal complexity. Because every fact seemed to billow away behind a shroud of half-truths.

Reaching in his pocket for change, he felt the crunch of paper. Of course, the letter in the indecipherable language. That would give him something concrete to pursue. He walked quickly towards the river, then unsure of the exact trajectory, hailed a cab. Only as he alighted on the tawdry boulevard near Arnhem's home, did it occur to him that the man might be less than pleased to find a letter which belonged to his daughter in James's hand.

ELEVEN

The insalubrious street where Arnhem lived was hot and dusty from the day's sunshine. It was also more crowded than James had ever seen it. Women had pulled chairs onto the pavement and sat outdoors with their sewing. Girls played skipping games across the stream of murky water which flowed from the gutters. A beggar held out a worn cap.

James found himself examining everyone for any visible contortions of limb or visage. Tossing a coin to the beggar, he forced his mind onto a different track

At Arnhem's door, an ancient jowly figure, all in black, reclined on a rickety stool, her back against the building. Her eyes were half-closed and James crept past her, only to hear a thundering 'oui' issue from her lips.

'Pas-là,' she said peering up at him with marked suspicion after he had asked politely for Monsieur Arnhem.

'When might he be back?'

'Never, would be best.' She gave him a scowl, then settled back against the wall once more.

James was tempted to wait, but there was nowhere to do so. He walked to the far end of the street and back again. Seeing a man with a coat and hat like Arnhem's, he almost approached him. A few centimes would certainly provide him with a translation. But he stopped himself. The breach of privacy was uncalled for. And the man might well know Arnhem.

He was about to give up and set off for the hotel, when he saw Arnhem appear from round a corner. He had his two youngest children in tow. James paused before greeting him. The children were remarkably attractive, the girl curly-haired, her cheeks dimpled, her dress a spotless white midi with a blue-trimmed sailor's collar. The boy, slightly smaller, was equally agreeable, with chocolate round eyes and tousled hair. He pulled against his father's grip, eager for a run, but Arnhem held onto him with the fierce protectiveness of a man who had already lost too much.

'Monsieur Norton,' the man spoke before James found his voice.'You were looking for me?'

James nodded. The little girl gave him a shy, fetching smile. 'I have something I wanted your help with.'

With an air of indecision, Arnhem looked from the children to James and back again. 'Of course, of course. We'll go to a café,' he murmured. 'Wait for me here.'

He shunted the children past the women in black who scowled at them despite their polite greeting. James saw them disappear up the stairs, heard the little girl ask, 'Why can't we come, too, Papa?'

For a moment, James felt a distinct pang of envy. It was mingled with instant remorse. He wouldn't have come had he known that it would involve tearing Arnhem away from his children. But the man quite rightly felt that their conversation couldn't take place in front of them.

Arnhem was back quickly, his coat flapping. 'The children have homework to do. But I mustn't leave them long.' He looked over his shoulder periodically as they walked along the street, then offered, 'I haven't told them about Rachel yet. I couldn't bring myself . . .' His voice trailed off.

'They're lovely children,' James murmured when they had already turned a corner. The thought leapt into his mind that Dr. Comte would be hard put to find any of the hereditary taints he spoke of with such assurance in Olympe's younger siblings.

'Here. We can stop here.' Arnhem looked around him nervously. 'Though perhaps it would be better inside. It's quieter.'

The interior of the café had never been touched by the sun. The tables were less than clean, the floor stained. The birdlike woman behind the counter had brightly rouged cheeks which clashed oddly with her smeared apron. A solitary old man, who had the tattered mien of a beggar, nursed a glass of absinthe at a table near the front. But James understood Arnhem's desire to be away from curious eyes and long ears. They found a place at the back. Arnhem quickly ordered tea and James joined him.

'What is it that you have for me?' The man asked, wasting no time. His look was grim. He slouched into his chair as if all he could hope for was another blow from fate.

'It's only this letter. I felt sure you could translate it for me.' James unfolded the sheet of paper and placed it in front of him.

Arnhem scanned the writing. An instant change came over him. He was now all hard-edged tension, his expression fierce. 'Where did you get this?'

'In Olympe's apartment.' James raised his hands in apology. 'We're trying to pursue all clues.'

'This is from Isak. Isak Bernfeld.'

'So he was in touch with Olympe again. As we were led to believe.'

'It would seem so. She didn't tell me.' Arnhem looked as if he was about to scrunch the sheet of paper into a ball and throw it across the room.

'What does he say?'

'He says he is back in Paris from Marseilles. He says he wishes to see her. He says he has something to tell her. Something she should know.'

James was suddenly excited. 'Does he give his address?'

'No. But I will find it out. Never fear.'

'So how did he expect her to get in touch with him?' James had the sense Arnhem was holding things back.

'He says he will wait for her outside the theatre. It was through the theatre announcement that he traced her.' Arnhem frowned. 'I didn't know he had followed her career, her change of name.'

'But he evidently did.' James paused, letting the weight of that sink into both of them. 'When does he say he will wait for her?'

Arnhem looked down at the letter again. 'He says Thursday.'

'Thursday!' James was as jubilant as if all the threads of the case had suddenly come together.

'No, no, Monsieur. I follow your train. But we do not know which

Thursday. The letter is dated over a month ago.' A storm cloud passed over Arnhem's face. 'She never told me,' he murmured.

James sipped his tea and waited. When the man didn't speak again, he plunged in. 'Do you know why she might have kept it from you?'

Arnhem shrugged.

'Might she have been afraid that you might try to convince her that . . . that she should move back into the fold.'

A strange laugh issued from Arnhem's lips. 'That is not an unintelligent question, Monsieur Norton. But Rachel . . . Olympe had moved beyond that. Well beyond that. There was no coming back.' He had the sudden look of a desert patriarch who had banished a black sheep from the fold.

'Perhaps Bernfeld felt otherwise. What kind of man is he? The other day you said he was a man of traditional values. But people can change.'

Arnhem studied him, his eyes luminous above the jutting arch of his nose. 'Why do you take such an interest in us, Monsieur Norton?'

James was unprepared for the question. He waved his arm vaguely. 'My brother . . .'

'Ah, I see. Of course. You are your brother's keeper. Loyalty to one's family can be a burden, Monsieur.'

'You have it.'

'I . . . I have little choice.' His eyes clouded over. 'And it is different for us. You should know that I did not care for your brother, Monsieur. Not in himself, of course. I know nothing of that. But for my daughter, the relations they had embarked on. I told Rachel . . . Olympe, he would do her no good. It was a mistake to put sentiment where reason should be. If she was to lead the life she had decided on for herself, then she had to be like those French women. She had to be thoroughly practical.'

James watched the emotions warring on his face. At one moment, he looked as if he might spit. At the next, he was rubbing his forehead, the way Raf did when the internal pressure grew too great.

'You understand my meaning?'

'I think so.'

'Yes. I told her on that path, because of the person she was, lay only destruction.' A sob escaped him.

James leaned forward on his chair. 'Are you telling me that you now think she killed herself? Killed herself for love.' He imagined Arnhem's words tumbling into Chief Inspector Durand's all-too receptive ear.

'No, no. Not at all. I didn't mean now. Not now. Not yet. She was happy. She was afloat on a wispy cloud in a summer sky. I was concerned for the future. Now there is no longer a future to be concerned about.'

His hand had shaped itself into a fist and he pounded the table with it. Once, abruptly, so that the tea cups shook.

James waited. When he said no more, he asked softly. 'Bernfeld. Tell me more about him.'

Arnhem's eyes narrowed. 'You are not a man to be deflected, I see that, Monsieur. Isak Bernfeld is a fine man. I will have nothing said against him. He helped me at the time that the first tragedy struck my family — when some lunatic burned down our business premises. No one was ever charged, Monsieur. No-one. They put it down to accident.' His gaze drifted.

James brought him back. 'And Bernfeld?'

'Bernfeld helped me. But trust me. After the funeral, I will find him. I have already made a start.'

'The funeral?' James asked.

'Yes, Tuesday. Madame de Landois . . . she is a generous woman. She approached the police for me. Will you honour my daughter with your presence, Monsieur?'

'I certainly will.'

Arnhem was already on his feet. He put some coins on the table, refusing James's offer to pay. 'No, no. And I will hold onto this letter.' He folded it into his coat pocket.

Unable to argue despite his sudden suspicion, James watched the letter disappear. What if Arnhem had kept things from him? He would never be able to verify that now.

The suspicion was contagious. 'Do you have anything else of my daughter's, Monsieur?'

James looked down and shook his head. He felt the man's stare on him, deflected it with a question as they walked out of the café.

'One more thing occurs to me, Monsieur Arnhem. You said Isak

Bernfeld moved to Toulouse. Yet in the letter, he mentions Marseilles. Do you know why he moved and moved again. Has he never contacted you?'

Arnhem quickened his pace, shook his head. 'Rachel's refusal of him was an insult. We didn't part on the best of terms,' he mumbled, then asked in a clearer voice. 'When will you visit my eldest daughter?'

'Tomorrow afternoon, I hope.' He didn't mention the earlier visit.

'Good. That is far more important.'

James nodded equably, then noticing a display of chocolates in the window of a small bakery, he paused. 'Please. Wait for me just a moment, Monsieur.' He made his purchase quickly and presented Arnhem with the package. 'For your little ones,' he said. 'Because I have taken you away from them.'

Arnhem stared at him without moving. There was a querulous pride on his face. At last, he took the package. 'Thank you. For their sake.' He bowed. 'But, Monsieur Norton, we do not need pity. We need justice.'

James tiptoed up the stairs of the apartment building. He stared at Ellie's door, and then, with an internal shrug not a little mixed with guilt, knocked softly at Raf's. He needed to speak to his brother. Ellie would keep him possessively at her side and his thoughts, already none too orderly, would be further scrambled.

While he waited, he wondered at the slight aversion he had developed for his sister's presence. It had never been there in the past. He trusted it was a passing aberration which would vanish with the present irregular circumstances.

He gave Arlette only a cursory nod as she opened the door and rushed in without speaking. He didn't want to risk being overheard.

'Monsieur Rafael is not here,' the woman said, her stance belligerent. 'And I was about to leave.'

He kept his eyes from the babe in her arms, the minute hand which seemed to be pounding at her bosom. 'Don't bother about me, Arlette. I'll just wait. Right here.' He pulled out a chair at the dining table and positioned himself so that he could look at Fromentin's imposing picture. Its aspect was altogether different in the fading, early evening light.

The woman hovered, and waving her away, he felt her sullen glance. Decidedly, she had not been trained to the civilities of a servant.

When she brought in a bottle of wine, a hunk of cheese and a baguette a moment later, he regretted his judgement and thanked her profusely. Realizing he had eaten nothing since breakfast, he had stopped for a quick steak-frites on his way here, but had left it half finished in his worry that he might miss Raf again if he were going out for the evening.

'Has my brother come back from the races?'

Arlette shook her head.

'But you expect him?'

'Oh, yes,' Arlette said with so much emphasis that he suspected she had no idea whatever of Raf's movements.

'Good,' James smiled.

Still she waited, so he asked her, 'Did you ever meet Olympe Fabre, Arlette?'

'Of course I met her,' the woman scoffed. 'She came here, didn't she?'

James nodded, uncertain whether her disapproval was directed at Olympe or at his own questioning.

'If you want to know what I thought of her, I thought she wasn't good enough for Monsieur Rafael.' With that she flounced towards the door, turning back only to add, her cheeks flushed, 'Not that I wanted her dead.'

'Of course not,' James soothed. 'That's a very pretty baby you have there, Arlette.'

The colour in her face deepened. 'I'll leave you now, monsieur. I'm meeting a girlfriend this evening. Monsieur Rafael said . . .'

'Of course. Of course.'

When he finally heard the click of the door, he relaxed into his chair and let the tumult of the day's events play through him. With a wayward nostalgia, he saw himself back at his desk at the law school. The orderly rows of books, the regular progression of his days had provided a shelter for him, a protective bubble which had burst in this last week to let in the raw anarchy of life. He had hardly anticipated all this when he had set out on his journey. Yet, he found himself oddly prepared, perhaps indeed hungry for it, relishing its unaccustomed texture.

It was almost as if the tragic foreshortening of that poor, unknown girl's life had thrust him into the thick of his own, had cut the rope that had kept him blindly anchored for so many years to Maisie's death and that of his lifeless daughter. And now he was loose on turbulent seas and oddly able to look again at his own deaths, to confront the images which had hovered for so long at the brink of his conscious mind, though he had never allowed them in. Closing his eyes, he let them in now and stared at the face of his unborn child, his dead wife. An uncontrollable sob shook him.

The moment passed and a chilling fear took him over — as if the wild, shrieking creatures within the walls of the asylum might break out to assault him, to take them all over.

He tightened his fist. Order, clarity had to be maintained. If he could do nothing for the dead, he could at least take a few small steps towards fulfilling Arnhem's injunction. Justice, the man had said, giving the word such force that James had felt he was thinking not only of Olympe's killer, but the charnel house of his wife's death, his mad daughter, the future of his remaining children, Captain Dreyfus bound for a new trial.

Yet what if Olympe's death pointed to Bernfeld? Would that satisfy Arnhem's call for justice?

Without realizing that he had moved, James found himself in Raf's study. A painting on the wall caught his attention. It was of Olympe. Yes, Olympe wearing the sad mask of a clown. The signature at the bottom was that of Max Henry. So Raf knew of the man, indeed had certainly met him. James allowed himself a rueful laugh.

He looked down at the desk. There was a sheet of paper in the typewriter. He read through it quickly, noticed more sheets to the side of the machine. Raf had been working, charting the most recent developments in the Dreyfus case, the attack on the President. Perhaps his visit to the races today would provide the final paragraphs for the unfinished article.

His eyes strayed round the desk. There was a newspaper, part of a column circled in thick black ink. James read, horror mounting in him. The bottom of a woman's severed body wrapped in a thick burlap sack had been found floating in the Seine by a fisherman. The police were conducting their investigations.

He shuddered and turned the paper over only to find a stack of postcards. The top image was a troubling one. It showed a woman in a lewd pose. He pushed it aside and the cards tumbled onto the floor. As he picked them up, he was forced to see that one after another they revealed women in various stages of undress striking lascivious postures. Their lips were pursed, their eyelids lowered in self-absorption, their legs bare or stockinged . . . James could feel his colour rising. Superstitiously he glanced over his shoulder. Of course he knew that men collected such images. But Raf?

He thought involuntarily of his mother, was glad he had already sent that reassuring, if somewhat curt telegram home, telling her there were a few immediate difficulties to overcome, but a matter of weeks should do it.

Suddenly his pulse set up an erratic rhythm. That face. He loosened his collar, turned on the desk lamp for a more accurate view. The photograph showed a young woman with wildly loosed hair, her face down-turned, her expression musing. She was dressed in a maid's apron and nothing else. In her hands she held a bowl of fruit. But it was the face James recognized. Olympe's face, just as he had seen it in the photograph in her apartment. He was certain of it.

Raf's relation to these erotic images abruptly took on a new and ugly twist. A perilous twist. James thought of Chief Inspector Durand and what he could make of this. He had an overwhelming desire to tear the picture into a hundred pieces and reduce each sliver to ashes. Instead he shuffled all the images into a drawer, despite himself taking a quick look inside to see what else his brother's secret life might reveal. He told himself it was a matter of Raf's own protection.

There was nothing of interest inside the desk, not even a stack of letters from Olympe. Perhaps the girl's talents didn't extend to writing.

He sat back in the chair and tried to think calmly about what he had discovered.

Was it possible that someone from her past, someone like Bernfeld, having been utterly rejected, perhaps in need of money, had returned, his passion still alive and now allied to vengeance and tried to blackmail Olympe for the work she had undertaken as a model for such lewd photographs? Oriane, the woman in the theatre, had mentioned blackmail. In the web of rumour she could have got everything wrong. It could be Olympe who was being blackmailed, rather than doing the blackmailing.

James took the photograph out of the drawer again and stared at it for a long moment. The melancholy sweetness of the face tugged at his heart. Yes. A blackmail threat that had gone savagely wrong. Abruptly, he placed the image into his jacket pocket and leaned back into the chair, closing his eyes for greater concentration.

Yes. When Olympe had refused to pay, either with love or money, Bernfeld had sent this photograph to Raf, a first step in his master plan. When the man had told Olympe of his action in order to demonstrate the seriousness of his intent, they had argued. Yes, yes. James could see them on the banks of the Seine somewhere, engaged in bitter conversation. Olympe had refused both his passion and his blackmail and in a rage, he had knocked her unconscious and thrown her to the waters. Yes, of course. And he had undressed her first, so that she couldn't be as quickly recognized. And then he had fled.

Arnhem had testified that Bernfeld was a good man, but good men were not unknown in the heat of passion to commit violent acts. Bernfeld had probably not intended to kill. Indeed he might only have accidentally knocked Olympe unconscious and then presuming her dead, in panic thrown her to the waters.

James closed his eyes and re-imagined the scene. The next thing he knew, someone was shaking him by the shoulder and calling his name. He jumped up, his head fuzzy from interrupted sleep.

'Don't worry, Jim. I'm not about to punch you for invading my office,' Raf snapped.

'Sorry. Sorry. I was just . . .' James's eyes fell on the telephone. 'I was wanting to use the phone. Couldn't get through. I must have fallen asleep.'

Raf chuckled. 'You were always a terrible liar, Jim. Could never trust you to cover for me with father. Did you like my piece? I've got to finish it off now. But we could have a drink first. Since you've obviously been waiting. You should have come to the races with me, Jim. It's been quite a day.'

'I saw the procession along the Champs Élysées. I didn't realize it was going to be a major event.'

'Beautiful horses. But not much action apart from that. No attacks on the President. Though there was a God Almighty kafuffle at the Pavillon d'Armenoville later on. That's where I've just come from. A row broke out. The aristos were dining in relative quiet, all passion having been spent at the races, when the mighty matter of Dreyfus's homecoming came up, and within seconds there was a brawl. Don't know how the news got to the champions of the people, but suddenly there they all were storming the pavilion as if it were the Bastille itself. I managed to get out, just as the police pounced, on what side I'm not sure, but probably in the general squall, on both.'

James followed Raf out to the front room and accepted a glass of wine. Raf chewed on a hunk of cheese and examined him astutely. As he did so, he frowned, his face growing abruptly solemn. 'I can see you've been pursuing matters of more immediate interest.' He sliced through the slab of cheese with a violent gesture. 'What have you found out?'

James told him briefly about his visit to the Salpêtrière, mentioning only that Judith had been unseeable, and then about the letter he had found in Olympe's apartment after Raf had left and how he had taken it to Arnhem for translation and had discovered it was from Bernfeld. Had discovered, too, that the man had probably seen her.

Raf stopped chewing, emptied his glass in one large gulp. 'All right. We have to find the bastard.'

'Arnhem promised that he would.' James paused.

'We'll make sure that he does. What other letters did you find, Jim?'

James coughed. 'There was a bundle from you. They're at the hotel. I'll pass them over.'

'Anything else?'

Raf was staring at him and James decided not to prevaricate. 'A handful from admirers. You know the kind. I imagine all actresses receive them. There were more I couldn't quite pack into the satchel in my hurry. I'd like to go back . . . before the police find them.'

Raf nodded, but his frown deepened.

James changed the subject. 'I . . . I was wondering about those photographs on your desk.'

'What photographs?'

'Don't play the innocent, Raf. You know very well what I mean.'

'I don't know that I do.'

'The pictures of those women. Undressed women.'

'You mean the pornography.' Raf laughed abruptly. 'Mustn't be coy, Jim. Does it appeal to you?'

'Really Rafael.'

'Oh, I see. You think I've fallen into the pits of unspeakable corruption. Sorry to disappoint, Jim. They're Touquet's.'

'Touquet's?'

'Yes, my journalist friend. You remember.'

Raf had misinterpreted his query.

'Yes, but why . . . ?'

'I told you Touquet was interested in all that. Brothels, prostitutes. The lot. He says that it's not only our dear Bertillon and his detectives who are making use of the new photographic technology. Oh yes, the police may use it to chart and identify the physiognomy of criminals. But there's a rather more lucrative, indeed burgeoning use — a trade in erotica. Touquet has been carrying out an investigation. What happens is that the pimps or brothel keepers provide their most fetching girls to be photographed. The girls don't get paid. Or maybe just a pittance. They think they're having a day out. They pose. Do what the photographer asks of them. And then the images are developed and duplicated, again and again. And sold. Here, there and everywhere. The mails are efficient. I wouldn't be surprised if your most respectable Harvard friends have some in their private collections, Jim.' He chuckled. 'Ask them when you get home. Ask them who they buy them from, too.'

James flushed.

'And report back to Touquet. His file is growing. Soon there'll be enough for a big exposé.'

'Do you know any of the girls in those pictures?' James blurted out bluntly, angry now.

'Sorry to disappoint, Jim. Can't say that I do.'

'You're sure?'

'Absolutely sure. I'm not a prude, Jim. But ask Touquet. He probably does. He can introduce you.' Raf was still baiting him.

James let it pass for the moment. Perhaps he was wrong. Or perhaps Raf was simply blind to a resemblance his lover's blinkers didn't permit him to see. He was about to ask him, rather more gently than he felt inclined to about the rumour of blackmail he had heard from Oriane, when Raf went on.

'By the way, I saw Touquet briefly yesterday. He's on to something, he thinks. He talked to some worried plainclothesman, who told him he was almost certain there was a new white-slavery ring bringing women in from the East. Jewish women. Some of them seem to have disappeared. He wants us to pose as clients, separately would be more efficient, and go to the designated brothels. Choose the most recent arrivals. Try to find out who their keepers are, who arranged for their travel, who met them once they got to Paris, and so on. He thinks we'll find out more than he can, 'cause we can pose as innocent, God-fearing Americans, just the type they might confess to, even if they're scared. And in the hope of getting out. Also, Touquet is too well known in those circles.'

James was taken aback. 'I don't see how that can help us with Olympe. You were so certain she had never been involved in anything of that kind. Have you changed your mind?'

'No. Of course not.' Raf leapt up and paced the length of the room. He was running his hands through his hair. By the time he turned back to James, there was something haggard in his dishevelment.

'You see . . . I don't think I've said this to you before, but Olympe was concerned about these women. I never understood quite why, except perhaps that some of them were her people. Maybe she also felt that there but for the grace of God . . .' His voice trailed off. 'In any case, I think she felt a certain burden of responsibility in her success. She sometimes went to visit one or t'other of them. Brought them small presents. Tried to talk them round into leading their lives differently. Almost like charity work. I admired it in her.'

He paused, then added abruptly, 'Though we did argue about it. I didn't like her to go too often.'

'Did you argue recently?' James asked with deliberate casualness.

Raf was pacing again. He nodded. 'Not too long before . . .' He waved his arms, his eyes hollow. 'Anyhow, Touquet thinks there's just a chance that some pimp or Madame didn't like Olympe's contact with the whores, maybe didn't like what they suspected she was up to or suspected she was up to more than she was and . . .' He stopped, sloshed more wine into their glass-es. 'I have to go and finish that article, Jim, while I can still see straight.'

'There's just one more thing.' James took a deep breath. 'You're going to have to be a bit careful, Raf. Chief Inspector Durand suspects you, thinks you might be implicated in Olympe's death.'

'Yes, Marguerite told me.'

'You've seen her?'

'At the races.' Raf looked away.

In that slightly furtive gesture, James sensed another confirmation of what he already more than half suspected, though it made his pulse leap erratically. How could Raf square it with himself? With his love for Olympe? And Marguerite, how could she allow parallel passions? There was too much he didn't understand.

He had to force himself to concentrate on Raf's words.

'The Chief Inspector's more of a fool than I thought. Marguerite thinks it's partly her fault. She's shown such interest in Olympe's case that Durand feels he has to work quickly. Any old theory will do. So he's come up with that utter piffle.'

'But he could make your life unpleasant,' James hesitated. 'They don't have habeas corpus here. They could take you in at any time.'

Raf scoffed, 'Just let them try. I'll have the ambassador down on them like a ton of bricks. Don't you worry about that.'

He studied James for a moment. 'You look spent, Jim. Why don't you just stay the night here? The spare room's all made up, I think. And it'll save you having to trek back for Ellie in the morning. Yes I know about that. I'm not quite the foul, neglectful specimen she makes out these days.' His face grew suddenly grim. 'Or maybe I am. Who can tell what these women want, eh Jim? Jealous. Jealous of everything. Take mother. She was always on at me about deciding on a career. And when I finally seem to have one, she suddenly wants me to give it up and come home and tend to her whims. That was one of the wonders of Olympe. With her I never felt there was a double agenda. She loved her work. And yes, she loved me. We were kindred souls.' His eyes filled with tears.

James rose slowly. He was about to ask about Marguerite when instead, in what he felt was an utterly unnatural gesture, he found his arm round his brother's shoulders.

'Where did you say that bed was, Raf?'

TWELVE

Professor Charles Ponsard's private consulting rooms were situated on the Avenue Hoche just beyond the Arc de Triomphe. The street had only recently been hewn from the surrounding countryside. Everything was greenery and flowering fruit trees and limpid light.

As Marguerite's carriage, kindly sent together with footman, pulled up in front of a prepossessing mansion in Second Empire style, Ellie squeezed James's hand with palpable excitement.

'If wealth has anything to do with skill, Jimmy, I think I'm in luck. The good doctor will be my salvation.'

Her manner belied the trace of irony in her voice and James, responding to the first, smiled solid reassurance.

With the footman's help, Ellie was quickly in her wheelchair and up the flower-lined path. A naked Venus on a high pedestal beckoned to them from its far end. Ellie saluted her. 'I need all the gods at my side, Jimmy. Even her.' She adjusted her hat to a slightly rakish angle and looked up at him for approval.

'You look quite lovely, Ellie dear. Really.'

Her laugh fluttered and came to an abrupt halt as a liveried servant opened the door. The man ushered them into a Pompeian vestibule, took James's hat and asked their names in a polite hush, James had the odd impression they were attending a soirée rather than a medical consultation.

Simultaneously, the bizarre notion that this might all be part of the treatment leapt into his mind only to vanish when they were shown into the waiting room.

The dark wainscoted space had the slightly menacing aspect of a medieval chamber. The light was tinged by the colours of the high, stained glass windows. Griffons and gargoyles and serpents clung to every piece of ornate furniture. Carved and painted wooden figurines held up candelabra in niches which might as well have been stations of the cross. Crests and bronze shields hung from the walls.

A rigid little man with scrawny arms and gnarled fingers squirmed in a baroque prayer stool, his face twitching spasmodically. On the opposite side of the room, sheltered within an alcove, a woman of queenly proportions sat utterly still in a high, stiff chair, one hand resting on the winged back of some scaly creature. The black folds of her dress looked as if they too were carved. Only the low murmur of her nurse's voice as she read from some book testified to her waking presence.

A shadow passed over Ellie's face as she took all this in. James moved her quickly into a far alcove and placed himself in her line of vision.

'The doctor has a taste for the Gothic,' he said lightly.

'Hmm.' The two spots of pink on Ellie's cheeks throbbed, soaking up what colour there was in the room. 'Let's hope it's only in furnishings.' Her smile trembled slightly. 'I rather like it, myself, Jimmy. Raf described Zola's house to me and I imagine it just like this. Smaller, of course. Isn't he fortunate to have met the great man?'

James kept up the patter until they were alone in the room. Then, unable to stop himself, he asked, 'How did you come to meet Olympe Fabre, Ellie? You said the other day that you had met her before Raf.'

A flurry of emotions he couldn't decipher played over her face, but she answered evenly enough. 'It was at Madame de Landois's. Soon after we got here. It was at one of Marguerite's five o'clocks. Isn't it silly, Jim, how they trot out all these anglicisms? Le five o'clock. Le smoking. Le jockey club — and all the time they despise the English.'

James brought her back, 'So Olympe came to one of the five o'clocks.'

'Yes. She sang. And Marguerite played the piano.' Her voice trailed off as if she were imagining the scene.

'And . . . ?'

'And then we chatted. Olympe had never met an American woman before. Her curiosity was quite delicious. And I . . . well, I'd never met an actress before.'

She stopped talking abruptly and clutched the arm of her chair with a hand grown transparent. The blue veins stood out against its pallor like welts.

James tried to change the subject, pointed to one of the crests on the wall. But she didn't hear him.

'You know what I wish, Jimmy,' she said at last, 'wish more than anything, even more than getting my strength back. I wish I had never induced Raf to go to the theatre to see her with me. That's what I wish.'

'Oh, Ellie. None of it has anything to do with you.' He tried to steer her into less perilous waters. Gossip. There was nothing Ellie liked better than gossip. He told her a little about the people he had most recently seen in Boston, asked her about Charlotte and Mrs. Elliott and Harriet and then, said, 'Tell me about Madame de Landois, Ellie. Have you ever met her husband?'

Her laugh tumbled through the stillness of the room. 'Jimmy, you should see yourself. Your eyes have turned the most glorious blue. You're utterly electric with inquisitiveness. Don't tell me you're growing sweet on Marguerite. Marguerite the magnificent.'

'Really, Ellie.'

'Really yourself, Jim boy.' She laughed again. 'And no, for your information, I've never met le Comte de Landois. In fact, I sometimes think he doesn't exist. She just invented him to make her life easier. She'd be quite capable of it, you know. She's fearsomely clever. Much too clever for the likes of us.'

'I've never heard you say that about anyone, Ellie.'

'Perhaps not. But then Marguerite is unique. And uniquely generous.' She paused. 'Yes. I can't fault her.'

'She speaks highly of you, too.'

'Does she?' She gave him an astute look. 'Yes, perhaps she does. As I said, she's generous. She took a real interest in Raf during his first stay here, introduced him to everyone who's anyone. Though not Olympe.' Tears leapt into her eyes. 'No. That had to wait for me.'

'Mlle Norton? Professeur Ponsard is ready for you now.' The servant moved to push her chair.

Ellie clutched at James's hand. 'Come in with me, Jim. I want you there.'

Professeur Ponsard's consulting room bore witness to the same decorative tastes as his waiting room. But here an accumulation of prongs and hammers and strange appliances littered a side table, like so many torture instruments. Behind the vast oak desk at which he sat hung an antique tapestry, slightly threadbare, depicting a classical scene. James made out a temple and a centaur before the man leapt up to greet them.

Surprisingly, the doctor had the open countenance and brown complexion of a countryman. His movements were quick, his eyes lively, and as he addressed Ellie in particular, there was a mixture of that authority and gentleness in his manner which induced ease and trust.

'I take it you wish to have your . . .'

'Brother.' Ellie filled in for him.

'Yes, indeed, your brother at your side, Mlle Norton. Quite right. Quite right. If it makes you feel more comfortable, that is all that matters. I don't think that today, for this first diagnostic visit, I shall need you to undress. No, no.' He looked deeply into her eyes. 'Now, take your time and tell me precisely what it is that is troubling you and how and when it all began.' He gestured at her with a friendly flourish of his arm, like a ringmaster.

'It be… began,' Ellie started with a hesitant stammer, 'yes, it began when I was at the Louvre with a friend. A pounding in my head, a terrible headache, worse than I'd ever experienced. Here.' She pointed to her left temple. 'Everything started to swim before my eyes. An indescribable dizziness, as if the walls were moving, closing in. I wanted to run, but I couldn't. My limbs were too heavy, utterly exhausted. I forced myself, made what felt like a final effort and fled from those swirling walls into the open air. I thought that the freshness would revive me. But no. Instead there was this tingling sensation in my right leg, as if my stocking were constantly slipping down. And both of my feet felt helpless, unresponsive, the toes prickling with their own life. I thought I would fall. My friend helped me home.'

'Yes, go on.' Docteur Ponsard was half kneeling before Ellie now, a small hammer in his hand. 'Please go on. This won't hurt at all.'

'What are you about to do, Doctor? I don't want to be undressed.' Her voice rose into shrillness.

'I'm just going to take off your shoes and stockings. Yes. We'll just lift your skirt up a little.'

Ellie seemed to shrivel in her chair. Her face turned chalk white as Ponsard touched her and eased her stockings down her legs. They lay in two rounded clumps at her feet.

'Carry on, Mademoiselle. Tell me about the progress of the pain.'

James watched him hammer and prod and pinch the length of her limbs. The sight of his sister's legs startled and moved him. They were preternaturally thin and seemed oblivious to the doctor's manipulations. But her face was alive to the doctor's hands. There was a sudden excitement in it, mingled with what he could only call mortification. It made him turn away.

'Do continue, Mademoiselle. You got home and then what?'

Ellie took a deep breath. 'That night, the pain was monstrous. It was as if someone were thrusting a knife under my toenails. Rats gnawed at my feet. If I turned on the light, I knew I would see them, but I was afraid. And my head hurt so. The slightest movement was an agony. Then the needles began, sharp, long, everywhere on my limbs, my nerves. Like giant wasps. I think I must have fainted, because when I woke, the doctor was there. Docteur Giroud. He was bathing my forehead with vinegar water and he gave me an injection which stopped the pain for a while. But a few hours later it started again. Two days after that, I lost all sensation in my legs. At first it felt like a blessing. But I couldn't walk.' She sobbed once. 'I haven't walked, since. And I'm so tired, doctor. So very tired.'

'Of course, of course.' Ponsard was soothing.

'Mercifully, the pain has stopped now. Will I walk again, doctor?'

'We will see. We will see.' He had placed some kind of octopus-like battery appliance with protruding wires and electrodes on the floor and he applied one cupped end now to her leg as he fiddled with a dial. 'Tell me, Mademoiselle, have you had any episodes like this in the past? Any other nervous pains like the ones you just described to me so graphically?'

'Nothing like this, doctor.' She looked up abruptly at James.

'Would you rather I waited outside, Ellie?'

'No, no. Stay James. You might as well know it all.' She was frowning, her eyes filled with fear, as the apparatus moved up her thigh. 'I . . . I have certainly suffered from mental anguish before, doctor. A kind of buzzing in my head. The ideas, no the words going round and round until the world feels as if it's disappearing into a great gaping void and me with it. There have been bouts of vomiting, too.' She bowed her face in something like shame. 'Black bile that needed to be spewed up. Yes, and terrible headaches. They stop me from sleeping. From eating. And the tiredness is extreme. As if all my nerve cells were hors de combat.'

The doctor nodded sagely, 'And you have attempted cures.'

'At home. In America. Yes. I went to a clinic in New York. They exercised us. A whole daily ritual of exercise and hot and cold baths. It did help. Yes. And once I had a complete rest cure. Nothing but food and sleep. Nothing.' Her voice trailed off, her face a pitted mask.

'And recently? Have you suffered some kind of shock?'

Ellie sank farther back into her chair. 'No, doctor. I had been well. Indeed happy.'

Ponsard was standing again, looking deeply into Ellie's eyes. 'Now Mademoiselle, now that we've had a little muscle-stimulating electricity, I want to send you to sleep. A deep, good sleep, which will relieve your fatigue. And perhaps it will help other things, too. We shall see. Here. I will put my finger here on this spot on your forehead. Do you feel the sleep coming?'

'I don't know.' Ellie's voice was tiny, childlike.

'Ah, but you do. Your lids are growing heavy. So very heavy you can't keep your eyes open. You are so tired. You need to sleep.' He passed his hand over her eyes, his voice incantatory, 'Yes, and your limbs feel so heavy too, you can't move your arms, not even your little finger. No, you are quite asleep. Soundly asleep. A deep, restful sleep.'

The doctor paused, then bent to lift Ellie's arm. James watched it fall as if it were subject only to gravity.

'Now Mademoiselle, I want you to get up. To open your eyes and to get up very slowly. Very, very slowly. Yes, that's it, give me your hand now.'

With utter astonishment, James saw Ellie rise from her chair and take a few slow steps. She was looking straight through him, her eyes unblinking.

'Yes that's good. That's very good. And now I want you to take a few turns alone around the room. Give those legs of yours a little exercise. Very good. Very good. Keep going until I ask you to stop.' Ponsard spoke in a deep, spellbinding baritone.

Suddenly James thought of a novel that had been all the rage some years back, a silly shoddy, yet strangely powerful book about a character called Svengali who had held a young woman under his hypnotic sway. He cast a baleful glance at Ponsard, who seemed altogether immune to his suspicions.

'You see, Monsieur, your sister's problem is not in her legs,' he said softly. 'There is no actual motor paralysis. If I am right in my diagnosis, she is suffering from hysteria. Her susceptibility to hypnosis is part proof of that. In your country, I believe they would call her condition a hysterical motor ataxia.' He looked up at James expecting acknowledgement.

'Her legs are indeed paralysed, but only when she is in her normal waking state. In this altered, this hypnotized state, as you see, she moves perfectly well, if a little weakly because her muscles are dwindling. Now tell me,' Ponsard smiled engagingly, 'is there any history of epilepsy in your family?'

'Not that I know of.'

'No spasms or fits?'

The ward at the Salpêtrière leapt into James's mind and he shook his head vigorously.

'No. I didn't really think so, from your sister's symptoms. But perhaps there is a history of nervous disorders.'

James shook his head emphatically.

'No, again. But these are things families like to keep secret, locked in the attic shall we say.'

James was about to rebut him, but Ponsard calmed him with a smile and a wave of the hand. 'The lack of a family pattern is not wholly unusual. As our great Charcot emphatically pointed out in his last years, hysteria is a separate condition, though for many years its sufferers mimicked aspects of epileptic seizures. Can you tell me, Monsieur, though your sister denies this, whether she has experienced some shock recently, had some sudden fright, something that might have affected her emotional condition and led to her paralysis?'

James shook his head again, 'I don't really know. I have no reason to suspect so. But, I've only recently arrived in Paris and the condition predated my arrival.' He was speaking to the doctor, but his attention was all on Ellie. She had taken several turns of the room now, her eyes wide, like some life-size doll. She seemed utterly unaware of the life around her, yet she didn't bump into furniture or objects. There was a small satisfied smile on her face which sent a chill through him.

'A disappointment in love, perhaps?'

James flinched. 'Can she hear us?'

Ponsard shook his head. 'No, Monsieur. She is altogether elsewhere.' His voice went down an octave. 'Yes, that's good, Mademoiselle. Very good. Keep on going. You will remember nothing of this, of course.' He turned back to James, the question still on his face.

'I . . . I'm afraid I can't help you. I will try to find out. But I don't think so. She would have said something. Ellie . . . my sister put aside any hopes of marriage some years back, I believe.' James fidgeted.

'Ah, yes. Our women are like that now. No man quite meets their expectations, yet at the same time they want to be like us.' He chuckled, his expression slightly sly. 'Unfortunately, it affects their constitution. Weakens them. But no matter. I suspect that your sister has a somewhat dramatic personality, that she is perhaps excessively sensitive, of a nervous disposition. In women like her, illness can provide some advantage, indeed some consolation. There can be a benefit to feeling fragile.'

'What benefit can there possibly be?' James protested. 'She can't leave her room without help. She can do almost nothing for herself.'

'So then you — or someone else — does for her.' Ponsard smiled as if all this were utterly self-evident. 'If there is anything my patients have taught me, Monsieur Norton, it is that there can be incalculable benefits, particularly for women, in illness. One doesn't have to put oneself through the indiscretions that those others, who feel armed against all eventualities, undergo because of their healthy constitution. And it keeps one's mind off other things. But I see you don't approve of my reasoning.'

'It's not that. It's just that Ellie suffers so acutely that I can't imagine how she could — if you are right — inflict such suffering on herself.'

'The human animal is indeed a strange one, Monsieur. Our science is new and has only begun to penetrate its mysteries. Her condition is neither willed nor voluntary, if that is what you are suggesting. It is outside her control. So we must try to do what we can for mademoiselle. I will prescribe a course of potassium bromide, really just to ensure that there is no epileptic base to her condition. If the bromide has no effect, then we know we are clearly dealing with a hysteroepilepsy. And, of course, there will be some treatments. They calm the imagination, occupy the mind.'

'Nothing more?'

'That is already a great deal, Monsieur. Sometimes there is a cure. The Nancy School will tell you that hypnotism can effect it. I am only in partial agreement. To be completely honest, since you have come through Madame de Landois, I will confess that I am not always certain what concatenation of life events and treatments brings the cure about.' He threw James a shrewd, assessing look. 'Enough to say that the most photographed and documented of Charcot's hysterical patients after some years became a laboratory technician. None of us understand whether it was by his intervention.'

Ponsard turned again to Ellie. 'And now Mademoiselle,' he murmured in that low soothing voice, 'you may return to your chair. You will feel calmer when you wake. Stronger. Refreshed.'

James watched Ellie sit down dutifully. The doctor quietly commanded her to close her eyes and at the touch of his fingers to open them again.

When she did so, she looked round with a smile.

'Have you had a good rest, Mademoiselle?'

Ellie nodded.

'Good. That is good. Here let me help you with your stockings.'

James saw the man bend to the task and wondered whether he would now tell Ellie of what she had been capable of in her hypnotized state. But all Ponsard did was to pat her gently on the shoulder, describe the course of bromides and suggest that she come to see him three or four more times. Her legs were once again lifeless.

Ellie had been looking at the handsome grandfather clock which stood in a corner of the room. Now she gasped. 'But Dr. Ponsard. I can't have been here all this time. You . . . you put me to sleep?' Her face grew suspicious, distorted.

'Yes, Mademoiselle, I put you to sleep. Applied a little mild hypnotism. It relaxes the nerves wonderfully. And you need rest above all. Don't overtax yourself. Put your books and your cares aside. Leave them to the men in your family. We need you to regain your strength, to cure you of that exhaustion you spoke of.'

James could see the warring emotions in his sister's face, anger and fear and hope all wrestling with each other. But she only asked in a timorous voice, 'So you have hope for me, Dr. Ponsard?'

'My hope is equal to yours,' he replied, bowing. And with the beneficent beam of a peasant priest blessing his flock, he urged them from the room.

Ellie didn't speak until the Avenue Hoche was well behind them. James sat tensely at her side, uncomfortable with his hidden knowledge. How was he to suppress his vivid memory of that other Ellie, the one who walked quite adequately, though with the drugged gaze of a somnambulist? It seemed to him a form of collusion with the doctor, but if it was in Ellie's best interest, he must keep quiet. He sighed inadvertently.

'Did I say something unspeakable, Jim?' Ellie's fingers dug into his arm. 'What did he do to me? He seemed so kind. I didn't realize he was going to . . .' Her voice rose. The eyes she turned on him were wide in fear. 'I don't like the idea of hypnotism, Jim. I don't like it one tiny bit. It makes one so defenceless.'

He patted her hand. 'But if it helps, Ellie. And rests you.' He followed Ponsard's cue.

The carriage suddenly swerved and she fell against him. Her cry was a howl of terror.

He helped her right herself. 'It was only a dog, Ellie.' He studied her face. 'What is it that you're so afraid of?'

'You can be brave, Jim.' Her voice held a scoff. 'You don't have to subject yourself to these people.'

She smoothed her dress with prim, nervous gestures and it tumbled through his mind that what she feared was that the doctor might touch her without her knowing. His thoughts wandered and he found himself with Olympe again, Olympe who had also, as Marguerite had explained, walked without being aware of it. Walked away. Walked to escape. And Ellie sat still to escape. Yes. He must talk to Marguerite about Ellie. She had recommended Docteur Ponsard, after all, evidently in the full knowledge of his techniques.

Ellie was speaking again, her voice low, barely audible above the coach's clatter. He gave her his attention.

'Once I really thought I would do something with my time on this earth, Jim. Something great. Something useful. Something beautiful. But nothing . . . nothing has come of it. There's nothing for a woman like me.'

'You'll get better, Ellie. I know you will.'

She didn't seem to have heard him.

'Had I been born a man, it would have been quite different. I could have done what Raf does, or you, or anyone. Do I shock you, Jim?'

James was indeed shocked by the bitterness in her tone, more than by her words, but she didn't give him time to answer.

'Maybe the hypnotism loosens one's tongue. It's meant to put to sleep that vigilant little watch dog we all carry within to keep us in order. You know, I'm not the only one to be subject to the whims of the doctors, Jim. Olympe was once. Yes even she, with all her accomplishments. She used to suffer from fugues.' Her laugh had an uncanny peel. 'I could do with a fugue.'

'Olympe told you about that?'

'She told me that and much much more. Strangely, given the vast difference in our backgrounds and temperament, we were sisters in spirit.

Perhaps because we had both suffered in the same way. She too had experienced those storm clouds hovering over her shoulder, then bursting into a drowning deluge.'

The fierce passion on her face made James uneasy. 'Did she tell you that, too? Or did you intuit it?'

'Tell, intuit. What difference does it make? We didn't spend our time together in courts of law. We recognized each other.' Her voice grew dreamy, took on the rhythm of hoofs on cobbles. 'She'd been down in the abyss, too. In the pits where the hammers clang through your head without cease and the waters are rising, rising slowly to envelope all of you. And there's no way out. No seam of gold or coal to tap to allow you to bribe your passage, even if you could. No way out at all.' She paused. 'That's what she must have felt at the end. The other night when the moon was full, I felt she was right beside me, talking to me.'

'What did she say?' James heard himself ask, struck by his own irrationality.

She looked up at him as if he had startled her awake. A small, troubling smile hovered round her lips. It gave her face an unsettling canniness. 'You really want to know, don't you Jim? She's cast her spell over you, too.' She laughed. 'I dare say you're more interested in dead women than live ones.'

'Don't be silly, Ellie.'

'Silly Ellie. Silly Ellie. Do you know how much I used to admire you, Jim? When we were young. Before Maisie. You used to come home and tell me everything about your classes. Aristotle and Plato and Seneca. I felt they'd become intimates. I knew you were going to become a great man. And then you went off and married that Maisie. She dispersed you. Why did you ever tie yourself to such a fool of a woman?'

She clamped her hand over her mouth. 'Sorry. I'm sorry. I shouldn't have said that. I've overstepped myself. Forgive me.'

James looked stonily out the window. Was Ellie right? Her words pierced him like poison arrows, thrusting their venom deep into his past.

She was babbling again, saying things he didn't want to listen to, her voice rising and falling as if she were several women in one. Maybe that

Ponsard had made her worse, turned her into that frightening Ellie he had only had glimpses of in the past, unleashed her tongue. He concentrated on the streets, only growing alert to her again when Olympe's name fell on his ears.

'Have the police learned anything more, Jim? Has Raf?'

Judith's name almost tumbled from his mouth, but he held himself back just in time. He wanted to know whether Olympe had ever spoken of her to Ellie. But Ponsard had said to keep her calm and evoking the Salpêtrière was hardly conducive to that. Not that she was calm, in any event. Yet he restrained himself, saying only in a soft voice, 'There may be a man from her past who unhappily stepped into her life again.'

'Oh. She never told me about that.' Her eyes glittered strangely.

'We're trying to locate him through her father.' The carriage turned into the Boulevard Malesherbes and with what he hoped didn't sound like relief, he said, 'We're here, Ellie. You'll want to rest now.'

'Will I, Jim? Yes, you're right. And Harriet should be here. So you needn't worry about me. No, you needn't worry.'

'She's a very good friend.'

'My own ministering angel. And not a fool.' She shot James a triumphant look.

THIRTEEN

Judith Arnhem perched on a stool in the corner of the cell-like room. Her eyes moved furtively, chasing invisible shadows on the floor. Like one of those women in paintings of the pre-Raphaelite school, her hair was wild — a dark, tangled undergrowth spangled with white by the moon. It occluded her face, which she kept bowed. Her hands were arced on her hospital smock, two stiff crabs, scuttling now and then to pick at the material.

Only when Dr. Comte spoke, did she look up. James was again struck by her uncanny resemblance to her sister, the same fine oval of a face, though somewhat thinner, hollowed out. The eyes were beetle black.

'I have brought you two visitors, Judith. Distant cousins from America.' Comte's voice was tinged with irony. 'Messieurs James and Rafael Norton. They wish to speak to you.'

Judith shook her head fiercely and like a trapped animal hunched farther into the corner of the room.

'Oh yes, you will speak to them since they have come all this way.' Comte moved towards her with a belligerent gesture, but Raf's voice stopped him in his tracks.

'You can leave us now, Doctor. We'll be perfectly fine on our own.' His tone was all calm intractable authority. James had the sudden realization that it was only when the two of them were alone, that Raf reverted to an earlier rebelliously wayward self.

'Judith will be happy to talk to us since we are
And privacy will be best.'

Dr. Comte seemed about to protest, but Raf
'We'll call you if we need you. We shan't be very lo
Thank you for providing the room.'

'I don't like that man,' James murmured whe
The doctor had made them leap innumerable hurdl
interview, had kept them in a corner of the baying
sign some incomprehensible form, had questione
death, then perniciously added that the fact of it sa
sis. The Arnhem family tree was a promising one
pools.

James had wondered at Raf's steely compos
Only a single look of savage dismay had scudded
when they first crossed the threshold.

Now Raf shrugged. He was staring at Judit
whether he too was struck by the likeness with O
gaze. For a long moment, no one spoke, then she l
to sit closer to her on the pallet of a bed. For lack
settled beside him.

'We're friends, Judith. Your father asked us t
was hoping to come too, but he was unable to. He
you had told him about Olympe's death.'

'Rachel.' The word was at once a correction
hoarse, strangely raucous in the small room. J
speed as they moved across her skirt. James had
if she had the freedom her legs might be moving
his mind, but didn't linger.

'Yes, of course, Rachel.' Raf repeated with
'Her death has been a great shock to us all.'

'They got her. Got her. Down with her. D
Defective. Degenerate. They'll get all of us.' Her vo
of an oracle and she had started to rock, at firs

'First there was Sarah, then Elisabeth, the
was counting on her gnarled fingers. 'And
Rachel,' she howled as she perched on the st
sobs with her hands.

Raf cast James a helpless look.

'Apart from Rachel, are these all friends o
asked after a moment.

She looked up, her face streaked with tear
men too. They told me. No names.'

Abruptly, she was up again. 'It doesn't mat
the small formal voice of a well-brought-up scho
me. I want to die. Thank you for coming. Good-

She gave them a look of heart-rending puri
the wall just as the door opened and a stout nur

'Dr. Comte has asked me to tell you that you
Messieurs. Are you all right, Judith? There'll be

Judith didn't answer, nor did she return
struggling against the nurse's attempt to lead her

James stepped back into the cubicle, 'Is
Mademoiselle?'

'He's lecturing now,' she replied curtly. 'He

'We need to see Vaillant,' James said to R
down the corridor.

'Why?'

'We need to check him out.'

'There's nothing in it. Judith is just . . . well
ous. Patients die. Or they're moved to other
because she's the way she is, she imagines th
woman. But we're wasting our time. Arnhem as g

'I'd still like to meet Vaillant,' James said stub
place. Why is it just the Jews that die?'

'We don't know that. We don't know who tho
She happens to be sensitive to their race. I guess
past.'

A sudden hubbub in the corridor stopped them speaking. Two patients were being wheeled past on trolleys. A slew of what looked like medical students followed them.

'When I was here the other day, Comte spun a theory for me, about Jews being disproportionately susceptible to nervous illness,' James said in a low voice when the commotion had passed.

'That could well be. Or it could be more spin-off from the Dreyfus case. If you went to as many mad patriotic meetings as I do, you'd be amazed at the garbage these pundits come up with. I'm not surprised it affects someone like Judith. But that doesn't make the man a killer. And it's Olympe we have to concentrate on.'

James paused.

'Did you notice how much Judith looks like Olympe?'

'You're going mad, too, Jim. This place is getting to you. Getting to me, too. We've got to get out of here.' Raf quickened his pace.

'You mean you didn't see it.'

'Of course I didn't see it. You're raving.'

They had reached the entry hall and James hesitated. 'I'm going to find out if I can get into Vaillant's lecture.'

Raf shrugged. 'Suit yourself. I've got other irons in the fire. I want to chase Arnhem on this Bernfeld man. And I'll stop off on the way to have a chat with Poupette, see if she's picked up any interesting news on the streets. Then, there's another rally tonight. Fancy it?'

'No, that's your domain.'

'It'll teach you something about the mad ideas that float around these days.' He paused, his eyes filling with troubled passion. 'The only difference is that outside this place they're given serious consideration and played out in the political arena.'

James slipped through a creaking door and found himself at the top of a medium-size amphitheatre. The room was about three-quarters full. He tiptoed to the nearest seat, close to the end of a row. All eyes were to the front where a man stood in front of a life-size diagram of what looked like a spinal column, though there were feet in various contorted positions placed around it. The man himself was tall, slender, and of military-bearing. He had a strong, handsome face which ended in a well-clipped point of a beard. His voice was stentorian. Dr. Vaillant, James quickly decided, was a prepossessing figure.

To his side on a narrow bed, a small, grizzled man lay huddled. Another man, wrapped in what looked like a caftan, sat listlessly in a wheelchair. Oddly there was a violin poised on his lap. Two assistants hovered about them.

'In conclusion, Messieurs,' Vaillant was saying, 'let me recapitulate a little of the material we have investigated in these last two presentations. The wandering Jews we have had occasion to examine in our midst bear witness to the positive and negative aspects of that great legend. Ahaseverus suffered from the imperative to 'Go on. Go on'. An unquiet instinct, an eternal restlessness forced him to wander the globe. More than any other people, the Jews amongst us are subject to this law of fluctuation whose manifestations are unpredictable. It can engender first-rate scientific and artistic aptitude; it can also produce mental aberrances. The two are not, I contend, unrelated and in Jews we find a general predisposition to hereditary neurologic disorders of all sorts — from ataxic tabes to neuropathologic chorea to hysteria — not to mention the American disease, neurasthenia.'

James balked and sat up straighter on the hard wood of the bench.

'Here at the Salpêtrière, our significant number of Jews present us with a unique opportunity to investigate a hereditary pool — not only through our inmates, but their relations. Vagabondage — as we have seen it in the 'filles des rues', those streetwalkers who poison our menfolk, and in those male patients who have travelled the breadth of Europe and sometimes gone as far afield as America and back, undoubtedly spreading their degenerate spawn on the way — is a specific hereditary condition characterized by an incessant need to wander from one home or homeland to another. Such people are never satisfied. Whether they have found a fortune, or a cure for their ills, their pathology means that they must needs go on, always in search of an elsewhere or a something else. On the way they develop a host of complaints, the American illness being only one of them. It remains for our science now to designate in our laboratories the anatomical source of the clinical picture such patients present.

'One day, Messieurs, I am convinced of it, one day we will discover a fingerprint of the moral history of a man or woman written into the coils and loops of that most fascinating of organs, the brain. I thank you, Messieurs. Ah oui, and Madame.' Vaillant bowed to a woman on his left with a smile which held the trace of a sneer.

James sat stonily in his seat only moving when people farther down the row forced him to. His mind was racing. He felt implicated in Vaillant's analysis — that bizarre yoking of Americans and Jews. It made him revolt viscerally against the doctor's argument. Reluctant traveller though he might himself be, he couldn't see anything generically wrong with movement. Americans wandered to arrive in America; they moved again for land, or work, or gold, or simply for the excitement of it all. Vaillant's notion that this constituted an illness was preposterous. Could this altogether sensible-looking doctor really be suggesting that James's own forebears had left England and Ireland because of some pathological predisposition to wander, rather than because of famine or intolerance? Was he intimating that the entire American continent was the result of some aberrant neurological condition? And if the basis of his argument about the one was incorrect, how could he be correct about the other, the Jews?

Raf was right. Mad ideas were afloat. Perhaps, James thought with a distinct sense of transgression, that very note he had so often heard struck in these last days — the note of hereditary transmission — was itself part of the madness.

At the same time, it was undeniable that Judith and the women he had seen in her ward were ill. Ellie was ill, too. The American illness.

His thoughts buzzing like angry wasps, he found himself in a mill of students. One of them was addressing him. 'Intéressant, non?'

Yes, James nodded. Vaillant was interesting. But . . . Suddenly he heard himself ask where the laboratories might be found.

The friendly student pointed downwards, then scrutinized him. 'Are you a student here?'

James shook his head. 'Just a visitor. But I would love to see the laboratories. At Harvard College we have nothing quite like this.'

'Harvard? In America?'

James nodded and the student grinned. 'How did you like what Vaillant said?'

'I can't say I was wholly convinced.'

The grin spread. 'Professeur Vaillant was once married to an American woman. She left him. She wandered. It explains a little, non?'

James wanted to ask if he had also been married to a Jewess, but found himself asking instead, 'Are you by any chance going down to the laboratories?'

'No. It's my time for the wards. But, wait a minute . . . There's our star pathologist.' He hailed a lanky man with a dour face and eyebrows so thick they all but formed a line across his brow. 'Are you going down to the lab, Steinlen?'

Steinlen gave a curt nod.

'Could you take Monsieur . . .'

'Norton,' James supplied.

'Monsieur Norton from Harvard down with you?'

Steinlen appraised him with decided suspicion. 'It's not open to visitors. Vaillant wouldn't be pleased.'

'I just want to have a quick look, but no matter. I'll get Dr. Vaillant's permission. We have friends in common.'

'Oh go on, take him,' the first student protested. 'None of the profs will be there now. And he's had to sit through Vaillant's asides on the American illness.'

'Vaillant's right,' the tall man said. 'The American doctors are in agreement. It's the hectic pace of American life.'

'Then we must have a great deal in common, Monsieur. I must say that I find Paris rather more hectic than Boston.'

'Ah but you see, you have chosen to come here. Many of your compatriots come here. *We* stay at home.'

'Go on, take him, Steinlen. You can show off your newest cadaver to Dr. Norton.'

'Is it a Jew?' James heard himself ask.

The dour face turned on him with a slight smirk. 'An old one. From

THIRTEEN

Judith Arnhem perched on a stool in the corner of the cell-like room. Her eyes moved furtively, chasing invisible shadows on the floor. Like one of those women in paintings of the pre-Raphaelite school, her hair was wild — a dark, tangled undergrowth spangled with white by the moon. It occluded her face, which she kept bowed. Her hands were arced on her hospital smock, two stiff crabs, scuttling now and then to pick at the material.

Only when Dr. Comte spoke, did she look up. James was again struck by her uncanny resemblance to her sister, the same fine oval of a face, though somewhat thinner, hollowed out. The eyes were beetle black.

'I have brought you two visitors, Judith. Distant cousins from America.' Comte's voice was tinged with irony. 'Messieurs James and Rafael Norton. They wish to speak to you.'

Judith shook her head fiercely and like a trapped animal hunched farther into the corner of the room.

'Oh yes, you will speak to them since they have come all this way.' Comte moved towards her with a belligerent gesture, but Raf's voice stopped him in his tracks.

'You can leave us now, Doctor. We'll be perfectly fine on our own.' His tone was all calm intractable authority. James had the sudden realization that it was only when the two of them were alone, that Raf reverted to an earlier rebelliously wayward self.

'Judith will be happy to talk to us since we are friends of her sister's. And privacy will be best.'

Dr. Comte seemed about to protest, but Raf put out a staying hand. 'We'll call you if we need you. We shan't be very long. Thank you, Doctor. Thank you for providing the room.'

'I don't like that man,' James murmured when Comte had left them. The doctor had made them leap innumerable hurdles before permitting the interview, had kept them in a corner of the baying ward, had made them sign some incomprehensible form, had questioned them about Olympe's death, then perniciously added that the fact of it sat well with his hypothesis. The Arnhem family tree was a promising one for proof of hereditary pools.

James had wondered at Raf's steely composure amidst the bedlam. Only a single look of savage dismay had scudded across his face, and that when they first crossed the threshold.

Now Raf shrugged. He was staring at Judith, and James wondered whether he too was struck by the likeness with Olympe. She returned his gaze. For a long moment, no one spoke, then she looked away and Raf went to sit closer to her on the pallet of a bed. For lack of another place, James settled beside him.

'We're friends, Judith. Your father asked us to come and see you. He was hoping to come too, but he was unable to. He wanted you to tell us what you had told him about Olympe's death.'

'Rachel.' The word was at once a correction and a cry. The voice was hoarse, strangely raucous in the small room. Judith's hands picked up speed as they moved across her skirt. James had a sudden impression that if she had the freedom her legs might be moving as quickly. Ellie leapt into his mind, but didn't linger.

'Yes, of course, Rachel.' Raf repeated with remarkable composure. 'Her death has been a great shock to us all.'

'They got her. Got her. Down with her. Down with her. Diseased. Defective. Degenerate. They'll get all of us.' Her voice had the droning force of an oracle and she had started to rock, at first slowly, then picking up speed as if she were atop a child's hobby horse. The small stool creaked beneath her. 'All of us. Me next. A huge fire. Hot. Incandescent. Only bones left.' Her eyes grew as vast and fearful as her troubled imaginings.

For a moment Raf was silent.

'Who do you mean by they?' James asked softly.

'I don't know you.' Judith stopped her rocking for a moment. 'You.' A finger arced with ferret speed to point.

'I'm Jim,' he heard himself use the name which fell more easily from French lips.

'But you know me?' Raf intervened. 'Rachel told you about me.'

A small smile curled her lips and suddenly, as she nodded, she looked like an ordinary young woman whose pallor and disarray might have been the result of a passing illness. 'Yes. I know you. You're a journalist. From New York.'

'That's right.' Raf returned her smile, his own charming, suasive. 'And I . . . I was very fond of Rachel.' He paused. 'There wasn't a fire, you know. Quite the opposite. It was water. She was drowned.'

'Water,' she repeated and started to rock again, her eyes flitting like a bird across the cage of the room. 'Water. It doesn't matter. Water kills. Washes the body. They keep the bodies. Take them apart. I've seen them.'

'Whom have you seen?' James asked gently.

'Them. Them.' She bent towards Raf, her voice lowered in a conspiratorial whisper. 'Them. The doctors.' She stopped, looked behind her, then towards the door, as if invisible eyes were watching her. They're killing us all. All.' She let out a wild moan and was suddenly on her feet lurching across the room in a drunken gait.

'It's all right, Judith. There's no one else here. Only us.'

'Not you. Not you.' She stared at Raf. 'Only us. Don't let my father come any more. Tell him. No more. One by one.' She slapped her hands together and the sound echoed through the room. 'One by one. Like flies. All of us.'

Raf moved to put a stilling arm round her shoulder, but she veered away from him. She was shaking now, her fear palpable, thick, cloying so that it spread across the small space to envelop them like a rank, oily substance.

'First there was Sarah, then Elisabeth, then Bette, then Rebecca.' She was counting on her gnarled fingers. 'And now Rachel. Rachel. Dear Rachel,' she howled as she perched on the stool again. She covered her sobs with her hands.

Raf cast James a helpless look.

'Apart from Rachel, are these all friends of yours in the ward?' James asked after a moment.

She looked up, her face streaked with tears. 'Not only this ward. The men too. They told me. No names.'

Abruptly, she was up again. 'It doesn't matter, Messieurs,' she said in the small formal voice of a well-brought-up schoolgirl. 'It doesn't matter for me. I want to die. Thank you for coming. Good-bye.'

She gave them a look of heart-rending purity, then turned her face to the wall just as the door opened and a stout nurse peered in.

'Dr. Comte has asked me to tell you that your interview time is up now, Messieurs. Are you all right, Judith? There'll be dinner soon.'

Judith didn't answer, nor did she return their good-byes. She was struggling against the nurse's attempt to lead her back to the main ward.

James stepped back into the cubicle, 'Is Dr. Vaillant here today, Mademoiselle?'

'He's lecturing now,' she replied curtly. 'He can't be disturbed.'

'We need to see Vaillant,' James said to Raf as they walked quickly down the corridor.

'Why?'

'We need to check him out.'

'There's nothing in it. Judith is just . . . well, just mad. It's quite obvious. Patients die. Or they're moved to other wards. They vanish. And because she's the way she is, she imagines they're being killed. Poor woman. But we're wasting our time. Arnhem as good as said it.'

'I'd still like to meet Vaillant,' James said stubbornly. 'Get a sense of the place. Why is it just the Jews that die?'

'We don't know that. We don't know who those people she named are. She happens to be sensitive to their race. I guess we'd be too, if we had her past.'

A sudden hubbub in the corridor stopped them speaking. Two patients were being wheeled past on trolleys. A slew of what looked like medical students followed them.

'When I was here the other day, Comte spun a theory for me, about Jews being disproportionately susceptible to nervous illness,' James said in a low voice when the commotion had passed.

'That could well be. Or it could be more spin-off from the Dreyfus case. If you went to as many mad patriotic meetings as I do, you'd be amazed at the garbage these pundits come up with. I'm not surprised it affects someone like Judith. But that doesn't make the man a killer. And it's Olympe we have to concentrate on.'

James paused.

'Did you notice how much Judith looks like Olympe?'

'You're going mad, too, Jim. This place is getting to you. Getting to me, too. We've got to get out of here.' Raf quickened his pace.

'You mean you didn't see it.'

'Of course I didn't see it. You're raving.'

They had reached the entry hall and James hesitated. 'I'm going to find out if I can get into Vaillant's lecture.'

Raf shrugged. 'Suit yourself. I've got other irons in the fire. I want to chase Arnhem on this Bernfeld man. And I'll stop off on the way to have a chat with Poupette, see if she's picked up any interesting news on the streets. Then, there's another rally tonight. Fancy it?'

'No, that's your domain.'

'It'll teach you something about the mad ideas that float around these days.' He paused, his eyes filling with troubled passion. 'The only difference is that outside this place they're given serious consideration and played out in the political arena.'

James slipped through a creaking door and found himself at the top of a medium-size amphitheatre. The room was about three-quarters full. He tiptoed to the nearest seat, close to the end of a row. All eyes were to the front where a man stood in front of a life-size diagram of what looked like a spinal column, though there were feet in various contorted positions placed around it. The man himself was tall, slender, and of military-bearing. He had a strong, handsome face which ended in a well-clipped point of a beard. His voice was stentorian. Dr. Vaillant, James quickly decided, was a prepossessing figure.

To his side on a narrow bed, a small, grizzled man lay huddled. Another man, wrapped in what looked like a caftan, sat listlessly in a wheelchair. Oddly there was a violin poised on his lap. Two assistants hovered about them.

'In conclusion, Messieurs,' Vaillant was saying, 'let me recapitulate a little of the material we have investigated in these last two presentations. The wandering Jews we have had occasion to examine in our midst bear witness to the positive and negative aspects of that great legend. Ahaseverus suffered from the imperative to 'Go on. Go on'. An unquiet instinct, an eternal restlessness forced him to wander the globe. More than any other people, the Jews amongst us are subject to this law of fluctuation whose manifestations are unpredictable. It can engender first-rate scientific and artistic aptitude; it can also produce mental aberrances. The two are not, I contend, unrelated and in Jews we find a general predisposition to hereditary neurologic disorders of all sorts — from ataxic tabes to neuropathologic chorea to hysteria — not to mention the American disease, neurasthenia.'

James balked and sat up straighter on the hard wood of the bench.

'Here at the Salpêtrière, our significant number of Jews present us with a unique opportunity to investigate a hereditary pool — not only through our inmates, but their relations. Vagabondage — as we have seen it in the 'filles des rues', those streetwalkers who poison our menfolk, and in those male patients who have travelled the breadth of Europe and sometimes gone as far afield as America and back, undoubtedly spreading their degenerate spawn on the way — is a specific hereditary condition characterized by an incessant need to wander from one home or homeland to another. Such people are never satisfied. Whether they have found a fortune, or a cure for their ills, their pathology means that they must needs go on, always in search of an elsewhere or a something else. On the way they develop a host of complaints, the American illness being only one of them. It remains for our science now to designate in our laboratories the anatomical source of the clinical picture such patients present.

'One day, Messieurs, I am convinced of it, one day we will discover a fingerprint of the moral history of a man or woman written into the coils and loops of that most fascinating of organs, the brain. I thank you, Messieurs. Ah oui, and Madame.' Vaillant bowed to a woman on his left with a smile which held the trace of a sneer.

James sat stonily in his seat only moving when people farther down the row forced him to. His mind was racing. He felt implicated in Vaillant's analysis — that bizarre yoking of Americans and Jews. It made him revolt viscerally against the doctor's argument. Reluctant traveller though he might himself be, he couldn't see anything generically wrong with movement. Americans wandered to arrive in America; they moved again for land, or work, or gold, or simply for the excitement of it all. Vaillant's notion that this constituted an illness was preposterous. Could this altogether sensible-looking doctor really be suggesting that James's own forebears had left England and Ireland because of some pathological predisposition to wander, rather than because of famine or intolerance? Was he intimating that the entire American continent was the result of some aberrant neurological condition? And if the basis of his argument about the one was incorrect, how could he be correct about the other, the Jews?

Raf was right. Mad ideas were afloat. Perhaps, James thought with a distinct sense of transgression, that very note he had so often heard struck in these last days — the note of hereditary transmission — was itself part of the madness.

At the same time, it was undeniable that Judith and the women he had seen in her ward were ill. Ellie was ill, too. The American illness.

His thoughts buzzing like angry wasps, he found himself in a mill of students. One of them was addressing him. 'Intéressant, non?'

Yes, James nodded. Vaillant was interesting. But . . . Suddenly he heard himself ask where the laboratories might be found.

The friendly student pointed downwards, then scrutinized him. 'Are you a student here?'

James shook his head. 'Just a visitor. But I would love to see the laboratories. At Harvard College we have nothing quite like this.'

'Harvard? In America?'

James nodded and the student grinned. 'How did you like what Vaillant said?'

'I can't say I was wholly convinced.'

The grin spread. 'Professeur Vaillant was once married to an American woman. She left him. She wandered. It explains a little, non?'

James wanted to ask if he had also been married to a Jewess, but found himself asking instead, 'Are you by any chance going down to the laboratories?'

'No. It's my time for the wards. But, wait a minute . . . There's our star pathologist.' He hailed a lanky man with a dour face and eyebrows so thick they all but formed a line across his brow. 'Are you going down to the lab, Steinlen?'

Steinlen gave a curt nod.

'Could you take Monsieur . . .'

'Norton,' James supplied.

'Monsieur Norton from Harvard down with you?'

Steinlen appraised him with decided suspicion. 'It's not open to visitors. Vaillant wouldn't be pleased.'

'I just want to have a quick look, but no matter. I'll get Dr. Vaillant's permission. We have friends in common.'

'Oh go on, take him,' the first student protested. 'None of the profs will be there now. And he's had to sit through Vaillant's asides on the American illness.'

'Vaillant's right,' the tall man said. 'The American doctors are in agreement. It's the hectic pace of American life.'

'Then we must have a great deal in common, Monsieur. I must say that I find Paris rather more hectic than Boston.'

'Ah but you see, you have chosen to come here. Many of your compatriots come here. *We* stay at home.'

'Go on, take him, Steinlen. You can show off your newest cadaver to Dr. Norton.'

'Is it a Jew?' James heard himself ask.

The dour face turned on him with a slight smirk. 'An old one. From

Odessa. An excellent specimen. Come along then. He has wonderfully splayed feet, with high arches and hammer toes. A tabetic.' The man went on, suddenly garrulous, drowning James in science.

James nodded without listening. The thoughts that crowded his mind were having an effect on his pulse. What if Judith were right? What if Vaillant was discreetly picking off patients in order to give a laboratory base to his theories? Whatever Raf contended, Olympe and her sister were remarkably alike. Might Vaillant have in some deranged way wanted to investigate a familial disease-pattern? There might be case notes somewhere in the hospital about a wandering Rachel.

No, he was raving. It was the influence of this place with its bleak corridors, its howling, confined lunatics. Even the courtyards, like the one they now crossed, were bleak, infested with scurrying shadows. And his speculations made no sense. Olympe's body had been found in the river. She hadn't disappeared into a laboratory.

Something else occurred to him. What if Judith had held forth her delirious speculations to Olympe? And the brave girl — he knew she was brave, everything in her life testified to it — had decided to investigate. As he was doing now. Had enmeshed herself in the whole venomous business and Vaillant had somehow got wind of a determination she might have formed to expose him. Expose his killing of patients. Jewish patients. What simpler solution to that threat than to plunge her into the waters of the Seine. No one would suspect him. No one from Olympe's world apart from Marguerite would even know of Judith's existence. And she couldn't tell Raf or her kinship with Judith would have to come out.

Did Marguerite know Vaillant? He would have to ask.

The only problem with his racing conjectures was that Vaillant didn't look like a killer. On the other hand the man beside him, the devoted student, had distinct possibilities in that direction. Or the bullying and fleshy Dr. Comte. Yes, decidedly Dr. Comte.

'Tell me,' James interrupted Steinlen's monologue. 'Do you ever have opportunity in the lab to investigate several members of one family.'

'Ah, there you have us, Monsieur. We have records, of course, of hereditary transmission — for Friedrich's disease and Thompson's disease;

many instances of depressed and demented parents producing ataxic children and so on. But to my knowledge, certainly during my time in the Salpêtrière we have only had one possibility of investigating the brain and internal deformations of a single family. That was a father and daughter.'

'Were they Jews?'

'Fortunately.' The man nodded, seemed about to give James his own cadaverous smile, when his face suddenly darkened. 'Have you heard that the government fell today?'

'No, I hadn't.'

'That, too, can be laid at the Jews' feet. Their financiers have influenced everyone. Loubet is in their pocket. There are several rallies tonight. You must come and swell our numbers. If we don't make our dissatisfaction heard, we are certain to have a government that wants nothing more than to reinstate Dreyfus and further weaken the republic. The medical faculty, I can tell you, is staunchly patriotic.'

'Indeed,' James murmured.

They had reached a far corner of a second courtyard and Steinlen unlocked a door, only to lock it quickly behind them.

An acrid chemical reek assaulted James's nostrils, invaded his eyes, produced tears which blurred his vision. He looked through their mist to see a rectangular room, a series of pallets at its centre. On one of them lay a corpse, obscenely naked, the skin tinged greyish green. It was a man, an old man, his belly protruding slightly, his legs thin, misshapen, his hands clenched at his side as if he were struggling against some insurmountable pain. The bristle on his jutting chin seemed strangely alive, each hair a manifest spike clutching onto life.

James gripped the table and averted his eyes. They fell on walls lined with jars. Brains of varying sizes floated inside them, like so many shrunken footballs. There were other parts, too, tangled tufts of fibres that he couldn't or wouldn't recognize. On the side tables lay a variety of instruments, scalpels and mallets and callipers and saws and heavy scissors, alongside scales, an assortment of bone parts, as well as what looked like vertebrae.

Suddenly, the room started to swirl in an ever more frenzied motion, the body, the jars, the instruments trapped in an unending circle of movement, gathering up everything in its wake, Maisie and Olympe and Judith and the women in the ward, round and round. A growing whirlpool of recurrence. And it was cold, so very cold, an arctic chill which ate away at skin and bone, preventing escape.

He didn't know how long he stood there, frozen in time, the whirlpool all around him, but gradually Steinlen's voice penetrated his daze. The voice waxed enthusiastic and as James at last focused on his face, he had the odd sense that this chamber of death and dismemberment was the man's preferred home.

He forced himself to listen to his words. Steinlen was describing what he was about to do to the cadaver, what lesions and irregular growths he expected to find, along with a calcification of the joints. But it was the brain that most interested him. The brain was undiscovered country, a mysterious region calling out to the adventurous scientist. He was certain that in this man he would find a shrunken left hemisphere. The left hemisphere was the material home of the higher, the rational qualities. It was always deficient in women and in the *débile,* the mentally defective.

Steinlen pointed and jabbed as he went and James had the dawning realization that he saw these sad remains of a man as a rich terrain waiting to be charted by his mapping skills. He took a deep, painful breath and reminding himself why he was here, asked with a telltale tremor, 'How many bodies do you get to work on?'

'Quite a few. The Salpêtrière houses the population of a small town.'

'Any young ones?'

'You mean children?'

'No, no, young people.'

'Of course. In a hospital like this, death is democratic.' Steinlen grinned exhibiting a row of strong yellow teeth.

'And Dr. Vaillant leads you in your researches. He comes here himself?'

'Oh, yes. Often enough. He's a skilful dissector.'

James nodded respectfully. 'And Dr. Comte as well?'

'He's better on the clinical side — but he provides us with a good number of our bodies.'

James's skin prickled, as if a scalpel had demarcated the circle of his heart. 'Do you get an even number of men and women?' he asked with a hesitant stammer.

'More women of late.'

'You keep records and charts, I suppose?'

Steinlen's lip curled in marked contempt. 'We are scientists, Monsieur. Of course we keep records.' He waved his arm towards a far corner of the room where James saw a closed door. 'But I have no authority . . .'

'Of course not, of course not.' James cut him off with a smile. 'I was only asking for future reference, in case any of our students wished to spend a few months at your great hospital.'

Steinlen seemed about to question him further, but James forestalled him with a hasty look at his watch. 'I must leave you now, Monsieur. It's later than I thought. My sincerest thanks.'

Relief bounded through him as he closed the door of that chamber of death behind him. He didn't enjoy it for long. He had taken only a few steps into the courtyard, when Dr. Comte's oily figure bounded into his view. A wish for invisibility did no good. The doctor was already addressing him.

'I see you are developing a great affection for our hospital, Monsieur Norton. Still here after so many hours?'

'I took the opportunity of attending Dr. Vaillant's lecture.'

'And visiting our laboratory?' The man eyed him with unpleasant suspicion and blocked his path.

'Most impressive,' James said evenly, edging round him. Then he stopped. 'Tell me, doctor, it's something that interests me. Have you come across many cases of ambulatory automatism?'

Comte lifted a single shaggy eyebrow. 'Only one, directly. You'll have to go to the men's wards for that.' His chuckle held a malign edge. 'Women, unless they take to the streets like your cousin Mademoiselle Boussel, tend to do their wandering in their dreams.'

'Is that so? Good evening, Doctor. Do take good care of Judith for us — and of dear Louise.'

'We take good care of all our patients, Monsieur,' the man called after him. 'Every single one.'

James didn't like his tone. He didn't like his tone at all. In fact there was nothing he liked about this place. He had a sudden vision of smuggling Judith out of its insalubrious confines — a Judith with her hair neatly coiffed, her dress a rustling silk, her fine eyes outlined with kohl. A Judith in effect who was a reincarnation of a lost Olympe. The vision followed him all the way back to his hotel.

A few hours later, the grime of the Salpêtrière scrubbed from his pores, his frock coat smooth over the glisten of a fresh shirt, James made his way round the neo-classical harmony of the Place Vendôme and into the Ritz. The well-appointed bar wasn't large, but it was crowded and dim and he doubted once more that he would recognize the man Marguerite had described in her letter. Olympe's friend, Marcel Bonnefoi, she had said, would be wearing a white carnation in his lapel. She had added that James wasn't to worry, Marcel would be certain to detect a tall, fresh-faced American amidst the bar's regulars.

James peered round the room, penetrated clouds of smoke to focus on lapels, on glittering jewels, on bored or laughing faces. What kind of man would embody the subtle, well-judged prose of those letters he had once again studied before setting off? He moved slowly towards the counter, his eyes drawn towards the tableau above it with its racing horses and floral extravagance, when a lazy wave from a far table caught his attention.

He turned towards the waver who reclined with marked indolence in a discreet corner chair, his legs in dapper striped trousers stretched before him. He had dark brows and thick black hair of remarkable glossiness which fell over one eye. In the other sat a monocle, which gave his face a leftward tilt. That apart, it was a well-disposed face, if rather feminine in the smallness of its features. James found himself thinking of the man Olympe's actress friend had depicted to him — the swell who had dropped Olympe off on the last day her fellow players had seen her.

'Marcel Bonnefoi?'

'Monsieur Norton.' The man's voice was husky as he stood to give James an all but imperceptible bow. He fingered the carnation in his buttonhole. 'Madame de Landois described you perfectly. I rue the tragedy which has brought us together. Please, do sit.' He signalled to a waiter who appeared with remarkable swiftness to take James's order of a Scotch.

James took in gloves the colour of fresh butter, a chest swollen under a white satin vest which had the word 'dandy' written all over it. He lost no time. 'I believe, Monsieur Bonnefoi, you might have been one of the last known people to see Olympe Fabre. Was it you who dropped her at the theatre on Thursday the first of June?'

The man pursed his lips round his silver cigarette holder in studied reflection, then blew out a perfect circle of smoke. 'It could very well be. Yes, yes. Thursday. Indeed. I dropped her at the theatre on Thursday. We had taken tea together.'

'How was she?'

Bonnefoi frowned. 'As far as I could see, she was no different from usual. Olympe was a special person, Monsieur. A true artiste. I wish you could have heard her analyzing the great Bernhardt's rendition of *Hamlet.* It was the last play we saw together and Olympe had studied every movement of hand and face, every inflection of voice.'

James cut him off. 'What did you talk about on Thursday?'

The man raised a slightly querulous eyebrow, so that the monocle dropped from his face to hang from its black ribbon. He replaced it carefully. 'If I remember correctly, we spoke, Monsieur, of *L'amour fou,* the play Olympe was starring in. The second, no the beginning of the third act of the play, to be precise, where Olympe says good-bye to her sleeping child. The last time I had seen her in it, it had struck me that Olympe could put more emotion into this scene. Her movements had been a little rushed. They didn't hold a sufficient poignancy . . .'

He puffed elegantly at his cigarette and James was suddenly aware of the smoothness of his face. It was untouched by beard. The hands too were delicate. They made James's own look huge, an ungainly spread of rough skin over bone.

An uncomfortable queasiness took James over. He stared at the man more blatantly than he had intended. The stare made Bonnefoi pause in his protracted exposition of the scene. He met James's gaze. James looked away abashed, hurriedly downing some whisky. 'Do go on,' he murmured, though he was only half listening now to the man's flow of rhetoric. It had struck him that Bonnefoi could well be one of those indeterminate creatures, neither quite male nor female. But there was something else. Something he couldn't put his finger on. Yes, he was almost certain he had seen the man before. At Marguerite's soirée perhaps. But it couldn't have been. She had said she only knew Bonnefoi distantly. It must have been somewhere else.

His mind flew through possibilities and all at once he heard himself cut the man off and ask, as flagrantly as some policeman, 'Were your relations with Olympe Fabre intimate, Monsieur Bonnefoi?'

The man brushed a speck from his trouser leg. 'Do you mean in the way of your brother, Monsieur?' A small smile tugged at his lips and James felt his face grow hot.

'So Olympe told you that?'

'I don't wish to be indiscreet, Monsieur. A lady's honour . . .'

'Of course, of course. Did . . . did she mention any other intimates to you?' James stumbled over his own words.

'Not to me, Monsieur. That was never the main subject of our conversations.'

'Did you know her long?'

'Several years now.'

'And was there anyone in that time, anything that might help to explain her death?'

'I wish I could assist you, Monsieur . . .' He shrugged trim shoulders. 'I really do. I have been thinking of nothing much else since I heard.'

'Did Olympe ever mention the subject of blackmail to you?'

'Blackmail?' Bonnefoi's voice rose into sudden shrillness. He corrected it. 'What do you mean, Monsieur?'

'I was told that Olympe might either have been blackmailing someone or the reverse, someone might have been blackmailing her.' James had a vivid memory of the obscene photograph he had found on Raf's desk.

It was as if Bonnefoi shared it. He was visibly disturbed, clumsily stubbing out his cigarette in the square ashtray. 'Where did you hear this, Monsieur?'

James waved in a vague manner. 'At the theatre.'

'Why would Olympe wish to blackmail anyone? Had she been in debt, she could have approached me.'

'That is what I don't know, Monsieur. I thought you might be able to help me.' As he said it, James realized that the man had helped him. Bonnefoi had assumed that it was Olympe who was carrying out the blackmail, not as James had thought, that she was its object.

Bonnefoi shook his head once, in a gesture of severity which put a definitive end to James's line of questioning. Evidently this indeterminate character didn't like the idea of blackmail. Blackmail was something he probably feared for himself. James scrutinized him closely. Could he inadvertently have struck a chord? Could Olympe indeed have been blackmailing Bonnefoi himself and it was he who had arranged for her death? He put the thought to one side. Only Chief Inspector Durand would have the authority to investigate Bonnefoi's finances. Yet the man didn't have either the face or the manner of a killer. Not like that fleshy doctor at the Salpêtrière.

'Did you ever meet Judith?' James heard himself ask.

'Judith?' the man repeated. He was gazing down at his feet reflectively as if the answer lay in the supple black leather of his trim boots. James, too, found himself looking at their glistening softness. 'Judith? Is she a fellow actress?'

'No, no. Olympe's sister.'

'Oh, I see. No, I had no occasion to meet Olympe's family. Nor, indeed, did I meet many of her colleagues. It was Olympe herself I admired. I am interested in the actor's art, Monsieur. Had my life been different, perhaps I, too . . .' The gravelly voice trailed off.

'Yes, of course.' James had the sense the interview had wound itself to an end. Yet he felt there was more he wanted to know of Bonnefoi, though he didn't know how to put his unease into words. Where had he seen the man? In the hospital amphitheatre this afternoon? That was it, perhaps. He had noticed him in the crowd, while his full attention was directed elsewhere.

Bonnefoi was already signalling for the waiter.

'May I call on you if anything else emerges, Monsieur?' James asked.

'Unfortunately, I leave Paris at the end of the week. But Madame de Landois will know where to reach me. In the meantime, if you see her before I do, please convey my best wishes.'

It seemed to James as he left the bar and walked past the ornate ironwork of the hotel's enclosed drive that the admirable Marguerite really did hold the keys to le tout Paris. He determined to telephone her as soon as he reached the Grand.

FOURTEEN

The weather had turned in the night. The skies wore a swirling cloak of steely grey. By the time James reached the ancient chalk quarry which was now the Cimetière de Montmartre, the heavens had begun a slow incessant weeping, as if they too mourned the passing of Olympe Fabre.

He was early. He had set off in good time, not sure how long the journey would take and now the attendant at the gates eyed him curiously before directing him towards the East Wall which housed the Jewish enclave.

James made his way through a hollow, past a tangle of trees and statuary which mingled pomp and whimsy, and eventually found himself in the gloom of a steep reddish, ivy-clad wall. Here and there stood ornate domed mausolea, their doors decorated with ironwork candelabra or stars of David. Massed around them were less elaborate tombs, simple slabs of white stone. Close to the wall, a solitary grave-digger leaned against his shovel. Before him lay a mound of freshly turned chalk-like earth, too white in the sombre light. James waited, the damp attacking his bones, the rain pattering as noisily as hail on his borrowed umbrella.

Gradually the mourners arrived. From his vantage point he could see them as they wove their way along the path. A gaggle of men and women whom he didn't recognize but whose dramatic attire and gestures, he decided, placed them as Olympe's colleagues from the theatre world. Artists, too, perhaps. He wondered whether the painter whose canvas he had purchased might be here. Yes, there was Oriane, her lips clamped shut as if she were afraid that a sudden giggle would erupt to desecrate the occasion.

He spied Marguerite, a dignified, lonely figure, sylph-like in a black cloak and simple hat. He raised an arm in greeting and she stepped towards him, her feet squelching the dank earth, her face as unmoving as if she too were sculpted in solemn stone. Only when she was beside him did he see the anguish in her eyes. It took him aback. He hadn't witnessed that in her before. Somehow it brought Olympe close, as if he, too, were now a cherished friend.

'Ah, mon ami . . .' Her black-gloved hand squeezed his as she stared into the pit. She was swaying a little. 'These occasions frighten me. The dead are so full of reproaches. Listen.'

From above he heard the cawing and flutter of crows.

'What is she saying to you?'

'You didn't protect me. You could have protected me.'

'We can never protect enough,' James said with so much feeling that her eyes stayed on him.

'Ah yes, you understand. Too early a death implicates us all.'

'Let's move back to leave room for Monsieur Arnhem.'

From a bend in the path, James saw a plain wooden coffin emerge. Six men held it aloft, foremost amongst them, Arnhem himself, ramrod straight beneath his burden. His eyes were fixed on an invisible distance. A small group processed behind the coffin. One man held the hands of Arnhem's children. For a moment, James wondered if this might be Bernfeld. The man had bulging, mournful eyes, a ragged beard, and his hat was fur-trimmed in eastern fashion. Drawing up the rear were Ellie and Raf and Harriet. Raf pushed Ellie's chair. As he came nearer, James was startled to see that he had a black eye. His lip was gashed. He heard Marguerite take a deep breath.

Ellie spied them and waved and a moment later they were all clustered together at the edge of the path, which was as far as Ellie's wheelchair could go.

'What happened to you, Rafael?' Marguerite asked in a hoarse whisper.

Raf shrugged. 'It's nothing. A little fight last . . .'

He stopped speaking as a high plaintive song pierced the air. Its words were incomprehensible but the sound itself seemed to crystallize grieving lament. The coffin was being slowly lowered. The men encircling the grave rocked in rhythmic prayer, their chant growing louder as the coffin reached bedrock. Watching them, James had a sense of exclusion, as if he were doubly a foreigner.

Still praying, one by one the mourners threw a handful of earth into the grave. Raf moved to follow in their wake. Ellie tugged at his sleeve, and he nodded, lifting her into his arms as if she were a wisp of a girl. A small smile lit her pale face. Harriet looked on in a severity tinged with disapproval.

As James watched Raf place a small lump of soil in his sister's hand, he had the distinct feeling that sometime in the last night or morning they had resolved their animosities. They seemed at one again. He wondered what had wrought the change.

But now it was his turn to bend to the cold, sodden earth and fling it at the coffin. The coffin which contained Olympe. He shivered, suddenly transfixed as he imagined her lying there beneath the thinness of pine. Could she hear the thump of the soil covering her, one handful at a time, beneath the lamentations of her kin?

Maisie's coffin had been thick, solid mahogany, edged with bronze. To ease his own conscience perhaps. It had been laid next to that tiny one he couldn't think about.

He heard a sob and wondered whether it was his own. He had come a long way to do his grieving, here in this strange country amongst foreign people with stern, unfamiliar faces. He looked to Marguerite for solace and noticed that her skin was damp with tears and rain. Was there something specific Olympe might be reproaching her for?

He moved them both along, cast a last lingering glance at the coffin and edged farther away up the knoll only to catch sight of little Juliet's face. She was gazing at him, her eyes two sombre pools of fear until suddenly, she smiled and waved. He felt as if the sun had suddenly risen to brighten the day. He smiled in return.

'A lovely child,' Marguerite murmured. She had caught the exchange.

He heard the faint note of yearning in her tone and met her eyes. 'Yes.'

'Her colouring is like Olympe's, but nothing much else, really. There's a brightness to her.'

He wanted to ask her why she didn't have a child of her own, but it wasn't a subject he could raise. Instead he clasped her arm more firmly and glanced at her profile. The skin was perfectly smooth. Porcelain. Something about it fixed his gaze, made him inexplicably uneasy.

'Look, Touquet is here, and Chief Inspector Durand,' she said softly. 'That won't make Arnhem happy. I wonder what Durand wants.'

'To take a good look at the mourners, I imagine. Perhaps to interview them.' James turned towards the cluster of dark bearded men in their shabby black coats and wished that he could allow himself to do the same.

Earth was being shovelled into the grave now and when it reached the surface, he saw Arnhem bend to pick up a large pebble and place it on the coarse ground. His lips were again moving in some kind of whispered prayer. Each of the pallbearers in turn replicated his gestures.

'It's to keep the dead from rising.' Marguerite shivered. 'A custom. Olympe told me about it once.'

They watched as the rite proceeded and when it seemed to have wound its way to an end, she said softly, 'I'd like to go and pay my respects to Arnhem. You know, I offered to have everyone back to my house. But he declined. Understandably, of course. Perhaps you might all like to come.'

James nodded. As they moved through the disparate clusters of people, Marguerite now silently greeted a few of what James thought of as the theatre crowd. He, himself, said hello to Oriane, and found himself wondering why Marcel Bonnefoi wasn't here. Perhaps no one had alerted him.

'Is the painter Max Henry here?' he asked Marguerite.

'He is. We just passed him. He's the little man, there, with the large hat, the cigarette dangling from his lips. But this is no time for your questions, James. He's harmless. I assure you.'

'How can you assure me?'

She shrugged. 'Intuition. Olympe's account. You can trust me. I knew her.'

'Did you know about Bernfeld?'

'That was before my time. Before we grew close. So I can't be certain in the same way.'

He nodded with a show of sagacity. But he was taken aback by her certainty.

When they drew close to Arnhem, James saw that Raf was talking to him. Ellie was back in her chair, Harriet at her side, and he walked over to them. Ellie's face was now set in grimness.

'I don't like that man, Jim.'

'Ellie! He's her father.'

'I don't think she liked him much either.'

'Shush.'

'Look. You can see. He's angry at Raf.'

'Maybe it's something Raf has said.'

She gave him a look which told him he was being perversely disloyal.

'What happened to Raf's face?'

'He got mixed up in some kind of brawl last night. Apparently there were a lot of them. Around various newspaper offices. Everyone beating everyone up. I want to go home, Jim.'

'Good.' James felt a smile of relief stretching, too wide for his face. 'I'll book your passage tomorrow.'

She gave him a sly look. 'Home with Raf and you.'

'Harriet will travel with you. Won't you, Harriet?'

'If Elinor wishes it,' the woman said stiffly.

'Oh no, Jim. I stay while you do. We all go together or not at all. In any case, I can help keep you and particularly Raf out of trouble. Harriet understands.'

Looking at Harriet, James wasn't certain she did. 'We'll talk about it later, Ellie. We're all invited to Madame de Landois's by the way.'

'Not me. I've had enough. Enough!' She looked round her with a shudder. Her voice rose. 'All of us, standing around like vultures picking at a corpse. Yes. All of us. Except me. I'm sitting.' Her laugh peeled with sudden bitterness. Disapproving looks flew her way. 'Olympe would have hated it. All those creatures in black.'

'Hush, Ellie.' Harriet murmured. She spun Ellie's chair round with an angry gesture and started to wheel her down the path.

James turned away shamefaced. Catching Arnhem's glance, he went over to the man to speak his condolences.

Arnhem's face was haggard, his eyes bloodshot. He listened to James, then gestured him up the incline away from the curious stares of his fellows.

'Your brother is a stubborn man, Monsieur Norton.' Arnhem's voice held a tautness, poised on the very verge of rage. 'I can speak to you. You are the elder. He is too stubborn, he will not let anything go. It will cause more problems.'

'I'm not sure I understand.'

Arnhem looked round furtively. 'I do not want him to pursue Bernfeld.'

'He's here?' James asked quickly.

'No, no. Though your brother doesn't believe me. He doesn't trust me. Look. He's trying to ascertain everyone's name.'

Raf was indeed talking to the old Jew in the fur-trimmed hat.

'But you've located Bernfeld?'

'I have. And I've spoken to him. He has nothing to do with poor Rachel's death. Nothing.'

'You're certain.'

'Absolutely.'

'Will your certainty convince the police?'

His eyes were suddenly fearful. 'What have they to do with it? They haven't asked me about him.'

'But they may. Raf will undoubtedly alert Chief Inspector Durand and . . .'

'No . . . no.' Arnhem's fists were clenched. 'That would not be wise. Please, tell him . . .' Tears suddenly leapt into his eyes.

'Perhaps then it would be best if we were to interview him . . . to put my brother's mind at rest. He's grieving. He's not himself.'

Arnhem's expression played over secret matter. He gripped James's arm. 'You . . . you can go and talk to him. You will not insult him. You will be respectful, considered. You will explain that we are deliberately keeping him away from the twisted minds of the police. You will not imply that you have greater rights over my poor Rachel than he does or I do, for that matter. And then you will see. You'll be able to set your brother's mind at rest.'

'Fine. Where does he live?'

'No, not at his home. That would be impolitic. You can find him at lunchtimes anywhere in the vicinity of the new national pavilions on the universal exposition site. He has a kiosque. Drink, food for the workers.'

'How will I know him?'

Arnhem let out a sardonic growl. 'You will know him, Monsieur. I assure you.' He drew a wide circle round his own face and walked abruptly away.

The rain had stopped. The gathered mourners had split up into desultory groups. They seemed unsure whether to leave or stay. There were to be no speeches, it seemed. Little Juliette and her brother were placing more pebbles on the grave, shaping them into patterns, as if they were at the seaside. Touquet was standing near them, gesticulating wildly to a man with a pugilist's features. Off to one side, Marguerite was conversing with Oriane.

Watching them, it came into James's mind that there was something clandestine in their gestures, as if some hidden matter were being shared. He walked slowly towards them. As he approached, their conversation stopped abruptly. Marguerite's smile came at him with too great a speed.

'I believe you've met Oriane Martine.'

James had time only to nod before he saw Raf beckoning to him with an urgent wave. He proffered excuses and hastened towards his brother. Chief Inspector Durand was at his side, a small but decided smirk on his face. Raf spoke in English.

'This madman wants to take me in for an interview with the investigating magistrate. Now. I think you'd better come with me, Jim, or in my present mood I'm liable to punch them both in the face.'

'Monsieur Norton. We meet again.' The small man bowed, his jaw thrust forward, his eyes glinting in near-gleeful irony. 'I believe your brother has explained. Our juge d'instruction, Maître Chardon is waiting for him.'

'I'll accompany you, of course.'

'That's not altogether regular, Monsieur.'

'I'm a lawyer, Chief Inspector. Therefore it can hardly be irregular. You have laid no charges on my brother, I take it. This is merely a preliminary interview.'

'It is what it is, Monsieur. Maître Chardon must build the dossier. And we mustn't keep him waiting much longer.'

'Let's get it over with, Durand.' Raf was already walking towards the gate.

'What about Ellie?'

'Alert Marguerite. She'll see to her.'

Maître Chardon's office in the interstices of the upper reaches of the Palais de Justice had a view far more appealing than its shabby interior, as if visitors needed to be reminded that freedom was out there — in the flow of the river, the bright awnings of the cafés, the kiosques of the booksellers and not in the confines of this dusty cubicle, with its paper-strewn desk and bare floors.

An extra chair had had to be sent for to accommodate James, who had imposed himself despite the lack of welcome. While they waited for its arrival, Raf paced a room too small for his strides. He gave off a sullen electricity. Like a caged animal's, his face proclaimed if you so much as touch, I'll bite.

James stared at the view and pretended a calm he didn't feel. Every glance he stole at Maître Chardon's pallid, spectacled face augmented his impression that they were dealing with a rat-like Robespierre of the judicial system, a man with a secret taste for the unsavoury, every whiff of which bolstered his narrow virtue.

At last the clerk arrived bearing the necessary chair. They gathered round the desk — the clerk, pen poised for note-taking, Chardon rifling through a thick pile of papers, Durand to his other side. James and Raf sat opposite the threesome.

'We will begin now, gentlemen. Yes?' Chardon's tone was pitched for a large, absent assembly of the terminally deaf. 'And just to remind you why we're here, let me put these in front of you.' He took some photographs from the midst of his papers and spread them on every available space on his desk. Raf and James scraped their chairs backwards simultaneously.

The photos all displayed Olympe's dead body bathed in an eerie yellowish light. The lack of natural colour seemed to make details more vivid, as if the camera's lens had taken in far more than James remembered seeing. There were close-ups of her arms and legs, oddly elongated. There were strange speckles, like bites, on her fingers. Her face, ghostly with its closed eyes, was mottled too. A shadow, like that of a pointing finger, fell on her cheek. Another circled her neck, like a strangling knot of dark pearl. Beyond her, half-hidden by a rumple of blanket, something white poked out.

'This is altogether unnecessary, Maître.' James was the first to find his tongue. 'We're fully aware why we're here.'

Chardon focused colourless eyes on him. 'You, Monsieur, I will remind you again, are here under special consideration and in an unofficial capacity. I will harbour no interruptions.'

James gave him a tight-lipped nod. He caught a whisper of a smile on Durand's face. He couldn't make out whether it hinted at mockery or at satisfaction with the proceedings.

'Get on with it, Chardon.' Raf was visibly distressed.

Chardon began with a series of innocuous questions about Raf's background — his place of birth, his childhood, his education, his family. But as these questions, which James had assumed were a mere matter of formal bureaucracy droned on, he felt a tingle of apprehension. The man was probing Raf about his childhood habits, his record of absenteeism at school, subjects he had failed or excelled at, his illnesses. It was all a long way from the matter at hand, yet seemed to have some malign purpose.

The purpose only began to grow clear as Chardon asked Raf whether he had suffered any falls in infancy, any instances of trauma.

Raf's tension exploded simultaneously. He slammed his fist on the desk. Papers and photographs leapt. Ink spilled. The clerk dropped his pen.

'Look, Chardon, if you're thinking of turning me into some kind of lunatic for the benefit of your dossier, you can think again. I'm a perfectly sane and rational man — except when little . . . little officials like you get my goat. Is that understood?'

Chardon's eyes were lowered, his hands neatly crossed on his lap. But his voice held a menacing edge. 'Believe me, Monsieur, if you co-operate with the investigation, things will go far more smoothly for you.'

'Really. Is that right? The next thing you're going to ask me is whether I've made any suicide attempts. Well, the answer is no. No, no, no. Nor did I collaborate in Olympe Fabre's suicide since there never was one. Have you taken that down?'

The scratch of the clerk's pen echoed in the sudden silence.

Chardon cleared his throat with a politely muffled cough. 'You have an excitable temperament, Monsieur Norton. Indeed your behaviour is altogether unruly. We shall certainly note that. In fact, I was going to ask you some further questions about your family, about all your forebears.'

Raf leaned back in his chair with an air of absurd nonchalance. 'Ask away. Waste everyone's time. But I can tell you there is no madness in the family, no dark history of murderers and suicides, not even any cousins behind bars. Or are there some I don't know about, Jim?'

James shook his head and wished he could tell Raf to show less contempt, though the line of questioning was certainly contemptible.

'Nor does anyone drink any more than you do, or maybe you don't, but certainly no more than our honoured French Presidents do. So the question of any hereditary predisposition to crime or abnormality or alcoholism is out. Does that answer your next questions, Chardon?'

Chardon shuffled his papers. 'Yet your sister, Mlle Elinor Norton, has been to see several of our nerve specialists.'

James edged forward on his chair. He hoped his gasp wasn't audible.

'Women's problems,' Raf muttered. 'My sister is a woman.'

'Indeed, born of the same parents, nonetheless.'

'You'll have to go and ask them, I guess. I wasn't present at her conception.'

'Raf!' James heard the syllable tumble from his lips.

Chardon met his eyes with a glint of triumph.

'And while you're at it, I suggest you have a word with our Ambassador. You know, Durand,' Raf turned to the Chief Inspector, 'I really had this wild notion that we were working on the same side. I don't know where I could have got it.'

Chardon cleared his throat, more loudly this time. 'All right, Monsieur Norton, since you seem averse to our establishing a thorough moral dossier, can you please tell me about your movements from the night of 1 June when Mlle Fabre vanished from view and during all the subsequent days until her body was found.'

'That's more like it, Chardon. A little good old American empiricism to scupper the battleship of your Gallic hereditary theories. All right, I last saw Olympe around mid-day on Thursday.' He hesitated. 'That was the day, you'll remember that Paul Déroulède was acquitted and his patriotic comrades gathered in not insubstantial numbers around Sainte-Antoine. I went to cover their celebrations, their demands for a plebiscitary Republic . . .'

'Did anyone see you there?'

'I'm hardly invisible.'

'Names?'

'For Christ's sake, Chardon. It was a public rally. I spoke to some guys, but . . .'

Chardon glanced at Durand with the glimmer of a smile. 'And that night, Monsieur Norton, where did you sleep?'

'What?'

'You heard me.'

'I don't remember doing much sleeping. But I went home eventually.'

'To the Boulevard Malesherbes?'

'Yes, to the Boulevard Malesherbes.'

'Can anyone confirm that?'

'I live alone, Chardon.'

'So there's no one?'

James was about to prompt and mention Arlette when a look from Raf made him bite his tongue.

'Go on. Tell us about Friday.'

Raf suddenly screeched his chair back and got up. 'This is utterly pointless, Chardon. But just to give you a sense of how very co-operative I can be, I'll tell you.' He waved his arms and started a countdown on his fingers. 'On Friday, I wrote and telegraphed my piece. Then I went round to see various friends at various papers. I'm a journalist, if you haven't realized. Now I know we may not be your favourite people. Or the Chief Inspector's here.' He gave Durand a provocative grin. 'But we're a necessary lot. And hardly criminal. And there's been a lot going on in this blasted city. You'll remember there was a major arrest on Friday night, and on Saturday, the court made its announcement about Dreyfus. When I heard, I decided a little journey to Rennes was in order, to see how the citizenry there were reacting to the prospect of having the great traitor foisted on them. Not good. Not good. Duels. Rows. Sunday morning I travelled back to Paris. I was due to meet Olympe, but she wasn't there. So I went to those memorable races. When I got back, Olympe still wasn't there.'

Chardon interrupted him. 'You have a key to her rooms?'

Raf hesitated. 'I do.'

'Please sit down, Monsieur. During the period that we're talking about, when was the first time you let yourself into Mlle Fabre's apartment?'

'Sunday. Sunday around lunchtime and again that evening.'

'Did you take anything of hers with you?'

'Of course not.'

Durand and Chardon exchanged a look.

'You're certain of that?'

'Of course, I'm certain. What are you suggesting?'

'I ask the questions, Monsieur Norton. And now I wish to ask you where that black eye and those cuts on your face came from?'

'They probably came from one of your thugs, Chardon.'

'Raf!' James exclaimed again.

'Well, I didn't get the man's name, did I, Jim? It was somewhere outside the court in the 10th where the Auteuil royalist gang are being tried. Great day. Government falls. Would-be presidential assassins on trial. Lots of life in the old streets. Do you ever get out in the streets, Maître?' He smirked at Chardon.

'But you had time to make a visit to the Salpêtrière Hospital. Can I ask what you were doing there?'

Raf and James stared at him in unison.

'I wanted to visit a patient,' James spoke up.

'Indeed. Kind of your brother to accompany you. The patient was your cousin, I believe.'

James swallowed hard. Comte. That oily Dr. Comte had been babbling.

Raf laughed loudly. 'More of a kissing cousin. Or don't you have that expression in French? I'll say this much for you, Durand. You're being assiduous. Just wish your instincts were on a par with your diligence.'

Chief Inspector Durand looked as if he were about to add another black eye to Raf's first. James distracted him. 'Do you know Dr. Vaillant, Chief Inspector?

Chardon answered for him. 'Why do you ask, Monsieur? Do you think the good Dr. Vaillant might step in and help us prove your brother's fundamental irresponsibility?'

'Hold on a minute . . .' Raf muttered.

'So you know Dr. Vaillant?' James overrode him.

'Dr. Vaillant is one of our foremost authorities in forensic medicine. He often acts as an expert witness. He is quite brilliant at assessing the fine dividing lines between controlled responsibility and madness.'

'I see.' James paused. 'There have been a rather large number of deaths on his wards of late.'

'It's a hospital, Monsieur. People, even cousins, do not go there when they are in the best of health.' There was a distinct sneer in Chardon's voice. 'In fact, many of them go there to die.'

'And death, I take it, has a preference for certain races above others in that great hospital,' James countered. 'If I were in your shoes, I would certainly check it out.'

The man removed his spectacles and wiped them slowly. Beneath them the vapid eyes were now tinged with anger. 'Let us get back to nearer matters, Messieurs.'

He gestured towards Durand who brought a sheet of paper out of a file and tidying the photographs into a pile, positioned the paper in front of Raf. With an air of distinct malice, he handed him a pen.

'Monsieur Norton, we would like you to write something for us. To be precise we would like you to write the words "This is what you need to copy and send".'

Raf looked at him aghast. 'Could you repeat that?'

Chardon repeated himself slowly and clearly, as if he were conducting a dictée for a six-year-old.

'You're trying to do a Dreyfus on me, Chardon.' Raf was up on his feet again. He was shouting. The room echoed with his voice. 'I'm not having it. Jim, go and get hold of the ambassador. They're trying to play a memorandum number on me, expertly pretend my writing looks like something incriminating. I'm not having it, Chardon. I tell you I'm not having it.'

'Where do these words you want my brother to write out come from, Monsieur?' James confronted the man. 'It's all highly irregular. My brother is right. In America this would not be countenanced. I wish to see the document from which you have taken these words before he offers his co-operation.'

Chardon looked at Durand, who made a slight nod.

'All right. But we cannot show you the words themselves. It would ruin the proof.'

'I really have had enough, Jim. This borders on the absurd.' Raf mumbled in English.

'It won't be the same as your writing, Jim.'

'It wasn't the same as Dreyfus's either. But he spent almost five years on Devil's Island all the same.'

'What are you saying, Messieurs?'

'Learn some English, Chardon. It might clear your mind of all this idiocy.'

'Really, Monsieur, I shall be forced to . . .'

Durand stood up and deliberately side-stepping Raf, handed James a sheet of typed paper. The top of it had been folded down and when James made to turn it, Durand uttered a loud, 'No. You can read what I have shown you. Only you.'

'Ridiculous!' Raf grunted.

James read the typescript quickly.

> *You may not remember me, since you did no more than solicit my favours at the Hotel D last night, but you will believe me when I say that I know the full gamut of your foul practices. I also know your true identity, as this letter proves. I have already exposed you to your nearest. If you fail to*

follow the enclosed instructions to the letter, I shall be forced to take the exposure further. A great many journalists would be eager to hear the story. Do not try to find me again. It is pointless.

'Where did you find this?' James addressed Durand.

The Chief Inspector turned to Chardon, who shook his head.

'A sample of your writing please.'

'Go ahead, Raf. They'll prove nothing.'

Raf scrawled a version of the words and handed the sheet to Chardon with aplomb. 'Do your worst, Maître.'

Chardon stared at the handwriting. 'By the way, Monsieur Norton, was the child Mlle Fabre bearing yours?'

'What?' Raf looked like a man who had just been punched hard.

'I think you heard me.'

'What child?'

'Mlle Fabre was with child,' Chardon spelled out in the tone of an impatient schoolmaster. 'Were you the child's father?'

'I didn't know . . .'

'Come now, Monsieur Norton. You expect us to believe that your beloved mistress failed to announce her pregnancy to you. That it wasn't a precipitating cause in your wish to be rid of her? Really, Monsieur, you take us for complete fools.'

Raf was incapable of speech.

'Did you suspect the child wasn't yours?'

'That is enough, Maître.' James stepped in. 'My brother had no knowledge of Mlle Fabre's pregnancy. This is the first either of us has heard of it.'

Durand was smiling.

Chardon shrugged. 'Very well, Messieurs. We will stop this interview for now.' He turned his pointed face to Raf. 'Though I must ask for your identification papers or rather your travel document, Monsieur.'

Raf found his voice. It was hot with rage. 'Oh no, Chardon. Oh no. You can't have it. You've done enough mischief. Before I know it, I'll be picked up by one of your henchmen and imprisoned for vagrancy.'

'You will have a letter saying the passport is in my care. It will serve as an identity card within Paris. No further, of course.' Chardon opened his desk drawer, passed a form letter to his clerk, who quickly filled it out. He gave Raf a clipped smile as he handed it to him and rose. 'We will see each other again soon, Messieurs. Very soon. I have no doubt that your recollection of matters pertaining to Mlle Fabre's death will have become clearer by then.'

'Wait a minute,' James called Chardon back from the door. 'I didn't get an answer to my question. Where did that letter you showed me come from?'

'Why from Olympe Fabre's apartment, Monsieur. Au Revoir.'

The clerk took Raf's passport and scurried after Chardon. Chief Inspector Durand stayed behind to turn a beatific grin on them.

'I don't know what you're so pleased about, Durand,' Raf growled. 'Why didn't you tell me before that you'd learned Olympe was pregnant. I take it you discovered it in the autopsy?'

Durand nodded.

'You'll have wasted everyone's time, most of all your own. Madame de Landois will hardly extend any more generous invitations to her parties.'

Durand stiffened. He thrust his chin forward, an instrument of blunt arrogance. 'We shall see, Monsieur Norton. We shall see. Meanwhile you'll accompany me to my office. I need to take your fingerprints.'

'What?' Raf stopped in the corridor, so that James all but bumped into him.

'Yes. It will only take a few minutes.' Durand stroked his moustache in evident satisfaction. 'And then I'll accompany you out. The fresh air will undoubtedly feel very welcome to you. You must inhale it while you can.'

FIFTEEN

'Bastards.' Raf kicked a piece of paper from the pavement into the gutter, narrowly missing the legs of a passing woman. He was fuming, walking so quickly that James had begun to breathe hard in order to keep pace. 'Those two are so trapped in their ideas of heredity and predispositions that they're halfway up the arsehole of the doctors. They're going to drown in shit. It gives them an excuse to lock everyone up and forget about them. Forget about the real reasons for crime. Forget about poverty and squalor.'

James said nothing and Raf went on, his speech as rapid as his gait. 'And they really do think men can have this hypnotic power over women. That all I had to do was look deeply into Olympe's eyes and she'd be hypnotized, act out whatever I tell her, throw herself into the river, under a train, murder her best friend. As if she had no capacity to think for herself.'

They had reached the Pont Neuf and to James's relief, Raf paused to lean against the balustrade and look down at the flow of the river. 'You know what it's all about, don't you? It's all because of the Bompard trial where that madwoman claimed she'd been hypnotized into murder by her lover. So now they're convinced no woman can think. If they'd met Olympe for two minutes, they'd know they were the ones who were barking.'

'But hypnotism does work,' James said softly, thinking of Ellie. He was about to tell Raf what he had witnessed, when his brother turned on him.

'What do you know about it, Jim? You're not suddenly on their side are you?' He met James's eyes, his own startling in their black fury. 'No, of course you're not. Okay, I'll give you that it sometimes works, on men as well as women, but it's got nothing at all to do with Olympe's death. Nothing.'

He stared into the waters again, as dark and turbulent with the day's rain as his own face, then veered round to look over his shoulder. 'We'd better keep moving, Jim. Durand's probably got somebody on our tail again. I wish I'd never got Marguerite mixed up in all this. It's made him stupidly diligent. I'd better stay away from her, too, or he'll decide she's implicated in some way.' He shivered suddenly, like a dog shaking water off its back. 'Come on. We can't go there now. Or you can. Without me.'

'No, no. I'll come with you.'

They walked towards the right bank, Raf glancing behind him every few minutes.

'Did you really not know Olympe was pregnant?' James asked at last. He realized a great proportion of Raf's present anger must have come from the revelation of that fact.

'I didn't. Which means that Olympe didn't either. I'm certain of it.'

'Unless the baby really wasn't yours?'

'I can't believe that, Jim. I really can't believe it.' He threw James an agonized look and rushed on. 'I need to hold onto something, hold onto my sense of her. Olympe was utterly honest. Honest because she was unafraid. So she couldn't have known or she would have told me at the nearest opportunity. It didn't show. It must have been very early. Maybe she wasn't sure.' He raced on, stopping abruptly when they had reached the stony formality of the Cour Carrée. 'What was on that piece of paper those fools showed you?'

James told him the contents of the letter. 'It definitely had the tone of a blackmailing document,' he finished.

Raf didn't say anything.

'Do you have any idea if Olympe was ever involved in blackmail?'

Raf suddenly darted across the current of strollers into a side passage. When James caught up with him, he was running his hand through his hair. 'Tell me all that again, Jim. Slowly. See if you can remember the exact phrases.'

James did as he asked.

'The Hotel D. That means something to me, but I can't place it.' Raf spoke with an effort.

With a quick glance round him, James impulsively took the erotic postcard he was certain was a photo of Olympe from his jacket pocket. 'What I can't get out of my mind, Raf, is this.' He flashed the picture in front of his brother. 'You see, someone could easily have spotted this, even someone like Bernfeld, and threatened to expose Olympe.'

'Let me see that.'

James held the picture in front of him, refusing to place it in his hand. He was afraid Raf would destroy it.

'That's not Olympe,' Raf's expression was grim. He started to walk again. 'You took that from my desk, didn't you? And I told you before. That's not Olympe.'

'But you admit that there's a striking resemblance. That someone who didn't know her as well as you did might be fooled.'

Raf nodded once, abruptly. He didn't speak again until they had reached the noisy clatter of the Rue de Rivoli. 'No. It doesn't make sense. If someone was blackmailing Olympe, threatening to expose her old sins, Durand and Chardon's little handwriting number back there doesn't make sense. I wouldn't be the one to blackmail her. So no need for my handwriting sample. No, if they'd got hold of that picture and mistaken her for that woman, they'd think that in some fit of jealousy, I did her in. Wait a minute, I see what you're suggesting. You're very devious, Jim.' He gave James a startled look. 'You're supposing that Durand thinks that in order to exonerate Olympe from past crimes I didn't believe she was involved in, I suggested a reverse blackmail ploy to her. A threat. Hence the line they had me write out, 'This is what you need to copy and send.'

'I hadn't actually got that far in my thinking.'

Raf wasn't listening. 'And then when she refused, or whatever, I decided she was guilty after all, guilty of a double sin, posing for pornography and conceiving another man's child. And in a fit of passion . . . No, that's ridiculous. You should burn that picture, Jim. Get rid of it.'

James was following another thread. 'Forget about the picture. The thing to concentrate on is the hard evidence. That was definitely a blackmailing letter. It was found in Olympe's apartment. You didn't ask her to send it. But someone might have. We have to find out who.'

'We don't know that. Olympe never mentioned anything of the kind. The dear Chief Inspector could just as easily have planted the thing there himself. To stitch up a case.'

James was about to say that Raf was too quick to exonerate Olympe of everything, to surmise that she had no other life than the one she had shown him. But he sealed his lips. His brother had enough on his plate. He looked utterly despondent now, so dejected that James insisted that they stop in one of the cafés of the Palais Royal for a quick drink.

It had been a long day. It was to prove even longer.

When they returned to the Boulevard Malesherbes, Ellie's maid, Violette, rushed out to them before Raf had even put his key into the lock. She had obviously been looking out the window or waiting for their footsteps.

'Quickly, Messieurs. Come quickly.' She gestured them into Ellie's apartment and James had a sudden flash of panic. He charged into the living room.

Ellie lay prone amidst her bolsters. Harriet was applying a compress to her forehead.

'What's happened, Harriet?' he whispered. Raf was right behind him.

Ellie's eyes fluttered open. 'Raf?' Her face looked ghastly, as if she had suffered some kind of seizure and the pain had etched itself in blue ridges beneath her eyes.

'I'm right here, Ellie.' Raf perched on the side of the divan and took her hand. 'What's happened?'

'Are you all right?'

'Of course I am, Ellie.'

'That's a relief.' Ellie's voice was a whimper. 'I thought something terrible had happened to you. I couldn't bear it, if it did, Raf. I couldn't bear it.' Tears were streaming down her cheeks.

'Now, now, Ellie. What's provoked all this?' Raf stroked her hair and she snuggled into him.

James found himself looking away, the scene somehow too intimate for him. He met Harriet's eyes, felt that she shared his embarrassment, but there was a tinge of something else, too. Disapproval, he judged from the stiff set of her shoulders. She beckoned him wordlessly towards the dining room and shut the door behind them. She stood there, wringing her hands, her eyes lowered.

'Tell me what's happened, Harriet.' His voice was encouraging.

'I admit, it is pretty grisly. I wish that silly girl hadn't brought it here.' She seemed to be talking to herself, exonerating Ellie as she went.

'Brought what?' James asked when she fell into abrupt silence. 'What girl?'

'Arlette. Silly woman. The concièrge brought this package up to her, addressed to your brother, of course. It smelled foul. Really bad. So she came running in here, shrieking, and dumped it on us. Ellie said we had to open it. So I did. I cut the string.' Her lips trembled. 'I don't know what kind of evil mind is capable of such things.'

'What things?'

'Go and see for yourself.' She averted her eyes. 'In the . . . in the water closet. I threw the worst away. But your brother needs to see the rest.'

James made for the toilet. The stench, as he opened the door, was overpowering. His stomach heaved. On the floor lay a large, crumpled sheet of brown paper smeared with excrement, to its side some rough cord and what looked like a letter. The words were printed in crayon by some semi-literate hand.

'Jew-Lover!' The first line blared. 'Scumbag. Pimp. Jew-trash fucker. This is what your kind deserve. But this is only a first installment. Watch out for the second. You'll be lying in it. We'll send all the traitorous pieces of you home wrapped in your stinking shit.'

James leaned against the wall for a moment, then holding his breath, crunched the brown paper into a tight ball. The top of it, he noted, bore Raf's name and address. Putting the letter to one side, he rushed downstairs and deposited the putrid mass in the nearest bin. When he came back, Raf was holding the letter.

'Well, Jim. Another great turn in our affairs.' He laughed. It was a sound like a nail scraping over sandpaper. 'Still, it's rather less serious than what Ellie led me to think. I was pretty sure there was a body neatly cut up in the cistern. Harriet's explained in her wonderfully sober way.'

'Do you know who might have sent it?'

'Haven't the foggiest. But I'm going to find out.'

'I think you should take the letter to Durand.'

'What! And have him lock me up for my own protection. You have to be kidding. In any case, he probably agrees with the content. Maybe he's even trying to scare me into a confession.'

'That doesn't sound probable.'

'No, but it's possible. Just possible. You don't know the wheels within wheels that make this society tick these days, Jim. The government's enlightened enough. But you can bet Durand's got not a few friends amongst those scurrilous patriots who blackened my eye yesterday. And it would suit him to have me out of the way. Then he can pin everything on the foreigners, even if they happen to be merely American foreigners.'

'You're beginning to sound like Arnhem, Raf. Durand may have some theories buzzing around in his head, but he's not stupid. All that hereditary stuff seems to be as common as garbage around here. For the rest, I don't think you should underestimate him.'

'Have it your way.' Raf didn't seem to be listening. 'Look, Jim. I'm gonna go across the landing and change and then I'm going to disappear. For a day or two or three.' He put out a hand to still James's protests. 'No. You can't come with me. I don't want you mixed up in this. And I've got to clear it up. I need to know how these thugs found out about Olympe and me. I don't know if it's to do with the questions I've been asking about her death . . .'

He paused for a moment as if some stray thought had leapt into his mind to obliterate all others. 'Or just scatter gun vituperation. But I'm going to find out. And it'll keep me out of Durand's way. No, I don't want you mixed up in it.' He repeated again. 'See to Ellie, she's got herself in a state. And then if you can manage it, drop in on Marguerite. Tell her what's going on. If you need me urgently, leave a message with Touquet at his paper.'

Before James could say anything, he was out the door.

Ellie was sitting up now, propped on her cushions like an odalisque. She held a cup tightly clasped in her two hands, as if for warmth, or as if the delicate china was too great a weight for a single one.

'You let him go,' she said, her face fraught, her tone accusing. 'How could you? If I had legs, I wouldn't have let him go.'

'A cup of tea for you, Mr. Norton? And some cake?' Harriet interrupted. 'For you too, Elinor. You must eat something.'

'It makes me retch.' Ellie didn't look at her.

'You'll be up and about soon, Ellie. Only a few more days until we see Dr. Ponsard again.' James hoped the note in his voice was sufficiently soothing. 'Raf had business to attend to.'

'Business. You call that business. I call it sheer folly. I don't know why you can't exert your authority, Jim. That's what you came here to do, isn't it? You came here to take us home. Not to let him run off again, run off into the sewers of the city.'

It struck James, for one tingling moment, that she sounded exactly like their mother. He attempted to come to terms with that and the unseemly emotions it suddenly aroused in him, when she added:

'I had a letter from Mother this morning. She's desperate to have us back.'

'I'd already told you that, Ellie. Tomorrow I shall arrange for you to sail with Harriet. Raf can't leave now for more reasons than you need to know about.'

'What reasons?' She shook her head savagely, the hair tumbling from its pins. Harriet took the cup from her hand. She paid no attention.

'There are no reasons left. Olympe is buried now. He won't accept it. He just won't accept that it's over. Won't accept that she might have preferred it this way. That she didn't want to go on.'

'These things take time, Ellie. It takes time to get over the death of a loved one.'

'He can get over it at home.'

'It's not that easy. The Inspector suspects Raf of being implicated in Olympe's death.'

'Of course he's implicated. I've already told you that. Everyone who knew her is implicated.'

'Not implicated emotionally. But in fact. More murder than suicide.'

Her face crumbled. Horror spread slowly over her features.

He felt brutal. But she needed to know. Understand that there was a world out there more intractable than her sensibility.

'First the package. Now . . . Oh Jim, I'm frightened. So frightened.' She drew the shawl tightly round her, as if it were a protective carapace. It couldn't cover the terror on her face.

'It'll be all right in the end, Ellie.'

The assurance was all in his voice. Her fear had wriggled across the room to heave itself onto his lap. He was forced to confront it. It weighed on him, so heavy and threatening that he clenched the arms of his chair like a man on a sinking dinghy. The events of the day whirled before his eyes, their menace suddenly manifest as if until this moment he had sheltered behind the shield of Raf's ire and energy. Behind the shield of necessity, too. The need to act the utterly calm elder brother. With Raf gone, the scene in the magistrate's chambers, Durand's hostility, that parcel of reeking hatred and excrement played out their full measure of danger. One woman dear to Raf was already dead. What would come next?

He took a deep breath, stirred himself from the chair. Harriet was speaking and he ordered himself to listen.

'I've suggested to Elinor that we could arrange to sail after she's had the two appointed treatments, which would make it the end of next week. The seas should be calm. And this is no place for her now. It's making her weaker with each passing day. What do you think, Mr. Norton? And you could come and make this place your own until you join us. It would save Elinor having to arrange everything.'

He met the solemnity of her eyes. There was the solace of competent good sense in them. And an undeniable strength. It buoyed him up. 'That sounds altogether fine, Harriet. And I dare say we won't tarry too long.'

Ellie, that rapt look on her face, was staring into the middle distance. It wasn't clear whether she had heard them.

James went out on the terrace and let the cool breeze play over him. A man in workers' blues was coming out of their building, a soft hat pulled low over his brow. Was this the kind of man who had delivered the reeking package? Was he a mere factotum sent by some higher-up to transmit a threat? Had Raf's questions about Olympe and the other dead women been so unsubtle as to warrant such a reply? Or was it an article for the French press that had occasioned the vile threat? But what content could warrant such an obscene act?

No, more likely that the culprit had acted on his own steam, was no messenger, but the very ruffian whom Raf had done battle with, who had given him his black eye. He watched the man in blue cross the boulevard. That somehow was easier to bear. An individual act of passionate loathing, hateful in itself, but certainly less dangerous. The accompanying letter certainly bore witness to that. Yet how could a random individual know about Raf's links to Olympe?

The man in blue looked up now, his eyes directly on the terrace where James stood. In a flash, James recognized his brother. He stepped back inside, gasping despite himself.

'What is it?' Ellie asked, alert once more.

'Nothing, nothing.' He turned back to her. 'I was just thinking about that package.'

'What package, Jimmy?' Ellie asked sweetly.

With a nod at the balding butler who had taken his hat and walking stick, James slipped silently into Marguerite de Landois' garden room and surveyed the scene. Marguerite was at the piano, urging a haunting melody from its keys, her body swaying slightly as her fingers produced a poignant dissonance.

The music brought unbidden tears to his eyes. For a moment, he had a vision of a girl at Marguerite's side, a dark-haired girl with tragic eyes lost in the sounds her bow summoned as it slid over strings in counterpoint to the piano's rhythm. This girl, he noted to his own surprise, bore no relation to the half-naked creature on the postcard in his jacket pocket. She was all innocence. Perhaps Raf was right. Perhaps James's own imagination had leapt to see similitude, where there was only racial resemblance.

The ghost Marguerite's playing had invoked for him disappeared. In its place stood the painter Max Henry. He was leaning against the piano, his eyes shut. In the smattering of chairs in front of him sat a few of the other figures he had seen at the funeral. The actress Oriane half-reclined on a chaise longue, her eyes leaping from object to object with distinct cupidity. The stout man with the pugilist's features, whom Touquet had addressed, was looking through an artist's folder. Touquet, himself, had either not come or had already left.

On the table at the far side of the room James saw the remains of a buffet, empty glasses, used plates, a half-eaten cake. There was a casual abandon to it all, so very different from the last gathering he had come to in this house. Perhaps it was the sudden glimmer of sunlight, softly pink to mark the day's end, dappling the garden. It made him feel he was in some country home, far from the nervous bustle of the city. He sank into the nearest chair and closed his eyes, letting the lingering adagio of the music play through him.

Like a small, rustling stream that had disappeared underground, the melody faltered on a melancholy chord and fell away into silence. For a moment, no one spoke or moved. Then, with a little shake of the head, Marguerite rose and the room stirred into motion.

She walked towards James, greeted him. 'That was one of Olympe's favourite pieces. We used to play it together. She liked to call it "Paris Requiem". Because it made her imagine other kinds of places. Countryside, woods — calmer, softer places.'

'She's said her good-bye now.' He hesitated. Marguerite's face looked slightly askew, vulnerable, shadowy with emotions that didn't want society. He mumbled an apology for his lateness, made excuses for Raf. Her eyes interrogated him, but she seemed to understand his inability to explain and ushered him over to Max Henry.

'Ah, Monsieur, I am honoured. You've paid me the greatest compliment an artist can have. You've bought one of my canvases.' He bowed. 'Olympe was a singular model. And much more. Her death robs us all.'

'You knew her well?' James asked.

The man's dark eyebrows rose into two distinct points, like antennae. 'Not well, no. Not in the way you mean. But well enough. She had a particular quality. The quality that makes actors, perhaps. She could mould herself by the movement of a shoulder or a lip into another character.'

'We're going, Max.' Oriane was at their side, together with the flat-nosed man, who James now learned was the theatre director. There was no time for more than quick introductions, since a performance called. And after a few minutes of flurried good-byes, James found himself alone with his hostess.

'No, no. You must stay.' She poured him a glass of wine, urged canapés on him. 'I have no desire at all to be alone.' She slipped into English. 'Tell me what happened with Chief Inspector Durand? Where is Rafael?'

James shrugged and as they sat down opposite each other in an intimate corner of the long room, he started to recount the day's events. She listened intently. When he mentioned that Raf had been asked to give the magistrate a sample of his handwriting, she blanched, her face starkly white against the black of her high-necked dress.

'Decidedly, the Chief Inspector is over-reaching himself. What did he ask him to write? What was the letter you saw?'

Did he trust her altogether, James wondered? Nonetheless, he summarized the letter's blackmailing content. She rose abruptly, started to pace, changed her mind and fetched cigarettes from the table. 'Tell me that again, James,' she said as she fitted her cigarette into an alabaster holder.

He lit it for her, lit his pipe as well while he spoke. He couldn't read her expression. It was as if the smoke and a self-generated mask had combined to hide her face.

'You're certain Durand found the letter in Olympe's rooms?'

'That's what he said. I can't be certain, of course.'

She was pacing again and he called her back, 'Why? Does the letter mean something to you?'

'No . . . I don't know. It just seems so implausible. But they didn't keep Rafael there, did they?' She swung round, her face suddenly so naked with emotion, that he averted his eyes. Yes, he had been too right. His throat tightened. She loved Raf.

Yet his rightness made even a greater mystery of things. Made him despondent, too, as if he had still hoped otherwise. He checked the tremor in his voice.

'You care for him very much.'

She met him on it, holding his gaze. 'I do.' She hesitated. Then her laugh rang out, a high clear sound which held only a little mirth. 'But if you are imagining things, Monsieur Norton of Boston, please stop. All that between us is long over. We are, as you say, friends. That is the miracle.'

James felt heat suffuse his face. Her directness left him a little breathless, but like a fresh breeze it cleared the air. He returned her smile, which had a note of weariness in it to match the mellowness of her eyes. 'Over because of Olympe?' he heard himself say.

'Yes, perhaps. Because of Olympe. Certainly the first and perhaps the second.'

So Olympe had displaced her in Raf's affections, though perhaps affections wasn't the right word. Marguerite still had a goodly part of those. Why had his brother preferred the younger woman?

'Yes. It should please you to know, as an older brother, that Raf is American enough to like his passions quite honest and open, and with a future attached. Though that future has now been stolen from him.'

She looped pearls round a finger. For a second James thought her pressure might break the strand.

'Did you know that Olympe was pregnant when she died?' He only realized how cruel the question was, coming hard on the heels of his last, when he took in the storm it provoked. Her hand shook. Her eyes grew black. A frown etched lines where he had never seen them.

'Did Raf tell you?'

'Chardin announced it. The autopsy revealed it.'

'Poor, dear Olympe. Did Raf know?'

James shook his head.

'That's a relief.'

'Why?'

'It must mean that she didn't either.' She was murmuring. Almost to herself. She puffed at her cigarette.

A verminous thought scuttled through his mind. He didn't want it there, but it forced its way in, making his lips dry, his heart pound. Could Marguerite through some overweening female jealousy have done something to unsettle or unbalance the younger woman. Something which had directly or indirectly led to her death? Could she have known about Olympe's pregnancy and suggested that Raf wouldn't stand for it. She had all the necessary intelligence and subtlety for such a ploy. And now Raf was returned to her. He had seen him, after all, scurrying towards her house at an unseemly hour.

No, no. He himself was becoming unbalanced.

'What is it, James? Something else has happened. You're hiding it from me. You can tell me.' He met the candid pressure of her eyes and suddenly wondered whether the jealousy he read there was all his own. Of Raf, with her. He sought for something to hide it.

'There was a rather unpleasant event when we got back to Raf's place. Far more menacing in a way than Durand's veiled threats.'

'Go on.'

He told her as lightly as he could about the parcel and its accompanying letter.

'So Rafael has gone off to try and find out where that came from.' She shook her head. 'I can't imagine that it is connected with Olympe's death. Sometimes your brother, James, is too hot-headed by half. These people, they are pigs. In a moment of collective frenzy, they might use their fists, even bombs. But an individual murder of an actress who has a certain reputation . . . no. I don't believe it.'

James nodded. 'But someone must have known of Raf's connection with Olympe. The letter was clear on that. Did he tell you that he's been trying to uncover if there's a link between Olympe's death and those of the other women, the Jewish prostitutes. That might have unsettled someone.'

Marguerite shuddered. She stubbed out her cigarette with shaky fingers.

He rushed to reassure her. 'Though you're probably right. The parcel was an empty threat. What worries me more, if I'm honest, is what Olympe's sister, Judith, told us. Is there anyone you know who might be able to gain access to the Salpêtrière's files? Specifically, the pathology files, the ones to do with Dr. Vaillant's wards.'

'I don't understand.'

James elaborated his suspicion that Olympe, led on by her sister's fears, had stumbled on dangerous matter and been brutally stopped. He didn't mention his notion that she might have been taken for Judith, but he did tell her about the repellent Dr. Comte and about Vaillant's lecture.

'That indeed is worrying.' Marguerite's lower lip trembled as she spoke. It gave her face a softness he hadn't dared to imagine. It made her, if anything, even more beautiful, like a girl who hadn't yet hardened into the moulds life demanded. 'Did you mention any of this to our Chief Inspector?'

James nodded. 'But it wasn't a trail which seemed to interest him. Dr. Vaillant works with the police and Durand seems more intent on giving Raf a rough time than anything else for the moment.'

'I'll try to speak to him tomorrow.'

'And at the hospital itself? Do you have any contacts.'

'I'll see what I can do.'

Darkness had fallen round them. James only grew alive to it when Marguerite reached to turn on a lamp. At that moment, there was a knock at the door followed by the butler's face. Marguerite went to confer with him.

'Will you stay and have dinner with me, James?'

He hesitated and she rushed on. 'I have no plans and I would really rather not be alone. Unless you would prefer a restaurant.'

'No, no. Dinner here would be grand. Thank you.'

'Good. I'm so glad. Make yourself at home. I'll just be a few minutes.'

He must have dozed off, for the next thing he knew someone was shaking him and he was stepping out of a deep, dank, hole — a grave, yes, where a succession of women lay. Maisie, sleeping peacefully. And Rachel twice buried, as herself and as Olympe and in two different garbs, one white and girlish and innocent, the other a concoction of veils shielding only nakedness from the musty earth which smelled painfully of excrement and lilac. But also Marguerite, her face shifting with the light so that she was a girl and then a wizened hag. No, no, it was his mother and Ellie, her mouth round in a soundless scream. All of them merging so that the grave became a catacomb with winding earthen paths and an assortment of doors behind which shadowy figures hid and mocked his slow, stiff passage.

His eyes felt sore from too much grit and too much seeing and he barely recognized the figure who muttered the soft 'Monsieur, Monsieur, si vous voulez-bien . . .'

James shook himself awake. The waves of sleep still pulling at him, he followed the butler up the stairs and along a corridor. 'If Monsieur would like to do his toilette . . .' The man opened a door, waved his arm in an arc and with a bow left him.

James found himself in an ample bedroom. Its dark blue curtains, narrow bed, and sturdy writing table, bore a distinctly masculine flavour. An inner door led to a bathroom and as if he were under an injunction to follow Pierre's orders, he did as the man had bade him. A razor, badger brush and shaving soap lay neatly laid out by the sink and he made use of them.

The brush seemed still to contain some moisture. Someone had used it recently. As if in a dream, he opened a wardrobe door and found a selection of men's clothes. He stared at these and wondered if he was still asleep, then wondered again if they might be Raf's, if this might be the room Raf used when he stayed here. Or perhaps Marguerite still kept a room for her absent husband.

He examined the clothes with a curiosity which made him leery of himself and decided they couldn't be Raf's, the shoes certainly were far too small, the boots too highly polished. With an uneasy sensation, he closed the door and went to sit at the writing desk, despite himself opening the drawers, as if he had been metamorphosed into a mannerless Chief Inspector Durand who would stop at nothing.

He found some writing paper and envelopes and then in the second drawer, a lone silk ascot of blue-patterned paisley. He lifted it to his nostrils and sniffed, then stared out into the dark street, the shadows of dream gradually dispersing into a reality he would rather not have confronted. Raf had worn a tie just like this one when he was last in Boston. James remembered it clearly, had thought to himself that with that tie and jaunty corduroy jacket, Raf must think he was masquerading as the Prince of Wales.

Dinner was not in the grand dining hall but in a more intimate chamber which James characterized for himself as a breakfast room. It wore all the traces of Marguerite's particular charm — a subtle understated taste which spoke of hidden depths and an intelligence which was still opaque to him. By the window there was a round table of medium size set for two with delicate china and glistening silver, at its centre a bowl of artfully arranged flowers. The furniture was mellow walnut with a light rococo touch. But the paintings were all in the modern style, bright daubs of colour merging into shape only if one kept one's distance. There were decorative clusters of vine and flower clambering over women's gowns and along walls. There were lilies like dabs of moving light in dappled pools. There was a dance hall in which women in rustling skirts kicked their legs high, their faces harshly animal-like in the yellowish glare of lamplight.

'Do you like my little collection, James?'

Marguerite had come into the room silently and he veered in surprise, his nod overhearty.

'Later I will show you the one I have of Olympe. It's not by Max Henry and I'm not really certain it will be to your taste . . .' her voice trailed off and then as if she were carrying on an argument with herself, she added emphatically. 'But I like it very much.'

'Olympe was obviously much painted in her brief life.'

She flashed him a dark look and he realized that he had made it sound a reprehensible matter, though he wasn't sure that was what he had intended.

'If you move in the circles in which Olympe increasingly moved, it's hardly rare. Actors, artists, bohemians, they mix and mingle.'

'And you?'

'Do you mean have I been painted?' She gestured him towards a chair and he suddenly took in her gown, no longer black, but a rustle of palest peach silk which made her skin glow. Her mood had changed with her gown.

He nodded. 'Not that any painter could do you justice,' he heard himself murmur in an uncharacteristic compliment. 'But what I also meant was that these are your circles, too. I find that slightly curious, given all this.' He gestured at the house, its ostensible wealth.

She laughed. 'Artists have always needed patrons.'

'You don't behave like a patron. You behave like one of them.'

'I shall take that, too, as a compliment, though I know you didn't intend it as such. You don't altogether approve of my friends, nor I take it of your brother's.'

'Are they the same on all counts?'

'Hardly.' Her smile was impish. 'I believe the other night at my soirée you met a few whom Raf would rather not countenance. He is not always tolerant, though I suspect his intolerance differs from yours. But that is as it should be.'

He considered this not altogether happily as Pierre came into the room balancing a tray. He watched the impeccable ease with which he served them, the heavy silver spoon dipped in the tureen, the carefully poured wine.

'What I think I was getting at,' he said when the man had closed the door behind him, 'was that I find it slightly difficult to understand the facility with which you move between what you call the bohemian . . . and these others . . . these . . .

'The gratin of the Saint-Germain.'

He nodded and returned her teasing smile. 'Yes, and my brother.'

'You might add yourself.'

'I hardly count. I'm just passing through.'

'Now it is you who are searching for compliments.'

'No, no.' He tasted the soup. 'Maybe it's the fluidity of social relations here that constantly surprises me.'

'I never thought I would hear that from an American. Yours is the country where people rise from nowhere. Where mobility is everything.'

'You mustn't believe the myths. We're as jealous of our hierarchies as the next nation.'

Her smile took on an edge. 'But by here, I take it you mean my home, not Paris in general.'

'I'm not sure.'

'And by social, you mean rather more . . .' Her laugh tinkled. 'You are suspicious of me, James. I'm not sure whether I should be flattered at the interest it shows, or made desolate. Let me tell you a little about myself. Perhaps it will help. Paris, you know, is not my first home. Like you, like

Raf, perhaps even like Olympe, I'm something of a foreigner. And we foreigners have to learn to mould ourselves and the world around us a little, if we are to survive.'

'You're foreign?' His tone conveyed all his astonishment.

'Yes, in a way I most decidedly am. If not to France itself, then to the mysterious ways of this city. I'm a country girl.' Her eyes teased him. There were flecks of yellow in them, like a cat's and they drew him in hypnotically as she began her story.

It was a story of an ancient and noble family, rich in lands though no longer in money. Marguerite was the last of her particular line. Her father had already been old when she was conceived and had girded his loins for a son, not the daughter who had emerged. He had pretended not to notice the difference and had proceeded to bring her up as if she were the boy he had set his heart on, particularly once her mother had died when Marguerite was eight.

She had been given the freedom of the vast estate and the sizeable manor. She rode and walked and swam and played with the peasants' and gamekeeper's children. She hunted with her father, learned to set traps, skin rabbit and pluck pheasant. By the time she was nine she could handle a pistol adequately. The rifle had come soon after.

Not that her father put no store on a more cerebral education. He was a passionate naturalist and her earliest memories were of collecting samples of the local flora and fauna with him — of watching ants construct their extraordinary labyrinths, or wood-lice at work on garden rubble. The house had a fine library and she was allowed free rein there as well. Governesses and tutors came and went, leaving her with a smattering of mathematics and chemistry, some Latin and more English, not to mention a love of drawing, particularly the butterflies in her father's collection.

All this went on happily enough until she was sixteen, when a cousin of her father's suddenly appeared from Paris and convinced him that this was no way to bring up a girl. Within a month, a wood had been sold off and, funds in hand, she was sent to Paris to live with her cousin and learn the ways of the capital. Translated into common speech this meant, of course, the art of finding a suitable husband.

'You can't imagine the shock of it,' Marguerite gave James a smile dazzling in its irony. 'Not only the city with its labyrinth of streets and daily round of sensations. But the complete physical re-education. I literally had to learn how to walk, how to smile, how to lower my eyelids and turn my head and lift what seemed an eternity of skirt, not to mention an assortment of china and silver.'

'You seem to have learned very well,' James met her on it as Pierre cleared the dishes. They moved to the corner sofa for coffee.

'Oh, yes. I had excellent teachers. I'll introduce you to my cousin one day. She's no longer in her prime, but she's a formidable woman. Quite frightening, in fact. And within a year she had me engaged, to an altogether suitable party — moneyed, sufficiently so to save our family estate, and titled, though perhaps not quite so grandly as my father. And wonderfully eligible.'

'The Comte de Landois?'

'The very one.'

'But you didn't get on?'

'The families got on. It was a fine match. And he cut a fine figure. So fine that for a time, I was really altogether passionate about him.' She looked away, her voice receding into a near whisper. 'He was a man of considerable experience and he taught me many things. More things than I think you would wish to know about, James.'

It took him a moment to guess at what she meant. He hid his discomfort behind a cloud of smoke. When he met her eyes again, they shone with a troubled light. He had a sense that a lock had been turned and he was peeking into a bedroom. The bed was dishevelled, a bare leg rested against a sheet. He gazed down at the floor, but her voice brought him back.

'And the count was proud of me, too, quite enchanted at first.'

'Yet the marriage was not a success,' James heard himself say in a voice that had a creak in it. Part of him wanted her to hurry on. This was a dangerous matter.

Her smile had a trace of weariness. 'There are things that go on between a man and a woman, as you well know, that are not altogether easy to explain. Olivier was, is, much older than I am. He's a man of the world, but where I was concerned he grew a little too forcefully restrictive.' She laughed, turned her face away, though not quickly enough, so that he saw pain flash across it.

After a moment she said in a small, dreamy voice. 'The sphere of my possibilities shrank. It became far narrower than in my childhood. We were obviously incompatible.'

'Yet you didn't divorce.'

Her laugh tinkled. 'Here we sometimes say that though love cannot last, marriage must. Olivier and I reached an accommodation. Now we get on very well. At a distance. He has learned to appreciate the country. And I the city. Which is why I began to tell you all this, I believe. Because I started off as something of a foreigner, not to mention an ardent observer of natural life, I'm drawn to the diverse company you wondered about.'

'Amongst which you include my brother.'

'Very much so.' She smoothed her silk skirt with an air of almost girlish modesty.

He watched her in silence for a moment and he reflected on all that she had said.

'You know, if I were Durand and I knew of your relationship with my brother, I would say that perhaps you had far more reason to want to see the end of Olympe than Raf himself. The passion in that case would make sense. The *crime passionel* as you call it.'

Marguerite's laugh held a touch of exhilaration. He suddenly imagined her with a pistol. 'I can assure you, James, that I have usually won my men in other ways.'

'But not, it seems, my brother.'

'The story may not be over.' Her eyes challenged him as if she were willing him to probe further or to meet her in a duel. 'You don't approve?'

'No, perhaps not. But nor would I have approved of Olympe.' He paused, chuckled at the bravery of the words that had leapt into his mind which he now spoke out loud. 'Perhaps I would merely have wanted you both for myself.'

She studied him with what he suddenly saw as the cool glance of the naturalist. 'You're a handsome man, James. And you have a rare honesty.' She rose and walked towards the windows, pulling the curtain back to peer out into darkness. When she turned back to him, there was a tremor in her voice, 'What you say about Durand is, of course, true. I'm surprised he hasn't been to question me.'

'Your status shields you. Then, too, he might not know about your relations with Raf.'

'But you, I take it, will tell him. If only to exonerate Rafael.'

He met her eyes for a long moment. 'Did your husband know Olympe?' he asked, not altogether certain what had impelled the question. 'You said he was still living here when you first met her.'

She caught the sense he hadn't yet altogether grasped himself. 'Yes, Olivier met her. But if you're suggesting that we quarrelled over her, you're quite wrong. She wasn't Olivier's type. And even if she were, James, that would hardly be a reason for a parting of the ways.' She got up abruptly and he sensed that in his haphazard speculation, he had touched some nerve, though he wasn't certain which it was.

'Forgive me. I'm being unpardonably rude. The day has worn me out, made me forget the gratitude we all owe you. I'm also worried about Raf. And about Ellie.' A sigh escaped him.

'Oh yes, dear Elinor. A fine woman. But I fear her emotions conspire against her. She is not like our French women who, given the necessary means, manage to order their lives to accommodate at least some of their desires. As you say, our habits are more lenient.'

James stifled a gasp. He had never thought of Ellie in such terms.

'How did the consultation with Docteur Ponsard go?'

He was about to tell her what he had witnessed, but bit back his words. The revelation somehow felt too shameful. Instead, he shrugged. 'Well enough, I think. She is to see him again for further treatment.'

Marguerite nodded sagely.

'Did he help Olympe?'

Her eyes filled with sudden tears. 'I believe so,' she murmured, then rose slowly and with evident fatigue. 'It has been a long day, James, and now it's very late. My coachman has the evening off, so he won't be able to ferry you. But you're altogether welcome to stay the night, if it suits you. Pierre will see to your needs.'

As if the man had been waiting to hear his name, a soft knock sounded.

Marguerite stretched out her hand.

James touched it with his lips. 'You're very kind.'

'Ah that, my friend. I'm not sure you're yet in a position to judge.'

Before he could counter her, she was out the door.

SIXTEEN

He woke to a clatter. In the sticky mists of dream, he thought of rocks falling on wood. A torrent of rocks on the wood of a coffin, imprisoning its occupant forever, burying her secrets in the silence of cold stone.

He opened his eyes with a shudder. The dusky room refused recognition. Not until his feet reached the silky texture of the bedside rug did he remember that he had spent the night at Marguerite's, that he had allowed himself to be beguiled by the notion that if he spent the night here, the house might somehow offer up a key to the enigma of its occupants, their shrouded connections. Instead he had fallen asleep almost as soon as his head touched the pillow only to wake to this present disorientation.

He padded over to the window, drew back the curtain and pushed open a shutter. The light was already bright. On the street below him a carriage picked up speed. The horses' manes flew, their smooth backs streaked by sunlight. He caught a glimpse of the driver. Marguerite's driver. Beside him sat a capped youth, who he was almost certain was Antoine.

It came to him that if Antoine was here and racing away in Marguerite's carriage, Raf must have sent him, which could only mean his brother was in trouble.

He dressed quickly and was about to put on his jacket when there was a knock at the door.

'Huit heures et demie. Comme vous avez précisez, Monsieur.' A young aproned maid, bearing a tray, stood at the door and reminded him of the appointed breakfast hour. She walked past him, deposited the tray on a corner table and poured coffee.

'Is Madame de Landois up?' he asked.

The girl gave him a curious, almost chastising look. 'She usually comes down at about eleven, Monsieur.' She curtsied and was out of the room before James mustered his thanks.

As he buttered the neatly sliced baguette and drank his café au lait, he ran through possibilities which extended from Raf's having suffered an injury to Chief Inspector Durand's men having cornered him at a place from which he now needed to flee without being seen. All the possibilities struck him as unlikely. What was far more probable was that Antoine was seeing to some prearranged errand and Marguerite had once again kindly offered her carriage. And from the maid's demeanour, it would be the summit of bad manners for him to trouble Marguerite in order to find out.

Some forty minutes later, he was out in the cool morning air and walking with a determined step in the direction he had set himself. The necessity of his course had come to him with his second cup of coffee. He had been a fool not to attend to it sooner.

The banks of the river were a hive of morning activity. Shoulders bent to the task, men unloaded timbers from one barge, pallets of brick from another as far as the eye could see. Voices rose in a chorus of orders and grunts. But the houseboat was moored exactly where he remembered it, probably by police command.

Tattered sheets hung from a washing line shrouded the cabin. As they fluttered in the breeze, he noticed a pair of supple black boots at their base, shiny against the whiteness. For some reason, he paused and an image of Marcel Bonnefoi sitting in the Ritz bar crowded into his mind. But the man couldn't be here. A moment later, the sheets parted and their owner emerged from behind them like an actor in a play. It was the young blonde woman he had last seen nursing her babe. She was wearing a coarse beige frock and gesturing someone through the curtain of sheets.

Chief Inspector Durand's barrel-chested figure emerged. James took a step backwards. The man was beginning to feel like a double, an erratic shadow who appeared before or behind him wherever he went.

He turned away. It was too late.

'Monsieur Norton,' the Chief Inspector hailed him and moved quickly in his direction. 'What a coincidence.' His cunning eyes narrowed. 'Or is it that you, too, are interested to know what people have come to visit the man who rescued Mlle Fabre's poor drowned body from the murky waters of the Seine? Your brother, needless to say, has been. And treated our boatman with rather more belligerence than was altogether necessary . . .'

Durand put his arm through James's and led him forcibly away from his original destination. 'Your brother is his own worst enemy, Monsieur Norton. He treats us, my men, myself, the whole apparatus of state, as if we were rank incompetents, or worse, criminals.' He shook his large head solemnly and tsked beneath his breath. 'It is hardly calculated to endear him to us or to our investigation. But then desperate men can hardly be counted on to be reasonable, can they, Monsieur Norton?' He cast a glance of mingled guile and complicity at James.

James shrugged off the man's arm. 'My brother's desperation, if that is what it is, is hardly rooted in the motives you attribute to him, Chief Inspector. He is simply a grieving man, a man in search of answers.'

'We shall see. We shall see.' Durand gave him a philosophical smile.

They had reached the quay and the Chief Inspector seemed to have little inclination to see James go. 'Walk with me, Monsieur Norton,' he said in a tone which was less invitation than command. 'There is no point your going back to the houseboat, I assure you.'

James allowed himself to be led. He could hardly do otherwise and he might be able to work the situation to Raf's advantage. 'My brother may have the rashness of youth,' he began, 'but . . .'

Durand cut him off. 'He is not a friend of the forces of law and order. You may not know this, Monsieur Norton, since you are a stranger to our city, but your brother's associates are the dregs of the journalistic world. That man Touquet, for example.' Durand spat emphatically. 'He's a gutter rat, chewing away at the very foundations of civilization, poisoning its waters.'

'You don't say?'

'I do. Why, even his wife left him. Divorced him on grounds of adultery. With prostitutes, I imagine. That's why he's so enamoured of their cause.'

'Really! Is divorce so easy to obtain here, then?' James thought of Marguerite.

'Pah. It's the bane of the republic.' Durand suddenly picked up a stone from the path and flung it into the midst of a construction site. 'Don't get me wrong, Monsieur. I am not an anti-republican. Oh no. Quite the opposite. I am a staunch servant of the republic. But this! Since '84, when the law was introduced, the divorce rate has spiralled. It attacks one out of every nine marriages. One out of nine. Marriage should be indissoluble. For the good of the community, you understand. The family, after all, is its cornerstone, the axis of stability. And the family now is severely threatened. Our birth rates have plummeted. Only the foreigners and the half-wits breed. Soon we will be half the size of our old enemy. That is a terrifying prospect. France half the size of Germany!'

'Indeed. You are married, Chief Inspector?'

A lightning scowl crossed Durand's face, but he answered blandly enough, puffing out his chest a little. 'Oh, yes. And I have two fine boys. But there is a related problem. You undoubtedly sniffed it out for yourself the other night at Madame de Landois' gathering.'

'I don't altogether follow you.'

'Women. They no longer accept anything. They refuse their place. In marriage and in everything else. They question everything.'

James had a distinct memory of the Chief Inspector pontificating on women's innate suggestibility. He didn't question the contradiction. 'Oh yes?' he urged Durand on, wondering where the conversation would take them.

'Yes. And the men in those circles are no better. Feminized, that's what they are. Overrefined, sensitive, lacking in moral fibre, nervous. Like the Jews. Like women. They can only point their guns out of drunken passion or at themselves. We must stop the rot, Monsieur. The enfeeblement.'

James murmured agreement.

'It's the nerves, Monsieur. They are shattered. The modern disease. We sleep badly, eat and drink too much or too little. The speed, the crowding, the noise, the excessive demands and excessive democracy, the emancipation of women, all of it rots the social fabric. How well do you know the beautiful Madame de Landois?' he asked with no transition.

James faltered, realizing this was where Durand had been leading. 'Not at all well, Chief Inspector. She's a gracious woman. Hardly like the images you've just conjured up.'

'You don't think so? What is the nature of her relation with your brother?'

James pretended not to have heard. Given the rush of passing traffic, it was easy enough. 'I know she was very attached to Olympe Fabre. She took the woman in hand when she was still a girl. Raised her to the heights she reached. Almost like a daughter.'

'A daughter, you say?' Durand frowned and was silent for a moment, as if he were performing a feat of mental arithmetic.

'I didn't mean literally, Chief Inspector. I meant in terms of the sentiment she had for Olympe.'

They had reached the Rue du Bac and James pulled out his watch. 'I will leave you Chief Inspector or I will be late for my appointment.'

'In the Sixth is it? Or the Seventh? You are seeing Madame de Landois? Do remember, Monsieur Norton, these aristocrats are not like us. We can so easily be taken in by their smooth manners.'

'Indeed, Chief Inspector. But you needn't worry. I am not so fortunate as to be meeting Madame de Landois. Just an American friend. A Mrs. Elliott,' James heard himself saying.

The Chief Inspector nodded shrewdly. 'By the way, Monsieur, I wish to interview your sister. My men were prevented access. Her companion said that number one, she was ill, and number two, she spoke no French.'

James had a mental image of Harriet, barring the gates like some armed, antique goddess to shield his sister.

'Yet despite her illness, Mademoiselle Norton came to the funeral.'

James stiffened, stretched to his full height so that he towered above the man. 'In a wheelchair, as you may have noticed Chief Inspector. Elinor is indeed ill. The doctor has insisted on complete rest. Her trip to the cemetery was against his specific orders.'

'Indeed, Monsieur. I see your women, too, are loath to listen.' He considered James for a moment. 'You understand, we still have no confirmation of your brother's movements from the day of Olympe Fabre's disappearance until midday Sunday. Your brother's housekeeper, I think you'll agree, leaves something to be desired as a witness. One of my men tells me he knew her well — when she was on the streets.'

'Indeed Inspector. My brother may be naïve, but he is kind-hearted. He took the woman in because of the child. He loves children.' Suddenly seeing the advantage of the line he had stumbled onto, James pursued it home. 'That is why it is clear to me, Inspector, that if Raf knew of Mlle Fabre's pregnancy, that would have made him even less capable of any violence than he already is.'

Durand considered for a moment. 'That is all fine and well, Monsieur, but we still have no witnesses to your brother's movements. What we do know from Mlle Fabre's landlady is that he certainly turned up at her apartment. What we don't know is what he may have taken away with him. Goodday, Monsieur.'

James watched him walk away, quickly, officiously, as if the pavement crowds must needs part for him. When he could no longer distinguish his figure, he turned and with a sigh, retraced his steps.

It was almost too late now to make a stop at the houseboat, though he was drawn there. Something about the place niggled at the edge of his consciousness and when he reached the embankment, he found himself making a detour toward the boat. He called out a 'bonjour' and walked up the ramp.

The young woman appeared again through the curtain of sheets. She was cradling her infant and she stared at James with visible apprehension. 'My husband's not here.'

'That doesn't matter.' He smiled. 'You remember me, don't you? I was here that night — when the body was found.'

She flinched as if he had hit her. He suddenly noticed the bruise on her cheek, her pallor, the untidiness of her hair. 'How's your little one?'

'Asleep.' She clutched the babe more closely to her, all the while bunching the sheets behind as if to prevent his entry.

'I . . . I just wanted to ask you some questions about that night. You know that young woman, she was my brother's . . . well, his sweetheart.'

Her eyes grew wider.

'He can't sleep, can't rest. He wants to know everything. Everything that happened to her. And I'm trying to help him. How did your husband find the body?'

She took a step backwards.

'Please tell me about it,' James urged softly. 'I'd like to hear it for myself.'

She hesitated, then blurted out. 'There was this banging, like an animal knocking itself against the hold, trying to escape. Horrible. I went to see what it was and there was this white shirt billowing. Then hair . . .' She stopped abruptly. 'Go away. Go!' she wailed, then stumbled back behind the sheets, leaving him only with an image of black boots running along the deck until they too vanished from view.

Mystified, he played over her words and manner as he walked, speedily now, along the uneven path which wound through the mammoth construction site that would soon be the universal exposition. The sounds of hammering and sawing were everywhere. Grit flew through the air like so many June bugs intent on attack. Dust rose in clouds from half-erect structures. Workmen shouted in incomprehensible languages.

The flags of various nations billowed, demarcating zones. Behind the Italian one, the intricate lacework of vaulting arches and unglazed windows seemed to combine with a whiff of Mediterranean herbs and a heavy meaty smell. Perhaps the interior was in fact a huge canteen. As the American zone gave way to the Austrian, then to the architectural vagaries of the Hungarian and the British, he felt he had entered a world of shifting façades where the senses could no longer be trusted.

He forced himself to concentrate on his task. He examined faces, though he had only a vague image of the one he was looking for.

Just past the Serbian flag and near the Pont Alma, he wound his way through a ragged queue of workmen and looking back to see the reason for their line, understood that he had probably reached his destination. The men were crowded round a makeshift table, heaped with baguettes and cakes and fruit. Behind it stood a small cart and an ancient, bowed draft horse. To the other side of the stall, atop barely smouldering coals, there was a vast urn, from which a white-shirted man, his sleeves rolled up, morosely ladled what could be soup. He was short, his beard scraggy and on his head sat a wide brimmed hat which resembled Arnhem's. James joined the queue.

When he finally got to the front, he said softly, 'Isak Bernfeld?'

The man met his eyes for a fugitive second.'Who wants him?'

'I do. I'm a friend of Arnhem's.'

The man scowled. 'What do you want to eat?'

'A cheese baguette. I'll wait for you over there.'

James waited and watched. Custom was good and the queue never seemed to diminish. The man he was now certain was Bernfeld looked round at him occasionally. The glance was both apprehensive and menacing. He wasn't a prepossessing man — not like Arnhem. James judged him to be about forty. His lips were thick, his eyes bulging, the skin pockmarked, the nose too brief. He was short-legged and stubby, though there was no excess flesh and his arms were strong. He moved about his tasks with the coiled energy of a man who hungered after larger gestures.

James had a moment's anguish as he thought of this Bernfeld with the delicate Olympe. One swipe of that thick arm and the girl could easily have toppled into the river, never to rise again. He stopped his baleful leap into imagination. It would serve no purpose to prejudge the man.

James munched at his long, thin sandwich. Napoleon's soldiers came into his mind. The Emperor General had thought of everything, had invented a bread without clumsy bulk, a rifle-shaped bread that could easily be strapped to a soldier's waist. His father had told him that. Had told him on their first trip to France. His father admired Napoleon, his efficiency, his attention to detail.

The queue was now only three-men long. James looked at his watch. The lunch break must be over. Girding himself for his task, he moved closer.

Suddenly he heard a bellow. A burly customer had erupted in a string of expletives. He banged his fist on the makeshift table and sent its remaining wares flying. 'Sale Juif,' the man roared. He turned to his companions. 'He's short-changed me. The Jew-skunk's short-changed me. You saw it.'

Bernfeld muttered something James couldn't hear and then the worker in blues was round the back of the table. He landed a punch on Bernfeld's chest. Without flinching Bernfeld returned it. His assailant staggered backwards.

A small crowd had already gathered to watch the commotion, spectators at a ring and now shouts rose from everywhere, thrusting the man towards Bernfeld, who pranced and feigned like an experienced street fighter. More punches fell. Two gendarmes burst into the fray, waving truncheons, ordering a halt, pinning the men's arms back, asking what had happened. The crowd spoke as one and pointed at Bernfeld.

James found himself addressing the policemen in the calm, authoritative voice of the courtroom. 'Pardon me, Messieurs, but I was standing just there when it all started. I'm afraid it was this man here, who threw the first punch, scattered the vendor's wares as well.'

The workman eyed him with a swagger. 'What's it to you? The Jew cheated me.'

'Out of how much?' one of the gendarmes asked.

The man shuffled his feet. An avid look flew over his face. 'Twenty centimes.'

'It's not true,' Bernfeld spoke for the first time. 'Not true, I tell you. But what does it matter. Here.' He whipped his arm away from the gendarme, drew some change out of his pocket, and flung it to the ground. 'Take it. Take all of it. Good riddance. Now go away. All of you. Go away. Leave a poor man in peace.'

With swift gestures, he dismantled the table, heaved it onto the back of the cart, along with the urn and the remaining provisions. While the other man was still scouring the earth for coins, he pulled the back of the cart to. The policemen looked at each other and shrugging, dispersed the small crowd.

Before James could stop him, Bernfeld was seated in the cart and urging his old draft horse on. James raced after him and leapt up on the seat beside him.

'I want to talk to you.'

The man mumbled something about a stomach which James couldn't make out. He gripped the wooden seat. Bernfeld was driving recklessly, urging his old horse on so that the wagon squeaked and shook. They turned away from the broad avenues and were soon in a part of Paris he didn't know. The streets were barely wide enough for the cart here, the pavements crowded with scruffy children and scurrying men.

With no notice, they abutted on a vast and ugly iron structure and came to a rattling halt. Everywhere around them were other carts and wagons heaving with crates and baskets. Of course. The Stomach was Les Halles, the city's central market. Pungent smells rose from the ground. Broken crates spilled rotting vegetables on wet pavement. A small girl picked up a stinking, goggle-eyed fish and popped it into her basket. Dogs tore apart hunks of raw meat, dropped from some vehicle. On another sat coops of squawking fowl, giving off a repellent smell.

Bernfeld leapt to the ground. James followed swiftly.

'Okay then. If you're still here, you might as well help.' Bernfeld indicated a pannier for James to carry.

Moments later they were through a door and walking beneath an immense glass canopy held aloft by iron ribs like some prehistoric monster too large for the delicate earth. The stalls were all but empty, the hall sparsely peopled. The Stomach was a nocturnal creature, James recalled reading. In the small hours while Paris slept, it would fill its belly only to disgorge it at dawn.

At last Bernfeld spoke. 'What do you want of me? I should thank you, but I am not grateful. You followed me, so the police will now think that we are in some racket together. They will harass me.' The man's eyes bulged with barely controlled irritation. His accent was like Arnhem's but thicker.

'I want to talk to you, that's all. About Olympe Fabre. Rachel Arnhem.'

Bernfeld speeded up his step. James followed him past stalls, past a pannier full of sheeps' heads, the eyes glittering strangely. They stopped at a counter to drop unsold provisions. Bernfeld counted out money for a capped and squat ruddy-faced man whose manner was distinctly surly.

Then they were out on the street again and through a crowded lane into another huge, girded structure. The place was a teeming labyrinth.

'All right. If we must, we must. But I have nothing to tell you. Nothing.' Bernfeld gestured him through another door into a crowded, insalubrious bar. He ordered two brandies and set one in front of James. They stood at the counter face to face, so that he could feel the man's breath on him as he spoke.

'I only met Olympe Fabre twice. Twice was enough.'

'But I was told you knew her well, you had proposed . . .'

'That was to Rachel Arnhem. She died — died many years before this Olympe.' Bernfeld's face was set in stone. 'Who are you, anyhow? What are you trying to pin on me?'

'My name is James Norton. My brother . . .' James stopped himself. Something about the man's previous statement had just made him aware that any mention of Raf's relations with Olympe would hardly be calculated to make him amenable. 'My family . . . we were friends of hers. Why did you write to her? Threaten her?'

'Ha!' A gutteral sneer emerged from the man's lips. His thick, gnarled fingers tightened around the glass. 'So Arnhem didn't tell you? No, of course not. He's become too good for money. Too well connected for memory. I wanted my money back. What do you think I wanted?'

'Olympe owed you money?'

'Arnhem owed me money. They owed me money. I gave him money. A tidy sum. Years ago. We were to be married. Rachel and I. Rachel and Isak. A lot of money. Did she marry me? No. Did Arnhem return the money? No. No. He needed it. He was desperate. Always desperate. And Isak was cheated. Cheated.'

James tried to make sense of this. 'So you went to Rachel, to Olympe, to get your money back?'

'With interest. Seven years. I was broke and she was rich. You've seen her apartment. Her clothes. Her friends. Look at you. Look at me.'

And you murdered her for it?'

'Murder? Who said anything about murder?' Beads of perspiration appeared on the man's forehead. A smell came from him, like the smell of fear. 'No, no, no. No, I tell you. You can't pin that on me. Just because I'm an old Jew, down on his luck.' He looked for a way out of the bar, but James already had his hand on his arm. He kept it there.

Bernfeld met his eyes. 'All I wanted was my money. Arnhem should have told you. I wouldn't murder one of my own, even if she had become a slut.' He slammed his glass down on the counter and called for another brandy.

'Where were you on the night of Thursday the 1st of June and for the five days thereafter? I want a specific account.'

'Where was I? How do I know? I was here. Or at work. Or in my grubby room. Look, mister, I may not be Captain Dreyfus, but I'm no more guilty than he is. Unless having a drink or two is against the law. And then you can lock-up the whole Stomach.' He grinned, showing ragged yellow teeth. 'Sure I may have threatened Rachel a little . . .'

How did you threaten her?

The grin turned into a scowl. 'She didn't believe what I told her. About the debt. I told her to ask her father. I told her I would give her a month to raise the money, if she didn't already have it hoarded away. Otherwise, she would have to marry me. That was the deal Arnhem made way back when I was on top of my fortune. That was the basis of the sum I gave him.'

'Did Rachel agree? Did she have the money?'

Bernfeld shrugged. 'She said she didn't have it to hand. I didn't believe her. But I told her if she didn't have it, she could raise it from one of her rich friends.'

James gripped Bernfeld by the shirt. 'So you forced the poor girl to resort to blackmail.'

'Who said blackmail? I said nothing about blackmail.'

'You sent her a letter which told her exactly how to go about it.'

Panic contorted the man's features. 'I didn't. Is that what Arnhem told you? I only wrote to her once. Once to arrange to meet her. And I wouldn't hurt her. Arnhem knows that. He must have told you. Not little Rachel.'

Tears had gathered in the man's eyes and threatened to overflow.

James's mind raced. Could he imagine the man lifting a violent hand to Olympe, physically menacing her perhaps while under the sway of alcohol, and somehow forcing her to her death. He wasn't sure. He could certainly imagine him applying pressure which threatened violence. He could imagine blackmail. He could also at last imagine Olympe flinging herself into the river's swirling waters. Better that than life with this anguished madman who seemed to love and loathe her in equal measure. Durand would have to be involved, after all, whatever Arnhem's imprecations. There was no way round it. If only to exonerate Raf from any collusion in blackmail.

The Olympe his mind had created would have been too ashamed to ask Raf for money he would probably readily have given. So under Bernfeld's pressure and instruction, she might have considered blackmailing someone else.

'If you're innocent of murder and of blackmail, Bernfeld, as you insist, I recommend we go to the police right now and you make your statement. Otherwise things will go badly for you.'

The man shuddered. 'If I go to the police, things will go badly in any case. They'll lock me up and throw away the key. Isn't that what they do with my kind.'

'Chief Inspector Durand will only want the truth,' James asserted a little uneasily.

An idea came to him. 'Tell you what, Bernfeld. Write down your address for me — and maybe just a sentence saying you had no part in the murder of Olympe Fabre. I'll take it to the Inspector, and instead of bringing you in, we'll both come and interview you. And don't give me the wrong address or suddenly disappear, because that will only provide proof, as you know.'

Congratulating himself on his cleverness in extracting a sample of writing he could now bring to the Inspector for comparison with the blackmailing letter, James presented his notebook and pencil to Bernfeld. The man gazed at it. Then with a shrug of pronounced hopelessness, he began to write. James saw incomprehensible characters appearing on the page. 'In French, Bernfeld. Write in French, damn you.'

'But Monsieur . . . this is the only writing I know.'

SEVENTEEN

James walked slowly back towards the Grand Hotel. He was tired. Very tired. Like some light skiff tossed by waves, his mind swirled and swayed in a stormy sea of impressions. There had been too many in the last days. But it was the relentless attempt to introduce order which caused the exhaustion, he suspected. The sheer effort of the will it required.

He gave it up for the moment and allowed the associations to play havoc with him. The back streets here were quiet, not like the hubbub of the river front where he had talked to the young woman, her babe cradled in her arms. Olympe had been with child, too, and it had perhaps precipitated her end. Like Maisie. The much-wanted child had brought death in its wake. Madame de Landois had no children. Neither did he. Nor Ellie, nor Raf, now. Would his mother, who presumably would appreciate some grandchildren, have commanded him to Paris had she known that Olympe was with child? Yes, and probably with even greater haste. Some children were better than others. Some were no good at all. Bad blood. No. It made no sense. Bernfeld, like James's own mother, would have been enraged at the thought of Olympe with child for the same and opposite reasons — a child conceived with someone outside the clan.

Money or marriage, Bernfeld had threatened her with. He could imagine the poor girl wondering whether Raf would have her against his mother's will and with a threatening Bernfeld to boot. Here were motives for suicide far more urgent than any hypnotic pass.

Something knocked at the corner of his mind. Something the woman on the boat had said.

But he was already at the hotel and a large, distinctly American contingent clustered round the reception counter demanded his attention. Three boys of varying sizes shuffled their feet and teased a small tearful girl who fled from the group into the capacious skirts of a black-clad dowager guarding a cabin trunk.

The sternly dramatic, angular features of this ravenlike figure thrust James into confusion. How could his mother so suddenly appear in Paris? He stopped in his tracks and took a long, ragged breath, arming himself with explanations. Then, slowly, he forced himself forward.

Proximity dispelled the illusion. The woman was not his mother, though the resemblance was marked. His heart still beating too quickly, he stared at his momentary misincarnation. She was indubitably a sign. A sign of his guilt. His last missive home had been all lying solace and procrastination, the lies bolder as his own awareness of the tangles Raf and Ellie were trapped in grew clearer. His mother had undoubtedly read the reality between the lines and if she wasn't actually here in person, there was probably a telegram awaiting him at the desk, one which might indeed announce her imminent presence.

He turned and moved grimly towards the counter. A vociferous argument between a red-faced man and the hotel manager was in full progress. A long ungainly queue for keys and mail had formed. With a shrug James changed course and made for the bar.

'Mr. Norton!'

James turned to see a parasol wielded with vigour in his direction from amidst a row of palm fronds.

'There you are, at last, Mr. Norton. Join us please.' Mrs. Elliott sat back into her chair and pointed to a place on the sofa beside Charlotte, who smiled at him brightly, displaying a row of strong teeth.

Unable to think of an excuse, James sat. It served him right, he thought, for having used Mrs. Elliott's name earlier in making his escape from the Chief Inspector.

'Charlotte and I hoped you wouldn't tarry too long. We're having tea, but you might like something stronger.' Mrs. Elliott waved at a garçon and barely waited for James to place his order before announcing, 'We've been to see your sister again, Mr. Norton, and we wanted to have a word about her.' Her face held a sombre warning.

'Oh, yes?'

'Yes. She's emphatically unwell.'

'Mother's right, Mr. Norton.' Charlotte's eyes were wide and James read something like fear in them. 'She . . . she couldn't concentrate. She hardly seemed to recognize us. And she was very angry at your brother. Very. We couldn't quite understand why. She just . . . well, it felt like delirium.'

'I told her maid to call the doctor instantly. Harriet wasn't there, you see.' Mrs. Elliott shook her head in dismal disapproval. 'I hope they haven't quarrelled.'

'No, mother, Harriet never quarrels. She was probably off with one of her other charges.'

'In any case, I think the girl understood me, because soon a man arrived. The trouble was he didn't speak English and he seemed to be asking us to leave. It was only as we got into the carriage, that I realized he didn't have a bag with him, so he might not have been the doctor after all.'

She gave James a querulous look as if everything were his fault. 'We think you should go to her, Mr. Norton. She shouldn't be alone. She should be with her family.'

'Of course. I'll go straight over.' James downed the Scotch that had just been placed in front of him. 'Thank you for letting me know.'

Mrs. Elliott put a staying hand on his arm. 'If you want my advice, Mr. Norton, you will get your sister home on the first possible sailing. I suspect the doctors here are all quacks. And she needs her mother.' She shot a glance at Harriet. 'This is no place for young women on their own. You understand me, Mr. Norton.'

'I do, I do. You're quite right. Excuse me now, I must be off.'

'You'll let us know how Elinor is, won't you?' Charlotte said while he hastily signed his name to the bill.

'Of course.'

He had only taken a few steps, when Mrs. Elliott called him back. 'That's him, Mr. Norton. The doctor, if he is a doctor. Perhaps he's come to find you.'

James followed the line of her finger and saw Chief Inspector Durand making his way through the lobby. His heart sank.

'Yes, yes,' he mumbled and hurriedly extricated himself, afraid that Mrs. Elliott might insist on an introduction. He had no choice now, but to make straight for the Chief Inspector.

'Just the person I was looking for,' Durand greeted him with a show of pleasure. 'I imagine your companions have already told you that I paid a little visit to your sister.' Durand missed nothing. He bowed ostentatiously in the direction of the ladies.

'Let's go somewhere quiet, Chief Inspector. But first I must make a telephone call. Tell me, did a doctor turn up while you were with Ellie . . . with my sister?'

'No, we were quite undisturbed, Monsieur Norton. A charming woman, your sister.' He smiled a satisfied little secret smile, which spoke loudly of information he wasn't prepared to reveal. 'Though, yes, I agree. She didn't seem altogether well. A doctor might be of assistance. Something to calm her.'

James had a bounding desire to wipe the smile off the Inspector's face. What could Ellie have told Durand to make him so happy? He thought it over while he put a call through to Docteur Ponsard. It would undoubtedly be something to do with Raf.

'It seems your sister knew Olympe Fabre very well.' Durand spoke as soon as James emerged from the cabinet. 'She didn't approve of her.'

'Really? She told me they were great friends. Look, Chief Inspector, unless there's anything precise that you need to ask me, I really must hurry. My friends tell me Ellie is delirious.'

'Delirious. No, no. They exaggerate. Voluble, certainly. Perhaps even a little confused.' He peered up at James and openly scrutinized his face. 'You seem to be the only member of your family who doesn't suffer from an excess of nerves, Monsieur Norton.'

'What did she tell you?'

'She told me at great length about an expedition she and Olympe Fabre had made to the Louvre.'

James had a sudden memory of Ellie telling Docteur Ponsard about the flashing pains in her legs. They had begun at the Louvre. Was Olympe the friend she had mentioned? The one who had helped her, Ellie had said.

'And does this explain anything at all about Olympe's subsequent death, Chief Inspector?'

'No, not really. But I was interested.'

They had reached the concierge's counter and James now stopped to check for post. There were three letters.

'I trust there will be a message from your brother, Monsieur Norton. It is really him I have come in search of.'

'Have your men lost his trail?' James asked innocently.

'Have you, Monsieur Norton?' The Chief Inspector retorted with a touch of menace while blatantly examining the envelopes as James glanced at them. 'Is there anything here from your brother?'

'No,' James said truthfully and tucked the letters into his jacket pocket. 'And I don't know where he is.'

'Neither did your sister. It struck me that she was quite inconsolably disappointed in him.'

'Ellie has always been a perfectionist, Chief Inspector.'

'And so remains unmarried,' Durand chuckled.

'I must go to her, Chief Inspector. There is something I need to tell you about, but there isn't time enough now.'

'If it's important, I can accompany you part of the way.'

'It's important.'

Durand followed him into the carriage the doorman had hailed.

'Before I tell you, Inspector, I want to remind you of the fact that several times now you've insisted to me that you're a Republican. I take it that you also mean by it that you have no grave prejudices against our poor Olympe's people?'

Durand stared at him cannily. 'What have you found, Monsieur Norton?'

'Can you reassure me?'

The Inspector nodded once, abruptly.

'I'm not sure exactly what I've found. I've traced an old suitor of Olympe Fabre's. But I wouldn't want you to stir up a hornet's nest by locking him up either prematurely or wrongly, just so as to fall in with police prejudices. You follow my meaning?'

Durand's face expressed uneasiness. 'I follow your meaning, Monsieur. But if the man is guilty . . .'

'There is as yet no substantial evidence. I will tell you everything, but only on condition that you promise to interview him first on his own ground.'

'You mean without Maître Chardon?' Durand grinned.

'Yes, your examining magistrate feels just a little blinkered to me, if you'll pardon my saying so.'

'All right, Monsieur Norton, I give you my word as a fellow Republican, that I shall do my best to be blind to this man's origins.'

James took his notebook out of his pocket, gave the Inspector Bernfeld's name and address and explained, 'Bernfeld was putting undue pressure on Mlle Fabre over a debt her father had incurred at the time when the man was courting her — in full expectation that they would marry. This menacing pressure, I believe, may well have been what led Olympe to try her hand at a little gentle blackmail. Once you've talked to Bernfeld, you, too, will see that my brother can have had nothing at all to do with that messy business.'

'So that's it, is it? Fighting your brother's corner again. Well, I can't say I'm surprised. Tell me, Monsieur Norton. How did you come upon this Bernfeld?'

James almost said 'through a letter', then bit his lip. 'Through an old friend of Olympe's. A childhood friend.'

'Indeed.' The Inspector tipped his hat. 'You have been busy. And is your own view that this Bernfeld is implicated in Olympe's death?'

James swallowed. 'Perhaps indirectly.'

'Indirectly. I think I see. I shall leave you now, Monsieur. Convey my respects to your sister. And do try to calm her a little.'

He paused to wink at James as he stepped from the carriage.

'You know, I have a feeling she may enjoy her hours in front of the jury.'

Harriet opened the apartment door to him. Her eyes were red-rimmed, her features swollen. She had evidently been crying.

'She's not well, James. I just got here half an hour ago. I've been trying to round up a doctor.'

'It's all right Harriet. Dr. Ponsard will be over as soon as he can.'

She gave him a grateful look. 'Ellie's just closed her eyes. Maybe she'll sleep now. We should leave her to do so until the doctor comes.'

'Tell me what's happened.'

Harriet sat down a little unwillingly. Her fingers picked at the top buttons of her blouse, as if the collar constrained her and trapped her breath. He had never seen her so perturbed. He found himself reaching down to pat her shoulder in reassurance. It was oddly yielding.

He waited until she had regained a little of her composure. 'Only if you can, Harriet. The Elliotts alerted me that she'd taken a turn.'

'It's just . . . I don't know . . .' She looked round, as if afraid that Ellie might overhear. 'When I got here, she started to rail at me. Told me it was all my fault.'

'What was all your fault?' James asked gently.

'Well, that's just it. I couldn't make it out at first. Then I realized it couldn't be me that she was addressing. She thought I was someone else. Or maybe she didn't see me at all.' Tears flooded her eyes. She wiped them away with a crumpled handkerchief.

After a moment, she astonished him by asking, 'Why did Elinor never marry, James?'

'I . . . I don't rightly know.' He sat down opposite her. 'Did she say anything about it?'

Harriet shrugged. 'Not directly. She was . . . well, I didn't understand what she was saying exactly. There were obscenities. So much hatred. Such resentment.' Her voice quivered. 'I thought maybe if I knew more about that side of her life, about why she hadn't married, it might clarify things.'

James thought back over the years. The question of Elinor's marriage or lack of it wasn't one he had ever put to himself directly. And it was so long since he had been privy to his sister's daily life.

'There was someone, a suitor, David Soames, if I remember correctly. It was when father was still alive. She refused him.'

'Why?'

He shrugged.

'Maybe he didn't match up to you and your brother's perfection.' There was a touch of acid in her voice.

James stared at her, grappling with some elusive meaning. 'No, no,' he stammered. 'I think Father didn't consider him altogether suitable. Or maybe it was Ellie herself. He wasn't, as I remember it, quite up to her wit. And in the event, nothing came of it. I think he went back to California. No, no. Wait a minute . . . That came later. After Father had his first attack.'

'His first attack?'

'Yes. Ellie was wonderful. She nursed him. Nursed him through it. Had a cot moved into his room. Mother doesn't like people being sick.' Only as James said it did he realize the truth of it. It struck him as a treacherous thought. He gave Harriet a shamefaced glance. But the woman was off on her own tack, talking almost as if to herself.

'So to Elinor it could seem that your father was at fault. Was the stumbling block on her path to marriage.' She flushed as she said it. 'I'm sorry, this is unpardonably rude of me. I shouldn't be interfering. It's just . . . it's just that I'm trying to make sense of what Elinor was saying.'

'What was she saying?'

'That. Blaming a man. Your father, I think.' She waved her hand, wouldn't meet his eyes.

He had a sudden vision of the histrionic blaze that would attend any such accusation of Ellie's, like an actress playing out her hour of tragedy in a litany of fierce adjectives. His father's dying, demanding body.

'Yet she adored him, you know,' James said softly. 'His little girl. His favourite.'

'Perhaps the two aren't mutually exclusive.'

He met her clear, intelligent gaze. 'No, perhaps not,' he paused. 'And in her delirium, she took you for him.'

Harriet was silent.

'What else did she say?'

Harriet shivered 'She talked about your brother. I think it was about your brother. It was all mixed up.'

The doorbell rang and she rose with visible relief. 'Let's hope that's the doctor.'

'Harriet,' he called her back. 'Thank you for your patience. Your loyalty to Elinor.'

For a moment, she looked as if he had insulted her, had somehow taken on the wrong tone. Perhaps she thought he was treating her as a servant. 'You've been . . .' he faltered. 'You've been a true, a generous friend.'

She turned away abruptly and made for the door.

Docteur Ponsard listened attentively to their joint account of Ellie's present plight. 'Has anything happened since we met on Monday to distress her particularly?'

'I'm afraid she insisted on coming to the funeral of a friend who died under somewhat suspicious circumstances.' James was about to go on and tell him about the disgusting package which had made its way into the apartment, but held back. He remembered what the pathologist at the Salpêtrière had said about the political affiliations of the medical profession — though he couldn't quite imagine that the kindly Ponsard would share such scurrilous views. In any event, there was no need. Ponsard was already making his way towards his patient.

In the dusky, curtained room, Ellie lay utterly motionless on the divan. She was like some pale effigy of herself. Her arms were folded across her bosom, her profile finely etched, as if some master mason had chiselled her replica on a tomb.

Panic clutched at James's throat. Not another death. In the stillness, he thought he heard the faint rustle of ghosts — Maisie, Olympe, floating through the air to embrace his sister. He rushed to take Ellie's hand. It was colder than stone.

'Ellie, Ellie dear.' His voice felt strangled. 'Docteur Ponsard has come.'

Her eyes fluttered open. 'Jimmy. Hello Jimmy. Have I been asleep?'

He nodded, relieved that she recognized him, and kept hold of her hand.

'Good-day docteur, or is it evening?' Ellie switched effortlessly into French. 'Did we have an appointment for today?' Her forehead creased into a puzzled frown.

'Non, Mademoiselle,' Ponsard took over. 'But you've taken a turn and your brother asked me to come and see you. Perhaps the bromide I prescribed has had an adverse effect. I shall examine you and see what we can do to make you comfortable.'

'Comfort, doctor. I'm not altogether certain I remember what that is.'

The sound of Ellie's familiar irony flooded through James like a benediction. He stepped aside to let the doctor take over.

Ponsard was smiling reassuringly. 'We'll do our best to remind you.' He whisked a thermometer and stethoscope from his bag. 'Perhaps Mademoiselle here can assist me.' He gestured at Harriet. 'I'll need to take a little look at your chest.'

Harriet made to lower the blanket and unfasten the buttons of Ellie's blouse.

Ellie stayed her hand. 'Where's Raf, Jimmy? Is he all right?'

'He's fine. Just fine. Working. What we need to worry about now is you. No one else.'

'That's kind of you, Jimmy. But perhaps you might worry about me from next door. Since they're going to turn me into an anatomical study.'

'Of course, of course.' James scuttled from the room. As he closed the door behind him, he saw Ponsard take the box with its protruding wires from his bag. So he was going to apply electricity again.

James shuddered and went to sit in the dining room. He wondered how it was that Ellie could now be so different from the person Harriet and indeed Mrs. Elliott had described. She seemed so very much herself again. Nowhere was there a trace of delirium, if it had been delirium. Ellie's hand had been so cold, not at all feverish.

Not so very long ago he had read an article about what the writer called 'altered states'. Two or maybe three distinct consciousnesses inhabited the same person, yet the core one was not aware of the others. Mediums moved into different spaces when their spirits, or whatever they were, spoke through them, it was said. So did witches and saints long ago.

But Ellie was none of those.

Was there any way of knowing why one state gave way to another and what controlled the slippery movement? Like becoming a new person every time you crossed the threshold into a new room. Yet there must be something that held all the rooms together. Even the room in which the paralyzed Ellie could miraculously walk. It was unutterably eerie that the Ellie who spoke to him and recognized him had no notion of that. Amnesia.

James searched his pockets for his pipe. He had forgotten it. He swore softly.

Maybe the mechanism which controlled the remembering and forgetting was as simple as that, as simple as his being completely unaware of how and why he had forgotten to tuck his pipe and tobacco pouch into his pocket. He must have left them behind in Marguerite's breakfast room late last night. So much had happened since then that it seemed an eternity ago.

He allowed himself the pleasure of thinking about the beautiful Madame de Landois for a moment and felt a languor creeping over his limbs. What had she done today while he was busy trailing the hapless Bernfeld and confronting the Chief Inspector? He let his mind play over the possibilities, saw her at the piano, at her easel. Saw her with Raf in his workers' blues in some insalubrious café.

He shook himself and remembered that one of the letters he had picked up at the hotel seemed to bear her hand. Quickly he pulled out the envelopes and tore open the appropriate one. Yes, it was from her. He read quickly.

Marguerite had not been sitting at her piano. She had found that the nephew of a friend was an intern at the Salpêtrière and she was going to see him to ascertain whether he was an appropriate person to undertake the delicate matter they had talked about. The delicate matter of checking through the files of the recent dead at the hospital. Along the way, she had also learned that Dr. Vaillant, despite his pronounced views on the subject of Jews, really did have an impeccable medical reputation.

James put the letter down and wondered whether he had leapt to wild conclusions simply because of the bewildering atmosphere of the hospital with its wards of raving patients. He considered Judith Arnhem for a moment and then with a helpless shrug, tore open a second letter.

It contained a telegram from his mother. Every sentence was a question or command, though the first might just as well have been the second, he thought treacherously. She wanted a firm date for their return, a prognosis for Ellie, and letters — particularly from Raf.

The third letter was a total surprise. It bore Touquet's signature and it asked James if he was still ready to help out with their investigations. If so, he should go to the Hotel Monpiquet and/or the neighbouring Lafleur. There followed a list of instructions and a warning. Should he by any chance encounter the burly Marcel Caro, he was neither to tangle with him, nor ask any leading questions which might in any way jeopardize what was proving a delicate operation. Caro, it turned out, was a former member of the vice squad, had probably left it to line his pockets more luxuriantly.

James read the letter through twice, then steeling himself, went to knock on the door of the sitting room. Once Ellie was settled and asleep, he knew exactly where he had to go.

EIGHTEEN

The night was hot, the air as close and muggy as an old blanket stale with perspiration. The street had not been electrified. Gas lamps cast yellow shadows furtive in their hurry, like the passers-by with their glinting downcast eyes and hunched shoulders. From somewhere a cat miaowled a high-pitched call. It merged into that of a wailing child.

James hesitated. The sign beneath the flickering lantern distinctly named his destination, but he didn't like the look of the heavy door with its curled and peeling paint, the darkened, shuttered windows. A caped policeman paused on the opposite pavement to cast him a suspicious glance. James squared his shoulders, wondered for another moment how on earth he had got himself involved in such unsavoury business, and let the solid bronze knocker fall.

A man in an indeterminate uniform, somewhere between bellhop and circus ringmaster, let him in, sizing him up with shifty eyes before leading him along a narrow hall. Halfway to the stairs, he opened the door on a large room.

James had an impression of peacock feathers and vast potted ferns, overstuffed sofas in plush, faded red, a musky perfume and women — women dancing languorously arm in arm to the tinkle of an upright piano; women lounging on chairs; women seated at a table in an alcove, an array of cards spread before them. Women in bright silks and floating white chemises; women wearing nothing but corsets which revealed pale gartered legs and plump bosoms; women with hair piled atop their heads or floating halfway down their backs or demurely braided. At the piano, too, there sat a woman with heavy bare arms and fat folds in her neck and an aureole of frizzled hair. One of these women now stood before him. He forced himself to focus.

'Bonsoir, Monsieur.' She smiled at him from a gash of red and beckoned him through. 'Venez, venez. I'm Madame Rosa.'

She was a solid woman of about forty with an ample body swathed in coral satin which swished as she moved. She had lustrous black hair, heavy eyebrows and the shrewd features of a shopkeeper.

'If I'm not mistaken, it's your first visit. I have no doubt that my girls will be able to meet each and every one of your tastes. It was wise of you to come early.' She winked at him, her expression openly lascivious as she directed him to a place on a sofa between two rouged creatures. They proceeded to disburden him of his jacket with little breathless moans of, 'So hot tonight. What a summer.'

A moment later, there was a glass of wine in his hand and the Madame was murmuring, 'Take your time. Look around, but if you want my recommendation, I think Clarice might suit you. Clarice,' she said more loudly and one of the dancing figures turned in their direction, a pale pretty blonde, with a tiny waist and the wide sleepy eyes of a child. She smiled languorously, touched her hand to her high, pert breasts and continued with her dance.

The woman at his side was caressing his thigh. Warring sensations attacked him — revulsion coupled with a stirring in his groin, a desire to flee and a strange, heavy passivity, which made immobility pleasurable, like the lull of a steaming bath.

He forced himself into alertness. He was here on business. And the place was slightly less sleazy than he had feared.

He stayed his neighbour's fingers with his hand and turned to examine her more carefully. She was a tiny redhead with a smattering of freckles on the bridge of her nose and pale dilated eyes which met his with an absent stare that sat oddly with her pursed and inviting lips. With a polite smile, he got up to explore.

A woman waltzed into his arms, a gamine of a French girl, he was almost certain of that. He took a few turns with her and looked round. On a distant sofa, half obscured by a palm, there sat a more promising figure. He moved his partner towards her. The woman had the dark waving hair, sharp nose, almond eyes and matt complexion that might mean an eastern origin. Beneath the exaggerated makeup, she looked astonishingly young, no more than seventeen he thought. Her bare shoulders were thin, birdlike and she had the slightly startled air of a forest creature trapped in the light. She held herself rigid, as if touch were not her trade. With a bow towards his partner, he sat down beside the girl.

She made herself small and moved away.

'Eugénie!' The Madame's injunction and an admonishing nod woke her from her reverie and resulted in a tilt of the head and a forced smile in James's direction.

James returned it, 'Bonsoir, Eugénie.'

'Bonsoir, Monsieur.'

There was an accent in her voice which boded well.

'Why don't you ask Monsieur to dance, Eugénie? You dance so well.' Madame Rosa turned to stage whisper archly at James. 'She's quite shy, Monsieur. New to us.' She winked at him again and bustled away as two customers appeared at the door. There were other men, too, he now noticed, some discreetly positioned in chairs, others dancing like him. From a first estimate, none of them seemed particularly remarkable, indeed rather more bourgeois than he had anticipated.

The girl moved delicately in his arms, not too close. He sniffed the cheap perfume of her hair and wondered how to begin his questioning.

As they danced, the vista of the room opened before him. From the card-player's alcove, he now saw a small man emerge, a buxom corsetted woman in tow. They disappeared through a back door. A moment later a different couple came through it, a stout, bearded man in a striped waistcoat and a statuesque brunette with the strong features of a biblical Judith who had just severed the head of Holofernes. James tripped over his partner's feet as he stopped to look at the man. The recognition shocked him. Dr. Comte. What was the man doing here?

He was suddenly aware that Eugénie was trembling, edging them in the direction of the piano, away from Comte. She buried her face in his shoulder, like a child seeking invisibility.

Could there be some nefarious connection between Comte and the brothel? James's mind raced. Did he perhaps supply girls from the Saint-Lazare wards to the brothel keeper? He thought of Olympe's friend, Louise Boussel, and superstitiously looked round for her. Then he averted his face, keeping his frightened partner in the shelter of the upright. Yes, it would make a kind of sense. He needed to talk to the woman Comte had been with. That was now imperative. But Eugénie was clinging to him.

'Where are you from, Eugénie?' he asked, to make use of his time.

The girl didn't answer. She had all but tucked herself against the wall and only kept up the motion of the dance with a slight, swaying of her body against his.

'Are you from Russia?' he hazarded.

Still she didn't answer. He realized she was standing on tiptoe and peering over his shoulder. Keeping an eye on Comte's movements, he thought. All at once her knees seemed to give way. Only the pressure of his arms kept her up. He half lifted her round in a twirl to see what had caused her panic. Standing by the door through which James had entered were Comte and a swarthy gorilla of a man, heads bowed in swift conversation. The swarthy man was glowering, angry about something.

Then Comte was on his way and the swarthy man was striding across the room as if he owned it, tapping a few bottoms as he went. He disappeared into the card-players' alcove with the statuesque woman Comte had come downstairs with.

The woman at the piano was murmuring something to Eugénie in a language James couldn't understand.

He took in her face for the first time. She was older, probably as old as Madame Rosa, gap-toothed and jowly, but with a blowsy bonhomie about her.

'Take the girl upstairs, why don't you, Monsieur?' Her stubby fingers pounded at the keys while she spoke and never lost a beat. 'She'll please you well, you'll see, even if she doesn't speak much.' She gave James a broad grin and murmured something in that foreign language again to Eugénie, who dutifully took his hand and led him to the corner door.

James followed recalcitrantly, his eyes straying towards the alcove. As they passed it, he saw Dr. Comte's partner. She was sitting, her legs provocatively crossed to show a length of thigh as she puffed at a cigarette. The swarthy man's hand gripped her arm. He was whispering something in her ear. Whatever it was he said, made her clench her lips in a stubborn expression.

The man could just be the infamous Marcel Caro, Touquet had warned him about. The description fitted.

He wished he could abandon Eugénie and join the couple. But the girl was tugging at his hand and Madame Rosa was suddenly beside them, nodding encouragement. He had an unhappy sense that if he left Eugénie now, she would pay dearly for it.

The girl led him up a short, steep flight of stairs to a warren of rooms, finally stopping at a nether door. She opened it with visible reluctance, then positioned herself on the edge of a bed which took up most of the room's space. She looked up at him with wide, fearful eyes, as she slowly unhooked her bodice. Pale breasts emerged, soft, pink-tipped. He put out a staying hand, but she misinterpreted his gesture and shyly brought it towards her. He touched soft, smooth flesh and despite all his intentions, felt himself grow hard. With a flicker of self-disgust, he sat down beside her and after a moment started to stroke her hair.

'Who is the man who frightened you so much downstairs, Eugénie?' he asked. 'I don't like to see you frightened.'

She didn't answer.

'Is his name Marcel Caro?'

She trembled and he put an arm reassuringly round her.

'How long have you been here, Eugénie?'

'Three months,' she whispered. Then, as if she had given away a secret and remembered her drill, she moved swiftly to work away at his buttons, to caress with a demure hesitation which moved him oddly so that he couldn't bring himself to stop her hands. And a moment later, she was on her knees in front of him, her lips playing, her mouth warm round him and he forgot why he was here, forgot everything except the sensation of fluttering fingers on his groin, of heat and wetness and rushing breath and that sudden clarity of emptiness which was half pain, half pleasure.

Afterwards as he watched her wipe her lips and fingers neatly on a cloth and fasten her bodice again before stretching back on the pillows, he felt a mixture of shame and desolation. Her look was still timid, but she patted the place beside her in open invitation. It was clear that she didn't want to go back downstairs yet. Of course not. It would mean confronting another customer. Or perhaps Madame Rosa would think she had been too quick and hadn't done her work adequately. With an inward sneer of self-derision, he took out his wallet and put what he thought must be a more than adequate sum on the night-table beside her.

She looked at the money and smiled abruptly, a warm spontaneous smile, like a girl who had been given the Christmas present she had ardently wished for. She patted the cushions beside her again.

'Three months in Paris,' James took her hand. 'That's not very long. Where are you from?'

She fingered the chain at her throat. A charm hung from it. With a start, James stared at its shape. Yes, it was a Hebrew character mounted on gold, a character like the ones in Bernfeld's letter that Arnhem had translated for him. A character like the one Raf had described to him on the charm Antoine had found in the depths of that underground shaft.

'You're Jewish?' James smiled.

The girl started, then nodded without returning his smile. He stroked her hair again, gently.

'Who brought you here?'

She shivered. 'From the Ukraine,' she whispered now.

'I'm from Boston. From America.'

Her eyes lit up and she suddenly clutched his wrist and repeated, 'America.' She repeated it again and again, as if the word itself were a charm. 'I have cousin in America.'

'Oh yes? Would you like to go there?'

Her delight turned to wariness again. James didn't understand the shift.

'That's a pretty necklace. Does the letter mean anything?'

'Chai,' she said. 'It means life. The man give it me. The man who supposed to bring me to America.'

'Oh?'

Tears leapt into her eyes. 'Instead bring me here. To work. To pay for my travel. But never be able to pay. Never enough.' The tears spilled down her cheeks.

James patted her hand.

'Did anyone come with you. From the Ukraine I mean.'

'Two girls. But I don't know where they go.' She looked around her, as if someone might be eavesdropping. 'Maybe you know them.' She whispered two names.

James shook his head.

'No. No, of course not. They change our names.'

'Who?'

She stared at him for a long moment, then shivered. 'That bad man. He meet us at the train.'

'Marcel Caro?'

She leapt up, wrung her hands. 'No, no, Maro. You know him?'

'Only by reputation,' James murmured, wondering if the girl had elided the name or whether it might be a nickname. He waited a moment. 'And that other man, the doctor? Do you have anything to do with him?'

She wrapped her arms around herself as if she was suddenly cold, but her expression was defiant. 'I'm clean. Clean.'

It came to James that Comte might extract services in return for medical visits. Yes, he could well be the brothel's state-appointed medical examiner — a position which would allow for exortion on a smaller or larger scale. He turned his attention back to Eugénie.

'Yes, yes. Of course you're clean. Don't be frightened, Eugénie. I only want to help you.'

Tears moistened her eyes. 'Help? No one can help. Too late.'

'It's never too late, Eugénie. While you have life. Which reminds me, did you by any chance meet a young woman here called Olympe Fabre? Or Rachel Arnhem?'

The girl shook her head slowly. 'Were they your special . . .?'

'No, no. It's not that. I've never been here before.'

Suspicion suddenly sharpened her features. She clutched at his arm. 'Are you . . . are you police?'

'No, no. Of course not.'

Distrust stayed on her face. 'You go now.'

As he adjusted his tie, she forced a smile of surprising coyness. 'Yes. And come back. Please.' She touched his lips with a light finger, her face that of a child who had mastered adult wiles.

This time shame suffused him. It brought moisture to his brow, a clenching of his jaw, so that he barely managed a brief bow, a mumbled thank you, before closing her door behind him. He leaned against it heavily, struggling to break free of the sullying currents of desire which threatened his purpose.

A lazy heat impregnated the noisy salon and with it came a whiff of mass perspiration. Two women stood by the piano and sang what was, judging from their lolling eyes and louche gestures, a racy ditty, though he couldn't quite make out the rush of words. The man he believed to be Marcel Caro was nowhere to be seen, but the woman he had noticed with him, and before that with Dr. Comte, was still there. She was perched on the lap of an older man who, with his spats and paunch and white whiskers, had the benign air of a grandfather. A gentlemanly grandfather. James wondered how he could go about getting her attention.

'Will you stay on with us a little, Monsieur? The night's still young.' Madame Rosa was at his side, waving a glass of wine into his hand. From somewhere behind her, the swarthy man whom he felt was Marcel Caro appeared. James stiffened. A little nod from her and the man vanished through the door from which James had come.

'I trust our Eugénie was to your taste. She's a sweet child.'

'Altogether satisfactory,' James heard himself say. He hoped she would report this to the man he had a sudden distinct sense had just gone to Eugénie. He would be checking on her, scuttling through her earnings, perhaps doing worse than that.

'Good, good. I'm glad to hear it.'

'And yes, I will stay on a little.' James's eyes moved in the direction of Dr. Comte's partner.

Madame Rosa followed his gaze and raised a questioning eyebrow. 'Not quite in the same order, that young lady. I see you're a man who likes his hors d'oeuvre followed by a good full entrée.' She chuckled, rubbed herself against him, so that he could see beads of sweat glistening at her cleavage. 'I'll let her know, but she may be a little while. She's with an old friend. Do sit down, monsieur. Enjoy the music.'

James lowered himself into an armchair. Women strolled in front of him, ruching skirts as they went, displaying legs, swinging hips. Clarice, the slender blonde, came to perch on the arm of his chair and let her hand play over the base of his neck. For some absurd reason, Marguerite de Landois flashed through his mind. He wondered how she might comment on his present adventure, wondered too what sensation her fingers on his neck might elicit. The thought astonished him and he buried it in a remote crevice of himself and sat up, his back ramrod straight despite the woman's caresses. She moved away with a full Gallic shrug of displeasure.

James waited and watched the activity of the place. Though appearances could hardly be foolproof, he estimated there were three Jewish women in the room, not counting the piano player and the absent Eugénie and whatever others were upstairs. He tried to see whether they too wore the telltale charm around their necks — a signal, if Eugénie's story was an example, that they had been brought to France as part of some white slave racket, in which Caro evidently played a role. And Comte? What was his part, the obligatory medical examination apart? Was he in cahoots with Caro, raking in a cut for silence every time a new slave was introduced into the brothels within his aegis?

He looked again in the direction of the statuesque brunette. Their eyes met this time, and with a slight tilt of his chin he nodded her over. She smiled a challenge, then turned lazily to ruffle the old man's hair and plant a kiss on his forehead. Within seconds, she stood before James, her hands on her swaying hips, her legs firmly planted, as if she had learned her brazen posture from a cancan dancer at the Moulin Rouge.

'Voulez-vous monter?' she asked, her gaze basilisk still.

James nodded. 'You've been recommended to me.'

'Really?' Thick brows rose into an arch. 'By whom?'

'Charlie,' James invented. 'An American friend. Awhile back.'

She shrugged. 'He didn't leave an impression. You're American?'

He nodded. Close to, he noticed that she was older than he had estimated. Her eyes had a bruised look.

She surveyed him with an experienced gaze which seemed already to have undressed him. 'We don't get too many of your kind here.'

'Oh? Guess I'll have to spread the word.'

'You do that.' Her laugh was hard, insinuating.

She led him up the stairs he had trod not so very long ago and then turned in a direction opposite to Eugénie's room. From behind a door he heard a rasping sound and then a scream. He stopped.

'Don't worry. It's Madeleine. She likes noise.' She eyed him curiously. 'You don't, I take it.'

James shrugged and followed her into a room which was about twice the size of the last one he had been in. One wall was all but covered by a rack of clothes. Costumes, he corrected himself. He saw a nurse's uniform, a nun's habit, a judge's cloak, a gendarme's cape, a frock coat and on the floor, a riding crop, handcuffs, an assortment of shoes and boots. One pair caught his eye.

'You like boots?' she asked, swift as lightning. She reached for them, raised them to his nostrils. James sniffed supple leather. 'Shall I put them on?' She lowered the boot to his crotch and rubbed it there.

James stepped backwards, shook his head.

'What's your taste then, Monsieur l'Americain?' From somewhere she pulled a leather thong and smoothed it between her fingers.

'I . . . I really wanted to talk, to tell the truth.'

'Talking . . . Is that an American form of brothel activity?' Laughter cascaded from her.

He found himself joining her in it. 'Perhaps. Why not. What's your name?'

'You can call me Berenice. Berenice from Nice.' She fluttered long eyelashes at him in some parody of the sultry Southerner and showed him to a chair. She herself sat down on the bed, drawing her skirts up, so that he could see red garters and a length of thigh. 'So talk away. Tell me your sins, if it excites you.'

James averted his eyes from her legs and plunged. 'Not my sins, exactly. I'd like to ask you some questions. You look like a woman who knows her way round this world.'

'You're a cop?' The laughter fled from her face.

'No. No. Promise. I'm a visiting American and all I want is to ask you whether by any chance you know a woman called Olympe Fabre, once Rachel Arnhem?'

She sprang from the bed and walked towards the window, straightening the curtain with an abrupt movement. There was a glimmer of fear behind the well-oiled mask which was her face.

'What's it to you?'

James reached for his wallet. 'I'm trying to find out how and why she died. She's a friend of the family.'

'Family! You can put your money away. Until later. I haven't seen her in years.'

'I was told she used to visit here.'

'Maybe she did and maybe she didn't.'

'So she wasn't a particular friend of yours?' He looked at her throat to check for the charm. There wasn't one. James thought quickly. 'She never tried to persuade you out of here?'

'I enjoy my work, Monsieur. Though I'm not enjoying this particular pass.'

James reached into his pocket and pulled out the erotic photograph. 'Is that what Olympe looked like when she worked in your trade?'

Berenice stared at the image and scoffed. 'That's not Olympe. That's Judith.' She clamped a hand over her mouth.

'Judith. I see. I see,' James murmured. 'Judith used to work here.'

'Not here. Another place.' She gave the bedclothes a savage tug, then her face softened. 'She was a sweet thing. Helpless. I took pity on her. I got her that posing job. Not that the money really helped. She wasn't cut out for the profession. So there you have it, Monsieur l'Americain. That's all I can tell you.'

'You're Jewish?'

She shrugged. 'What difference does it make? But no, if you must know, I'm not. I'm a good little Catholic girl. Want to hear my catechism? No, I can see you don't.' She walked over to him and drew out his wallet, helped herself defiantly to a few bills. With a shushing finger over her lips, she walked to the clothes rack and hid the money in the swathes of the nun's habit.

'So you never saw Olympe Fabre here?'

'Okay, sure. I saw her. Once. Madame Rosa was all atitter. That's how I found out the woman I was looking at wasn't Judith. Thought she'd just somehow managed to grow too grand for me.'

James swallowed a little sigh of triumph. So he had been right. The Olympe of the present and the Judith of the brothel days bore an uncanny resemblance. 'Go on,' he urged Berenice.

'Anyhow, Rosa thought that maybe this Olympe had come 'cause she wanted to pick up a little extra cash on the side. Women do, you know. In the afternoons. Good upstanding ladies,' she sneered. 'Rent themselves a place. Take away our trade. But no. That's not what she'd come for. She'd come to talk to Simone.'

'Simone?'

'Our pianist. Well not always just a pianist. She's quite a hand if you fancy her type. Been round the track a few hundred times.'

'So Olympe came to see her?'

'Yup, apparently they're old friends. That's it, Monsieur l'American. Your time's up. I'm a working woman.' She pulled him from his chair, so that he stood face to face with her. 'Too bad, you didn't want to play. I rather like those icy eyes of yours and the upright posture.' She slipped her hand into his shirt. 'And you're in good shape for a man of your years.'

James stopped her hand. 'Better than Dr. Comte?'

She moved away. 'I don't know any Dr. Comte.'

'I just saw you with him.'

'Oh him!' There was a faint tremor in her laugh. 'He's just a form filler. We all need form fillers in this great Republic of ours.'

The door suddenly burst open and over her head he saw the man he assumed was Caro lunging across the room. Berenice stepped aside with a gasp. Before James could move, the man was shaking him like some child's rattle, slamming a fist into his jaw, another into his belly. The last landed with such force that the walls went reeling.

James fell back onto his chair, tried to catch a painful breath and simultaneously charge at the man.

But Caro, despite his bulk, was too quick and experienced a fighter. He all but lifted James up and shoved him towards the door. 'Let that be a warning,' he hissed. 'Get out of here and don't come back. Nobody scares Maro's girls. Nobody tampers with them. You hear me?'

'Nobody but you and your friend, Comte, eh?' James heard himself snarl.

The door slammed behind him. He lurched down the hall. The walls swerved towards him.

Clinging to the banister, he tried to assemble his scattered wits. He should go back and give the man a wallop. His pride cried out for it. Yet even if he could dent that solid girth, it would serve little purpose. The police then. But Touquet had already intimated that Caro was probably in cahoots with the locals and he now knew the swarthy pimp was Caro.

No, no. The sensible thing was to talk to Simone, the pianist, before the bull of a man made his way downstairs. And then he would go to Durand. For all his mad speculations, Durand wasn't crooked. He was all but certain of that. Then together they would confront the evil Comte. Like some maleficient presence, the doctor had shadowed every point of their investigation. Who knew but that a little further digging would show that the girls in Caro's white slave racket ended up on slabs at the Salpêtrière when they took the first brave steps towards exposure or escape — steps that Olympe had encouraged. Yes, at the Salpêtrière, where they could provide ready physical proof for theories of degeneracy.

James straightened his jacket and made his way downstairs. The room looked slightly desolate now, empty of the favourites who were elsewhere engaged. Only a few girls lolled on the sofas. The men looked dazed, worse for drink perhaps. He could use one, but he didn't want to have to confront Madame Rosa. He sidled towards the piano, where the large woman was playing a bittersweet number, and leaned against it, catching her eye.

'I'd like to speak with you privately, Madame,' he said, hardly moving his lips.

She looked up at him lazily. A gold tooth glittered as she smiled. 'I'm busy, Monsieur. I hope you liked our little Eugénie.'

'I want to talk to you about Olympe Fabre.'

Her stubby fingers missed a beat.

'Come again.'

'You heard me. I know the two of you were friends.'

She looked quickly round her shoulder, her fleshy arms quivering with the motion, her face now as tight as a mask. 'Not here,' she murmured. 'Not tonight.'

'When then?'

'I have nothing to say.'

'Better to say it to me than to the police, however.'

'Who are you?'

'A private investigator. Shall I speak to Madame Rosa?'

'No, no.' She flashed him a plea, her face sinking into jowly gloom as she struck a dissonant chord.

'Name a place then. For tomorrow.'

She looked round again. 'Café Dauphine. Near the Comédie. Eleven-thirty.'

'If you're not there, I'll come straight back here. With a friend.' James's stance threatened.

'I'll be there. Poor Olympe.'

NINETEEN

Exhaustion tugged at James's limbs like metal weights. He leaned heavily on the hotel counter and tried to clear the fog that had invaded his mind. He was certain that he had left his room key here, but now it was nowhere to be found and the lengthy business of identification had only just begun. He searched his pockets once more. Could he have mistakenly taken the key with him and dropped it somewhere in the brothel — or left it at Marguerite's house with his pipe? He tried to think back to his departure from his room — almost two days ago now, but all he could focus on was that he felt soiled, irascible, bruised.

'Eh, bien?' He growled at the night clerk who had just re-emerged from some nether office.

'It's all right, Monsieur. The porter will see you up. You may find your key safely in your room.' He waved James's papers at him. 'We'll just hold on to these until everything is settled.'

James grunted a response and followed the porter. In the nighttime dimness, the hotel felt eerie. The empty elevators, the long, darkened corridors with their rows of neatly polished shoes awaiting their owners, were like some image of an afterlife in which the sleeping dead had not yet risen from their tombs. He shivered with sudden cold as the porter fitted a key into the lock of room 411.

It turned smoothly. He nodded his thanks and let himself in, switching on the bedside light as he made gratefully for the bathroom.

There was a rustle of noise behind him. Before he could turn, his arms were clamped behind his back in a muscular vice. He struggled against it. To his surprise, it relaxed. He veered round.

'Sorry, Jim.' Raf was rubbing his eyes. His hair was dishevelled. He was wearing James's pyjamas. 'I must have been dreaming. Something about sabres and lopped heads.' He grinned. 'Good thing I recognized you.'

'What are you doing here?'

'It seemed a good place to be.' He glanced at the watch on the bedside table and whistled. 'Do you realize that it's after three.'

James spied the whisky bottle on the table. 'Not too late for a drink. I need one, what with you scaring the daylights out of me.' He poured them both a measure. 'What are you doing here?' he repeated as he handed his brother a glass.

'Well, I tried to go home, but there was this surly-looking guy hanging around the apartment, so I changed my mind. One of the Chief Inspector's crew, I imagine. By the way, I've located the nasty little band of creeps who sent me that odiferous present.'

'Oh?'

'Ya. A mean-minded trio of right-wing journalists. Didn't like my position on Dreyfus — or on anything else for that matter. And don't like the fact that I'm foreign and attacking the honour of la belle France. So they thought they'd teach me a lesson. A practical joke, you might say.' He let out a guffaw. 'They hired someone else to do their delivery work, of course. I gave them a talking to and threatened retribution. Not that in my present circumstances I can imagine the police taking action.'

'Do they have anything to do with Olympe's death?'

After a moment's hesitation, Raf shook his head. 'Not directly anyhow. They're just windbags. They create a climate in which others can act on the hatred they foment.' He pounded the pillows, then propped them up and smoothed the sheets. 'Guess you'd better have the bed, Jim. It's your room after all. I'll finish the night on the sofa.'

'How come you didn't go to Marguerite's? You spend enough nights there.'

Raf shot him an acerbic look. 'Do I detect a note of malice in your tone? Or is it just good, clean curmudgeonly envy?'

'Neither. I'm tired. I've got to have a wash.' James closed the bathroom door behind him.

When he came out again, Raf was stretched on the sofa and smoking a cigarette. The desk behind him, James now noted, was littered with the letters he had taken from Olympe's apartment.

'I can't sleep anymore.' He surveyed James. 'Just to put your mind at ease, I did speak to Marguerite and she said it was better I didn't come round. I had a feeling she was worrying about Durand, about the fact that I'm being followed.'

'Why?' James asked. His guilt made him aggressive. It was he after all who had planted the seeds of worry in Marguerite. 'It's not as if Durand doesn't know about the two of you.'

Raf blew a smoke ring into the air. 'To tell you the truth I don't quite understand what's got her suddenly worried. It's not like her. I think she's hiding something from me.'

'Really?' James had a sudden image of the men's clothes hanging in Marguerite's spare room. They were too small for Raf. 'Do you think she has another lover?'

'Another lover.' Raf mimicked his tone. 'You're sounding jaded, Jim. So quickly, too. It's not a question of another. Marguerite and I aren't anymore. Haven't been since I met Olympe.' He paused over the name, his face suddenly despairing. 'Marguerite must have told you that. Would have if you had asked. But it's not the kind of thing you ask, I imagine. I know how much you disapprove of me.'

'Yet you stay at her place.'

'Sure. It's a big house. And it's sometimes convenient. We like to talk. We're good friends. Don't give me that disbelieving face, Jim. It doesn't suit your sweet temperament.'

'A jealous friend, I imagine.' James followed his own line of thought. 'You with a younger woman. One you could consider marrying, one she had to a certain extent shaped.'

'There isn't a trace of jealousy in Marguerite.'

'I'm beginning to suspect you're the innocent.'

Raf glared at him. 'She knows I'm devoted to her. She's like — well, she's like a fairy godmother to me. She's given me so much, taught me everything.'

Even with his limited knowledge of women, James had the distinct impression Marguerite would hardly be happy with that description. But he kept his counsel.

After a moment, Raf said. 'So you think she has a lover?'

James shrugged. 'All I know is that there were men's clothes in the spare room. A smaller man than you. Suits, boots . . .' He yawned.

Raf chuckled. 'So you haven't guessed?'

James wasn't listening. It had suddenly come to him. That matter that had niggled at him for days. All at once, it was there, clear, beyond the sleepy haze of his mind, like a sentence in bold capitals he should have been able to read before. He leapt up. 'That's it, Raf. We have to go back to the barge. First thing tomorrow.'

'Why?'

'The boots. The boots the woman on the boat was wearing. They were sleek, supple, expensive. Not at all in keeping with the rest of her grimy clothes.'

'So? So someone gave them to her.'

'No, no. It's something else. I suspect they came from Olympe. From her body. Before or after her death, I don't know. It's something the woman said, too.'

'What are you talking about, Jim? Where have you been anyway? You're all wired up. A bit like the electricity pavilion they're building for this great new century of ours.'

James sighed, promised himself that he'd visit the barge first thing in the morning, then told Raf where he'd been, told him tersely about Bernfeld and about Touquet's letter and his visit to the Hotel Monpiquet. About Caro and Dr. Comte.

By the time he had finished, Raf was pacing, his face a livid scowl. 'So you think that Caro and Comte together . . .' He slammed his fist on the desk. 'Let me get this straight. Caro's running a white slave ring. Trafficking in women. Comte services their medical needs and if they act up or are past their use, he takes them off to the Salpêtrière. And eventually they end up as useful subjects for scientific autopsy. Small brains, lesions, whatever. It's too ghastly. And the powers that be turn a blind eye. Anything's better than having to change the immigration laws. And Olympe must have somehow got mixed up in it, made them fear exposure, so they did her in. Like they did those other women in. Bastards.'

'We'll have to build the evidence step by step, Raf.' James tried to calm him.

'That reminds me,' Raf stopped his pacing and reached to extract Olympe's notebook from the litter on the desk. 'I went through this earlier. The initials H.C. definitely appeared. Henri Comte. She must have gone to see him. That's it, Jim. Tomorrow we go and bludgeon a confession out of him.'

James took a deep breath. 'As I said, Raf. Slowly. We have to get Durand on board. We haven't any proof yet of a link between Caro and Olympe. Except that she went to the Monpiquet. We don't know why she went there or what she did. We need to get our hands on the hospital files too, check out Judith's story and see if any of the deaths in the hospital were of girls who had been prostitutes. I imagine there are others involved, probably Madame Rosa . . .' His voice trailed off, cracked in discomfort.

James's cautionary note visibly irritated Raf. 'Who's this Madame Rosa, then? Is that your source, the one you slept with?'

'What are you talking about?'

'Don't look so deeply offended. Loosen up. It's not a crime. We have bodies. We have senses.'

'We have other more important parts, too.' Anger leapt from James's voice. He realized it was directed as much at himself, at his shame over Eugénie, as at Raf.

'You mean a soul, I imagine?' Raf scoffed. 'You really think a just God would have had Olympe murdered? You really think that? You're a fool then.'

James kept himself still. 'I meant a moral intelligence. A mind. We have minds. They give us a sense of what is right. Of justice.'

'Justice, indeed. What's justice for the rich man is hardly justice for the beggar. Let alone the female beggar.'

There was such deep-rooted rancour in Raf's sudden attack, that it robbed James of his last ounce of energy. His legs felt weak, as if the very foundations on which he had erected his life were crumbling. He lay back on the pillows. 'Would you rather I went home, Raf? I'm obviously just in the way here. Whatever I do, whatever I say, you just snipe at me. And none of it is really my business. I'll take Elinor with me and we'll board the first available ship.'

They stared at each other across the room.

'Sorry, Jim. Sorry. Don't know what's come over me.' Raf turned his back on him and fiddled with the papers on the desk. 'Old habits, I guess. Half the time, when I'm with you, I feel I've been turned into a kid again, the useless and rebellious black sheep of the family, so I lash out or run off. As if you and Father were both standing over me, judging, shaking your heads, robbing me of any breathing space, telling me whatever I touch is wrong.'

He turned back to James, his face suffused with guilty emotion. 'Sorry, Jim. In fact you've been incredibly helpful through all this. And of more use than I've been.'

James stared at him through a fog of incomprehension. Blurry incidents from the past floated through it. An image came to him of the two of them standing before their father in his study. Raf was being reprimanded for some minor misdemeanour. But their father's love for him was palpable. It was there in the very heat of his sorrow over this trifling transgression. James rarely transgressed and rarely felt the warmth of that love.

'You're wrong about that, Raf. Father adored you. Of the two of us, you were his decided favourite, let alone mother and Ellie's.'

Perplexity played over Raf's features. 'That's not how it felt to me, Jim. Ellie, maybe . . . but we won't go into that. Father saw you as perfection itself, the perfection I could never aspire to. God, I resented it.'

James shook his head, bewildered by this declaration, saddened, too. 'In fact, Raf, I was always a little jealous of you. Still am probably. Your talent for life. Even Maisie adored you.'

'That's the whisky talking.' He topped up James's glass with a shaky smile which did nothing to eradicate the frown etched on his forehead. 'You're trying to tell me that all these years, the two of us have been doing a little green-eyed family dance, each of us imagining the other as parental pet?'

'Maybe. Probably.'

He met James's eyes, his own darkly serious. 'You know, I like you, Jim. Like getting to know you again. And I really am glad you're here, even if it's not altogether evident from my actions. I guess I haven't been feeling too good. And I've been taking it out on you.'

'It's hardly been an easy time.'

'No.' Raf sat down, his elbows on his knees, his chin propped on his hands. He gazed at the muddle of papers on the desk. 'Sometimes, I feel everything's running away with me. This Bernfeld business and the money, the blackmail, the thugs and their white slaves, all that on top of Olympe's death. It makes me realize that there was so much about Olympe I didn't know. She kept so much from me. So much.' He leapt up to scrunch one of his own letters into a ball and fling it across the room, then with a sheepish look went to pick it up.

'Maybe it was her way of being kind,' James said softly. 'She didn't want to shatter your illusion of perfection. The sense you had of her.'

'So she didn't ask for my help. Was afraid to tell me, as if she thought I wouldn't love her if she did.' He rubbed his eyes. 'The way I sometimes used to be afraid of you. Still am now and again. My perfect big brother.'

'The far from perfect big brother,' James grumbled, 'needs to get some sleep. You too, Raf. Let's hope things look clearer in the morning.'

The dauphine had all the accoutrements of a chic establishment — striped awnings, clean, marbletop tables with curving ironwork, comfortable wicker chairs, an ample indoor area, where floors and counters sparkled, not to mention polite waiters and a clientele whose hats and parasols had evidently come from the best of establishments. James found himself agreeably surprised. He chose an indoor table in a quiet corner, drank a welcome café au lait, his first of the day, and waited for his appointment with the pianist.

He didn't, he realized, even know her full name.

Raf had gone by the time he woke. It was already late. The note he had left had uncharacteristically thanked James for his patience and for buoying up his little brother. Raf explained that he was off to see Touquet to talk their findings over. He was planning to drop in on Louise Boussel again, too. And maybe later, they could all arrange to see Durand together and make a concerted attack on the direction of the Chief Inspector's investigations. Only he could influence the magistrate.

James glanced at his pocket watch. It was fifteen minutes past the appointed time. He began to think he had been naïve, a little too trusting. He should have bullied any information the woman had to give while he had her in front of him — whatever the consequences. Just as he reminded himself that at that point he had not been too keen for another confrontation with Marcel Caro, a stolid matron in a metallic blue dress appeared in front of him. It took him a moment, the sight of a gap-toothed half smile, to recognize in this stout, somewhat callous-faced, but really altogether ordinary personage, the pianist he was waiting for.

'Monsieur . . .' She didn't meet his eyes.

'Please. Do sit down. I had all but given you up. Madame . . . ?'

'Simone. It isn't always easy to get away. To get away privately. I had to invent an errand. Some ribbon, some buttons for the girls' clothes. I do a lot of sewing.' She looked at her roughened hands with a melancholy expression.

He ordered a pot of tea at her request, added some patisserie in the hope of easing her visible nervousness, then asked softly, 'How long did you know Olympe Fabre?'

The woman's dark, hooded eyes filled with tears. 'Poor little Rachel. Such a sweet child she was. Continued to be, too. She wasn't ashamed of us. I couldn't believe it when I heard.'

James waited until she had wiped the corners of her eyes with a dainty hanky.

'When did you last see her?'

'Oh it must be a month ago, now. Maybe more. She came to visit. She dropped in on us every now and again.'

'Us?'

'Well, me, really. She had this plan that when she had earned enough money, she and I and her sister, Judith, would take a place together and I would look after them both. It was her secret dream.' Her plump cheek dimpled and she met his eyes at last.

James had a sense that the dream was as much her own as Olympe's.

'You know Judith?'

'I knew Judith first. We worked in the same . . . the same house once upon a time. Not Madame Rosa's. Judith's stay was brief. She became too ill.' She paused as the waiter placed slabs of tart before them. Her eyes took on an avid glint. But she restrained herself. 'What is your interest in us, Monsieur?'

'My brother was in love with Olympe. We're trying to find her killer. We're helping the police.'

She shivered. 'I see. I wish I could help you.'

'You may be able to.' James eyed her keenly. 'Was Olympe interested in the other . . . the other members of your establishment?'

'She was a friendly soul, Monsieur. She talked to them from time to time. Tried to cheer them. Brought little presents.'

'No more than that?'

Her eyebrows rose. 'She wasn't like that, Monsieur. Not like some of the girls. At least I don't think so.'

James wasn't sure he had caught her meaning. 'What about Marcel Caro? What do you know about him?'

Her fingers tightened around the fork she had picked up. Her face grew wary. 'I don't know the name.'

'But he was there last night. A heavy man. Oily skin. Dark hair. A boxer's face. From what I understand he's a regular.'

As if James's words had conjured the man up, he suddenly saw the mirror image of his portrait peering through the front of the café. Yes, it was Caro, a suited Caro with a straw hat on his head, his sallow cheeks bright in the warmth. He was sitting at one of the *terrasse* tables near the open door, his profile turned towards them. James wondered if he could hear their exchange. He must have followed Simone here.

Either that or they were working together.

'I can't say that I've noticed him,' Simone was saying. She swallowed a sizeable piece of tart. 'I usually have my back to the salon.'

'I think you're lying.'

'Really, Monsieur. That is quite uncalled for.'

Bile rose in him, hot and black. He felt like slapping her, wiping away the show of propriety, the dainty way she brought the serviette to her lips. The source of his venom was a mystery to him.

'And what's called for, I suppose, is more sullied girls. Girls wooed from their distant homes and sold as slaves to your establishment. Slaves. You're a coward and a liar, Madame.'

'And you understand nothing. Nothing. And let me remind you that you seem more than willing to use these sullied girls,' she scoffed, pushed back her chair.

James gripped her arm. He pinned it against the table and simultaneously flashed a look towards the man on the *terrasse.* Caro was still there, a cigarette dangling from his mouth.

'Explain to me what I don't understand.'

She glanced at his hand, seemed to consider the outcome of a struggle, then settled back, not without a flash of poison in her eyes.

'What you don't understand, Monsieur, with your gilded spoons and your fine clothes and your independent income, is that these girls, these girls wooed from their distant homes, as you so beautifully put it, are far, far better off as living flesh than as dead meat chopped up in some pogrom. They're really no worse off than servants here. They're not slaves. Now will you let me go. Please. You're hurting me.'

She had taken on the air of an injured princess. It sat unhappily on her stolid features.

'Live, imprisoned flesh,' he underlined, his grip still firm. Caro had bent farther towards the door. James considered whether he might be better placed today if a fight broke out. His pride itched for it, despite the dictates of intelligence.

'Olympe talked to you, I can see. Foolish girl. I told her she was being foolish. There was no point in putting ideas into the girls' heads. They weren't clever enough to hold them there. They weren't like her. One of them even ran off after taking her advice and got herself . . .' She clapped a hand over her mouth.

'Got herself killed,' James finished for her grimly. He raised his voice. 'Killed by Marcel Caro. Abetted by Dr. Comte, perhaps.'

He looked towards the door. He was astonished to find that Caro had disappeared. His rage seemed to vanish with the man and the thought that he might be wrong about the sad, old professional in front of him surfaced. Perhaps Simone wasn't in cahoots with Caro.

He loosened his grip and Madame Simone sprang up more nimbly than her weight would seem to allow. She looked quickly round her. 'Don't meddle in what has nothing to do with you, Monsieur,' she hissed. 'I shall forget this meeting. You would be wise to do the same. Good intentions sometimes pave the road to hell.'

He had learned nothing he didn't already know, James reflected as he strolled in front of the Louvre and paused amidst a cluster of people to watch a clown advertising a travelling circus. The chalk-white face made him think of Ellie. He would have to go back to her soon. But first he had to cross the Seine.

At least Madame Simone had confirmed his and Touquet's speculations. He knew that Olympe had been encouraging at least one girl to make a break for freedom. If there had been more than one, if she had visited a variety of establishments where Marcel Caro plied his vile trade, then the man had ample motive for murder. And James could imagine the ease with which he would carry it out.

He walked quickly, averting his gaze from the murky flow of the river. It was a hot day again, but the sky had a sallow flatness to it, as if it wanted to hide its better face from the tawdry goings-on below.

The barge was still there, though no drying linen shrouded its grey-brown planks today.

He strode on board and called out a hello. He was out of luck. It was the lumbering husband who came out to greet him and none too politely.

'What d'ya want?' he grunted, all suspicion.

'Just a word. You remember me? I was here with Chief Inspector Durand. On the night the body was found.'

'So what's it to you?'

His wife had come creeping round the corner and she put a quietening hand on her husband's arm. 'Perhaps Monsieur would like a cold drink?' she said softly.

'No drinks. We're not millionaires. What's your business?'

James glanced down at the woman's feet. He cleared his throat. 'I was just wondering. Can you tell me where your wife got her boots?'

'What!' The man took a stride towards him, his face ugly.

James put out a staying hand. 'It's just that I don't believe they're hers.'

'I told you they'd find out,' the woman whimpered.

'Shut-it. What do you want with them?'

'I just want to know where they came from.'

'It's none of your bloody business.'

James felt a streak of rage flash through him. Suddenly he was on the man, shaking him by the shoulders, threatening him bodily as he should have done Caro, lifting him off the ground. 'I'm making it my business,' he shouted. 'And in five minutes flat the police will be here, unless you tell me exactly where those boots came from.'

'They came from the dead girl,' the woman murmured. 'I didn't want them. He forced me. He polished them for me. Said they were as good as new.' She was shivering. 'We don't have much . . .'

James released the man. 'What else did you take from Olympe Fabre?'

The man straightened his blue shirt, shrugged. 'You don't want to know what I took from her. It won't make you happy. It was shameful.'

'What?'

'You heard me. A scandal. Better not to know.' He was surly, but he kept his distance.

'Jean means that when we found her, she was wearing trousers. Black trousers and a frock coat and a shirt. It was only because of her hair that we knew she was a woman. So Jean said we should take them off her and sell them. I tidied them up a bit, sewed the tears. He didn't get much money. Not much at all.'

'I see,' James said, not seeing. 'Who did you sell them to?'

'Some bloke. It doesn't matter.'

'Was there anything else?'

A look passed between husband and wife and the man shook his head too abruptly. 'Nothing. Now get out of here. We don't want any more visitors. Waste of time, all of you.'

'I guesss I'll have to come back with the Chief Inspector, after all.' James made to move.

'Tell him, Jean.'

The man lunged towards his wife. James leapt to intercede and dragged him away from her. 'You'd better come with me. Right now. They have excellent cells at the Sureté.'

He shoved the man towards the gangplank.

'No, Monsieur. No, please.' The woman clutched at James's sleeve. 'Give it to him, Jean. Or we'll all end up getting arrested. The baby . . .' She was sobbing. 'It's not right. I told you it wasn't right. You shouldn't profit from the dead.'

James pretended oblivion and prodded the man along.

'All right. Go and get it,' he lashed out at his wife as they reached the bank. 'She's going to get it. Get your paws off me. Now.'

James kept his grip while the woman disappeared round the corner of the deck. She came back a moment later and held out a bracelet, a pretty mixture of silver and emeralds.

'Here, here. Take it. Please, Monsieur. Don't have him arrested. Please.' Her voice trembled. Tears rolled down her cheeks. 'They'll take the baby. I couldn't . . . We didn't mean anything by it. Really. Jean thought it would prevent a scandal. He wanted me to have something nice . . .'

James looked from one to the other of them. 'You're sure this is everything?'

The woman nodded while her husband grunted. 'The slut was hardly wearing Marie Antoinette's diamonds!'

'Jean! Yes, yes.' She turned towards James. 'That's everything. On my honour.' She crossed herself quickly. 'Please, Monsieur . . .' Her eyes implored him.

'All right. I'll let the Chief Inspector know you told me all this willingly. That your intentions were . . .' he paused. 'That your intentions were good.'

'Thank you, monsieur. Thank you.'

He left with the sound of her thanks mingled with her husband's curses ringing in his ears.

Drunk on too much information, James walked unsteadily. He was oblivious to his direction, to the play of human traffic around him, to the shouting voices which told him to watch his step as he lurched into a mountain of construction material. His throat felt raw. This last bit of unpalatable knowledge stuck in his gullet. He couldn't digest it.

He remembered one of the first things Raf had said to him about the case. The drowned Olympe was bereft of clothes. Someone had all but stripped her and then killed her or in the reverse order. That didn't matter. What mattered was that a woman bent on suicide didn't take her clothes off before flinging herself into the river. Therefore her death had to be murder. But Olympe's body, it now transpired, hadn't floated downstream ungarbed. After all this, her death could still be a suicide.

That much he could absorb. But the fact that she had been dressed in a man's clothes was the rub. Why? What did it signify?

His thoughts scurried, restless as rats. He sniffed at dark corners. What was it the pianist had said? Olympe wasn't like that, wasn't like some of the girls. What were some of the girls like? He thought of the statuesque Berenice, little Eugénie.

Could Olympe's interest when she visited her friends have been something quite other than charitable? He pushed the thought away into a dusty crack. In any event, in no way did such matters deny Caro's violent activities.

He needed to see Durand. He looked round to get his bearings. Somehow his feet had carried him in the direction of Madame de Landois' street. Perhaps he should talk to Marguerite first. It might help to clarify things. Yes, if she was at home that's what he would do. He could also perhaps catch up with Raf at Touquet's office by telephone from there. But no, no. He couldn't tell Raf this latest bit of information. Not the full content of it. It would throw Raf into even greater turmoil.

A carriage clattered round the corner, narrowly missing him as he made the turn into the street. In front of Marguerite's *hôtel particulier,* a man walked, his stick clicking out a repetitive rhythm on the pavement. As James approached, he turned and retraced his trajectory, glancing up at the double doors of Marguerite's house, before once more turning back.

James recognized Chief Inspector Durand and slowed his steps. Could the man be spying on Marguerite's movements, too? He watched to see if this time Durand would disappear round the far corner, but the man was back again. He saw James and waved, hurrying towards him.

'Ah, Monsieur Norton. Perhaps the fates are being kind to me at last.'

James was taken aback. The Chief Inspector had never before manifested such pleasure at seeing him.

'Yes, yes. You may be able to help me. You Americans know about democracy.'

'What is it, Chief Inspector?' James was mystified.

'Come, let's indulge ourselves in a little glass of something and I will tell you.' Durand stroked his moustache nervously and urged him along. 'It's to do with Madame de Landois.' He glanced back at the looming bulk of the house and all but bumped into a capped, hurrying youth. It was Antoine. The boy didn't acknowledge James.

'Just over there, Monsieur Norton.' The Chief Inspector pointed to a small café, half-hidden behind a stationary carriage. He didn't speak again until they were seated at an angle from the pewter-topped counter and two glasses of cognac stood before them. Durand took a large gulp of his, then gazed at James. His eyes narrowed abruptly.

'We lifted your brother's fingerprints from Olympe Fabre's apartment, Monsieur.'

James waited for more, but it didn't come. 'That's hardly a surprise, is it, Chief Inspector? My brother has done nothing to hide the frequency of his visits to that place.'

Durand swallowed a retort. He seemed to be struggling over something.

'That can hardly be what you brought me here for, Chief Inspector.'

'It isn't.'

'What then?'

The man considered him shrewdly. 'Olympe Fabre's landlady tells us that a man pressured his way into Olympe's apartment. He crossed her palms with silver, needless to say. He may also have walked off with some things. Letters for instance. I've found it distinctly odd that Mlle Fabre kept no letters from your brother . . .' His voice trailed off, but he fixed James with an interrogator's snakelike gaze.

James averted his eyes, forced his voice into casualness. 'Did you ask Rafael whether he ever wrote to her?'

'Come, come, Monsieur Norton.'

'Do you have a description of this man?'

'What we know is that he was well-dressed, rather debonair in fact. Perhaps like you.'

'Really, Chief Inspector. Me — debonair?'

'You haven't been driven to take any souvenirs from Olympe Fabre's apartment, then? Perhaps souvenirs for your brother?'

'Do I strike you as that kind of man, Inspector?'

'To tell you the truth, Monsieur Norton, I don't rightly know what kind of man you strike me as. Perhaps that's because you're a lawyer. Sly characters, lawyers. But that's why you can help me, Monsieur Norton.'

'Have you interviewed Bernfeld?'

'I'm afraid I haven't yet found him at the address you gave me. I've left a man there, to watch out for him. However I don't believe this Bernfeld of yours can be complicit in the blackmail in quite the way you wish to make him.'

'Really? Has your graphologist determined something? Surely he hasn't found that Rafael's writing matches the blackmail note?'

'Given your brother's base estimation of my men, Monsieur, it will astonish him to learn that no, we didn't find a match. His writing has distinctly not been shaped by a French school.'

James permitted himself a smile. 'He'll be pleased and relieved to hear that he's been cleared.'

'Not cleared, Monsieur. Not altogether.' Durand tapped out a military rhythm on the table.

'You're wasting your time, Chief Inspector. And your men's in following him.'

'Let me be the judge of that. In such cases the passion of love too often turns into its opposite.'

James shrugged. He wondered now whether he ought after all to tell Durand about what he had discovered about Olympe's clothes. If the man still held to his ridiculous theories about Raf hypnotizing her into a suicide pact, the fact that she was dressed, whether as a man or a woman, would probably only strengthen his notion.

'But I am going to take a chance on you, Monsieur. Yes, I am going to entrust you with a confidence.' His eyes glinted at James, pebble dark above the sharp cheekbones.

'Only if you think I can bear it, Chief Inspector. You know my priorities in this matter.'

'What are they exactly?'

'To clear my brother's name and to discover the truth about Olympe's death.'

'In that order?'

'The two are synonymous.'

'For your sake, I hope you are right. But as for that blackmail letter . . . Quite by chance this morning, because I received a note from Madame de Landois, I made an extraordinary discovery.' He moved closer again. 'Her writing and the writing on the blackmail letter are one and the same.'

James put his glass down unsteadily. 'No!'

'Yes. I fear so.'

'Your expert has confirmed it?'

Durand looked shamefaced. 'I haven't put it to him yet. You see, our Commissioner has warned me to be polite. To take care. You understand?'

James understood that the Chief Inspector had been cautioned by superior powers. Madame de Landois would not make a comfortable suspect for whatever crime or misdemeanour.

'I don't want her to think that we are prying unnecessarily into her affairs. Yet the matter could be highly significant. I was hoping that you . . .'

James cut him off. 'Do you think Madame de Landois was showing Olympe how she could raise money to pay back her family debt to Bernfeld?'

'No. No. Surely, if Olympe had confided her need of money to her, Madame would have lent it to her. Don't you think?'

'One can never judge from the surface about the state of people's finances.'

James thought of some of his former clients, thought rather more anxiously of his last conversation with Marguerite. Could his speculations then have carried more than a grain of truth? Could Marguerite, in some moment of crazed passion at losing Raf, some sense of vengeful betrayal, have committed an act which would incriminate her rival, an act which had so agonized Olympe that she had plunged to her death. Trapped in a web of dire possibilities, he almost failed to hear Durand.

'Perhaps. In any case, I would like you to put it to her.'

'Me?' James was aghast.

'Yes, yes. You can do it diplomatically. And you can tease the whole story from her. You can even say that I sent you as a messenger.'

'Kill the messenger, you mean?'

Durand raised an eyebrow. 'Surely you are not afraid of her?'

'No, no. But it will be a challenge.' He met the Chief Inspector's eyes and decided in that moment that, in spite of everything and despite his occasionally bizarre ideas, he liked the man, even trusted him. 'You will have to do something for me in return, Inspector.'

'Oh?'

'Yes. It may be equally, if not more important to our investigation. And rather more dangerous, I suspect.'

'You want to see me dead, then.'

'No, no.' James told him what he had discovered at the Hotel Monpiquet, told him about Marcel Caro, his traffic in women from the East, Jewish women, one certainly and perhaps several more, already dead, and how Olympe might have delved too deeply and incurred the man's murderous wrath. He told him too about Dr. Henri Comte. 'So you need to do some careful questioning, Chief Inspector. And some investigating.'

Durand looked more worried than if James had suggested raising an expedition against the Germans. 'Caro. I know the man. Very slightly. He used to be with the morality police. Not my jurisdiction.' He gnawed at his lips as if to get rid of a foul taste, rifled through his pockets for cigarettes. 'This isn't one of Touquet's wild speculations, is it?'

'No. It's based on the evidence of my ears and eyes. Not to mention a rather bruised jaw.' James rubbed his cheek delicately. 'Though Touquet put me on the trail, I have to admit. You're not afraid, are you, Chief Inspector?'

'Afraid, of course not.' He puffed out his chest, then grinned ruefully. 'Though to be altogether honest, I'm no longer certain whether the challenge of Madame de Landois might not have been far preferable to a visit to one of our brothels.'

TWENTY

Marguerite de Landois' balding butler kept James waiting longer than usual before directing him to the library. Here, too, the wait was long. He picked out a random volume of Descartes and let his eyes skim. But his mind was elsewhere. He wondered what was keeping her — this woman who had bemoaned the fact that her very womanhood made her days long and lax.

As he looked out onto the garden, he determined that once she was with him, there would be little point in beating about the bush. Marguerite was far better at indirections than he was. He would fulfill the Chief Inspector's errand immediately, ask what needed to be asked, and then rush over to Ellie, whom he was once more aware of having neglected. He hoped Ponsard's ministrations had calmed her.

He wondered if in part all his rushing about were simply an escape from her pressing condition. Now that he considered it, her condition frightened him almost more than anything else. Yes, more than Durand's suspicions about Raf, not to mention Caro's savage behaviour.

'James, I'm sorry to keep you. It was unavoidable.'

James started. He hadn't heard the door opening.

'And you look distressed. What's happened? I've asked Pierre to bring tea.'

Marguerite's cheeks were flushed as if she had just emerged from a hot bath, her hair piled high, moist ringlets framing her face. Her scent wafted towards him. It made him think of lilies of the valley, shaded woods, like her celandine dress. She was their nymph. He shunted the thought aside as she gestured him towards a chair.

'I'm on an errand,' he said more bluntly than he would have wished.

'Oh? An unpleasant one, I take it.'

'Slightly delicate.'

'You can be frank with me.' Irony glimmered over her features. 'Though I confess, I feel there has been rather too much unpleasantness these last days.'

'Yes. Far too much.' He surveyed her to catch her mood, then cleared his throat. 'It's an errand from Chief Inspector Durand.'

'Oh dear, our good Chief Inspector has you in his clutches.'

'That's not how I would have put it.'

'Put it for me then.' There was suddenly something hard in her voice.

'You remember I told you about that blackmailing letter Durand had found, the one from which he asked Raf to write out a sentence?'

'How could I forget?'

Pierre appeared with a tray. She waved him into haste, murmured an impatient, 'Leave us, Pierre.' He was hardly out of the room before she intoned in a cold voice, 'The letter. What about it?'

'Apparently, the writing matches your own.'

She slumped back into her chair, then changed her mind and got up. Her movements were agitated. 'I had hoped it wouldn't come to this.'

He wished he could see her face, but she was standing by the window, her back to him. At last he said softly, 'So it really was written by you?'

'Yes, yes, it was.' She turned, her face pale, tears crowding her eyes. 'So long ago. I had all but let myself forget it.' She sat down at a distance from him, smoothed her dress with trembling fingers.

'When?'

'Years.'

'Why?'

'It's hard to explain, James.' She was up again.

'Perhaps you'd rather explain to Durand.' He hadn't intended the note of cruelty that had crept up on him unawares. He had been thinking of

Olympe, the corrupt moves her older and undoubtedly admired benefactress had engaged her in.

She stared at him, calm now as if his coldness had bestowed that on her. 'Perhaps that would indeed be better, but since he's sent you . . . Only promise me that you won't breathe a word to Raf.'

'I can't honestly do that, Marguerite. Not until I know what it's about.'

Her calm crumbled. She was digging her nails into the palm of her hand. 'Pour us some tea, James.'

She took the cup gratefully and drank a few mouthfuls. Only then did he notice that his pipe and tobacco had been discreetly placed on the tray. He reached for them.

'It's not easy to talk about. And you will hate me afterwards.' Her eyes beseeched him. Then she shrugged and put the cup down on the table. 'What matter!'

He could see from her face that it mattered acutely. 'Give me the freedom to decide on that myself, Marguerite.'

'Ah, freedom!' She was up again, pacing restlessly. 'That's what it was all about. Years ago, as I told you. I can hardly remember myself then. I was a different person. Baffled by everything. Vulnerable. Small inside. Shamed. Trapped. Like a dog who had leapt into a pit sniffing a banquet of delicacies and found only fleas and rats, but was too small to leap out again, could only bark helplessly, endlessly, scratch until the sores bled.'

'No, you don't understand. You've never been there. Never felt the pain of entrapment.' She stared at him for a moment, her eyes savage. 'It started before I met Rachel, as she was then. I think I told you that my marriage was not going well. One of the reasons it was not going well was that my husband had a taste for boys.'

James gasped.

'Oh, it's hardly unusual. Though I didn't know about such things then. I was really remarkably innocent. I only knew that he had stopped loving me. Had grown cold. Never touched me.' She shivered. 'I was doubly desperate because I thought then that I wanted a child. In my reckless grief, I started to follow him. Late at night, when he left the house after dinner. I was certain he had a mistress and I wanted to know who she was.'

She laughed oddly. 'One night I managed to track him to a certain hotel in the Ninth arrondissement. But I didn't dare go in. I followed him there on several occasions. One daytime, I went there on my own and made enquiries. Don't ask me the bravery and heartache it cost me. The whole thing was so demeaning. But I couldn't let it go. Couldn't. Anyhow, eventually I managed to find out that it was a particular kind of establishment. A brothel where boys and men met.'

'The hotel D . . .'

'Yes. I have to say that the innocent country bumpkin that I was drew back in shock. I started to loathe my husband. Loathe him with a fury. I couldn't bear his punctilious little voice, his mannerisms, the way he straightened his tie, or sipped his wine, having sniffed it first, his nose like a rat's. I couldn't bear his politeness. I couldn't bear the way he would choose what dress or jewellery I should wear then fasten it round my neck, his fingers cool, precise. His very presence scratched at me until I thought I would go mad.

'It was around that time that I met Rachel. We grew close. And eventually, I told her. I told her because I needed to tell someone and she wasn't of my circle. I told her because I thought if she was up to it, she might be able to help me. I had concocted this plan. I knew that Olivier was a vain man, enamoured of his status, and would dread nothing so much as public exposure. I needed someone who could witness his presence at one of the brothels he frequented, and then pretend blackmail, having, of course, simultaneously stated that I had been alerted to his betrayal.

'Rachel thought it was a game, an acting game. We got her some men's clothes and she wore them to perfection. She wasn't afraid of those establishments. Her sister . . . but that's another story. In any case, it didn't take long until she found Olivier out, flirted with him a little. And then I wrote that letter for her to copy and send. One to me as well. When the letters arrived, I confronted Olivier. It was terrible. He wept.'

She hid her face from him.

'Now, now that I am wiser about the vagaries of desire, I am deeply ashamed of myself. But then . . . then I was brutal. Righteous.'

She sat down opposite him, her eyes vast, her face drawn. Oddly, she looked younger, like a frightened girl, tortured by emotions that wouldn't leave her alone.

'By the end of that dreadful night, we had reached an accommodation. He would pay the messenger the sum mentioned in the letter, which was, in fact, small enough. And we would live apart. That would be best for both of us. He determined to travel for some months and then settle in the country. He was afraid, of course, that the blackmail would continue. I told him I would deal with that. He could trust me.'

She poured them more tea, her hand not altogether steady. 'It's not an act or a period of my life I like to remember. I never thought I would have to. I had always assumed that Olympe had thrown out the letter.'

She paused. Her features grew pensive. 'It seems odd that she carried it with her over all those years. When you mentioned that Durand had it and had attributed it to Raf, I knew that sooner or later I might have to dredge all this up. I admit I hate having to confront ugliness, especially in myself. I somehow hoped that it wouldn't happen. It has.'

She glanced at him and rushed on. 'Oh, I know, James, know that blackmail is a foul crime. It ruptures and besmirches the ties that bind society. It's also a betrayal. But at the time it felt like the only way out.' She gave him a grim smile.

'Quite what you decide to tell the Chief Inspector, I leave to you. But do emphasize that none of it bears any relationship to Olympe's death. And I sincerely wish he won't need to confront Olivier with it. Who knows, Olivier may even lie to save face. I can't say that I would blame him. As for Rafael,' she arranged a stray lock, 'my greatest wish is that . . .'

She didn't finish her sentence. Instead she looked up at him like a prisoner in the dock. The jury had already pronounced and she was awaiting sentence. James had become both judge and potential executioner. He delayed the moment.

'How can you be so certain that all this bears no relationship to Olympe's death? Maybe your husband decided to take his revenge. He could somehow have found out that the letter came from her.'

Marguerite shook her head. 'Never.'

'You're very absolute. Do you know more than I do?'

'Oh, I'm not saying he couldn't have found out, if he had really tried. If he had persisted. But Olivier is a changed man. He's altogether happy with his new life. The country suits him. And he comes to Paris less and less frequently. I think I would have known if the insult, the threat, had rankled and festered through all these years. Will you tell Rafael?'

'I haven't decided yet. The truth is, Marguerite, I've barely taken it all in.'

Her chuckle held a trace of self-contempt. 'I don't know why I care so much for his opinion. Can you explain that to me?'

'I suspect you're a far better philosopher of the boudoir than I'll ever be.'

'And you despise me for it.'

'I don't think so. I don't know yet.' As he said it, he wondered at his own equanimity. What right had he to judge her, given the vagaries of his own desire?

She got up again, her skirts swishing as she strode through silence. After a moment, she opened the French windows and beckoned him onto the small ironwork terrace. The garden lay beneath them in all its June glory. A bird sang melodiously.

'It's strange, James, but I feel lighter. Confession must be good for one. You know, I haven't slept these last nights for worry about when and how it would come out.' Her voice fell into a whisper. 'I guess in a way, I'd been worrying for a long time.'

'But not worrying so profoundly that you might want to do damage to Olympe?'

'Of course not.' She turned on him.

'Yet, she held on to the letter. So perhaps she was worrying that you might one day. Want to do her damage, I mean. The letter was her safeguard.'

She shrugged. 'I'd never considered that. But you must be right. The rich, after all, are never to be completely trusted. Olympe knew that.' She gave him one of her astute looks. 'Maybe you're better acquainted with the murky depths of the soul than even I am, James. What will you do now?'

He moved back into the room. A restlessness had overtaken him. He wanted to go, to walk, to think. But there was too much he still had to ask her. Now more than ever. He examined the painting which hung over the fireplace. He hadn't really taken it in before. It showed a man leaning against a mantlepiece, a little as he was doing now. The face was intent, bony. The eyes stared straight out of the canvas with an arrogant expression. 'Is that Olivier?'

'No, James. I'm sorry to disappoint. It's my father. I painted it before I left home. It's not very good. But I have a certain fondness for it. He scowls reassuringly at the upheavals in my life.'

'It doesn't look to me as if he's scowling.'

'No?' She came to stand beside him, examined the portrait. He could smell the fragrance of her hair, see the delicate whorls of her ear, the down on her cheek, the gentle rise and fall of her bosom. She turned and suddenly touched his lips with hers. He had the sensation of wings fluttering softly across his face. He would have liked to hold them there, but he hesitated and she was already away, leaving him with an indefinable sadness.

'I think you should probably go and see the Chief Inspector now, James. He'll be waiting.'

He shook himself inwardly. 'There are a few more things I need to ask you.'

'If you must.'

'Yes. You may be the best placed to answer them. About Olympe.' He cleared his throat, reached for his pipe and filled it methodically. 'I have discovered that contrary to appearances, Olympe was wearing clothes when she died.' He struck a match. 'Men's clothes.'

'Indeed.' Marguerite looked wholly untroubled by his revelation. 'Are you telling me that suicide now seems more likely?'

'Perhaps that, too. I was really wondering about the clothes.'

Marguerite giggled. The sound was so unexpected that he choked a little on his smoke and coughed. Her laughter grew louder. She stifled it behind her hand. 'I'm sorry, James, but you should see your face. With all your wisdom, you're so wonderfully shockable. It quite cheers me.'

'So this doesn't surprise you?' James struggled for composure.

'No. Should it? Olympe often donned men's clothes after that first time. Particularly late at night, if she was alone. It made getting round the city far easier. No one bothers you if you're a man. Neither other men, nor the police. She made quite the swell in her top hat.'

'Did Raf know about this?'

'I can't tell you that for certain. We never talked about it. But he certainly knows . . .' She stopped herself.

'Knows what?'

She laughed again. 'Haven't you guessed yet? I would have thought that Rafael might have mentioned it by now.'

'Mentioned what?'

She walked over to the desk, took something out of a drawer, and strolled back towards him, her posture subtly different, a thrust to her shoulders, a stiffness in her hips. There was a monocle in her eye. 'Enchantez, Monsieur Norton.' Her cheek twitched slightly.

James blinked, his gaze racing to her feet as if he might see supple black boots there, striped trousers. 'Marcel Bonnefoi? You?'

She nodded, let the monocle fall. 'I'm sorry, James. It was Olympe's and my little joke.' She giggled again and he had a sudden rushing sense of an unthought-of aspect of their relationship. Girls inventing pranks. Playing. Perhaps more than that.

'I half guessed,' he murmured. 'There was something, some resemblance I couldn't place. Does Raf know?'

'About Marcel? I'm not altogether sure. Olympe may have told him. I haven't. I did it just for her. To amuse her, really. To give her an untroubling admirer. It wasn't exactly Marcel I thought he might have mentioned.' Her eyes twinkled mischievously.

He stared at her. 'Antoine. Antoine, of course.' A candle suddenly illuminated dusky regions in his mind. 'All those times, I saw him rushing to and from the house. In the carriage. And just before. When I was with Durand. That's how you knew . . . Why you were so long.'

She nodded. 'You'll forgive me that, at least.'

'I'm not sure,' he mumbled. 'I feel duped.'

'It wasn't intended that way. It's just for convenience. The adventure is secondary. There's so little I can allow myself to do as Madame de Landois. You do see that? And I can help Rafael out. Disappear into a crowd. Move quickly without the weight of these skirts. You don't realize how fortunate men's fashions are.'

'But Marcel Bonnefoi? Why serve him up to me?'

She shrugged. 'You wanted to meet him. He obliged. I couldn't just blurt out the game to you. Not then. You can give off such a severe aura, James. I thought it might altogether scupper our friendship. Don't you see?'

He didn't see. The air was thick with duplicity and something else, an unnaturalness. Through the miasma he sniffed at treacherous liaisons. 'Did you know about Olympe's visits to the brothels?'

'What?'

'I think you heard me. She went to see friends.' He gave the word the emphasis of quotation marks.

'I wasn't her keeper, James.'

'But you were, outside the cast of the play, the last person we know to have been with her? How was she? What did you talk about?' His voice had turned inquisitorial.

Marguerite leaned back into her chair. 'Don't think I haven't gone over and over it in my mind. She was fine, happy really, full of plans. Not in the least a woman on the verge of suicide, if that's what you mean. She even mentioned the word *marriage*. She said she thought she might go with Raf to America, after the play had finished its run. To see what life there might be like. To see if it was really the wondrous land of dreams. To see whether it might be the answer to her family's plight. She was excited.'

'Did you say anything to blunt her hopes?'

She looked down at her hands. The gold wedding band glistened on her fourth finger. 'I've never been to America, James. There was little I could say.'

'I meant about marriage to Raf.'

'No. No. I said nothing. Well, perhaps only to intimate that in my case marriage had not been altogether a success. But she knew that. And she didn't mention anything about a pregnancy. Don't look at me like that, James.'

'Like what?'

'As if to suggest that in some jealous rage, I might have wished her ill. Yes, yes, of course I confess to a passing pang. That would hardly be unnatural. But you have to understand that Olympe was like a daughter to me. Certainly she thought of me as something of a mother. A partial replacement, in any case. And she never knew that there had been anything between Rafael and myself — except friendship. Which is in truth what there is.'

'She never knew?' James felt as if he had sunk into the depths of perfidy.

'Well, no. Rafael never told her. In consideration of me, as much as anything else I imagine. Sometimes I wish I had never told you. There was no real need.'

'I guessed.'

'You suspected,' she corrected him. 'Suspicions in our world are as pervasive as air. We may feed on them, but they're proof of nothing.'

He changed the subject. 'Have you learned any more about the Salpêtrière files. From your intern friend. He isn't you as well, is he?'

'No, he isn't. Though the idea did cross my mind. Then flitted away. That's a serious matter. I should hear from him tomorrow. I've upset you, James. That wasn't my intention. Almost more with my masquerading than with the blackmail, a far more serious offence in my estimation.'

He couldn't meet her eyes. 'I need to phone Touquet's office. Do you have the number?'

She gave it to him with the expression of a penitent and left without a nod.

Watching her go, James felt breathless, as if he had penetrated into some protean region beneath the waves where shapes shifted with fugitive speed, too quick for the senses to settle on. Or as if he had been swallowed up in the inner recesses of some oriental harem, a labyrinth where the dance of veils was perpetual, beckoning him onwards towards the core of some feminine mystery which metamorphosed into billowing gossamer as he approached, hiding rather than revealing. Door after door in an endless corridor, veil after veil, so that he lost his bearings, was dizzy with the pursuit of an ever-changing object for which neither his eyes nor his values could provide a solid measure.

He picked up the telephone and put it down as quickly. He wasn't ready for Raf. What was it the Chief Inspector had said to him one day? Yes, he had complained of this world of his where women were no longer women and men not men. Perhaps he had more in common with the Chief Inspector than he had suspected.

With a sudden longing for home, he wished for clear demarcation lines, for things to be as they seemed. He wondered if that might ever be possible again.

Harriet opened the door to him. It was a relief to see her scrubbed face, unencumbered by wiles or mystery.

She put a finger to her lips. 'Elinor's asleep.' She ushered him into the dining room.

'How has she been?'

She lowered her eyes, smoothed a wrinkle in the tablecloth, then looked up at him again, shaking her head. 'Not well. She slept through part of the night, then woke to scribble in her journal. She didn't acknowledge me, hasn't acknowledged me all day. And she won't eat.'

'What did Dr. Ponsard say?'

She shrugged. 'Well, he did examine her thoroughly. She was quite calm. You remember that. You were still here. He prohibited the wearing of corsets.' She flushed slightly, then raced on. 'And he gave her some sleeping powders. Something for the temperature, too.'

'No prognosis?'

'He came back around noon to check on her. She didn't recognize him. Or at least she pretended not to . . . I don't know James, I really don't know.'

'And . . .?'

She smoothed her dress with something of an injured expression. 'He had a box with him, coils. He told me to bring a large bowl of water. Her bare feet were put into it. When he caught me staring, he told me to leave them. I think he applied current to her body.' She shivered, then looked round and lowered her voice. ' I think he may also have hypnotized her.'

'Oh?' James imagined Ellie walking around the room with those sleepwalker's eyes.

'Yes. Because when he finally called me back, he told me that she had taken a little cold broth and brioche and that I was to monitor her and report to him when he came in tomorrow. While he was talking, Elinor started to retch, to vomit everything up on the floor. Ponsard reprimanded her sternly. Elinor gave him a smile. It wasn't a nice smile, more like a challenge, as if she was going to show him.' She shuddered again. 'I cleaned up and then he ordered me out once more.'

'Poor Harriet. I'm sorry. Where was Violette?'

'She was running some errands.'

'Did Ponsard say anything more?'

'Before he left, he said he was a little worried that there might be some blockage in her esophagus. He had wheeled her out on the terrace. He thought a little air and change of scenery might do her good. When I went in to her, she was scribbling in her journal again. She's slept or scribbled all day since. She won't eat or take her medicine, not even the digestive powders he prescribed. She doesn't know me.'

Harriet's eyes had filled with tears and she turned away to wipe them.

'Why don't you go home and rest, Harriet. I'll keep an eye on her. You must be exhausted.'

'No, no. It's not that. I'm comfortable enough here.' She gave him one of her direct looks. 'My own quarters are nothing to write home about. Though I would like a walk. I have a few things to see to. But I'll be back in an hour or two. I'm sure Elinor wouldn't like you to . . . to see her like this.'

'She's been poorly before, Harriet. And she's come through. She always comes through.' He said it with more certainty than he felt.

After Harriet had left, he tiptoed into the salon. Ellie was asleep in her chair beside the divan. Her head drooped down on her chest. She was wearing a belted burgundy robe. The ruffle of a white nightgown peeked from her sleeve. Her notebook was perched on a table by her side, which also contained an assortment of powders and pitchers. There was a stale smell in the air.

He picked up a book, chose a far chair and settled into it. He didn't look at the book. His spirit was heavy, his head full of too many riddles. He used the quiet moments to try and sift through all the things he had learned in the last twenty-four hours. He had no sense of how long he sat there, but the next thing he knew, Ellie's voice roused him from his reverie.

'Jim, you're home. I'm so glad, but there's no good news for you I fear.'

Ellie was swaying in her chair, one hand clasped round her stomach as if she were in pain, the other playing erratically with her hair pins.

'No, no.' Tears flooded her eyes. 'Maisie's no better.'

'Maisie? Maisie?'

Ellie sobbed, clapped her hands to her ears. Her back was arched in agitation. 'She's fading, Jim. Fading. It's all my fault.'

'Your fault?'

'Yes. I never told you. I was afraid.' She grasped the arms of her chair as if to lever herself up, but her hands stayed there, clenched into white fists. Her eyes were preternaturally large. She spoke in fits and starts. 'My embroidery. I dropped it. Dropped it on the stairs. I didn't realize. Didn't know. Maisie tripped. Tripped on it. The babe, too.' She slumped backwards, limp as a sack.

'Tripped on it,' James repeated, his mind in turmoil.

'Yes. There. I've told you. You should go up to her. She'll want to see you.' She tilted her head. Her smile had a milky sweetness. 'She loves her Jim.'

For a fleeting moment, as if Ellie's conviction were contagious, James had the impression that were he only to locate the stairs of the Boston house and ascend them, he would find Maisie resting amidst lace and linen. Maisie with her gentle faraway gaze, her frail pallor.

He took a deep breath. But there was no air in the room. With a brutal clatter, he threw open the windows and turned on his sister. 'Maisie's dead, Ellie. We're in Paris. Paris. Do you hear me? And you know that perfectly well. You know that.'

Her hands clasped her stomach, she swayed. 'You're angry with me, Jim. You have a right to be angry. But pity me, too. There's a worm in my stomach. It's eating away at me. Eating.' Her eyes pleaded with him, and then grew opaque. 'You rest. You must be tired after a day at the office. I'll go to Maisie. Yes.' He could barely make out her words.

With a sudden movement, she propped herself up from the chair. For a lightning second, James thought she was going to walk. Instead, she lunged to the floor in a heap of blankets.

He rushed towards her. She had collapsed into a faint. He dampened a cloth in water, applied it to her temples, her wrists, whispered her name, carried her to the divan and laid her gently on it. Covering her lightly, he sat to watch over her in a mounting panic.

He couldn't follow the wanderings of her delirious mind, as fluid and capricious as a wraith which knew no boundaries of time or place. Could it be that in an attempt to come to terms with her own condition, Ellie had transported herself back to an invalid Maisie — a Maisie who had lain abed for months with near-perfect equanimity?

When her eyes fluttered open, he breathed a sigh of relief. But she didn't focus on him now. As he brought a glass to her lips, he felt he had become transparent.

She drank in short thirsty gulps, and then lay back, her gaze fixed on the ceiling.

'That's right, Ellie, you rest now. Sleep a little if you can.'

She offered no response.

'If you need anything, I'm here. Just call me.'

Her silence was as disturbing as her speech. He went back to his chair and watched her out of the corner of his eye. A pale glint of late sunlight fell on her and streaked her with a vertical gash so that it seemed to cut her in half. She didn't move. Not even when tears cascaded down her face. He hesitated, and then went to wipe them.

'You're kind,' she whispered.

He waited for her to say something more, but she receded into her silent place. Her breathing grew even and he realized that she must have fallen asleep.

Fetching a piece of paper, he settled at the table. He was determined to make use of his time, to put some order into the disparate strands of their enquiry. Everything seemed to have taken on a fraying centrifugal force and his mind ached for cohesion. He was about to write down the names of the key players for whom he harboured any degree of suspicion, when instead he found himself printing Rachel Arnhem-Olympe Fabre at the top of the page, and beneath this what amounted to a chronology of her life and its points of intersection with the people he had encountered at such a fast and furious rate in these last days.

Before he had finished, he heard the click of the door. He tiptoed out and saw Violette, a basket filled with groceries in her arms. He greeted her, said he would be dining with Mlle Harriet and returned to his musing.

He was just thinking about the fire which had obliterated Madame Arnhem's life and set the two sisters on a such a treacherous path, when a sound from Ellie pierced his concentration.

'What are you doing?' she asked in a neutral voice.

'I'm just writing something, Ellie dear.'

'About what.'

He swallowed. He still didn't know if she was focused in the here and now or not. 'About a case.'

'A case?'

'Olympe. Can I get you something to eat, Ellie. Or a drink. Violette's back.'

Her brow furrowed with the effort of attention. 'Will you pass me my notebook?' she surprised him by asking. 'I want to write, too.'

'You mustn't tire yourself, Ellie.'

She said nothing, not even when he handed her the book and the stubby pencils which lay beside it. She propped herself on an elbow and gesturing him away, opened the journal and began to write. A noise in the corridor made her stop. She was all alertness. 'Who's that?'

'I imagine it's Harriet.'

She slammed the cover of the book down. 'I don't want to see her. Don't let her in here.' Her nostrils quivered. There was fear in her eyes, like a rabbit trapped in light.

'All right. But she only means you well.'

'I want you with me. No one else. Please stay. You do me good.'

'Of course, I'll stay.'

'Thank you, Raf. Thank you.'

James froze in position. The Ellie who wanted him by her side was the Ellie who thought he was Raf.

'And you're the only one I'll ever allow to read this,' she whispered looking up at him with a tender expression. 'You're the only one who understands me. You understand about the worm. The worm who comes in the night.'

James murmured helpless assent.

PART THREE

TWENTY-ONE

For the next days, he was taken up with Ellie. He ministered to her, sat or slumbered by her side in a state of semisomnolent vigilance, fed her the potions and broth Ponsard had prescribed and which she took from James and no one else, even though she still addressed him as Raf. Whoever he was, it seemed that his presence had a calming effect. Ponsard testified to as much on both his visits, which brought with them the whiff of an emissary from some promised, some imminently rational land. Since Ellie was peaceful, Ponsard decided that she was best left to rest and mend in her own way, before he undertook any further treatment.

'The mind is still a mysterious entity to our science,' he told James. 'We tiptoe, we blunder and do what we can. But who knows whether your sister may not be her own best physician, with a little help from time. When the mists of delusion have cleared, we will see what else we can do.'

Ellie paid no attention to the doctor. She only hummed a little during his visits, some childhood tune, which had the ring of a skipping rhyme.

'The wind blows low, the wind blows high, little Jessie says she'll die . . .'

She hummed across Harriet, too. James — or rather the Raf he was meant to be — was the only person she addressed with any degree of alertness, and that only to ask for her notebook or a cooling drink.

As he sat by her side, he wandered back over her past episodes and had a vision of his mother sitting just like this, the house darkened in enforced slumber, the knitting growing in her hands with the speed of a magic beanstalk.

Once, too, when he had come home to visit from Philadelphia and finding no one else about, had rushed into Ellie's room, he had surprised his father in a similar posture, newspaper still in hand, eyes half closed. Ellie, her features askance, was mumbling something incomprehensible, and his father, instantly alert, had rushed him away as if from some secret scene of perfidy. He had offered no explanation, except that Ellie wasn't herself.

It astonished James that throughout those years, he had never penetrated quite so deeply as now into the terrifying reality that simple expression obscured.

Sometime during his bedside vigil, James slipped away to phone both Touquet's office and the Grand. He left a message for his brother, simply to tell him where he was. He also wrote a note to Chief Inspector Durand explaining that Madame de Landois had indeed penned the blackmailing letter, but it dated from some six years back and was part of an elaborate hoax which bore no relation to the present situation. He wondered at his own formulation and at quite what induced him to preserve the woman's honour. Perhaps it was simply that if the worst had to be discovered about Marguerite, he wanted to be the one to discover it. The shadowy nature of this wish didn't fail to strike him. He concluded, not without an aching irony, that since he couldn't hope to compete with Raf in the winning of women's favours, maybe he was trying at least to equal him when it came to knowledge.

As for the ever-present puzzle of Olympe's tragic death, it had come to him during the musings of these long days and gruelling nights, that a hidden key to her relations with Marguerite and indeed with Raf, let alone the prostitutes she had visited, probably lay buried with her sister Judith. Or indeed with her childhood friend Louise Boussel. He could imagine the Olympe he now thought he had some grip on confessing to these old confidantes, telling them things she couldn't mention to her new friends. Or simply thinking matters through in their uncritical presence. He didn't quite know why he had come to this conclusion, except that he knew Olympe was a loyal soul. He determined to see both women as soon as he could leave Ellie.

But something intervened. In Saturday's five o'clock post, there was a letter from Raf asking him to meet him at the Grand by eight. 'Tonight is the big night,' Raf proclaimed in the cryptic tone of someone who suspected his letter would be intercepted by alien eyes. 'I know you wouldn't want to miss it.'

James fingered the bracelet the boatman had given him and which still lay in his pocket. He took it out to examine it in the light. Could Raf have given it to Olympe? And should he now, in all conscience, return it to his brother and convey everything he had learned?

Like some ultrasensitive instrument that could read his inclinations even before he was aware of them, Ellie was suddenly not only awake, but aware of who he was.

'Jim,' she beckoned him to her side. 'Jim, where are you going? What's that you've got? And where's Raf? Where has he gone?'

'I don't quite know, Ellie. But I'm going to meet him at the hotel later.'

She surveyed him, her eyes darkening with her appraisal. 'You never did like spending much time with me, Jim. Always running. Leaving me to father or to Raf.'

'That's not quite fair, Ellie.' He was taken aback by her accusation, but also relieved that she now recognized him.

'Isn't it?' She turned her attention to the bracelet and snatched it from his hand. 'Where did you get that, Jim? That's my bracelet. Raf gave it to me for my birthday. I thought I'd lost it.'

'Yours?' He prevaricated. 'I found it lying about. It's pretty. Very pretty.'

'Help me put it on, Jim.'

The trapped fire of the emeralds danced in the light. He fumbled with the catch.

'Never mind, Jim. You won't have to put up with me much longer. Everything will be fine now. Now that the bracelet's come back.' She started her humming, and then stopped abruptly. 'Tell Raf there's something I need to say to him. Say to him alone. It's urgent.'

'All right. I'll see you later then, Ellie.' He planted a light kiss on her brow. 'I'm so glad you're feeling a little better. Harriet will take care of your needs.'

'Ah, Harriet. Dear Harriet. So utterly dependable.' She sighed, her eyes playing over the bracelet once more.

The bustling Saturday evening streets dispersed the cloistered air of the sickroom with a tingling rapidity. Women's hats looked brighter and more elaborate than an array of exotic birds. The frothy confections of the neighbouring patisserie enticed. Near the Madeleine, a harlequin of a juggler threw striped pins in the air with such speed that their colours metamorphosed and dazzled. When a flower girl thrust a bouquet of fluttering sweet-peas towards him, he purchased them for their sheer evanescent beauty.

The Grand appeared before he had expected it. He lingered for an extra moment in the life of the boulevard. He found himself wishing he could lose himself in its careless extravagance, as if a roof and walls signalled a suffocating tomb from which he had too recently been released. These last days with Ellie, in fact the entirety of these last weeks, since he had witnessed Olympe's dead body, had given him, he realized, a sense of his own precarious mortality and with it a sense that life was precious. It led him to confront the fact that he had not felt it to be precious before. Since Maisie's death he had successfully shrouded himself in some stiff impermeable carapace where sensation didn't penetrate. Years in limbo. Years of waste.

He half remembered a line from Shakespeare. 'I wasted time and now time wastes me.' An unnameable fear coiled in his stomach. With it came a fleeting image of Marguerite brushing against him as they stood by the fireplace and an anxiety about what Raf's 'big night' might entail.

He hurried through the lobby of the hotel. Seeing the crowd at the elevator, he made for the stairs. By the time he reached his room, he was panting slightly. He turned the knob only to find the door locked. He knocked. There was no response. A second knock still failed to rouse his brother. Puzzled, he tried again, then after a glance at his watch which showed five minutes to eight, slowly made his way back down to reception. What could have led Raf to alter his stated plans?

The clerk handed James an envelope. Beneath the formal reticence, his eyes were avid with curiosity. James turned away to read his letter. The note was briefer than a telegram. 'Emergency at Salpêtrière. Raf.'

Without pausing to deliberate, James headed for the door.

A motley crowd had gathered in the stifling corridor outside Dr. Vaillant's ward. Passage was all but impossible. Nurses in billowing headdresses jostled with white-gowned doctors and orderlies bearing a stretcher. All of them were pressed backwards by a caped policeman, standing at the door of one of the cell-like cubicles. Working his way through the gaggle, James saw a lightning-like flare flash from the partially open door. Into the hush that followed it came a commanding, 'Don't touch anything. Not a thing.'

Chief Inspector Durand's voice. James pushed forward, his pulse racing faster than a greyhound. Before he could reach the door, a man barged past him, his elbows like battering rams. Dr. Comte. His face was set in an ugly scowl. James uttered his name, but the man was as oblivious to his surroundings as a locomotive at full steam. He rammed his way between the women and charged down the corridor.

Torn between following him and making his way past the gendarme, James was momentarily transfixed by a second flash. He could smell the burning powder now, like rotting eggs.

'Chief Inspector Durand's expecting me,' he shouted above the head of an orderly.

'Name?' the policeman barked officiously.

James told him.

He opened the door a fraction wider to squeeze through. James's innards lurched. He saw the loose hospital gown first, swinging in the air as if a wind had propelled it upwards and refused to let it go. Beneath it, two limp stockinged feet turned in a ninety degree arc and back again with hypnotic slowness. Time was trapped in that infinitesimal motion.

He forced his eyes upwards. From a knotted sheet hung a woman, her bent face all but obliterated by a fan of dark hair. The hair crackled with life. It was the only life left in her.

'There's no room for anyone else in there now.'

James barely heard the gendarme's words. His thoughts were too loud. Judith Arnhem. Judith was dead. Judith who had predicted her own death, who had forewarned them. How had they allowed this to happen?

Immune to admonishments, he propelled himself back through the crowded hall in search of Comte. Why had Durand allowed the man to go? He pushed open the door he thought he had seen Comte enter. The cackles and screams of a ward besieged him. For a moment, in the pandemonium, he was disoriented. A stout matron emerged from the sea of rocking figures to block his passage. He asked for Dr. Comte. With a shake of the head and a stern 'not here', she marched him backwards.

James tried a second and a third door. Both were locked.

From the far end of the corridor he now heard a new commotion. 'Make way. Make way,' a voice ordered. Stretcher-bearers moved in his direction. A sheet covered the figure between them. Keeping pace with the desolate retinue was the sticklike pathology student, Steinlen.

James gripped his arm. 'You remember me? That's a friend of mine, you have there. I'd like to come with you.'

The bony youth gave him a harassed look. 'That's against orders. Specific orders.' He shook James off. 'Besides, she's no one's friend now.'

'Whose orders?'

'Police.' A smug smile tugged at his lips. 'They're the only ones allowed in.'

James retraced his steps. He reached the cubicle just as the photographer struggled through the door, a tripod balanced in one arm. While he exchanged a word with the gendarme, James slipped unnoticed into the room.

Bent almost double, Arnhem sat on the palette of a bed and swayed slightly. He didn't look up. His gnarled hands covered his face as if he might never lift them from there again. Raf stood next to Chief Inspector Durand. Both of them were staring up at the ceiling where a beam traversed the room. Screwed into it was a hook of the kind that might once have been used for holding a candle tray. Stretched on the floor beneath them was the sheet he had last seen round Judith's throat. It was tightly wound and regularly knotted like some giant's primitive necklace. A toppled stool lay beside it. The air was stale, fetid with an aroma which could only be the stench of death.

'Jim. You got here.' Raf spoke first. 'Olympe's sister is dead.' Raf's eyes were vast with childlike wonder. A vein throbbed at his temple. 'Monsieur Arnhem and the nurse found her hanging when he came to visit. It's too awful. He had the presence of mind to insist on getting the Chief Inspector here.'

'And I sent for you, Monsieur Norton. Your brother intercepted the message.' Durand scowled at both of them. 'A foul business. The matron told us the woman had been ranting of nothing but death for weeks. Which is why they had her in here on her own.'

'Had her in here alone so they could do away with her more easily.' Arnhem's guttural hiss startled all of them. 'You're fools all of you.'

'Be reasonable, Arnhem. I know it's not easy when your child . . . your children . . . The point is if the medics wanted to get her, they could just give her an injection of something. A lot less trouble and you would have been none the wiser.'

'Did you interview Dr. Comte?' James was so transfixed by the grief in Arnhem's face, that his voice came in a whisper.

'Comte raged. He had apparently just come on duty when I arrived. He gave his nurses a regular dressing down.' Durand stroked his moustache reflectively. 'I wouldn't have liked to have been in their shoes. He told them when patients were put into solitary it was not so that they could be forgotten for days on end.'

'What did the nurses say?'

'Mademoiselle Laplanche . . .' Durand checked his notebook, 'said it was the weekend and they had all been run off their feet and that they were two short of staff, because of illness, and that they had indeed looked in on Judith Arnhem at noon and she was sleeping peacefully.'

'I presume you've asked the pathologist to run a check on what chemicals she had inside her.'

'You really don't need to teach me how to suck eggs, Monsieur Norton.'

'And your police pathologist will be assisting the young Dr. Steinlen?'

Durand grimaced. 'In due course. Dr. Comte tells us Steinlen is very able. A ferret for detail.'

'Dr. Comte is not to be trusted.' Arnhem leapt up, suddenly as fierce in his stance as an unleashed tiger. 'I have tried to explain my daughter's fears to you, Chief Inspector. She may have been ill, but she could also be alert. More alert and sensitive to her surroundings than the rest of us. She had a kind of sixth sense. Rachel always talked of it. It was I . . . I who was resistant to Judith's observations.' Arnhem tore at his hair.

The air in the small room had grown intolerable. James looked with longing at the small, high window. Without thinking, he reached for the stool and was about to stand on it when Durand barked, 'I want to fingerprint that. Don't touch.'

'Of course.' James stepped back. 'Sorry. It occurs to me that when we last came to see Judith Arnhem, this wasn't the cubicle she was in. The last one didn't have a window. Nor was there a beam. A beam with a convenient hook to hang from. Judith might have been induced, or rather, things might have been made easy for her . . .' His thoughts trailed off. 'Even if someone didn't actually hang her while she was drugged.'

There was gratitude in Arnhem's haggard features. 'That's it precisely, Monsieur Norton. That's what I have been attempting to say. Dr. Comte trampled over all my questions.'

'Until proved otherwise, Dr. Comte is a respected servant of our national hygiene program, Arnhem.'

The man looked as if he was about to jump at Durand's throat.

'It's not your fault, Monsieur Arnhem,' Raf said softly. 'None of us altogether took Judith at her word. Except Jim, here. And Olympe, as you said.' He put his arm round the older man's shoulders. 'I think a brandy is in order, Jim.'

'Yes. Yes. All of you go. My men will be here soon and I need the room cleared.' Durand waved them off. James hung back behind the others.

'Listen Chief Inspector, if you're going to have a second, a private interview with Dr. Comte, I'd like to be there.'

'Oh?'

'Yes. The thing is that not only did I see Comte at the brothel the other night, but we think that Olympe may have gone to see him. Her daybook . . .'

'What daybook?' Durand cut him off with a vocal lunge.

'Oh, just an appointments book that . . . that my brother came across.' James swallowed hard.

'In her apartment?'

James nodded as Durand's eyes bulged threateningly.

'I want that in my office at the latest tomorrow morning or I'll have you arrested for hindering a police investigation.'

'Of course, Chief Inspector. Of course. But as for Comte . . .'

'I think, Monsieur Norton, that you have more reason to trust me than the other way around.'

'You'll ask him about his meeting with Olympe as well as everything else? You'll ask him delicately.'

Durand thrust his head back with Napoleonic aplomb. 'As I've said before, you hardly need to teach me my business, Monsieur Norton. Please remember that I harbour suspicions about everyone. Everyone, regardless of rank. And continue to, despite your letter about Madame de Landois.'

'Indeed, Chief Inspector.'

As if to provide further evidence of Durand's words, Raf stuck his head back round the door and grumbled, 'Listen, Durand. I don't know how many men you've got to throw around. But you could just call the one standing right out there off my tail. He followed me here and he's about to follow me out. And it's a waste of time I tell you. Since I know he's there.'

Durand's demeanour was icy. 'I don't know what you're talking about.' He waved them off with a final admonishment to James. 'The daybook. You won't forget.'

Outside, angry clouds had gathered, dusky charcoal against the indigo of the sky. By the time they reached the gates, the first fat drops had begun to fall.

Raf hailed a carriage. He was holding Arnhem's arm, as if to keep him upright. 'You come with us, Monsieur Arnhem. I'm sure the children will be all right with your friends for a little while longer.'

He gave James a meaningful look and James reiterated the invitation.

'No, I must go to them.' Arnhem was adamant. 'I have been away too long already.' In the lamplight, his eyes glistened with tears. 'I can take no more chances. No more chances.'

The carriage clattered over cobbles. The storm burst upon them, as noisy on bonnet and pavement as the splatter of gunfire. Horses whinnied in protest. Walkers ran and huddled beneath streaming awnings. Pavements and road took on a glistening sheen.

Arnhem was muttering, talking to himself like some ragged Lear on a blasted heath, his lips barely moving, his open eyes streaming tears. 'Yes, that's best. That's best. We will all follow Judith. The dybbuk. Her mother in her. One by one. Taking them away. To her.'

Raf and James looked at each other.

'We can't leave him,' James whispered. 'Why don't we take them all, the children too, to Marguerite's. And she may have had some news from that intern. It's become more urgent now.'

Raf glanced at his watch. 'I promised Touquet . . .'

'Get a message to him.'

'We don't even know if Marguerite's in.'

'We'll wait for her. Someone's bound to be there.'

At their joint insistence, the children were picked up, half asleep, from a bemused neighbour and bundled into the waiting cab. They sat astride their father's knees, one on each, and cast curious looks at the brothers.

'Where are we going?' the little girl asked.

Arnhem didn't answer, but his arms clutched his children as if they might be lifted from him at any moment.

'We're going very fast,' the boy said with something like wonder.

'I don't believe I know your names.' Raf smiled at the two.

'I'm Adam,' the boy said self-importantly. 'And my sister is Juliette.'

'Nice names.'

Juliette gave James a bewitching smile. 'What's yours?'

James introduced them both.

'I never thanked you for the chocolates,' Juliette said, her eyes serious. 'They were delicious.'

'Delicious,' Adam echoed.

'Hush,' Arnhem grunted, as if the sound of his children's innocent happiness only augmented the weight of his burden. 'It's no time to talk of chocolates.' He added something in a language they didn't understand and the children sat up straighter, their faces suddenly taut with fatigue and something else that James couldn't understand. He wondered for a moment what exactly Arnhem had finally told them about Olympe's death and whether his words now were a grim reminder of that incontrovertible fact, soon to be followed by one equally bleak.

They were crossing the river and the children tried to peer through the rain-spattered window, all the while maintaining their stiff posture. Shadowy lights played over the great buttresses of the Notre Dame like will-o-the-wisps. A motor car overtook them with a loud hoot of its horn. The children jumped. The horses whinnied loudly and reared. They could hear the driver cursing. For a moment all movement ceased.

Juliette's mouth fell open. 'Is it an accident, Messieurs?' she asked in a tremulous voice, the fear in her face, unequal to the occasion.

'No, no,' James soothed. 'Nothing to worry about. We'll be there very soon.'

'Where are we going?'

'To see a friend of your sister's. A friend of Olympe's. She's called Madame de Landois.'

Tears filled the girl's eyes. She turned her face away from them.

'You'll like her, I think, Juliette. And I'm sure she'll like you and Adam.'

'Liking is no matter,' Arnhem suddenly proclaimed. 'Why are we going there? I have forgotten.'

'Madame de Landois may have some information for us,' Raf said lightly. As the carriage started to move again, he kept up an innocuous patter with the children, pointing out sights, an umbrella tossed by a gust of wind, a café where great philosophers had sat debating the future of France. 'Do you know the name of your new prime minister?' he asked.

'Waldeck-Rousseau,' Adam answered with no hesitation. 'Papa says he is a fine orator and a good republican.'

'He's right.'

'Words can no longer help us,' Arnhem muttered.

'We're here.' James made an effort to be cheerful. He leapt out of the carriage, lifted the children one by one. 'You'll see, it's a lovely house.'

The children stood back in awe as Raf exchanged some words with the uniformed footmen.

'Marguerite's entertaining,' he said to James in a low voice. 'I've had a message sent up. We'll wait for her in the orangerie. The children will be more comfortable there.' He held back a little as Arnhem and the children were shown through. 'One of her guests is Dr. Vaillant,' he whispered to James. 'One can never accuse Marguerite of wasting her time. But I think it's best for the moment that we stay out of the way.'

It was in part a question and James responded, 'Why don't you go up?'

Raf shrugged. 'Let's wait and see what she advises.'

Juliette and Adam were standing at the threshold of the long room. They went in only with a little prodding. Their eyes were vast.

'It's so . . . so pretty. So bright. So many lights,' the little girl sighed. She touched her fingertips to the side of the grand piano and for a moment, James held his breath. It was as if he had suddenly seen the young Rachel described to him by Marguerite walking into this room for the first time.

'And so many flowers. Look Papa.'

Arnhem didn't answer. His eyes were blind to the room. He perched on the edge of a hard-backed chair and stared into the middle distance.

This younger Rachel, James remarked, was neither troubled, nor beset by shyness. Nor was her brother. He was leafing through a book that had been left on the side table. 'Insects,' he intoned, as Raf approached him. 'A dung beetle. A huge one. It's head is just like a scoop. You can see each of its legs. And the antennae.' The lad was excited.

'I used to know quite a few of those personally,' Raf laughed.

Adam gave him a sceptical look. 'Is it true that they can eat more than their own weight in twenty-four hours?'

'That's what they say. And at the start of summer they bury themselves and an apple-size ball of dung that they've made and feed on that.'

'Raf here used to have a beetle collection,' James offered. 'I can't say it altogether pleased our sister.' He stopped himself as the thought of Ellie plunged into his mind. Ellie feeding on her own accumulated thoughts, like some shiny Egyptian scarab.

The arrival of two of Marguerite's maids bearing trays replete with cold meats, fruit and patisserie caught the children's attention.

'I hope you're hungry.'

Juliette nodded while her brother simply stared as the food was spread out on the side table.

Raf poured brandy for the men. He urged Arnhem to drink and then to eat.

'You must eat, Papa,' Juliette chided. 'We need you to be strong.'

There was a stunned expression on Arnhem's face. It didn't disappear with the jolt of alcohol, but the sallowness of his skin took on a tinge of colour.

'May I have two, Papa?' Adam asked still, staring at the pastry. 'I can't make up my mind.'

'Three,' Raf replied for him. 'Make a feast of it. But don't get yourself sick. There'll be more in the morning.'

'Are we staying here tonight?'

'You certainly may, if you wish. If your father agrees. Personally I think it would be a good idea. What do you say, Arnhem? Then the little ones can get some sleep as soon as they've had a bite.'

'I'll only stay if Papa is staying.' Juliette was shyly determined. 'I don't like to leave him when he's so sad.' She turned to whisper to James as if she were his own age. 'He's been very sad, you know. We've all been.' She pushed her plate away. 'Did you know my sister Rachel?'

'I knew her well,' Raf answered for him. 'I miss her very much.'

Juliette's eyes filled with tears.

Raf ruffled her hair. 'I'll convince your father that you're all to stay.'

'Well, this is a surprise.'

None of them had seen Marguerite come in and now they all stood, even Arnhem. She was at her grandest in a dress of deep, shimmering blue, an ornate necklace at her throat, the encrusted lapis less luminous than her bared shoulders. Her hair was swept up in smooth coils which accentuated the fine structure of her face. She gave them all a dazzling smile, though she refused James's eyes. She focused in particular on the children. 'I am so pleased to meet you both properly at last. Juliette, I believe. And you're Adam. Good evening, Monsieur Arnhem.' She paused as she took in his demeanour. 'Has something happened?'

Raf took her arm and led her to the far end of the room while James occupied the children. Juliette's attention, however, kept returning to Marguerite in an open fascination which held not a little trace of fear.

When they returned, Marguerite was distinctly in charge. 'Now Monsieur Arnhem. I won't take no for an answer. I have kept you waiting too long. And now the children are tired and undoubtedly more than ready for bed. Pierre will have two rooms ready for you in no time and once they've been tucked in, we'll have our little talk. Yes. That's all arranged then. Tell me, Juliette, do you prefer a white nightie or pink?'

'I don't mind,' the little girl stammered.

'Your sister preferred white. Oh yes, she used to stay here too from time to time. When she didn't feel like making the drive home. It's quite nice, really. You'll see. And if you like, you can take some cherries up with you. And a drink, of course. You, too, Adam.'

'Adam's been enjoying your insect book.'

'Really. My father drew those. He'd be pleased that you liked them. We can look at them again in the morning.'

A half hour later, thc children had been whisked off to bed and the four adults sat in the library and nursed a fresh round of drinks. Marguerite's face had taken on an edge of grimness. As she got up to pace, James had a vision of a female warrior, a Joan of Arc girding her strength for battle. The image merged into that of the trousered Marcel Bonnefoi and he felt himself grow hot with embarrassment.

Marguerite still hadn't acknowledged him directly. Her confession stood between them like a barricade, too high with spikes to be tackled. He sensed that she must be wondering if he had yet told Raf of her collusion with Olympe in the blackmailing of her husband. He hadn't, of course, and part of him hoped that the need to would never arise. He didn't want to be thrust into the punishing role again, the elder brother who inevitably punctured ideals and sent them hurtling into the mud.

Watching Marguerite now, he also felt a new kind of admiration for her, as if the marks and taints of her had given her a greater depth; as if tawdry truths augmented mystery, rather than dispelling it. The fascination she held for him had grown despite his earlier disapproval of her treacherous behaviour.

'Do we know if anyone came to visit Judith in the days before her death?'

James forced himself to focus on Marguerite's question. Raf exchanged a glance with Arnhem, then answered. 'The Chief Inspector did put that to the nurse. She said she thought there had been someone yesterday, when Judith was still in the main ward. She didn't know his name. All she said was that he was dark and black-hatted.'

'It was Bernfeld.' Arnhem's voice was barely audible.

'Bernfeld?'

'Yes.' The man's eyes were as sombre as a tomb. 'He more or less told me he was going to see her when he came by the other day.'

'What passed between you?'

'Family matters.' Arnhem was curt.

'Look here, Arnhem. There's no reason to be difficult,' Raf burst out. 'We're trying to help.'

A tense silence settled on the room. His back to them, Arnhem stared at the massed ranks of books. When his voice came at last, it felt too sudden.

'Bernfeld bears me a grudge. Rightly. Quite rightly. I owe him a debt I still can't repay.' The features he turned on them were desolate.

'When Bernfeld came by, I railed at him. I asked him how a man of honour could go and vent his rage on an innocent woman, torture her with a debt she didn't even know about. Why hadn't he come to me for repayment? Why go to Rachel? He railed right back. He accused me of setting the police on him.' Arnhem threw James a hostile look.

'But strangely it was against Rachel that his principal ire was directed. After all these years he still hadn't been able to swallow her dismissal of him. His pride had been shattered. Only she could make that good. And he had initially wanted vengeance as much as money. He told me so bluntly.

'So he wanted her dead, I shouted at him. No, no, not dead, he replied. Certainly not dead. Because now he was doubly lost. Through his own fault. Now no one could make good the wound or the debt. He might as well be dead too.' Arnhem emptied his glass.

'But what about Judith?' James asked.

'I'm coming to that. I'm coming to that.' Arnhem ran his hand through his tangled mane. 'We screamed at each other. We said things we shouldn't have said. You know, once Bernfeld used to respect me, honour me. When my wife was still alive. We were an example to him. That's why . . .' He paused, then raced on. 'We were like two madmen that night. And then in the midst of the recriminations and the insults, he suddenly asked me with a kind of tortured sadness whether Rachel had ever talked about him in all those years.

'It was as if he was begging for some form of recognition. But I couldn't give it to him. I told him that Rachel didn't talk to me about such things. They were women's matters. If she talked to anyone, maybe she talked to Judith. He remembered Judith. He started to ask me all kinds of questions about her and I told him honestly that she was ill by turns, but often quite sensible. He grew strangely quiet then and the idea lodged itself in his mind . . . maybe it came from me . . . that perhaps he and Judith could live together. Perhaps they could do each other good. Judith used to be pretty, you know. She was the beauty. Anyhow the idea came. Like a joint fantasy. Which is why I suspect it was Bernfeld who went to see her.'

Arnhem looked at them each in turn, as if waiting for judgement.

'What are you saying, Arnhem? We have to alert the Inspector. Bernfeld needs locking up. You're telling us that the man was a twice-rejected suitor, who took out his viciousness first on Olympe and then on your poor mad daughter.'

Raf didn't pull his punches. Marguerite shushed him with a look and James muttered that Durand had already put a man on Bernfeld's tail.

'No. No. You misunderstand,' Arnhem wailed. 'It's my fault. All my fault. What I'm saying is that Bernfeld upset Judith with his proposals, which were also mine. Upset, she was often wild, so they put her in isolation. And that's what facilitated her death.'

'Yet Raf said earlier you had discounted suicide.' Marguerite spoke softly.

Arnhem stiffened. 'I don't know. From what I've said . . . maybe. But I still don't think so. That hook was so high. How could little Judith, a Judith who was sleepy from all the chloroform they give her to quieten her down, have managed it?' He shook his head. 'No, no. I feel there must have been something else. Someone else.' His shoulders suddenly slumped, his tone grew raw. 'Though I agree that poor Judith had little left to live for. Very little.'

His face told them he felt much the same about himself.

They all fell into a heavy silence. James broke it by addressing a direct question to Marguerite for the first time. 'Have you learned anything, Marguerite? Anything from that intern you spoke of? Anything from Docteur Vaillant?'

She didn't answer him. She was staring at Arnhem. 'Monsieur Arnhem, may I remind you that Dreyfus struggled through all those years on Devil's Island, struggled while much of France turned its back on him. Take him as your example.' Her manner was terse.

'He didn't lose his children. Only his public honour. That is perhaps expendable.'

'You still have two. That's two more than many of the rest of us. You must garner your strength for them. Remember, Monsieur Arnhem, suicide is ruthless. It murders us all. That's why we find it so hard to accept, why we refuse to believe that either Olympe or even Judith wished that for us. Your remaining little ones could not bear that legacy from you. I suggest you go to them now. If I remember my own childhood correctly, I suspect that Juliette is lying awake in bed waiting to sleep until she has made sure of your presence.'

Arnhem rose slowly. 'You are probably right, Madame.'

'She is right,' James underlined. He was once again struck by Marguerite's depths. He wished that everything about her demeanour didn't suggest that she now considered him an enemy.

'Pierre will show you to your room. Try to sleep well, despite your grief, Monsieur Arnhem. We all need your wits and your fitness.'

No sooner had Arnhem left them, then Marguerite turned the full force of her gaze on James. She didn't speak for a moment. She was reading his features as if they were runes replete with secret significance. At last she shook her head slightly, like an animal emerging from the sea.

'To answer your question, James, I don't know. Yes, my friend's son has reported back to me, but his researches are still cursory. He doesn't have much time to go through files, and can only do so when it seems appropriate to the business he's conducting. I asked him to check not only Dr. Vaillant's wards for the last two years, but another comparable one. Otherwise we have no way of knowing whether the deaths in one are out of proportion with the ordinary course of things. People die in hospitals. That is a given.'

'What did he find?'

'So far he found that there were five more deaths in Vaillant's wards than in the other one. But that is not a significant enough number, I think, to make a difference.'

'Was there a discrepancy in ages?'

'Not a significant one according to my intern. The deaths are largely of people over fifty, though there are a few in their twenties and thirties — all women.' She shifted her position, rearranged her skirts reflectively.

'And what about the proportions of Jews?'

'Again, in percentage terms these tally with the numbers of inmates.'

'So Judith was wrong.'

Marguerite shifted again, her agitation now more evident. 'I'm not sure. Not now. Not in the light of her own death.'

'Out with it, Marguerite.' Raf's impatience hovered on impoliteness.

'I'm just trying to put it all together. It's all happened in the last four months. Three young women, two of them self-confessedly Jewish, have died. Two of them had only recently been admitted, the third had been there longer. She wasn't in Vaillant's ward. In any event, all three were listed as suicides. Two had hanged themselves. One had somehow self-administered a killing dose of morphine.' Marguerite paused. 'One was named in the files as a prostitute; the other two as milliners, which could be a euphemism.'

Raf bolted from his chair. 'Come on, Jim. There's no time to lose.

We can just about make that appointment.'

'What appointment?' Marguerite, too, rose.

'Nothing. Nothing. We have to meet Touquet. He has some information. We need to move quickly.'

'Hold on Raf. I want to hear Marguerite's impression of Docteur Vaillant. We have to think this through.'

Marguerite had put a staying hand on Raf's arm. Like a nervous colt, he shook her off. She surveyed him for a moment, then turned to James. 'Docteur Vaillant is a gentleman. His views may not be mine, but I don't really believe he would do anything underhanded. Not deliberately. Coincidentally, since before you came that wasn't the first thing on my mind, I asked him about suicides at the Salpêtrière and he shook his head in something like mourning and echoed Monsieur Arnhem. Many of these people haven't much to live for, he said. And he added that their minds are confused. Noisy. They want to shut out the noise. The description made me feel rather sympathetic towards him.'

'Come on, Jim. It's not Vaillant we're interested in. It's that bastard Comte. That's whom Olympe went to see. She must have been on to him. Maybe she even knew the girls.'

'What are you talking about, Raf?'

'I can't explain now, Marguerite. Can we borrow Martin?'

She shook her head.

'Why not? Oh no. No, you can't. Not this time. It's too dangerous. And you have the children here. It's absolutely forbidden.' He threw James an apprehensive glance and James suddenly understood. Raf had inferred that Marguerite was about to don one of her male disguises and follow them.

'Let's go, Jim.'

'Come back. Come back as soon as you've done,' Marguerite called after them as they raced down the silent hall.

TWENTY-TWO

Heavy rain had turned to persistent drizzle. Mist drifted from the pavements, curled from the corners of the streets, hovered yellow round lamp-posts. The weather and the lateness of the hour had all but emptied the city of life. Like luminous disembodied parts, the gloves and batons of two uniformed gendarmes rose from the dark before their strolling owners.

The carriage moved swiftly, bumping and tossing them so that the glistening dome of the Opera tumbled askew as they took a sharp turn into the boulevards where late-night revellers still gathered despite the weather. Here the lamps of the music halls were alight and the garish colour of the posters leapt and danced. A woman laughed, flashing brilliant teeth as she lowered her umbrella and climbed into a cab.

His thoughts clotted with everything that had occurred in these last hours, James prodded himself from reverie. 'I still don't know what this mysterious rendez-vous with Touquet is about.'

Raf flinched. He, too, had been immersed in his private world. 'It's not exactly a rendez-vous. Touquet may not be there. But he's had information that Caro will definitely be and perhaps Dr. Comte. Apparently both frequent the place on a fairly regular basis.'

'Where is there?'

'It's known as the "Jaune". It's a brothel. They specialize in foreign women. Touquet reckons at least four of the girls belong to Caro. Maybe more. And Saturday is the big night.'

'Why may Touquet not be there?'

'Well, he may be. But we're not supposed to recognize each other. Caro has found out who he is and he doesn't like it.'

'Judging from the other night, he doesn't like me much either.' James fingered his jaw.

'But you have the advantage of being a paying client. Not to mention an American one.' Raf winked.

'I'm not in the mood for . . .' James couldn't bring the word out.

'You don't have to. It's probably best if we go in separately and just hang around downstairs, keep our ears peeled. And then when Caro leaves, we follow him and corner him alone. Two of us should be able to beat some information out of him.'

'What information exactly are we looking for?'

'Come on, Jim. Wake up. We're going to ask him about Olympe.'

'And you think he's just going to tell us. Say, "hello friends, it was me. I did it." Just like that.'

'Don't be ridiculous, Jim.' Raf shook his fist. 'We're going to persuade him.'

'And then what?'

'Let's see how it goes. We'll play it by ear. If we get what I think we're going to get, we drag him kicking and screaming to the nearest Commissariat.'

'I don't know, Raf. The man's not exactly a midget, nor compliant. I think we listen and report back to Durand.'

'Who'll procrastinate and procrastinate until the villain moves down to Marseilles and out of his jurisdiction.'

'And what if he's with someone? What if he's with Comte, who knows us well enough?'

'We'll play it by ear. Just keep yours attuned.'

They had entered a warren of streets so narrow that the houses seemed to tilt and meet overhead, blocking the sky. The carriage inched along, as if the cobbles themselves had grown precarious. A woman with a mass of blonde curls stepped out from the darkened recess of a door. Her tongue played over scarlet lips. She beckoned with a salacious gesture. A few moments later, the mime was repeated, though this time the woman lifted her skirts to reveal a swathe of leg. A man emerged to drag her into the shadows.

At the next turn, the carriage stopped. Raf leapt out with bounding alacrity, his eagerness for action barely containable. James noted that his fists were clenched again.

He paid the driver, waited until Raf was in, then followed more slowly.

The entrance to the brothel took him through a dank hall. Red wallpaper suppurated moisture like drops of blood. As the inner door opened, the mingled smell of warm flesh and absinthe and cheap perfume enveloped him. It brought with it an image of Eugénie, so very young and so very frightened, as she had stammered out her sorry tale. Rage kindled inside him, banishing hesitation. Caro was a brute.

This was a bigger salon than that at the Monpiquet. From somewhere came the brash sound of an accordion, but he couldn't see the musician for the teeming crowd. They danced, they sang, they drank, they sprawled on sofas and chairs and on corners of the floor, bodies clasped so closely together that it obliterated the need for bedrooms. There was no attempt at refinement here. The men were in shirtsleeves. Half of them looked like gangsters. The women's eyes were darkly kohled, their mouths crimson slashes, their clothes little more than bustiers with a gauze of skirt advertising an assortment of shapes.

A burly, bearded man in a striped fisherman's shirt extracted a sum from him almost before he had crossed the threshold. When James tipped him, he raised an eyebrow in mock astonishment.

'Les garçons, alors? C'est par là.' He pointed to a door behind him and placing his hand on his hip, swivelled it like some frenzied bee.

Shocked, James shook his head vigorously. No, no. He certainly didn't want boys.

'This way then.' He jostled James through to a sofa, whisking off a clinging couple in the process. He whistled between his teeth and in a moment, a brunette with the plump features of a sleepy cat curled beside

James. The cheek she turned to his displayed a livid scar.

James took a deep breath and looked round him. Raf was already dancing with a coltish redhead. Her features were voracious. As she pecked at his neck, she left the trace of her lips on his collar. He swung her round towards James and mouthed, 'Signal, when you spot him.'

James tugged his partner onto the dance floor. It was a way of moving and observing. The place was too noisy for speech. The girl pressed close to him and seemed to want to guide him towards a door through which couples came and went with surprising speed. James lifted her in the opposite direction. Her hair tickled his face like feathers. When she looked up at him, her pupils were unnaturally large and bright, fixed in an unseeing stare. With a start, he thought of Ellie. He tucked her face down on his chest.

He could see the accordion-player now, an elf of a man with a cigarette dangling from his lips, the ash precariously poised. At either side of him stood a woman. They were mirror images of each other; skinny tousle-haired urchins with veined necks, their breasts on display like apples on platters. They were singing, their voices raucous. The ditty must have been salacious, because they moved in obscene pantomime.

He caught a refrain.

'Pierreuses,
Trotteuses,
Les ch'veux frisés,
Les seins blasés,
Les pieds usés.'

Something about streetwalkers with tired breasts and tired feet, James translated for himself and simultaneously caught a glimpse of Touquet's sallow profile in the shadow of a pillar. He abandoned his partner and made his way towards Touquet. Before he could reach him, another woman danced herself into his arms. This one had a Mediterranean complexion and a frizz of dark hair. She looked no more than fifteen. Around her neck was the telltale charm. He asked her name.

'Manou,' she murmured.

Her eyes, too, were dilated, oddly luminous.

'Excuse me, Manou. I must talk with someone.'

She clung to him and he realized her feet were unsteady. He propped her gently on the arm of a sofa and hastened towards Touquet. Raf reached him at the same time.

'Damn it. He's gone. Vanished about ten minutes ago.' Touquet was visibly agitated. 'He came downstairs, had a word with Madame Boule and then he just upped and disappeared. Must have slipped out. And Comte never turned up, as far as I know.'

'Let's go after him. He can't have got far.' Raf was already making for the door.

Touquet gave James a sceptical look, and then shrugged. 'Okay, we've got nothing to lose. You're late.'

'It was unavoidable.'

'Meet you outside. We should stagger our departure. There are eyes and tongues in these walls.' Touquet veered off towards the singers.

Before James could reach the door, a great tub of a woman in a strawberry red dress accosted him. Something about her jowly face reminded him ominously of Mrs. Elliott. He found himself bowing.

'Ah, Monsieur,' she preened. 'Not leaving us already, are you? I know, I know, my best girls are upstairs. But if you wait just a little longer, I'm sure . . .'

'On another occasion, Madame. Thank you.' He bowed himself out, kept his hands on the latch behind him, to make sure it didn't move. As he stood there for a moment the door diagonally opposite him opened and a thin, dapper, top-hatted man stepped out. He lifted his hat to James ceremoniously. Behind him, James saw whorls of cigarette smoke, strange, lithe creatures moving as if in a cloud, their eyes brightly outlined, their cheeks rouged, their gestures feminine though they wore trousers. He steadied himself. The top-hatted gent tweaked his moustache and pointed his walking stick invitingly through the door.

James shook his head and raced down the darkened corridor. Marguerite came into his mind. Marguerite and the husband she and Olympe had blackmailed into departure. Emotions warred within him.

Disgust and pity and over it all a sense of awe, as if he had come across a mysterious, uncharted island, filled with a multiplicity of life forms which hadn't yet found their way into public classification systems. Yet these were secretly known to many of the people he had met here and Olympe ran like a scarlet ribbon between them, linking them all.

'Jim.' Raf's voice nudged him from his thoughts. Nudged the top-hatted man behind him, too. They both turned to see Raf leaning against the corner lamp-post. The man gave James a knowing smile and with a nod took off in the opposite direction, his walking stick tapping out a desultory rhythm on the wet pavement.

'What took you so long? Good, here's Touquet at last. Which way, Touquet?'

Touquet shrugged. 'We could try Renard's. It's not far. And he apparently goes there, too, from time to time. There's a short-cut through the back here.'

Touquet cut into a narrow alleyway. But for the glimmer of a light from an upper window, the lane was blacker than the night, the buildings on either side weighing in on them like looming ramparts. They walked in single file over uneven cobble stones, slippery from the rain. A rat slithered out of a gutter and ran between them. From somewhere a dog barked. They didn't speak. The atmosphere weighed on them, far heavier than the warm, curling mist.

They had arrived at some sort of tiny square or courtyard, a stone figurine at its midst. Touquet led them across it and then to the right where they plunged into another dingy alley. When they reached the next corner, a scream pierced the silence. It hurtled through the lane like a banshee, ricocheting off the stone walls, gathering an echoing force as it went. They stopped in their tracks. A thud followed, like a sack hitting stone and then the sound of running footsteps, a clacking on cobbles which reverberated through the canyon of the buildings.

'Come on,' Raf roused them. He was already dashing in the direction of the sound. They raced after him, all but colliding with his motionless form in the next lane.

James's foot touched something soft, but inert. He looked down, felt as much as saw an ungainly bundle. Old clothes, heaped on the ground. Raf was kneeling.

'Touquet, get the police. Quick,' he lashed out.

'Where? Why?'

'It's a body, you idiot. Where's that brothel of yours?'

'At the next corner.'

'Well, get over there. Bring a lantern back with you.' He shouted after him.

From a window above them, a light flickered. A curtain had been pushed back. Through the shadows, James made out a shape. 'Venez,' he shouted and waved. 'Bring a lamp.' He repeated his injunction.

'Jesus, Jim. This is just what we needed.'

'Is he alive?' He kneeled to take hold of a cold, dank wrist. 'There's still a pulse. Faint though. Should we turn him over?'

'I don't know, Jim. The guy needs a doctor. Au secours! Un médecin!' Raf yelled at the top of his lungs.

Light suddenly illuminated them. A man, a boy really, with tousled hair and sleepy eyes was holding a lantern above them.

'Bring it closer,' Raf ordered. He gestured to James and together they slowly turned the body over.

The man's suit and waistcoat were rumpled, but it was a good enough suit and the shirt was white, except for the red stain which crept up its midriff. At the dark centre of the stain, the shirt was slashed. So was the flesh beneath. Blood oozed from the man's belly in a pumping rivulet.

'Jesus!' Raf repeated. 'What do we do?'

'Try and bind it, I guess.' In a split second, James had his jacket off and was unbuttoning his shirt. As he did so, he noticed a small crowd had gathered round them. A second lamp had arrived. A woman was gesturing at him. 'Here, here. This will be better.' She was tugging at her petticoat. 'It's bigger. He's a large man.'

She handed Raf the garment and knelt down beside him. 'Prop his head up slightly. Just in case. And untie his collar.'

Someone passed them a rolled-up jacket and James moved to tuck it under the man's head. It was only then that he became aware of the man's face. The pucker at the brow, the stubby nose, the corpulent cheeks, blotched with dusky blue now. He let out a noisy breath. 'Raf, Raf! It's Dr. Comte.'

'What?'

'Yes, it's him.'

'Police. Make way. Make way.' A stentorian voice reached them. The crowd moved aside and in a moment a young, lavishly moustachioed man in a bowler hat and ordinary clothes was at their side.

'You.' Raf scowled, and then grinned. 'Well, for once I have to say I'm happy to see you. We need an ambulance here. And you'd better try and get someone to wake Chief Inspector Durand. This man here isn't quite a corpse yet and his name is Henri Comte. Dr. Henri Comte. Meet my shadow, Jim.'

After that, everything happened quickly. Touquet reappeared with a gaggle behind him. The narrow lane heaved with people and voices. A baby's cries echoed through the air. Someone proffered brandy. Three men arrived with a stretcher, closely followed by two caped constables. Dr. Comte was heaved on to the stretcher and borne aloft to the end of the lane where a hospital vehicle waited.

'We should go with him,' James said.

'You're right.'

No sooner had they begun to move forward, than they were surrounded by the three police officers.

'You're under arrest.' The moustachioed plainclothesman announced.

'Arrest. Don't be ridiculous.' Raf tried to push him aside.

'This woman here saw you both kneeling over the body.'

'Of course she did,' James said evenly. 'We found the man here, officer. We heard a scream and came running. We put out the alert.'

'You'll come quietly.' The man seemed a little confused, but he wasn't about to let them go. 'You can repeat that at headquarters.'

'Search us for the weapon, you oaf. If you find a knife on us, then you've got a reason to take us in. The man was stabbed, remember. If you don't and you still insist, you can bet your life, you're going to be back in uniform. And in a hurry. Touquet, get over here.' Raf waved to his friend.

'We're going to headquarters,' the officer repeated stubbornly.

'It looks like headquarters is coming here,' James murmured. Over the heads of the lingering onlookers, he glimpsed Chief Inspector Durand's staunch form. He was coming from the end of the lane opposite to the ambulance. James waved him forward.

'I've rarely been so pleased to see you, Chief Inspector.'

'Indeed. What's happened, Flammard?' Durand addressed his officer, who quickly relayed his view of events.

'That's all nonsense, Chief Inspector,' Raf burst out. 'The Nortons of Boston are hardly in the habit of stabbing doctors in alleyways.'

'So what exactly were you doing here? I don't relish being woken in the middle of the night just because you're out playing, Monsieur.' Durand peered up at Raf. His face was bullish.

'Let me handle this, Raf.' James took the Chief Inspector aside and explained briefly, stressing that they really should all accompany Comte to the hospital. He might have some valuable information, if he was in any state to be questioned.

The Chief Inspector rubbed his chin reflectively. 'A knife wound, you say?'

James nodded.

The youth who had first held the lantern came up to them. 'I saw it all, Monsieur. Well, most of it. The scream woke me. I live up there.' He pointed. 'I heard footsteps running in that direction. And then more of them coming from over there.' As he pointed again, James saw a broad-shouldered, capped form emerge from the shadows.

For a second, the message his eyes conveyed lacked distinctness. Then he bounded forward, using his shoulders as a ram to clear a space through the crowd. He charged the man with his head, forced him against the wall. Thick fingers gripped his arms, pressed him backwards. This time he landed a fist square into the man's chest. There was a return punch at his jaw, a kick at his groin.

Like a flash of forked lightning, he saw the glint of steel. 'Caro,' he shouted, ducking as the knife lunged at him. 'Caro,' he screamed again and felt stone scrape against his back, his head.

'Bastard,' Raf was yelling. 'Pimp.'

James heard steel clatter on cobbles. And then he heard nothing more.

TWENTY-THREE

He was back on shipboard. He could feel the heave and toss of the waves, a gentle rhythmic swaying which wasn't unpleasant at night, except that it tugged at his innards and his head felt too heavy to lift. Then came the mutter of indistinct voices. An alien smell attacked his nostrils. He wondered distantly if some waste pipe had burst, wondered too at the ache which cut through him, as regular as the ship's sway. But he was too tired to pay it heed. Sleep carried him away.

The next thing he knew, cold hands were prodding his chest. He flinched away. Steel weighed on his eyelids. With a grunt, he forced them open. A world he didn't recognize swam slowly but not fully into focus, so that he thought he must be dreaming. A white-coated man stood over him, next to him a vaguely familiar but unrecognizable figure with a pointed weasel-face and drooping moustache. Beyond them, a sea of beds floated in murky light.

The white-coated man's voice was brisk, but oddly maternal. 'It's only a surface wound. But your head must be hurting. I've given you something for the pain. Best to sleep.'

James's eyelids obeyed the injunction with no prodding from his will.

When he woke again, pale sunshine streamed through windows, making dust motes dance. Raf was sitting by his side, anxiety etched on his handsome face.

'There you are, Jim. I was beginning to think we'd lost you for another day. How're you feeling, old man?'

James considered. 'Rather like an old man. Where am I?

Raf chuckled. 'Well, the first thing to say is that you're something of a hero. But like all heroes you needed just a little wound to make us believe it. So Marcel Caro provided one. He by the way is safely behind bars. Even our favourite Chief Inspector couldn't doubt the evidence of his own eyes. An attack with a five-inch blade on an American citizen may not be murder, but it sure is an attempt. And the attempt has landed you in this not altogether pleasant hospital. We'll have you out soon enough, Jim. The doctor says as long as you're not seeing double and you can walk, you'll be fine. Though you'll probably be groggy for a bit. It's your head that got the worse of it. That's what knocked you out. He gave you a soothing concoction.'

James eased himself up on the uncomfortable roll of a bolster, battled with dizziness. He felt quite the opposite of a hero, whatever that was, though it probably had to do with bounding bewilderment and a creaking stiffness in the joints. He closed his eyes again for a moment. The dash through the wet streets, the body, came back through a fuzzy distance.

'Comte.' His mind sprang to attention. 'What's happened to Dr. Comte?'

'I'm afraid he hasn't fared quite as well as you have.'

'You mean he's dead?' James lurched forward, gasped at the pain.

'Take it easy, Jim. Your wound's not mortal, but it'll take a few days to heal. No, Comte's not dead, though I suspect Marcel Caro hoped he would be, which is why he came back to check on the state of his wished-for cadaver. He wasn't expecting quite such a crowd to happen upon the scene so very quickly.'

'You mean Caro tried to kill Dr. Comte?' Confusion whipped through James, thicker than egg yolk. 'I thought . . . I thought they were a team.'

Raf shrugged. 'I'm pretty sure the knife that made that little indentation in you was the one that did the damage on Comte. For once, the Chief Inspector seems to agree. Let's hope he's got Caro talking. Touquet and I briefed him, a little too hastily in the midst of all this, about the list of dead girls. Let's hope that Comte wakes up to talk. He lost a lot of blood.'

A nurse appeared bearing a tray. A bowl filled with some grey-coloured gruel sat on it. It looked as appetizing as sewage. James shook his head. A hammer seemed to have taken up residence inside it. He pushed the tray aside with as polite a 'non' as he could muster.

'Was that breakfast?'

'Lunch, I suspect.'

'So I've been out for what . . . a day and a night?'

Raf nodded.

There was a moan from the next bed. A man tossed and writhed. He howled out a name. A nurse came running.

James winced. He didn't want to be here. There was so much to do. He placed his feet gingerly on the floor, tested their strength.

Raf held on to him, his expression worried. 'I'm not sure you're quite strong enough yet.'

'I'm not going to get any stronger here.' He gritted his teeth against the pain at his side. Stitches, he imagined. He hadn't dared to check yet.

'Look, Jim. I'm going to find that doctor, take his advice. You just wait.'

'Find out about Comte, while you're at it.' James inched back onto the bed. 'I've been wrong, Raf. All my suppositions were wrong. Marcel Caro and Comte couldn't have been in cahoots. I don't know where that leaves us. I really don't.' His spirits felt as flat as a withered prairie at the end of August. 'Just when I sensed we were getting somewhere.'

It was Raf's turn to be patient and philosophical. 'Let's wait and hear what the Chief Inspector has to report. There are things going on here that we're not seeing clearly. But I sense we're on the right track, Jim. I really do. Caro and Comte were probably in on the trafficking together. And the murders. Then they fell out over something. Isn't that always the way with villains?' With a clumsy show of tenderness, he patted his brother on the shoulder and hurried down the aisle between the crowded rows of beds.

James wasn't discharged until dusk had fallen. Raf had brought him a fresh shirt, a suit, all the necessary garments. He told him he had chucked his other clothes. No point in being reminded of rents and slashes and blood.

Despite protests, James suffered the humiliation of being wheeled to the hospital gates in a chair. It made him think of Ellie and he asked Raf if he had checked in on her.

'I'll send her a bleu as soon as I've dropped you at Marguerite's. We won't worry her, just let her know that you've had a little accident and need a few day's mending.' Raf gave him a swift assessing look as he helped him into the carriage. 'You're too good at guilt, Jim. She'll be all right. We have other things to think about.'

'Why Marguerite's? I don't want to go there.' James settled testily into leather and realized simultaneously that it was the Landois carriage they were in. 'I'd really rather be on my own.'

'You need a little looking after, Jim. And Marguerite's got the staff. Besides, she insisted.'

The carriage lurched into motion. James flinched, held himself rigid. He was grateful for the traffic which kept their progress along the boulevards slow. The evening was clear, the sky a deep, darkening blue and after the persistent rain, strollers were making the most of the weather. Everything looked a little unreal to him, even the most mundane things, as if he had been away for a long time. At the edge of the Jardin du Luxembourg, the chestnuts swayed with a sumptuous motion. The smell of hot, apple-filled beignets wafted through the window from the vendor's kiosque with a sweetness that made his mouth water. A cyclist in a peaked cap and goggles raced past them with supernatural grace. A woman in nurse's black bent over a large pram and shook a wooden rattle. Her dimpled smile had an extraordinary delicacy.

'You haven't taken against Marguerite, have you Jim?' Raf was surveying him. 'I realize she might be a little, well, let's say sophisticated for your tastes. But she's a good soul. You can trust me on that, if nothing else. She's a brick, really.' Raf's voice carried the ring of earnest passion. 'She's helped me more than I can tell you.'

James attempted a chuckle. 'I have no doubts at all on that score. It's just that I'm not feeling quite up to such stimulating company.'

'I think you'd find trying to get to the Grand rather more stimulating. The boulevard's been cordoned off. A bomb exploded somewhere near there last night. Anarchists, I imagine. I had a prowl when I went back for your clothes. I should be covering it. I may go and have another ferret round once I've dropped you. But I'll make sure to tell Marguerite all you want is rest.'

Rest of a kind was what James got. He didn't lay eyes on Marguerite. Pierre accompanied him to the room he had stayed in the previous week, told him a light supper would soon be brought up and that the doctor would be visiting first thing in the morning. Then he was left to his own devices. He sipped a little of the hot broth, nibbled at the chicken and dozed. He dozed through the night, his dreams galloping in reckless directions, taking him down treacherous streets where blood ran in the sewers like so much rain water. Looming giants hurled knives at him and he caught them and hurled them back only to wake, bathed in perspiration.

When his eyes closed again, he was on a rickety barge in wintry waters. Something thudded against the stern and he raced towards the sound, chased by a grotesque woman with a gap-toothed grin. She got there first and with an icy chuckle heaved a body from the waters, a beautiful girl, weeds dangling from her hair like tresses. A sheet floated behind her. It trailed from her neck which was arched in an odd position, but her eyes were open and they wept giant tears. It was a waif's face. Eugénie. All around her now stood a circle of onlookers — a woman in a top hat like a circus ringmaster, a frail creature with rouged cheekbones and gnarled skeletal fingers which tapped the arms of a wheelchair, a bearded, wild-eyed figure, with outstretched hands and a soundless wail of a mouth. There was a stout bearded man, too, in a white coat, a malevolent smile on his face as he reached for a syringe, but he fell into the waters and they closed round him in a whirlpool.

He started awake. His throat was parched. He reached for the glass by his bedside and drank noisily. Then he was asleep again. A woman lay at his side. He stroked her hair. It was crinkly and rough, but as he stroked, it turned silken. Maisie, he whispered, but she turned to dust in his hands and from somewhere a babe cried. Then he was standing in the dock in a court-room. A tricolour fluttered above a moustachioed judge in black robes and a strange, round hat. The judge consulted the stern matriarch at his side. She had the features of his mother, but they spoke whispered French and in unison they pointed a finger at him and passed sentence. A stabbing pain rent his chest. Feet marched towards him over wooden floors. 'Monsieur Norton. Monsieur Norton.'

It took James a long moment to recognize Pierre's voice. 'Excuse me, Monsieur, but Docteur Blanchard has arrived.'

Pierre waved through the maid with a tray. 'I'll have him hold on for a few moments, while Monsieur has his coffee.'

'Thank you, Pierre.'

The doctor, when he came, was gentle, but thorough. He checked his pulse, shone a light into his eyes, examined the back of his head, dabbed at it with some stinging lotion, then washed and changed his dressing. For the first time, James looked down at his chest and saw a sizeable welt of mottled blue and yellow, the puckered skin at its centre held together in ugly leather notches. He averted his gaze. The doctor tsked beneath his breath, wound gauze round him, counselled rest, and said he would be back the following morning.

James lay there, sipping coffee, crumbling bits of brioche and feeling sorry for himself. At last, with a grunt of impatience, he got up. He gazed out the window. The sky was blue, laced with the fluff of clouds. He made several turns of the room, checking his balance. He was fine, he determined. Within minutes, he had his clothes on. Quietly he made his way downstairs.

From the orangerie came the sounds of a familiar sonata. Marguerite must be at the piano. There was a pause and a child's high clear voice rose from the room. Juliette. He recognized her at once and faltered, drawn by the thought of a morning in such inviting company. Then, with quick decision, he continued on his original course. He chose to walk the distance rather than risk the bumps and jolts of a cab. The slow but steady progress also helped to chase the clouds from his mind.

The Quai des Orfèvres had the dusty gloom and rancorous commotion of a headquarters of disaster. Uniformed officers jostled and prodded unwilling suspects. Villains shouted and cursed. Plaintive women, shoulders hunched and eyes lowered, huddled on benches. Self-important police clerks extracted requests or charges and noted them with a laborious slowness calculated to intimidate.

James's terse demand for the location of Chief Inspector Durand's office was met only with narrowed eyes and an order to wait. He waited. He repeated his request, this time with an emphasis on the fact that he had an appointment. He waited some more. The scene he had forsaken in Marguerite's orangerie grew more inviting with each passing minute. At last, with a surge of anger, he shouted at the delaying official, only to be met with an innocent gaze and a pointing finger. Chief Inspector Durand had just come in. James turned to see him hurrying across the hall.

'Chief Inspector.' James hailed him.

Durand gave him the full benefit of his surprise. 'Up already, Monsieur Norton? Good, good.' His expression belied his words. The man looked exhausted. His eyes bulged, his cheeks were sallow, his tie was askew as if he had been tugging at it for need of air.

'Can we go somewhere to talk?'

'Talk, talk, of course.' The Chief Inspector seemed distracted, but as he ushered him up stairs and along a corridor, he chuckled sardonically. 'If only you were a little the worse for wear, Monsieur Norton, the case against Marcel Caro would be that much stronger.'

'What are you talking about? You can throw the book at Caro. Two attempted murders. Suspicion of several successful ones. Not to mention trafficking and pimping. Come on, Chief Inspector. You hardly need my dead body for evidence.'

'Calm yourself, Monsieur. Of course, we can hold Caro. But as for the trial, the only thing we've got is his assault on you, which he claims is self-defence. You went for him first. You're a lawyer, Monsieur Norton. You understand the difficulty.'

Durand waved him through into a not-insubstantial office. James was astonished at its aspect. The papers on the mahogany desk were stacked with a fanatic's precision. Pens and a bronze inkwell stood next to a vase of perfect flesh-pink roses arranged with a woman's eye. There were prints and drawings on the walls which displayed a collector's refined taste. Even the leaves of the plane trees outside seemed to have been arranged for effect.

Durand pointed to a comfortable armchair. 'Except for the assault on you, we have no witnesses. No proof.' He shrugged. 'But we can go and see Maître Chardin later. For your deposition.'

James didn't sit. He stared at Durand in disbelief. 'I don't understand you, Chief Inspector. Either this attack has addled my brain or there's something wrong with your interrogation techniques. I suggest we go and interview Caro together right now.'

Durand shook his head. 'The vice squad officers are with him.'

James examined him closely. He thought of Touquet's warnings about the corruption in the morality police. Caro would inevitably have old friends in their ranks, let alone new ones who were probably extracting not a little material benefit from his scabrous activities. 'Are they the problem?'

Durand's only answer was to finger his lavish moustache reflectively. 'You should sit down, Monsieur Norton. All this agitation can't be good for you.'

'Waiting isn't good for me either. Or for anyone else. Is the problem with Caro's friends in the vice squad?'

Durand shrugged. 'We'll see, we'll see. Never forget, Monsieur Norton, that the vice squad is a useful tool of public order. These officers are right in the thick of the criminal world. They see things in those brothels, on the streets. They hear things . . . about the plans of anarchists and royalists and any variety of agents of public disorder. Politicians are, how shall I say it, "attached" to them.'

'And they line their pockets. I worry, Chief Inspector. I worry about those young women trapped in this labyrinth of corruption. They have nowhere to turn.'

'I worry, too, Monsieur Norton.' Durand was visibly downhearted. 'I worry about the progress of our murder enquiry. It seems to lead only to more deaths.'

It came to James again that he genuinely liked the man. The strategy presented itself to him in a flash. He sat down and looked Durand in the eye. 'We're going to get you a promotion, Chief Inspector. I suspect your new cabinet, not to mention the upstanding Monsieur Waldeck Rousseau, would not be averse to seeing at least one branch of the force demonstrating that its position on the Jewish question is the best of Republican ones.'

'I don't understand you. What are you suggesting, Monsieur Norton?'

'My brother has probably already mentioned much of this to you, but let's take it step by step.' James told him about the prostitutes who wore the Hebrew character on a chain round their necks. The charms came from Caro. A similar charm had been found in the metro shaft where the supposed suicide of the prostitute had taken place. He emphasized that with a little help from their journalist friends, Durand's investigation would take on the aura of a campaign. A police intervention to stop the traffic in Jewish women could not but be popular with the new government and even with a substantial sector of the public. It would be in keeping with Dreyfus's return from Devil's Island and his new trial. It would demonstrate that the police treated all sectors of the population with equal respect. It would also demonstrate that the police, Chief Inspector Durand foremost amongst them, were not afraid of seeking out corruption in their own ranks.

Durand listened with distinct scepticism. 'This is all fine and well, Monsieur Norton. But an investigation deals in facts and witnesses, not vague accusations.'

'I can help you round up some witnesses immediately, Chief Inspector. Trust me. But you may need to persuade them a little — a promise of papers might not come amiss, perhaps even a change of address, a move to some small town where the witnesses are not at the mercy of Caro's henchmen and your morality police. What do you say? No, don't answer me now. Just come with me.'

An hour later, they were outside the Hotel Monpiquet. In the daylight, the building had an innocuous air. It was a slightly shabby edifice, indistinguishable from its neighbours. The door was locked. It took three long rings to rouse a response.

While they waited, Durand questioned him. 'I thought your primary interest was in the death of Olympe Fabre. With the best will in the world, I can't see how any of this helps you.'

'Didn't Raf mention it? Olympe Fabre used to visit this establishment. She had an interest in the girls' welfare. Her sister you should know, after the tragic death of their mother, worked in a similar place for a short while.

One of the women we need to interview here knew both the sisters from that time. And Caro could well be implicated in Olympe's death as well.'

'I see. So that's what your brother's been up to.'

'What we've both been up to.'

Durand threw back his shoulders as the door opened. He held his walking stick like an offensive weapon. 'Police,' he announced to a young aproned woman with heavy-lidded eyes whom James didn't recognize. She stood to nervous attention.

'We wish to see Madame Simone,' he said imitating Durand's tone.

The woman looked from one to the other of them, seemed about to say something, then changed her mind and with a shrug led them in.

The red-upholstered main room was all but deserted. It looked tawdry in the light. Two girls in loosely fitting robes sat by the window palms and played cards. Neither of them was Eugénie.

'Wait here, Messieurs. I'll fetch her.'

'No, no.' James was adamant. He didn't want the tricky Madame Simone to disappear before their eyes. 'We'll come with you.'

'As you please,' she repeated the shrug, her tone sullen.

She led them up the stairs James remembered and then up a further three floors. The last staircase was dusty and uneven and James began to rue his earlier determination. His body ached. The wound felt raw.

Their guide paused before she reached the end of the corridor, pointed at a door, then scuttled away with an anxious glance over her shoulder. 'Don't tell her I brought you,' she whispered.

Durand knocked at the door with his stick. 'Madame Simone,' he called authoritatively.

'I'm not dressed,' a voice grumbled at them.

'Open up. Police.'

'What?'

'You heard me.'

'One moment, please. Just one moment.' The voice was suddenly polite. 'Did Madame Rosa send you?'

Durand grumbled an indeterminate sound and the door opened.

In the gloom Madame Simone looked like a pudding that had escaped its mould. She was wearing some shapeless yellowish garment which matched the pouches beneath her eyes. Her chin careened down her neck. Her mouth had lost its outlines.

'You,' she hissed at James. She collected herself to try a smile at the Chief Inspector who brushed past her into the room. It had the aura of a den in which all the treasures of a lifetime had been stashed. Shawls draped from drawers. Hats with an assortment of smooth and speckled feathers lived their own life in a dingy corner. Cheap beads cascaded from the rim of a mottled dressing-table mirror. A half-open wardrobe poured clothes. The bed was a jumble of greying sheets. Catching his eye, Madame Simone smoothed a limp brocade spread over it. It couldn't obliterate the musty smell.

'My apologies, officer. I had a lie-in this morning.'

'Chief Inspector.' Durand moved to open the windows.

'Chief Inspector. Will you sit?' She hastily cleared two upright chairs and the clutter at the small table. 'There. That's better.' She smiled at the Chief Inspector, studiously avoiding James, though she left the second chair for him and perched herself at the edge of the bed like some outlandish antipodean bird.

'This is a good-size room you have here, Madame Simone,' James heard himself say. 'I guess it comes with long service.'

The woman didn't answer.

'Exactly how long have you worked as the pianist here, Madame?' The Chief Inspector had his notebook out.

'About five years, Monsieur.'

'And before that?'

'Oh here and there,' she was deliberately vague. 'Madame Rosa has been very kind to me. We help each other.'

'Indeed. And you also help a certain Marcel Caro?'

Simone flashed an invidious glance at James. 'I don't know that name, Chief Inspector.'

'Perhaps you know the man in question by a different name. We shall have to take you down to the Quai des Orfèvres to have a look at him.'

The woman's face turned even pastier than before. 'I have so much to do today. Perhaps you could describe the individual to me.'

Durand offered a terse sketch and James reminded her, 'The man we know as Caro came with you to the dauphine when we met.'

'No one came with me. But I think you must be describing Maro. Yes I know Maro a little. Just a little, mind.' A tension had mounted in her body, so that she looked a little less like a blanc-mange. She played with the bangle at her wrist, smiled her co-operation at the Chief Inspector.

'And this Maro,' James said, 'introduces girls to your premises, looks after them in a manner of speaking.'

'I don't know that for certain.'

'You don't know that for certain,' the Chief Inspector mimicked her coyness. 'May I suggest to you in plain language that what you do know for certain is that he's a trafficker and a pimp.'

The woman didn't answer.

'Come now, Madame. We have the man behind bars. And we'll have you behind an equally rigid set in no time.' The Chief Inspector was standing. He moved closer to her, his attitude menacing.

Simone flinched.

'Unless we have your co-operation, Madame, of course. All we need from you is a statement, a signed statement.'

She looked around her wildly, searching for an escape route.

'You have no need to worry,' James murmured. 'Caro or Maro won't be out of prison for some time, if ever.'

'But Madame Ro. . .' she stopped herself, pretended a cough. 'Is that where it ends, Chief Inspector?' she asked in a strangled voice.

'Almost. The statement will have to be repeated in front of the investigating magistrate and perhaps again in court. And, of course, just a small point, you will tell us where this Maro of yours gets his girls.'

'I don't know that,' her voice suddenly boomed.

'But, Madame Simone, don't you remember? You told me very clearly at the café, that these girls, like Eugénie, were far better off here than in the Pale of Settlement or whatever points east, because of the pogroms, because . . .'

'I said nothing of the sort.'

'Funny, I recall . . .' James paced, put on his best thinking face. 'It was when we were talking about your friends, Rachel and Judith Arnhem. Judith is dead, too. Did you know that? Dead like that poor girl who tumbled to her end in the metro shaft. You knew her, too, didn't you? You told me that Olympe, that Rachel had put ideas into her head.'

'Judith dead?' The woman trembled. 'But he couldn't . . .' She started again. 'Maro didn't know Judith,' she said bleakly.

'But he knew Olympe Fabre.'

She covered her face, whimpered. 'I don't know. I don't know anything.'

'I think you had better get dressed, Madame.'

'But . . .'

'No buts. We'll carry on this interview at headquarters. It will throw a different light on things.' Durand patted her shoulder, suddenly amiable. 'There, there, Madame. It's not you we're after. It's that Maro. We need your help, that's all.'

'Eugénie blabbed to you, did she? Did she?' She was shouting at James. 'I knew that girl was no good. As soon as he brought her.'

'Brought her from where?'

She buttoned her lips.

'We'll just wait here and you go behind your pretty screen and you put on some clothes. Some nice clothes. We want to make a good impression on the magistrate.'

'I'm only earning my keep, Chief Inspector. Nothing outside the law. Nothing, I promise you.'

'Of course.' Durand soothed.

James positioned himself at the oozing dresser. There was a jewellery tray on it and his eyes strayed over the contents. He gasped. There, at the bottom of the tray, half buried amidst an assortment of bangles and earrings, lay chains with the telltale Hebrew character.

'Chief Inspector. Over here.' He pointed to the charms.

Durand smiled, and with a finger to his lips, put the chains in his pocket. 'You go and find the other one. I'll meet you downstairs.' They were whispering.

James hesitated. His head was pounding again. 'You'll be gentle with her.'

'Sweet on her, are you?' Durand mocked.

'No, but she's very young.'

'This was your idea, remember. And she's a direct witness to the trafficking. Go on.' Durand's face was suddenly as cheerful as if Waterloo had been won.

James knocked softly at the remembered door on the first floor.

'Tell Madame, I not well. Sick,' a voice called.

James inched open the door. Eugénie was lying in bed, her hair a tangle over the bolster. She sat up, stiffly. 'Not working yet. Not working.' Her eyes were vast in her thin face.

'I just want to talk to you.' James let himself in and closed the door silently behind him.

She drew the sheets up to her chin.

'I need you to come with me, Eugénie. To tell the police what you told me the other night. About how you got here. No, don't be afraid. Afterwards you'll be free. We can find you work, perhaps. Other work.'

'Not police. They send me back. My father . . .' Her face grew contorted. 'He kill me. Maro say. No police.'

'Maro's in jail. Now, get dressed. Please. I promise you'll be all right.' He took some money out of his wallet and placed it on the bed.

She stared from it to him and back again. Then with a shrug, she nodded. 'I bring everything. Not come here again. Promise.'

James nodded, without quite knowing how he would make good his vow, though do so he must, for too many reasons. He turned his back. He could hear the spring of the bed, the sounds of her dressing, the snap of a case. He wondered for a moment what either of the women could tell them about Comte.

'Ready.'

Eugénie was wearing a worn brown serge dress that barely reached her ankles. Her hair was neatly clipped back in a tail. Her face was bare of makeup. She looked like nothing so much as a schoolgirl and he realized she must be wearing the clothes she had arrived in. She smiled at him faintly. 'My own dress. Only my own,' she pointed to a small round bag with a tie at its top. 'Better so.'

As they neared the bottom of the stairs, the Chief Inspector's voice reached them. It was raised high in angry threat. A woman's voice matched it.

Madame Rosa, her black skirts spread like a vulture's threatening wings, was blocking the door, barring the Chief Inspector's progress. He had his arm through Madame Simone's who cowered a little.

'You'll not get away with this Chief Inspector. I run a perfectly legal business and you have no grounds on which to take my right hand with you. None at all. I shall lodge a complaint. My complaints, I should add, find their way to very high places indeed. You may find yourself not only reprimanded but demoted.'

'Which high places are we talking of exactly, Madame?' The Chief Inspector was surly, but for a moment James feared he might give in and wash his hands of the whole business.

'And who's this now? Oh no. No. You don't take Eugénie with you. She owes me . . . she owes me a substantial sum which she hasn't worked off yet.'

'And whom did you pay that sum to, Madame?'

A black look crossed Madame Rosa's face. 'That is not what I meant. There is always an investment in taking on a girl. None of which is your business Chief Inspector. You shall have Commissaire Caille to deal with.'

The Chief Inspector took on his Napoleonic posture, one hand in his jacket, his weight balanced on a single leg, his head held so high that the bowler seemed to metamorphose into a tricorne. 'Indeed, Madame. I begin to quiver already. But I will have to take my chances. A murder enquiry is a serious matter.'

'I'm coming with you.' Darts flew from her eyes and landed on James. 'You!' She scowled. 'I remember you now. I should have trusted my instincts. So very humble. So very gentlemanly. I knew it was all a fraud. Well, I'm coming with you.'

'I don't think that would be wise, Madame. Not now. Not today. For a woman of your delicacy and your contacts, a night behind bars might not prove the pleasantest of experiences.'

'Leave it, Madame Rosa,' Simone intervened. 'And don't worry. The

Chief Inspector has promised me . . . He only wants a simple statement. It will do us no harm.'

'No harm at all, ladies, if the crimes are not yours.'

'This is an honest establishment, Chief Inspector.' Madame Rosa's face turned crimson. Altogether honest. Nor are you to believe a word the young one says. For one thing, she speaks no French. You'll have to get Madame Simone to translate.'

Durand tipped his hat. 'It's kind of you to offer her services, Madame. But I think I may just have an equally reliable translator to hand.'

TWENTY-FOUR

The lower reaches of the police station, which bordered on the Palais de Justice and were connected to it by devious passages, held a subterranean chill. Natural light had never penetrated here. The shadows the lamps cast were long and deformed by the repetitive guillotine of iron bars.

Despite the woollen shawl she had wrapped around herself, Eugénie shivered.

'We won't be long, Mademoiselle. All you have to do is identify the man as the one who met you in Paris and took you to the Hotel Monpiquet. You translate that for me, Arnhem.'

Arnhem clutched his black hat and did as he was told. The roll of the incomprehensible language went on for far longer than Durand's words and James, who trailed behind them, had the impression that Arnhem must be adding a few comforting asides of his own.

There had been a touch of brilliance in the Chief Inspector's sending for Arnhem to act as their translator. The notion hadn't occurred to James. Eugénie had not only relaxed and opened up instantly to relay her ghastly tale, but it had permitted Arnhem and Madame Simone to confront each other. Both James and Durand had been surprised by the fact that Arnhem didn't know the woman who claimed a long friendship with both his daughters. But it made sense. The girls would hardly come running home and recount their friendship with a whore to their father.

But the sight of a grieving Arnhem had nonetheless had an effect on Madame Simone. Perhaps he woke memories of her own father, of a distant family. In any event, she became softer, more tractable. She confessed that all of them at the Monpiquet were afraid of Maro, even Madame Rosa herself, though Simone suspected that their relationship was a long one, and dated back to the days when Rosa was a simple prostitute who had no establishment of her own. Indeed, Simone let slip in one of her more voluble moments, she had speculated that it was Maro who had helped her set up and provided the essential protection.

She had caught herself then and protested that though Maro might be lustful, he had no need to stoop to murder. She was certain he wasn't implicated in Olympe's tragic end. There was no need. He had no reason to fear her. He had too many friends in high places. She repeated that several times. When they pushed her on the death of the girl in the metro shaft, she merely shrugged. Yes, she had been one of Maro's girls, but again he had no need to kill her. She was worth far less to him dead than alive. And he hardly needed to fear exposure from that end. Who would take the word of an illiterate prostitute, a Jew at that, against a former police officer, a man with so many contacts? No it made no sense. The girl had simply done away with herself. And, yes, it had been wrong of Olympe to put ideas into her head. Not everyone had the talent and intelligence of an Olympe. As for Judith, that made even less sense. Maro might have temper outbursts, but he was a practical man.

There was an air of disingenuousness in all Simone's comments, James thought, but they had their own logic — the pragmatic, amoral logic of a woman who had an experience of brutal circumstances, but was yet oddly cloistered from the rest of the world. Caro or Maro, for her, was exactly the grand, the powerful and frightening figure he wished to appear. She could not see beyond the fear he engendered. He hoped that if this episode did nothing else, it would save Eugénie from growing into Simone.

They had reached the cell Durand had had the man transferred to. There were no bars here, but a solid wooden door with a peephole at the top, so that Eugénie could see the man without herself having to suffer the panic his presence so evidently produced in her. She was so small that she had to be lifted to look in. Arnhem did that and held her there for several moments.

When she nodded, he brought her down gently. In that tenderness, James had the sudden impression that Arnhem had found a replacement for at least one of his daughters.

'It's him. Maro,' Eugénie said in French, her face fierce. She poured out a stream of words to Arnhem.

His translation confirmed that this Marcel Caro was indeed the man who had met Eugénie and her two friends and had brought her to the Monpiquet. She wished they could find the other two girls and free them too. Maro had done unspeakable things to her. Had indoctrinated her, Arnhem said, though the girl's flush told them that perhaps her description had been more graphic.

They trudged back to the Chief Inspector's office, grateful for the clang of the door and the turn of the heavy key behind them. 'What do we do with her now?' Durand muttered to James. 'We can't keep her here and the nuns who usually serve in such circumstances might not be suitable.'

'She'll come with me.' Arnhem had overheard them and was definitive.

'You can't take her back to Madame de Landois,' James burst out.

'I wasn't thinking of that.'

'And she shouldn't stay alone at your place. That wouldn't be safe.'

They had reached the Chief Inspector's office and Arnhem paused at the threshold.

'I know where there's a room with two other women. Women of her own kind.'

'You mean prostitutes.'

'No, no. Shame, Monsieur Norton. Eugénie is not a prostitute. She's simply an unfortunate creature. We must try and change her fortunes. No, good women, honourable women. Of our faith.'

'We have to be able to reach her at all times.' The Chief Inspector urged them in. 'I'll need an address.'

'Of course.' Arnhem paused. 'But you know the address. It's the same building as Isak Bernfeld's. The women are neighbours of his. And they have a small spare room. I saw them today.'

'You went to see Bernfeld today?'

'He came to me first. To mourn. The Inspector had told him . . . interrogated him about Judith's death.'

James sank into an empty chair. Every part of his body ached now.

'We needed to talk to each other. I walked him home.'

'And . . .' James urged him on, but Arnhem had sunk into some kind of reverie. He kept looking out at the trees which fringed the window and then back at Eugénie who stood utterly still in the corner of the room.

'What did he say about Judith?' James asked again.

'He said she was perfectly calm, perfectly reasonable, but sadder than a soul in hell. She remembered him apparently. He held her hand and they wept together. Wept over Rachel.'

'So until the Inspector told him, he knew nothing of Judith's death?'

Arnhem shook his ragged head. 'Nothing. Nothing at all. He was utterly devastated to learn of it. He cried, sobbed in front of me. He said he had helped to end the lives of both my daughters. I wept then too.'

'And you would trust Eugénie to this man?' James was aghast.

'He will look after her with his own life. He will protect her. And the women are there. It is altogether respectable. Have you any better ideas, Monsieur Norton?'

'Yes, let her go with him.' Durand interrupted them. He had been reading a letter on his desk and he crumpled it now with an angry gesture. The anger was in his voice too. 'But you're responsible for her, Monsieur Arnhem. Should we need her, you'll bring her to us.'

'On my word.'

'That's fine. Off with you both.' With a brief good-bye, he waved them from the room, then pressed the buzzer on his desk. 'We're going to send Madame Simone off, too.'

'What's got into you, Chief Inspector?'

'That letter's got into me. All in vain, I knew it. Madame Rosa was right. Caro is all too well connected.'

'Who was the letter from?'

'The deputy head of the vice squad. He says we have nothing on Caro except alleged assault, which will most likely be proved to have been in self-defence. Nor can one trust the word of prostitutes. And so on. And so on. I knew it. I knew it in my bones. There is no way that any of these prostitutes' evidence will stand up. And Caro probably has so much dirt on everyone — on policemen, on politicians — that we'll never get to trial.'

'We need Dr. Comte.'

'We do indeed.' The Chief Inspector paced, straightened one of the prints on his wall. 'One of my men is at the hospital with him. The last word, about two hours ago now, was that he was still out. And if Comte dies, that's it. Only he can identify his assailant. If he saw him.'

He slumped into his chair, despondent. All energy had left him.

The two men looked at each other in silence, then James burst out. 'We have to keep going, Chief Inspector. Dr. Comte may still rally. And Touquet and my brother will find the other girls Caro sold. I think they already know who they are. If the women are as personable, as young and obviously innocent as Eugénie, a good lawyer will know how to let them impress a jury. And you really can't let Madame Simone go just yet. She knows too much, far more than she told us I imagine. She's a sly one. And she did have the charms in her room. We don't want her suddenly to disappear.'

He stopped his outburst as Madame Simone appeared at the door with an officer.

Durand tapped his fingers on his desk in a desultory rhythm. He eyed Madame Simone for a long moment. 'I fear we need to keep you here just a little longer, Madame. No, no, don't protest. I'll make sure you're very comfortable. A good hot dinner. Think of it as a rest from your labours. I know that in the morning, there'll be more that you want to tell us.'

Simone spluttered, but with a wave of Durand's hand and a murmur of 'women's quarters', the constable dragged her away.

James grinned at him. 'I guess I'll be off too, Chief Inspector. I'm feeling a little the worst for wear.'

'Yes, you should be in bed. I told you that this morning.'

With the gesture of an aesthete picking up a particularly repulsive object, Durand reached for the crumpled letter and smoothed it slowly. 'Don't think they're going to get the best of Durand quite so easily, Monsieur Norton. No, no. Not so very easily. I've just thought of somebody I must go and see. Yes, for the honour of the Republic.' He picked up his hat and with a brief bow at James, preceded him from the room.

James had intended to go back to his hotel. He remembered just in time that the doctor was to come and see him in the morning at Marguerite's, so he changed his instructions to the cab driver. In fact, he felt in need of a doctor right now. Repose was obviously bad for one, he reflected. It freed time to focus on the body's plaints.

When he arrived, Pierre told him that Madame wished to see him. She was in the library. With the children, he added. His tone was even, but there was something disdainful in the position of his chin. It made James smile. Pierre was proprietary of his mistress. He was also probably the sole person to know about all of Marguerite's doings, her masquerades, the place of Raf and Olympe in her life. Yet not even the Chief Inspector, he imagined, would be able to wrest secrets from that imperturbable presence.

Marguerite was sitting at the long table, a child on either side of her. In front of them lay vast tomes open at pages of fine drawings — insects for Adam, flowers for Juliette. All of them were busy drawing, but they looked up as James came in and greeted him with happy smiles.

'That'll be enough for today. You go to your room now and wash and get ready for dinner.' Marguerite whisked them off. 'I need to talk with Monsieur Norton.'

Juliette stopped to give him a curtsey as she and her brother dashed from the room.

'They seem altogether cheerful,' James offered.

'They're sweet children.' Marguerite's look was rueful. 'I enjoy them. Does that surprise you?'

He hesitated. 'No. Should it?'

She laughed. 'Given your knowledge of some of my other activities, I thought that perhaps . . .' She changed track. 'I'm grateful to you, James. For your discretion.'

He bowed.

'It was, well, kind of you, not to mention all that past business to Rafael.'

'I may still have to.' He tempered his honesty. 'But will only do so, if it's absolutely necessary.'

'Let's hope the necessity doesn't arise.' She surveyed him. 'You're looking a little the worse for wear.'

'I am tired, I confess. I may just take to my room, if that's not rude of me.'

'Is there anything you wish to tell me. I've heard nothing all day of developments.'

James gestured her to a chair, then sat down himself.

'There isn't much to report.' He summed up in a few sentences. 'But there is something I wish to ask. I want you to think again about whether Olympe ever said anything to you about her visits to the brothels? Or why she did it, particularly of late.'

'I imagine it was for the reasons we've all talked about. She may have wanted to share her good fortune, her newly found wisdom with those poor girls.' Her face grew pensive. She seemed to be examining some intricate pattern in the Persian rug at her feet. 'There was something else, but it was an aside. I paid little attention to it, but it could just be linked. Her sister had asked her to trace an old friend of hers. She was worried that the woman might have died. Judith, as we know, was preoccupied by death and Olympe thought if she could find this friend, it would calm her. But she never said the friend might work in a brothel.'

'She wasn't afraid of the brothels?'

Marguerite raised her eyes to meet his and he was once again struck by her beauty, the vivacity of her intelligence. 'There was no fear in Olympe once she shed the pain of those early years. At least I never saw it. The worst in some way had already happened. But you're fretting away at some knot, James. Tell me about it. And help yourself to a drink.' She pointed to a carafe and glasses on the table behind him.

James poured them both a glass. He relished the burn of the alcohol in his throat. It juddered away fatigue, distanced the ache. He poured himself a second glass. 'I've been worrying away at motive. A motive to tie Marcel Caro to Olympe and Judith's deaths. I had thought that perhaps Caro was angry at Olympe's interference with his girls, that he worried about exposure. But given what we've heard today about his status, his connections, that no longer makes sense. If Chief Inspector Durand can't get a fix on him, Olympe would certainly not have been able to. And there's nothing to tie him to Judith, now that Dr. Comte is out of the picture as an ally, I'm stumped. Altogether stumped.'

He leaned back in his chair and closed his eyes. Images raced through his mind, the brothels he had visited, the chase through the dark alleys, the thump of a body on wet stone. He sat up abruptly. 'Unless one of my original ideas is right. One of the girls in the brothel mistook Olympe for Judith. Judith at her best. Maybe it was Judith, way back when, who witnessed some terrible crime Caro had committed. And when Olympe appeared at the brothel, Caro mistook her for her sister, killed her or had her killed, only to discover that the wrong woman had suffered, so now it was Judith's turn.'

'But in her condition, Judith could do him no harm. Did anyone at the hospital identify him as visiting her?'

'That's where the link with Dr. Comte might come in. Comte could easily have seen him and recognized him. He knew him well enough, after all. I saw them together. So Caro had to do Comte in, too.'

A small smile played round Marguerite's lips.

'What is it?'

'No, no, it's nothing. Well it's simply that I always thought lawyers had cold minds, prized facts above imaginative truth. Whereas you, James . . .'

'So you think this is nonsense.'

'No, no, it has a kind of grand logic.' Her eyes sparkled. 'Perhaps I can help you out. Women are rather good at noticing what other women are hiding. I could talk to the girls, about Caro, about Judith.'

'You can't go into one of those places.'

'Why ever not?'

He suddenly grasped her intention. 'No, not even in one of your disguises. Definitely not.'

She laughed. 'You sound like a husband, James.'

He vaulted up, wincing slightly. 'Forgive me. I'm tired. I should get some rest.' At the door, he turned back. He hoped his composure was intact again. 'Your hospitality is formidable, Marguerite. I'm . . . I'm grateful to you. My brother is a lucky man.'

The laugh was still on her face. 'The hospitality is for you, too, James,' she said lightly. 'By the way, Raf should be joining us for dinner. At eight.'

He bowed. 'Do you know where he's been?'

'He rang earlier and asked for you. He was rather put out that you weren't in.'

'Oh.'

'You were supposed to be in bed, here, recuperating. While he was in yours, evading his various pursuers.'

James met her smile at last. 'And what has Raf been up to?'

'Investigating the bombing. And he was hoping to see Touquet before he set out.'

'Yes,' James mused. 'Touquet may have some more ammunition for us. And we need him now. We need his fiery pen.'

The message from Chief Inspector Durand arrived early, just after the doctor's visit, an admonition to rest and another change of bandage. The Chief Inspector was alerting him about Dr. Comte. He wasn't off the danger list yet, but he was awake. Durand was going to see him at 11 a.m. James was welcome to join him.

He took up Marguerite's offer of her carriage. She was going to stay in this morning. She wanted to be with the children. Last night, Arnhem had broken the news of Judith's death to them. On Marguerite's advice, they had agreed to tell them only that she had died. It seemed pointless to speculate in front of them about the manner of her death. Then, too, they hardly knew Judith, except as a vague presence, always hospitalized, always ailing. They were, Arnhem admitted, slightly afraid of her.

When Arnhem had made the announcement, little Adam had nodded, the frown convulsing his entire face. 'She wanted to join Rachel, didn't she, Papa?'

Arnhem had murmured assent.

'We miss Rachel, too,' Juliette had murmured.

'But now she has Judith, so she won't be so lonely.' Adam was definitive.

Arnhem had recounted this over dinner, once the little ones were in bed, and they had all wondered over the wisdom of children.

'Maybe Adam's right. Maybe that's the whole truth of it,' Raf had said. And Arnhem had countered him vehemently, pointing out that even if for a moment they agreed it might be true, it threw no light at all on Rachel's death.

But it was what Raf had told him, when they had snatched a few moments alone together later and caught up on developments, that had haunted him through the night.

Raf had been to see Ellie who, according to Harriet had responded well to Dr. Ponsard's latest ministrations. She had indeed been almost her old self when Raf had gone in to her. And she had asked him to convey her love to James. After that, because he was feeling flat, Raf had made a visit to the Montmartre cemetery. He had brought Olympe a bunch of flowers. He was certain Olympe, who adored colour, would appreciate flowers rather more than the slew of pebbles which they had been told to place on her grave. He had lingered there awhile plagued by melancholy thoughts. And then he had noticed amidst the pebbles which covered her grave, a sparkling object. When he had reached down, he had found a bracelet he had given Ellie for her birthday, a rather lovely piece, studded with emeralds.

Raf had taken the bracelet from his pocket and shown it to James, who had stared at it in bewilderment. Finally, he had muttered something about Ellie perhaps placing it on the grave at the funeral. She hadn't liked the idea of the pebbles, he recalled for Raf's benefit.

But the matter of the bracelet disturbed James profoundly. It squatted on the doorstep of his mind, stealing in whenever he opened the door a fraction and wreaking havoc with his thoughts. He tried for a semblance of order once more as the carriage bumped him towards Dr. Comte. According to the houseboat couple who had found Olympe's body, they had pilfered the bracelet from her corpse and kept it hidden until James had confronted them with their several thefts. There was no reason for them to lie about this, since it was to their benefit to keep the bracelet secret. Then, a good few days after the funeral, Ellie had claimed the bracelet as hers, something which Raf corroborated. Finally, the same bracelet had made its way to Olympe's grave.

How had it got there and why? He pushed aside the thought of an Ellie who wasn't Ellie wandering through darkened streets and forced himself to concentrate on more immediate matters.

It was five to the hour when James reached the hospital floor Durand had noted. The Chief Inspector was already there, standing by the matron's desk. He came towards James with his slightly swinging gait, his hands behind his back, where his walking stick trailed.

'The doctors are with him now. He's still pretty bad.'

'I don't know that I should go in with you. I may not inspire him with confidence.'

'Leave that to me.'

'If there's time, will you try and work out what his relationship with Olympe Fabre was. One of my hunches is that she came to see him on behalf of the women in the brothels he visited.'

'Chief Inspector Durand.' A white-coated figure hailed them. 'You'll remember what I said. Ten minutes, no more. And try not to overexcite him.'

Comte had his own room. A wimpled nurse hovered over him. Shrouded in white sheets, he looked shrunken, his face a mottled blue-grey against his pillow. Only the pucker at his brow seemed alive. It throbbed red. He raised swollen eyelids a fraction as Durand addressed him. His eyes moved from one to the other of them through a wet film.

'This is Monsieur Norton. He found you on the street. He saved your life.'

Comte moistened cracked lips. 'I hope the last is true,' he said in a hoarse whisper.

'We know you're not altogether yourself yet, but there are a few questions we need to ask you urgently.'

Comte waited without nodding.

'Did you see your assailant?'

'That bastard Caro. I smelled him.'

Durand couldn't hide his jubilation. He was grinning from ear to ear.

'Why did he attack you?' James asked.

The question met with silence. But perhaps Comte had only been mustering his strength and choosing the briefest way to make his point, for when he spoke at last, the words were rushed, falling over each other.

'His women were too young. Getting younger and younger. Beneath the legal age limit. I gave him three months to change his ways. He didn't. He knew I was about to report him. And not to the police.' The bleary eyes grew wary as they darted towards the Chief Inspector.

'To whom?' James asked. Comte's reply had astonished him. Its content had entered nowhere in his speculations. If he was telling the truth, Comte was altogether a different man than he had surmised. 'Report to whom?' he repeated.

'I'll tell you if I'm still alive by the end of the week.'

'A politician?' Durand asked. 'We're on your side.'

Comte didn't answer. He closed his eyes.

'One more thing,' Durand pressed on, 'and then we'll leave you in peace. Leave you to recover. A young actress called Olympe Fabre who had a sister in your ward, Judith Arnhem — both of them now sadly dead — came to see you. What did she want?'

Comte raised his eyelids a fraction. 'A prognosis about her sister. She wanted to know how she would respond to travel. To a trip to America.'

James let out a startled breath. 'A trip to America?' he repeated stupidly. 'What did you tell her?'

'Told her I wasn't a fortune teller.' Comte's lips moved towards a grin which turned into a grimace. 'Thought you were part of the plan.'

'Do you have any idea who might have killed her? And who might have killed her sister, Judith?'

Comte closed his eyes again. The nurse beckoned to them. 'Enough now. He's had enough.'

'Just one more question,' James persisted. 'Did you see Caro anywhere at the Salpêtrière on the day of Judith Arnhem's death?'

The eyes didn't flicker. Even the throbbing pucker on his brow had lost its colour.

'You must go now.' The sister's words were a command. She bore down on them, her stiff skirts swishing against the tile of the walls.

Comte's reply came as they tiptoed towards the door. It was a strangled whisper. 'Too much death, too much, even for a doctor.'

When they had reached the Pont de Notre Dame, Chief Inspector Durand pulled out his pocket watch. 'We must lunch first.' He put out a hand to still James's protests. 'It will help us think. We need to eat and to consider. Come, we will go to my favourite bistro. They will give us a quiet table.'

The quiet table was on an even quieter square behind the Palais de Justice. Leafy plane trees rustled in the breeze. Sun dappled the triangular green. It was hard to imagine that a moment ago they had been amidst hurtling traffic and rushing crowds.

Chief Inspector Durand studied the menu intently. 'Will you permit me to order for you?' he asked in the tone of a man inviting him to a Masonic initiation.

James nodded. He had just realized that Durand was amongst those Parisians for whom few matters could equal in seriousness the consideration of what food should be placed before them. Indeed, until their order was made, the wine swirled and sniffed and tasted, the white serviettes carefully positioned on their laps, the thick paté and crusty bread bitten into and proclaimed delicious, Durand's remarks were only about food.

When their first course was finished, he carefully wiped every crumb from his moustache and took a notebook from his pocket.

'So, where were we?'

'We still don't know . . .'

'Slowly, Monsieur Norton, slowly. Let us see what we do know first. We know that your brother and Olympe Fabre were lovers and that she was with child. We now also know that she was considering a trip to America and hoped to take her sister, Judith, and therefore probably her whole family, with her. We know that Isak Bernfeld was putting financial pressure on her . . . and therefore a move could only be good. We know that Olympe Fabre had a rather murky and disturbing past which even on recent occasions put her in touch with a world of vice and prostitution. We know that your family, or should I say your sister and your mother, were not altogether enamoured of the possible merging of your two clans.'

'Wait a minute. Hold your horses. What are you . . .?'

Durand held out a calming hand.

'I said let us see what we know. I am the detective, Monsieur, and I must be methodical. We must start with Olympe Fabre. It was because of her that I was brought on to this case.' The Chief Inspector topped up their glasses, sipped.

'So . . . We know, but only from his own lips, that your brother last saw her around midday on Thursday, the first of June, the last day on which any of her theatrical colleagues or indeed anyone we have interviewed saw her. After that your brother is conveniently untraceable until Sunday.'

'I cannot really believe that you still suspect Raf.'

'I have not said that I suspect him or that I don't suspect him. I am merely rehearsing what we know.'

'Have you checked to see whether Raf did in fact report for the *New York Times* on the various stories he said he was covering that weekend, on the town of Rennes, on the acquittal of your fanatical Déroulède?'

'My men have. But all he wrote could have been garnered by the way and from our own newspapers. Let me go on, Monsieur Norton.' The Chief Inspector let out a loud sigh. 'We also know that your brother left fresh, indeed untouched fingerprints, in various places in Olympe Fabre's apartment and . . . and . . .' he overrode James's protests again 'that he took letters and a notebook from the apartment, thereby obstructing the police investigation. We have still not had access to these.'

James swirled his wine in imitation of the Chief Inspector, cleared his throat. 'I shall give you all that, Chief Inspector. I simply forgot in the midst of all this. I should also tell you that it was not Raf, but I, who took those things from the apartment. No, I am not covering up for my brother. I have to admit that to begin with I didn't altogether trust your . . . well, shall we say your efficiency. Your theories seemed to me to be a method for obscuring, not revealing the truth. Then, too, my brother's letters are rather personal, perhaps overly sentimental. I shall let you see them, if you wish, and of course, the notebook.'

Durand stared at him with narrowed eyes for a long moment. Then he let out a guffaw. 'Perhaps you also arrived in Paris rather earlier than we all surmised, Monsieur Norton, let us say on a certain Thursday morning. I know, I know. We must defend our kin. It is admirable of you. Ah, the daube. You will tell me whether you have ever tasted a better one.'

The waiter spooned chunks of beef and onion and carrot in a thick sauce from a copper dish. He added parsleyed potatoes. Durand watched, his face avid, as James tasted.

'Excellent,' James said honestly. 'A true feast.'

'Good, good.' The Chief Inspector tucked in. 'Now, where were we? Oh yes. The things we know. We also know that Madame de Landois and Olympe Fabre were involved in some kind of blackmailing ploy, though Madame evidently refused to tell you at whom it was aimed. Nor do we have any more than her word about the date of this feminine escapade. What we do know is that Olympe Fabre kept the letter in her possession. We could speculate that Madame is not telling us the whole truth and that for whatever reason of need, Mlle Fabre had determined to use the past against her patroness, had perhaps even begun to do so in order to get that scoundrel Bernfeld off her back and that this hardly suited Madame de Landois. So she, too, has motive.'

The Chief Inspector was evidently pleased with this little speech for he dug into his daube with gusto.

James watched him and considered. 'I am forced to take you into my confidence, Chief Inspector.' He lowered his voice. 'I would wish what I say to go no further. I was trying to preserve Madame's honour, but she did in fact tell me the gist of the blackmail.'

'Really!' Durand scowled.

'Yes, I'm afraid so. It was aimed at her husband. She wished . . . well, she wished to be rid of him. He was . . . he preferred boys. And the blackmail, which involved very little money, was a way of coercing him into living a separate life.'

The Chief Inspector stared at him for too long. Then he wiped his lips primly. 'These aristocrats. Their blood has grown weak. They have become feminized.' He tsked beneath his breath. 'And this is why the beautiful Madame de Landois has no children. Still, still . . .' he squared his shoulders, 'none of this explains why Olympe Fabre held on to the evidence. She may still have used the letter to pressure Madame de Landois.'

'We are no longer in the realm of what we know, Chief Inspector. We have careened off into speculation.'

'You're right. You're right. If only we had found Olympe Fabre's clothes, they might have provided us with a clue. Were they ripped? Had she taken them off willingly? They weren't in your brother's apartment. Oh yes, we searched there, of course.' Durand smiled. 'Though not Madame de Landois' premises, since the lady could so easily deflect us with an assertion that whatever we found belonged only to her.'

James evaded the matter of the clothes. 'Let's be practical, Chief Inspector. The next thing we do know is that Judith Arnhem was found hanging at the Salpêtrière, that Comte was one of her doctors, that Marcel Caro, who was engaged in trafficking girls, Jewish girls from the East, attempted to kill him. Comte tells us that the murderous assault was an attempt to silence him. We have only his word. It could just as well have been because Comte saw Caro at the Salpêtrière, where he had gone to silence Judith — Judith who in her brothel days may have witnessed a crime he committed. You see, the younger Judith and Olympe were very much alike. Caro might have mistakenly had Olympe killed off and then realizing his mistake, gone for Judith.

The Chief Inspector shook his head. 'There are too many if's in all this, Monsieur Norton. And a man in Dr. Comte's condition has no reason to lie.'

'In my experience, Chief Inspector, people always find reasons for lying. During my earlier meetings with Dr. Comte, he did not strike me as a particularly moral individual. He fulminated against the Jews, said that far too many of them found their way into prostitution or into that dank asylum where he works.'

'Hardly a new observation.' Durand was studying his plate where only the sauce remained. He dabbed it up with bread.

'But his idea seemed to be that they were doomed to this as a matter of birth. A ridiculous notion, utterly unscientific. You see very well from our own brief example with Caro, how it is poverty, duress, trickery, coercion which puts these girls on the streets or into the brothels. And I dare say, it is the conditions under which they then live which drive them mad.'

'We are not engaged in a scientific debate, Monsieur Norton. We are engaged in an investigation. Are you now suggesting that Dr. Comte was killing off his own patients? I don't believe it. Not for a moment. I had his record checked. He is an excellent public servant. A man devoted to national hygiene. That is why he works in that pithole of Saint-Lazare. That is why he conducts sanitary checks in the brothels. As well as carrying on his clinical work at the Salpêtrière. Why, he could be in private practice and earning far more and far more pleasantly. No, no. The man is a good Republican.' Durand moved closer. 'You know his father died of syphilis.'

James reflected on all this in silence. At last he murmured, 'There's something there. In that hospital. I can't put my finger on it. Has your police pathologist done a post-mortem on Judith Arnhem?'

'Calm yourself, Monsieur Norton. You'll curdle the flavour of this crème brûlée. I put some pressure on him. He should have gone to the Salpêtrière this morning. Now let us concentrate on Marcel Caro.' Durand frowned. His voice grew lugubrious. 'You know what we need, Monsieur Norton? We need a moral vaccination for women, one which could inoculate them against the hypnotic influence of scoundrels like Caro. Indeed against any of those lurking interlopers who wish only to lead them astray and whom unfortunately they find so seductive.'

'Really, Chief Inspector!'

'I am taking a big chance on all this, Monsieur Norton. If only Comte had named the politician he was intending to register his plaint with. Our corrupt officers make my life difficult. Exceedingly difficult. Now even a dying man refuses to trust me.'

Which was why, James thought, the Chief Inspector had chosen a visiting and not altogether reliable American as a lunch companion.

TWENTY-FIVE

Caro sat at a table in a grim little interrogation room. He was handcuffed. Beside him stood a uniformed officer. There was a gleaming white truncheon in his hand. He swung it against his palm from time to time in a display of menace.

The swarthy Caro looked not in the least frightened. His broad shoulders were bolt straight. There was an arrogant snigger on his square face. His lids were lowered in a mask of indolence. Only the flash of the pupils beneath signalled anger.

'Marcel Caro,' Chief Inspector Durand declaimed.

'You know my name. I know my name. Get on with it. We've wasted enough precious time as it is.'

Durand gestured James towards the chair beside him.

'Who's he?'

'He is helping us with our investigations.' Durand enunciated slowly. Another uniformed officer had followed them into the cramped room and was taking notes. 'This is the man you attacked in the early hours of Sunday morning.'

'He attacked me. I defended myself.' Caro's posture threatened. 'Next time, I'll defend myself better.'

'Marcel Caro.' Durand was sharp. 'You are charged not only with this first assault, but with the attempt on the life of one, Dr. Henri Comte, who has named you as his assailant. You are also charged with illegally bringing underage women into the country and selling them on to houses of ill-repute which continue to line your pockets. We have several witnesses. We will soon have more.'

Caro scoffed.

'All of these women wear your mark, a charm with a Hebrew letter on a chain around their necks. We now have several of these in our possession, together with statements testifying that they have come from you.'

A slight frown formed on Caro's low forehead.

Durand continued. 'One such charm was found on the site where a certain Mlle Eliane plunged to her death. What was your relationship with Mlle Eliane?'

'None.'

'Witnesses say otherwise.'

Caro glowered. 'All right. I knew her.'

'Did you see her on the night of 29 March 1899?'

'Stupid question. You know how many women I see.'

'This would have been a rather unusual place for a meeting. The construction site of the new Vincennes-Porte Maillot line.'

'I don't remember.'

'I trust you'll remember after you've spent a few more weeks here.'

Caro jerked forward. 'You've got nothing on me.'

'Only aggravated assault and attempted murder. Have you ever met a woman called Olympe Fabre?'

'What?'

'You heard me.'

'The actress. Only if she was a whore.' He laughed loudly at his own joke.

'We contend that on the night of June 1 you beat her and forced her into the waters of the Seine, thereby killing her.'

Caro leapt to his feet. 'What?'

A truncheon fell on his shoulder. He sat down again with a bump.

'Now you're going to try and lay all the unsolved crimes in Paris at my feet. I wasn't born yesterday, Durand. I know what you're up to. I didn't work in this force for all those years to no avail. I won't have it.'

'That's enough, Caro. Last Saturday, you broke into the room of one Judith Arnhem at the Salpêtrière, tied a noose round her neck and hanged her from the ceiling.'

'Oh no. Oh no. That's that bastard Comte trying to put all his sordid little crimes on my shoulders. And don't tell me he didn't enjoy my girls, eh? It's just that he gets his kicks by prodding his instruments up their . . .'

'We've heard enough. Take him back to his cell, officer. We'll interview you again, tomorrow, Caro. Maybe you'll have come to your senses by then. Maybe you'll have remembered a few things you want to tell us.'

James lingered in Durand's office. He shook his head. 'Despite what I'd like to think, my instincts tell me he had nothing to do either with Olympe Fabre or her sister's death.'

The Chief Inspector shrugged. 'You never know, he may give us a few little gems tomorrow. His type needs beating down. Which reminds me, I have an appointment with a certain politician.' He brushed the lapels of his dark suit, adjusted his tie and giving James a smile which mingled vanity and mystery in equal measure, dismissed him. 'No, no questions. And yes, as soon as I have the post-mortem results, I'll let you know.'

In the hall, James all but bumped into a rushing figure.

'Ah, Monsieur Norton. Good, you can direct me to the Chief Inspector's office.' Touquet lowered his voice in complicity. 'I have a list for him. Of the women.' He touched his neck. His white shirt, James noted, was remarkably clean and he had had his hair trimmed into spruceness. 'You know the ones I mean. The articles, by the way, will begin immediately.' He gripped James's arm. 'You have been a great help to us.'

'It's that one.' James pointed. 'You had better hurry. The Chief Inspector has an important meeting.'

All the heat of the day had gathered on the square flanked by the great H-shaped front of the Notre Dame. The pavements sizzled through leather soles. Vendors fanned themselves with their hats. Children, their faces reddened, dragged their feet despite mothers' tugs. James felt as if he had been abruptly and forcibly immersed in a vast Turkish bath.

With sudden inspiration he headed for the shelter of the cathedral. Inside its massive stone walls, coolness reigned. He stood still, letting the chill envelop him and listening to the dense silence which reverberated through the darkened nave. The sudden explosion of light on the first great clustered pillars of the choir was like the materialization of an insubstantial presence. It invoked awe. He walked slowly towards the light and looked up at the sides of the transept, its majestic windows stained a deep, imperial purple.

He had last been here with Maisie, all those years ago. The cathedral had frightened her by its immensity and they hadn't stayed long. Now, he went to sit in a pew and gazed at the magnificent vaulting, the great soaring Gothic shafts. They lulled his mind into emptiness. He didn't know quite how long he had sat there but when he rose, he felt calmed, as if the sordidness and the pain of these last days could somehow be contained by this great structure which spoke to him of human accomplishment, of hope and possibility.

He left the square behind him and walked in the small tree-dappled park by the river. He leaned on the balustrade and watched the fast-moving waters. Could it have been here that Olympe had taken her plunge? No, certainly not. To his right, a feat of modern engineering, perhaps no less ingenious than the great cathedral, was under way. Scaffolding loomed from the waters beneath which a tunnel was worming its progress. With the new century, an underground train would speed between the two banks of the river. For the moment, the construction site barred passage downriver. So Olympe's fall would have had to take place beyond it or on the other side of the Île de la Cité. Why hadn't he thought of that before?

His steps took on a sudden quickness. He backtracked across the square and hailed a cab. He had no idea why he felt a sudden need to pay a visit to Olympe's resting place. Yet he did, no matter that the drive to the northern edge of the city was long and slow. He kept his eyes shuttered, wanting to hang on to his strange, quiescent mood which brought with it a startling clarity.

A burial was taking place in the lower reaches of the cemetery. He avoided the black-clad mourners, the carriages, the giant wreaths of flowers, the priest intoning a benediction, and made his way up the path towards the looming wall. He found the still-unmarked grave soon enough. Raf's flowers were there, a froth of colour decaying on the dry earth. He leaned against the wall and waited for Olympe's presence to speak to him.

She was a stranger, yet he felt he knew her as intimately as he had ever known a woman. What matter the difference of situation, of nation or heritage? He could visualize her proud grace, imagine the fire in her eyes when she appeared on stage or the tinge of melancholy which stole upon her features in repose. In her brief life she had done so much, had explored realms which he himself would never experience except as a visitor. He sensed her courage and her thirst for life. She had cared for her family and had carried them as a burden, even wanting to transport them to America should she make her way there. She hadn't reprimanded her father for the debt which had fallen so heavily on her shoulders. She had helped her benefactress in the only way she could, even if it involved her in an illicit intrigue. And she was carrying his brother's child, though she hadn't told him. Could it be that she herself was not yet aware of it?

Something in James ached. He noticed that his fists were clenched, that his nails had left ridges in his palm. He walked slowly round the grave, wishing that he, too, had brought flowers.

It was then that he noticed it. The pebbles. The ritual pebbles they had all placed on the grave were no longer there. Only one or two remained. And the earth, despite the heat of the day, had a moisture about it, as if it had been recently turned. More recently than a week ago. Certainly more recently than Olympe's burial.

What was it that Arnhem or someone else had told him? James shivered despite the warmth. The pebbles were there to stop the dead from rising before the appointed day. He stilled himself. He bent to touch the soil. Yes, the topmost clods might have a dry greyness to them, but their underlayer was damp. He walked until he found another recent grave, not yet covered by a tombstone. With a swift, guilty look round to check that he was alone, he bent to feel the texture of the earth. It was quite dry. Dry and chalky. It crumbled into dust between his fingers.

With a grim determination which bordered on rage, he hurried from the cemetery. He considered going straight back to the Quai des Orfèvres to catch the Chief Inspector. But Durand would probably still be out. Instead, he stopped off at a post office and sent the Chief Inspector a bleu. The letter would get to him in two hours. With luck Durand would read it before he went home for the evening, not that anything would be managed before tomorrow. And then? A pit opened up in James's stomach. It had the dimensions of Olympe's unquiet grave.

The area around the Grand Hotel had an air of busy normality. But for the proliferation of uniformed officers, who paraded in twos at regular intervals along the length of the boulevard, there were no traces of the anarchist incident Raf had mentioned. After a moment's hesitation, James shunned the entrance of the hotel. He didn't want to see Raf yet, who might just be in his room. He wasn't ready for disclosures nor the painful speculation which would inevitably follow.

Instead he headed a little farther along the Boulevard des Capucines and allowed himself to be ushered into a café which displayed a placard announcing 'Cinématographie — fondée par les Frères Lumières de Lyon.' Beyond the tables, rows of chairs had been set up for a theatrical presentation. He sat down near the front, just as the screen before him flickered into life. There was a collective gasp from the audience. A locomotive lurched towards them, gathering speed as it went. A woman screamed. So lifelike was the train's motion, that James too ducked uncomfortably in his chair. He had seen magic lantern shows before, but never anything quite like this.

The locomotive dissolved into pinpoints of light. From somewhere behind him, there came a loud whirring sound and then the screen filled again, this time with a dappled, magical spray of water. A man was holding a garden hose. Its stream caught passers-by unaware. Their faces were so close, James could feel their astonishment, the impact of the water. They skipped and ran and the man laughed. He laughed and laughed, like a vaudeville comedian, and the audience laughed, too. They all tumbled and laughed and waited in breathless anticipation. Because it was clear that at any moment, the sprayer would become the sprayed. When the sunlit stream finally soaked him, tension exploded into raucous applause.

How could he be applauding a mere illusion, James wondered. And laughing, laughing so that his stitches tugged and prickled, laughing in the midst of these past weeks' sorrows.

After the flickering blacks and whites and greys of the cinématographe, the brightly painted world of the boulevard itself looked illusory. People and carriages hurtled at him. Mouths moved in exaggerated motion without producing sound. He dived into the safety of the hotel, collected keys and post, and went up to his room.

Raf wasn't there. James washed. He examined himself in the mirror and felt for a moment that his powers of observation had been sharpened by the screen. His face had an unfamiliar cast. It had grown more gaunt where the light caught his cheekbone. The bruise at the edge of his jaw had a yellowish tinge which moved into purple at its centre like a discoloured pool of stagnant water. He shaved round it carefully, his eyes looking out at him with cool, blue amusement. He refused their steadiness. They reflected nothing of his preoccupations.

With a shrug, he went to find the portrait of Olympe. He positioned it on the desk in such a way that he could study it when he stretched out on the bed. Seeing Olympe's notebook, he popped it into his jacket pocket. Tomorrow he would give it to the Chief Inspector.

Taking his post with him, he lay down. Olympe stared out at him with that direct gaze which only augmented her mystery. He looked back at her, then with a sigh, tore open the envelopes.

His mother's first. He breezed through the script hardly taking it in and put it aside. Mrs. Elliott asking whether he might join them for lunch today. Too late. He didn't recognize the handwriting of the last. It was Harriet's, conveying Ellie's greetings and saying they missed him.

He lay there a little longer, gazing at Olympe, then with sudden urgency, he donned fresh clothes, and having left a telephone message for Marguerite saying he would stay at the hotel tonight, he went out into the streets.

Harriet opened the door to him. Her face was drawn, her hair a little dishevelled. She tidied it with a nervous gesture as he mouthed a 'How is she?' He realized as he said it, that it would have been polite to ask after Harriet's own welfare first.

'Fine, just fine. Rather gay.' The words ran counter to her expression. It made him uneasy. Harriet, he had assumed, was incapable of duplicity.

'She'll be delighted to see you.'

'But you're not?' James heard himself enquire.

'No, no.' She flushed with embarrassment. 'It's just that I seem to have been running all day. And it's been so impossibly hot. Please, please. Do go in to her. I'll join you soon.' She hurried off.

Ellie was not in her usual place. Her chair had been wheeled to the round table at the opposite end of the room from the divan. She sat there, her head bowed over a notebook, her pen scratching the page at a furious pace. She didn't look up until James had murmured a 'Hello, Ellie dear,' and when she did, it was as if she didn't recognize him. His heart sank.

'Harriet tells me you're much improved.'

'Harriet was ever one of the world's great optimists. She doesn't see the mud at her feet, even when she's fallen into it. Hello, Jim. How've you been?' She acknowledged him at last.

'Not too badly. Though Raf probably explained. I had a little run in with a gorilla. Which is why I haven't been in to see you.'

She took this in good stead, as if she were the old Ellie once more. 'A gorilla, Jim. Why, you could manage two. Even if you were strapped by lianas in the deepest jungle. You never had a chocolate éclair for a spine.'

He noticed as he sat down opposite her that she was heavily made up. Her cheeks were rouged, her eyes outlined in kohl, her lips painted scarlet. The effect was unnerving. Beneath it, he could see the pallor. Her hands trembled slightly, whether in excitement or weakness, he couldn't be sure.

'So Dr. Ponsard has proved as good as his recommendation?'

She blinked, as if she hadn't understood him.

'Dr. Ponsard has helped?'

'Oh yes, yes.' She closed the notebook, placed it on the chair beside her. 'A veritable healer. A magnificent man. He just has to touch me and all the aches and pains leap out of the window to find another subject. So much pain in the world. One wouldn't want to hoard it for an elite.

One welcomes the great bringers of democracy.'

'Your wit has found you again.'

'My wit, Jim? You flatter me. Still flattery is all. I thank you.' She touched her forehead with a dramatic oriental flourish. 'By the way, do you find Harriet altered? She's become so humble. It makes me want to kick her. But then I can't kick, can I, Jim?' Her titter rose into shrillness, brought a hastily covered hiccup to her lips.

James masked his concern. 'Has Dr. Ponsard given you some medication, Ellie?'

'Shelves full of medication. Little jolts of electricity. Not unpleasurable, I assure you. But . . .' She lowered her voice and brought her head nearer to his. 'I daresay his best prescription has been for three large goblets of rouge a day. If I didn't know better, Jim, I'd think you men had hatched a full-blown conspiracy. Raf prescribed that aeons ago. How is my younger brother, by the way? Has he found Olympe's murderer yet?'

There was no change in her face with the question, as if the whole matter of Olympe's death had become a subject for trivial gossip. His sister's forced loquacity, James determined, was due to tipsiness. And tipsiness was far better than the delirium he had witnessed.

'Has he?'

James shook his head. 'Though I think we're getting close.'

'Close to discovering what I've known all along.' Ellie honoured him with a regal smile. 'Close to discovering that she chose her end herself. And if you don't, you'll be here forever. Oh Harriet, dear, there you are. Why don't you ask Violette to open a bottle for us? Jim is thirsty. I can see it in his face. And hungry perhaps. We've eaten, Jim, but the house can rise to a little nibble. Oh, I almost forgot . . . Go on, Harriet. Go.' She snapped at her friend and turned back to James.

'We're planning a fête for Saturday night. You and Raf and the Elliotts and Marguerite and all our friends. No, there's no getting out of it. You must be here. Both of you. It's my farewell party. Farewell to Paris. Hasn't Harriet mentioned it? I'm going back. Mother wants it. You want it. Everyone wants it and I'm going back. Sailing next week. Charlotte and Mrs. E have had enough, too, and are coming along. They've got their wardrobes, they've been to Worth's, they've done the museums and they want to spend the rest of the summer in Provincetown. Toodle-oo to Paree.'

'Why, that's wonderful, Ellie. I'm sure you'll feel ever so much better once you set foot in Boston. And Mother will be so pleased. She's missed you. She been lonely.'

'Do you think so, Jim?' Her voice was suddenly hard. 'I suspect she's missed Raf just a teensy weensy bit more. But never mind.'

'Is Harriet going with you?

'Would that make you join us, Jim? No, no. Don't splutter. I know you're just a little sweet on her.'

'I may join you in any case. If everything is in order here.'

'In order.' She laughed. 'No, no, Jim. Don't join me. That would be foolish. You're far better off here. For a little while longer, in any case. It's made you . . . Oh thank you, Harriet. Just put it here and let Jim pour. Will you join us? No?' She leaned forward conspiratorially and announced in a stage whisper, 'Harriet doesn't approve of my medication. She thinks it robs me of my wit. Nay, my seriousness. She wants to discuss President McKinley. I've told her there's no one there to discuss. The man is living proof of the adage that anyone can become president of the great United States of America. Anyone white and male, that is.'

Harriet's face had grown as stiff as a poker. Her eyes were shuttered.

'Do join us, Harriet. Ellie has just told me the good news. I'm sure you've considered travelling with her . . . If there's anything I can do to help you make up your mind?'

'No. No. My mind is made up. Thank you, Mr. Norton. I'll . . . I'll join you in a few moments.'

The woman had barely left the room when Ellie laughed. 'There, you see. I've offended her again. She offends more easily than a king's faded mistress. It's quite extraordinary.'

James cut her off. 'There's something I'd like to ask you about.' He poured them each a glass.

'Ask away. No hesitation necessary. You're rather good at hesitation, Jim. No, no, that's not quite right. You barge right in and then you hesitate as if perhaps you oughtn't to have done the barging. It's grand really. Like some dance. Two steps forward, one step back. With delicacy.'

'That's enough, Ellie.' It came out as a bark and she slumped back into her chair.

'Yes, you're right. Enough.'

'I only meant . . .' He handed her the glass.

'What did you want to ask me?'

He raised his glass to her. 'Come on, Ellie. Let's drink a toast. To Ellie who's come back to herself.'

She drank like a greedy child, then raised her eyes at him above the top of her glass. 'Where do you think I was, Jim?'

He laughed nervously. 'Wandering. Dreaming.'

'Yes, I like that. If one's feet can't wander, then one's dreams do. Do you think there's a rule in there, Jim? One for general application.'

'Perhaps.' He cleared his throat. 'You're not wearing your pretty bracelet, Ellie. The one Raf gave you.'

'Am I not?' She examined her arm. 'No. I guess I'm not. I hope it hasn't been mislaid again.'

'Where could you have put it? I'll find it for you.'

'Don't bother. Just ask Harriet. Harriet knows everything, finds everything. In fact, it's getting rather irritating.'

'You exaggerate, Ellie.'

'Do I? Yes, you're right. It's what I do best. I exaggerate.' She laughed, storm tears gathering in her eyes. She contained them.

'You know what, my darling brother. I do believe it's my bedtime. I have to build up my strength for our party. You'll be there, won't you, Jim? And you'll bring Raf? That's an order. Now get Violette for me and see if you can put a smile in Harriet's eyes or I dare say I shall ask her not to join us on the night.'

'You can't do that.'

'Can't I?' For a moment she rose to the challenge, her face like a figurehead's on a Viking prow. Then she shrank back into herself. 'No, you're probably right. I can't. Need is a terrible thing, Jim. Leave me now.'

He found Harriet in the dining room. There was a book in front of her, but her eyes weren't on it. Behind her spectacles, they were clouded in misery.'

'She's a little drunk, Harriet. It makes one voluble.'

She nodded once, briefly. He sat down opposite her. 'Would you like to go home and get a good night's sleep? I can stay with her.'

'Hasn't Ellie told you? No, of course not. She told me she wanted me to stay here. She begged me, ordered me to sublet my rooms. Well, I did that. Just a few days ago.'

'I see.'

She took off her glasses and met his eyes.

'Well, if you don't sail with her, you can stay on here. Until . . . well, until it suits you. Don't worry, Harriet. We'll work it out. I know she's grateful to you.'

'Do you?'

The force of her utterance made him a little unsure. He got up again, looked out into the darkened courtyard. It gave back only his own reflection.

'Tell me,' he began softly. 'Have you seen a bracelet of Ellie's? An emerald one that Raf gave her.'

She scraped her chair back from the table, shut her book forcibly. 'Yes I have. Didn't she tell you?'

'You mean she offered it to you. Gave it to you?'

'No, that's not at all what I mean.' She wrung her hands in agitation.

He sat down again. 'What do you mean then?'

'You won't like it. I didn't like it.'

'Tell me in any case.'

'She made me. She made me bring it to that woman's grave. She said it was rightfully hers and she wanted to give it to her. I told her it was a mad idea and she said I was in no position to judge her ideas or anything else. We argued. It wasn't pleasant.' Her face blazed. 'I wish I hadn't done it. I wish I had behaved like the servant I've become and lied, lied blatantly and kept the bracelet. There. I've said it now.'

'You did the right thing, Harriet. Don't worry about it any more. She's still ill, you know.'

'That's what I keep having to remind myself.'

'We all do that, Harriet. We've all had to do that for a long time.'

TWENTY-SIX

Chief Inspector Durand leaned on his stick. His face wore the sceptical discontent of a busy man urged to gamble once more on shares in the bankrupt Panama Canal. In front of him, two men with spades flung earth from Olympe Fabre's grave. James stood by, his face averted.

It was four o'clock on another blistering afternoon and it was true that by the time they had arrived at the grave, the soil held few traces of the moisture James had witnessed the previous day. Nonetheless, he had implored the Chief Inspector to make good his hunch, even though he wasn't certain to what it might lead. With an exaggerated Gallic shrug, Durand had agreed. His look implied that James would owe him several favours in return for this wild goose chase.

A thump of the spade indicated that the men had reached the casket. They cleared the remaining earth and passed two thick belts round the middle of the coffin. They edged it up slowly so that it rested on the surface of the ground. Insects scuttled around it. Fat brown worms wriggled, racing from the light. With a nod from Durand, who had a handkerchief to his nose, the men levered open the wood.

The smell came first, an odour of decay which made James, too, reach for his handkerchief. He wished he could cover his eyes with it, for Olympe lay there despite his dark intimations. She was shrouded in a white sheet discoloured and mottled here and there with blotches of what might be bodily fluid. The sheet heaved with the ghost of breath.

'Maggots,' Durand whispered. He seemed to be following the trajectory of James's gaze. 'She's here. Let's go.' His words stopped abruptly. They both saw it at the same shrivelling instant. The shroud had come away at the top. Olympe's face was partially visible, the eyelids closed, but where her eyebrows should have been, there was a jagged laceration, so deep that it severed the entirety of her forehead over which the hair lay askew.

James leaned back against the wall. He couldn't look and he couldn't not look. He watched a bird flap onto the branch of a tree. He watched Durand gesture to the men to raise Olympe's head. One of them swore, 'The top's come away.'

Durand placed his handkerchief on the ground and kneeled. He muttered something under his breath. James was grateful that his squat body blocked his view of the poor, dead girl, for his eyes had strayed to her again now against his will. After a moment, the Chief Inspector stumbled upright and spat on his hand, wiping it with the top of the hankie.

'Cover her up,' he ordered the men. His voice was unusually shrill. 'We can go, Monsieur Norton. Quickly, quickly.' He wouldn't meet James's eyes, nor, despite his query, did he speak again until they had left the cemetery behind them. He walked with a kind of desperation. At the first café, he gestured James in and rushed for the WC.

James ordered two brandies at the bar and had downed his before the Chief Inspector reappeared.

'Let's sit for a moment. And coffees, garçon, bring us two.' He carried his glass to a far table. 'You were right,' he said as he sat down. 'Someone's been in there. Our pathologist didn't do that to her. Wouldn't.' He shook his head darkly.

'Who would?'

'Did you see, then?'

'See what?'

'Her head . . .' Durand gulped down his brandy.

James nodded. 'But why? Why?'

'That's what we're going to find out.'

'Do you think it's vandalism? Those same hooligans who sent the package of excrement to my brother?'

Durand didn't answer.

'Or some strange rite, a ritual desecration aimed only at Jews. Like some of the horrors perpetrated on the Negroes after our civil war?'

Durand stared at him, his eyes glazed. 'There's something I don't think you saw, something I haven't told you yet.'

'Go on.'

'The cut.' He touched his forehead and winced. 'Her brain . . . it's been removed.'

James's gasp drew a curious look from the barman. Like some automaton, he repeated Durand's words in question form.

The Chief Inspector nodded. He fiddled with the brim of his hat which lay beside him on the table. He removed a speck of lint. 'There's something else. I only learned this morning. It didn't seem relevant then.' He met James's eyes, his own incandescent. 'Our pathologist's report on Judith Arnhem. There was a quantity of chloroform in her blood, but we had reason to deduce that in any case. What surprised me in his report was the fact that when he arrived, they had already removed her brain. I asked him about it. He said it wasn't an unusual procedure in research hospitals.'

'Let's go.' James was already on his feet.

'Where?'

'We're going to make a visit to Dr. Vaillant. It's just as I suspected. There is something fishy going on at the Salpêtrière. And if Dr. Comte is out of the picture, that leaves us with Vaillant, whatever his pre-eminence.'

Dr. Vaillant was on the point of leaving his office for the day when James and Durand caught up with him. With the commanding air of a general, he told them he had no time for an interview. His frock coat and top hat, his impeccably trimmed beard, backed up his excuse of an impending and urgent meeting.

The Chief Inspector seemed to be on the point of deferring to rank. James bristled. 'We only need five minutes of your time, doctor. Those five minutes may mark the difference between life and death.'

Vaillant shrugged. 'Really, Monsieur, you astonish me. But let it not be said that Dr. Vaillant is indifferent to life.' He ushered them into his office and gestured towards two chairs. The room itself was as prepossessing as its inhabitant. Shelves towered with heavy tomes. The desk was huge and intricately carved. Oils on medical themes ranked the walls. One of them depicted a beautiful woman whose torso was an anatomy of bones and ribs. A bronze life-size nude of a well-muscled man stood by the window like some protective antique deity.

'What can I do for you?' Vaillant asked. He stood opposite them, dwarfing his seated visitors.

'When I last came to one of your lectures, you talked of the good fortune of the Salpêtrière in providing a hereditary pool for neurological study, specifically a Jewish pool,' James began.

'Indeed.' Vaillant was utterly unruffled. 'That is the case. But five minutes is not sufficient time for scientific deliberations, Monsieur. You must come back another day.'

James overrode him. 'What we need to know, Doctor, is whether your theoretical speculations are based on the firm foundation of studies of the brain. More specifically, do you anatomize the brains of all your patients?'

Vaillant waved an impeccably manicured hand. 'Many. I really cannot see of what interest this is to the police.' He scowled at Durand.

'Do you also extend your researches to the brains of their relatives?'

'I don't understand you, Monsieur.'

Durand spoke at last. 'What my friend here is trying to say is that the grave of a recent murder victim, the sister of a patient of yours, one Judith Arnhem, has been tampered with, the brain taken.'

'Really, Chief Inspector. I am hardly in the habit of robbing graves.' Vaillant pulled on a glove, eased it over his fingers. 'Now if that is all, Messieurs, I must ask you to go.'

'But in the interest of your research, you would not discourage such practices?' James persisted.

'Good-bye, Messieurs. I would remind you that we do not live in the Dark Ages. Dissection is a scientific tool. The Salpêtrière is at the forefront of medical progress.'

'Which, of course, means that you keep impeccable records.' James nudged the Chief Inspector.

'Yes. We shall need to call on those, Dr. Vaillant.'

'Well, if your men can read and understand them, Chief Inspector, you are welcome to them.' Vaillant gave him an arrogant smile. 'This truly marks a new era for French science, Chief Inspector. I will tell the minister tonight that our guardians of public safety are making great strides.'

With this parting shot, Vaillant hurried along the corridor.

'He knows nothing about it,' Durand muttered.

'I'm not so sure,' James countered. 'Not sure at all.'

Had James had the name of Marguerite's intern he would have gone in search of him straightaway. He didn't. An interview with Dr. Comte was similarly out of the question, particularly since James suspected bullying tactics were in order. The man was still on the danger list.

But the matter of Olympe's rifled grave not only troubled him. It perplexed him greatly. Both Dr. Comte and Marcel Caro, his two prime murder suspects, were out of the picture. Yet he was certain that there had to be a link between whoever had desecrated Olympe's grave and body, and the person who had killed her. Chief Inspector Durand had raced off. Having received the wholehearted backing of his politician and Touquet's promise of an imminent press campaign which could only do his career good, the Chief Inspector was now under greater pressure to gather evidence about Caro's white slavery ring than to solve the mystery of Olympe and her sister's deaths.

Left to his own devices, James wandered towards the ward which had until so recently been home to Judith Arnhem. He opened the door a fraction, caught the first moans and paused to gird himself in sensory armour. Once inside, he forced himself to look at the women one by one. Were there any here who, like Judith, might be alert to the deaths or disappearances of their fellows and be able to give him some clues? Poised, like some primitive statue on the fourth bed to his right, he noticed a mountain of a woman, her face impassive, her eyes turned inwards. She was utterly still, unlike her shrill or rocking fellows. Just as he reached her, the white-wimpled nurse he had encountered on a previous visit came hurrying towards him.

'You remember me?' he smiled. 'I'm with the police. I'm investigating the death of Judith Arnhem.'

Her eyes narrowed. 'I wasn't here that day. What do you want to know? We're run off our feet here. What with dear Dr. Comte ill, we're in turmoil.'

'Yes, I do understand. I just wanted to know if any of your patients were close to Mlle Arnhem. Any who might have talked to her that day or just prior to it.'

'Talked, yes, but made sense, probably not. This is an asylum, Monsieur.'

'Yes, yes. I'm aware of that. Still . . .'

'Ask me. I knew Judith. We all thought she was getting on so well. Well, for here, if you see what I mean. Then, suddenly, about two months ago it was, the delusions took hold of her.' She shook her head sadly. 'I'm not surprised she did it, you know. All she could talk about was death. Dr. Comte didn't agree with me, but I thought it was the fire that set her off.'

'What fire?'

'Oh, just a small one. It was put out quickly enough. Out there.' She pointed to the windows at the far end of the ward. 'I suspect one of the inmates threw a match onto a heap of old mattresses that were being chucked. Anyhow, they caught fire. And the straw . . . well, you can imagine. And Judith was in a bed at that end. She . . . we had to pacify her.'

'I see. Tell me, Mademoiselle, who performs your post-mortems?'

She looked at him strangely.

'After they die, patients are examined, I take it.'

She nodded. She was fingering a small gold crucifix which hung from her chest. 'I don't like it. I've never liked it. They cut them up something fierce. For research. But it's not right.'

'Who does it?'

'Not Dr. Comte. Dr. Froissart, I guess. And the professor. Others too. That skinny intern who's always sticking his nose into everything. Very serious, he is.'

'What's his name?

'I don't remember. Labiche or Spitzer or something. There are so many of them.' A particularly piercing howl caught her attention. 'I must go, Monsieur.'

'Thank you, thank you, Mademoiselle. You've been very helpful indeed.'

James walked and mused. All his thoughts abutted at dead ends. They had discovered so much, yet the mystery of Olympe's death was like an ever-receding horizon. As soon as he felt close to a solution, it melted away again into the distance. If her murder, like her sister's, really had something to do with a malign form of research, why hadn't her murderer simply taken the desired organ before shunting her into the Seine? It didn't make sense.

He had a sudden desire to talk things over with the ever-lucid Marguerite. He wasn't too far away now, but he grew impatient and hailed a fiacre. He arrived just as two young bloods in top hats emerged from her door. There was something vaguely familiar about them. Perhaps he had seen them at Marguerite's gathering. It all seemed so long ago.

Pierre showed him into the small salon on the first floor. Marguerite was reclining in a chaise longue, a cigarette in an ornate holder between her fingers. She seemed deep in thought, but she rose as he came in and greeted him warmly.

'James. Perfect. I was contemplating a long evening alone. The Arnhems left me a few hours ago and the house feels far too quiet. I shall miss the little ones. But Arnhem felt it best to take them home. He feared that they would get a little too used to the splendours of my life and find the return to their lodgings unbearable. As it is, he thinks they will always and ever only associate Judith's death with a holiday in a grand house.' Her laugh was rueful. 'Maybe he's right. But it wasn't wrong of me to have them here, was it?'

She seemed genuinely to want a response.

'Not at all. Not at all. I'm certain it kept Arnhem from sinking into the abyss as well.'

'You know,' she gestured him towards a chair. 'Sometimes I think Arnhem feels I'm to blame for half of his misfortunes. That I'm somehow responsible for Olympe's death. He thinks that if she hadn't met me, she'd still be alive. Maybe he's right about that, too.' She threw him a sombre look.

'That's hardly a rational thought. Her fortunes might have been worse elsewhere.'

'They could hardly be worse.'

James reached for his pipe. 'Your thoughts are very gloomy this evening.'

'You're right. I need cheering. Why don't we treat ourselves to an evening out, James? My favourite restaurant will certainly find a table for us. If you don't mind the rumours flying about the delicious and mysterious twosome we make.' Her laugh had an edge of shrillness.

'Is Raf not about?'

'Rafael is not about, as you say. He rang just over an hour ago. He's on a piste with Touquet. Things are moving quickly.' There was a slight weariness in the eyes she turned on James. 'If he spends yet another night in those brothels, I shall begin to fear for his welfare. No, no, James. Don't look so grim. I'm not being serious. I'm at loose ends.' She stubbed out her cigarette. 'What's that you have there?'

'Olympe's notebook. I just realized that I'd forgotten to pass it on to Chief Inspector Durand. It's been sitting in my pocket all day.'

'May I have another look at it? I've been thinking about it. Last time, I hardly glanced at it. You merely chanted a lot of initials at me. But I have a sense that if I look at it properly, something may occur to me. I knew Olympe fairly well, after all. There's one thing in particular . . .' Her voice trailed off. 'May I?'

James handed her the notebook. She shivered slightly as she clasped it in her hand, but she gave him a coaxing smile. 'So are you agreed? Shall I get myself ready? If you prefer, I could transform myself into the dashing Monsieur Bonnefoi.'

'No, no.' James was shocked.

Her smile played with him. 'That's settled then. You shall take me out as Madame de Landois.'

'Most definitely as the gracious Madame de Landois.'

She was rather a long time in returning, but when she did, she was regal. Her hair was impeccably coiffed. A small intricately curved hat sat atop it. An ivory cape fell from her shoulders in a long, elegant sweep.

Strands of pearls decked her throat.

'I have decided on the Ritz,' she said. 'So that we can eat in the garden. And so that I can make up to you for the minor fiasco of our first meeting there.'

'That,' James said with a hovering smile, 'will be altogether delightful.'

A panoply of candles adorned the stretch of white-clad tables. Light flickered over leaves and illuminated flowers. Birds warbled their evening song. Amidst the rustic charm, silver glittered and glasses sparkled as brightly as the jewels, bare shoulders and white cravates of the assembled diners. They had made a small detour to the Grand, so that James, too, would be in appropriate attire. Now he was grateful that they had.

As the waiter led them through the fragrant garden to their table, an assortment of strangers pursued them with their eyes, or proffered greetings to Marguerite. She nodded and smiled like a princess on a state visit.

'Good,' Marguerite said as they sat down in a quiet corner. 'We've run the gauntlet.' Her eyes were mischievous. 'Shall we celebrate with champagne?'

Once it had come and they had placed their order for caviar followed by truffled duck, she leaned towards him. 'You should know, James, that I didn't spend all that time dressing. I was studying Olympe's daybook.'

'Oh.' Her tone demanded attention and he leaned closer. 'You found something.'

'I'm not certain. I have to confess I'd been feeling somewhat miffed that Olympe hadn't trusted me enough to tell me about her pregnancy. I know we've speculated as to whether she herself was aware of it or not, since she hadn't mentioned it to Raf either. But increasingly, I'd been feeling that she must have known or at least suspected. Olympe wasn't an ingénue, blind to the facts of life. Quite the opposite.'

'Perhaps if she knew, she didn't tell you because she sensed that you might let it slip to my brother. Before she was ready.'

'Your opinion of me sinks lower and lower.'

'No, no, it's not that. Really not. It's just that maybe she planned to . . . well to rid herself of it, so she preferred no-one to know.'

James stopped to stare at her. He was astonished at the thoughts that he managed to voice in front of this beautiful woman. Not that she had flinched. Her composure, her openness were altogether extraordinary.

He was suddenly aware of the waiters hovering around them. Had they understood what he was saying? No, no. Surely they didn't speak English. He waited until the silver dishes of caviar on ice had been served, waited until they had each swallowed a mouthful and made the requisite small talk. Then, he lowered his voice.

'But what did you discover?'

'Some ten days before she disappeared, on a Monday in any case, which was her free day, Olympe went to see a doctor.'

'Who?'

'I don't know. But the notebook shows a staff with a serpent twined round it. The symbol of the medical profession. Olympe liked to draw. Maybe she was hesitant about noting the doctor's name, which would make it all the more likely that she was going to see him about her suspected condition.'

'Yet she didn't say anything about it when you saw her on the Thursday, saw her as Marcel Bonnefoi?' The question tumbled out before he had taken its implications into account.

'No.' She considered, her eyes thoughtful. 'But Marcel and Olympe never discussed women's matters. It wasn't a rule. But that's how it turned out. Marcel was an admirer and sometime advisor largely to Olympe, the actress. To say anything about her condition would have brought us out of the pleasure of the masquerade.' Marguerite sipped her champagne. 'Still, it was an exceptional moment. I guess you're right. She didn't want me to know.'

'She must have wanted to tell Raf first.' James consoled her. 'She must have been waiting to find the right moment.' He had a sudden vision of Maisie hiding her face, barely moving her lips as she whispered her news to him. 'That would have been only right.'

'Or you're the one who's right. She was having darker thoughts.' She pushed her plate away. 'You know, James, this is the first bit of information that makes me think that after all, she might have chosen it. Chosen death, I mean.'

They sat in silence, the glitter of their surroundings forgotten. Finally, James shook his head. 'No, no. I don't believe it.' He hadn't told her about what they had discovered at Olympe's grave that afternoon. He wasn't going to tell her. But it was another in the many factors that tipped the balance for him.

He watched the waiters remove their plates, bring on the next course on a vast silver platter, pour glasses of rich Bordeaux. He searched for an easier subject, heard himself say, 'I noticed two young men leaving when I arrived at your house earlier. I thought I recognized them, but I couldn't quite place them.'

She laughed. 'You would make a wonderful spy, James. I shall have to remember this. That was my young intern, Georges Legrand, and a friend of his. I'd asked him to drop round so that we could talk through his findings.'

'Oh? Was there anything new of interest?'

'Not really. His friend sang the praises of Professor Vaillant. He was rather impressed that I knew him. Strange, bony young man. He kept playing with his knuckles. But there's something else I must tell you. About Olympe's daybook.'

'Yes?'

James's eagerness met with her sudden discomfort. 'I'm not sure. I could be wrong. And it may not please you.'

'Tell me in any case.'

She picked at her duck, arranged slender greens into a neat pile. 'You remember you asked me about the initials that came up in those last days and I couldn't identify some of them?'

'Yes.'

'Well, I had another look. Looked in French, rather than English, if you see what I mean.'

'I don't really.'

'Well, the sounds of the letters are different in French, *i*'s are *e*'s and so on.'

'I see.'

'And when we spoke about it, we spoke in English. But when I looked again, I read in French. So that your sister's name appeared as a mingling of two initials. For all her other talents, Olympe was not a great writer. She rarely even managed a letter. Hence, that earlier embarrassment of mine.'

He stared at her.

'About the letter to my husband. It was why I wrote it out for her to copy.'

'I see.'

'What you don't perhaps see is this.' She opened her small pearl-beaded purse and took out the daybook. She flicked through pages. 'Look, here. This is how I noticed it. I'm MDL. And this, this LI is your sister, Ellie. We all had lunch together that day. That's really how it came to me.'

'Of course. How clever of you to notice.'

'You may not think it very clever of me in a moment.' She flicked through some more pages. 'Here. On the day Olympe vanished. The LI comes again. Which means that Elinor may well have been one of the last to see Olympe alive. Did she mention it?'

James looked from the notebook to Marguerite and down again in consternation, as if one or other of them might provide him with a revelation. His stomach seemed to rebel against the difficulty of digesting this new piece of information. 'I don't think so,' he said at last. 'She hasn't been very well these last weeks.'

'No. And it's probably nothing. Olympe was obviously waylaid.'

'Marguerite, I had to come and pay my respects. You're looking ravishing.' A tall bearded man was suddenly upon them. 'And Monsieur Norton. Charmed to see you again.'

'Gustave. James, you remember Gustave Fromentin. Will you join us for a few minutes, Gustave?'

'Happily.' An ever-present waiter pulled out a chair. 'I just wanted to tell you that the picture was finished.'

'That's wonderful. When can I see it?'

After an initial sense of displacement, James felt something like relief. He needed to brood and the quick flow of repartee between Marguerite and the painter gave him a breathing space. The breath, however, clutched at his throat.

It was only later as he lay in his hotel room bed, his eyes fixed on the ceiling, and tried not to scratch his wound which had started to itch, that it came to him. The young man he had seen leaving Marguerite's — of course he knew him. He simply didn't know him in formal attire. He knew him in a white coat. He knew him from that cold room which stank of chemicals and death. He knew him as the fervid dissector of corpses. Steinlen. The man who had followed the dead Judith Arnhem on her stretcher. The young doctor who idealized Professor Vaillant and swallowed his theories about Jews wholesale.

Rueing his blindness, James could barely wait until morning.

TWENTY-SEVEN

'I don't like to admit it, Monsieur Norton, but your brother has been singularly useful in the matter of the prostitutes. When he puts his mind to it, his reasoning is excellent, almost as good as a Frenchman's.'

'On his behalf and on mine, I'm grateful that you've come round, Chief Inspector.'

The note of irony was lost on Durand. It was Friday afternoon and the carriage was taking them to the Salpêtrière. Despite James's plea of urgency, the Chief Inspector had been too busy to arrange for the visit sooner. It entailed bullying Professor Vaillant into a meeting as well as rounding up the police pathologist to accompany them. Arthur Marquand was sitting opposite them now — a desiccated turtle of a man, whose entire energy seemed to be located in his bright, darting eyes.

'You approved of the article about you and this whole sordid matter which appeared in this morning's *Figaro*?'

Durand nodded, warred against the gleam of vanity which flashed across his face. 'It was almost accurate. Some of my colleagues, however, are less than pleased. Any intimation of police corruption has a way of inducing a closing of the ranks. I may soon find myself a pariah.'

'Or you may find new supporters.'

'Let us hope so. But I must tell you about my most recent interrogation of Caro.' Hard lines etched themselves around his mouth. 'If nothing else, I shall always be content that we have managed to secure that brute behind bars.' The Chief Inspector looked out on the jostle of a marketplace. His expression was that of a man who had just saved its clustered citizens from certain disaster. 'I trust the judge will confer the severest sentence. My new friends will have to arrange for the best judge, of course.'

'What did Caro reveal?' James was all tense anticipation.

The Chief Inspector smoothed his moustache. 'Well, we now have some twelve young women, some very young, mere children, who wear his mark — the chain you know. They are all willing to testify. And the latest news is that Dr. Comte is mending, so he will be able to act as a witness as well. Faced with all that, Caro has given us some names — contacts whom he claims are the planners, while he is just a lowly cog in the machine.'

'Good, very good.'

'But that's not all.' The Chief Inspector's smile was wily. 'Confronted by my insistence that he was responsible for the deaths of Olympe Fabre and her sister, according to one of your earlier understandings of the case — that is, that he did away with them because he feared that Mlle Fabre would use her friends and status to expose his doings, he catapulted. He refused any link with the deaths of the sisters. But he confessed that he might have been responsible for the death of the young woman in the metro shaft. She was running and he was chasing. He caught up with her at that spot. They fought. She fell. It was never his intention, he claims, to kill her. But fall she did, and not of her own volition. So we have manslaughter, at least. Are you not going to congratulate me?'

'I congratulate you, Chief Inspector. But we still have work to do.'

They had arrived at the gates of the Salpêtrière. The pathologist, Marquand, leapt out with the speed of a lizard just warmed by the sun into activity. James and the Chief Inspector followed more slowly.

'You've briefed him, have you? He knows what's at stake?'

'Yes, yes, Monsieur Norton. Calm yourself. I assure you. He is an excellent man, more at home with corpses than with the rest of us. One doesn't need words to interrogate a corpse.'

'And you told Vaillant not to alert the young Dr. Steinlen. He mustn't know our suspicions.'

'I did my best. The good doctor doesn't countenance orders easily.'

James took out his pocket watch. 'We'll be five minutes early.'

Marquand evidently knew his way. He led them along an intricate route through the labyrinthine complex. They passed a group of inmates taking the afternoon sun in the gardens. One grizzled man, lazing on a bench, thrust out his hand in an erratic motion just as James approached. James stepped back. But it wasn't James at whom he was aiming. The fly caught, he examined it, brought it to his mouth and swallowed. A beatific grin appeared on his face.

James hurried after the others who had now entered a building. He didn't recognize the door, but it led them quickly to the chill of the subterranean floor. They looked at each other, then Durand knocked and without waiting for a response turned the knob. The door was locked. He rattled it, knocked again.

At last a voice grumbled, 'One moment, one moment. I'm busy.'

'So are we. Hurry up,' Durand barked.

Steinlen stood at the door, blocking their passage. 'What is it? Oh, it's you, Docteur Marquand. I was in the middle of a delicate operation. Professeur Vaillant asked me to check on something for him.'

'That's all right. We just wanted to have a look at Judith Arnhem again. This is Chief Inspector Durand and his colleague, Monsieur Norton. You've kept the cadaver, as I asked?'

'Yes, yes, of course.' Steinlen wiped his hands a little nervously on his coat. It had patches of blood on it. He didn't seem to recognize James.

'Bring her out then,' Durand commanded. He gestured at Marquand who instantly started strolling round the long room, holding up jars to the light, turning over what looked like nothing so much as slabs of liver in butchers' trays.

'Here she is,' Steinlen lifted a sheet from an end table. 'I . . . I've been doing some work on her.'

James glanced at the figure which only half resembled a human. She was turned on her stomach. The skin of her back had been cut away to reveal the spinal column beneath, a pale twisted line with innumerable branches. The hair had been shorn, the scalp sawn in half. He averted his eyes. The queasiness which had accompanied his entry into the laboratory reached dramatic proportions. He stumbled onto a stool and covered his face with his hands. Somewhere above his nausea, he heard Marquand ask, 'What have you done with the brain?'

'Just over here, Docteur.'

'Messieurs.' A stentorian voice from the other side of the long lab called them to attention. 'I apologize for the short delay. It was unavoidable. Now what can I do for you?'

James looked up. Professeur Vaillant had come in, impeccable in his white gown. It gave him a saturnine aspect, emphasizing the blackness of his military beard. Steinlen, he noted, was standing as he would for a general, though his face had taken on a sallow cast and his lower lip trembled slightly.

'We were just having another look at the body of Judith Arnhem, the patient, you remember, who was unaccountably found hanging in one of your wards. We were wondering why Steinlen, here, had removed her brain before Docteur Marquand had had a chance to join in the autopsy. You've met Docteur Marquand, Professeur?'

'Indeed. Show them the brain, Steinlen.'

Steinlen moved clumsily across the room, half tripping over a stool.

'My young colleague is sometimes a little too eager to get on with our researches, Chief Inspector. I'm sure you must have some fledgling detectives who do the same.' Vaillant smiled slightly as if bestowing a favour on the Chief Inspector with his comparison. 'Ah yes, here it is.' Vaillant took the large jar Steinlen had handed him. He twirled it round in his hand so that the chemicals lapped round the floating shape. 'Interesting. The left hemisphere is well developed, surprisingly so for one of our patients. I shall have to look into her records. Mlle Arnhem, did you say?'

'Don't you label your organs, Steinlen?' Marquand grumbled. 'How am I to know this part belongs to Mlle Arnhem, if no one has labelled it? In fact, it rather surprises me. The colour is somewhat paler than it ought to be for one so recently deceased, particularly since you removed it so quickly.' A frown wrinkled his features, so that he looked more than ever like a turtle.

His eyes bulged. 'And look, look just there in the back, Professeur, the sawing has been so clumsy that some of the folds have been destroyed. There really was no need to be so hasty in your dissection, Steinlen.'

Vaillant examined the organ more closely. Steinlen stood by. He had taken a corner of the sheet from the pallet on which the cadaver lay and was twisting it. Twisting and twisting so that it became a tight coil. James watched, riveted.

'And here,' Marquand spoke again, 'halfway up the temple lobes. Saw marks again. Bad practice. You know, Professeur, I found far too large a residue of chloroform in the young woman's blood for any administration of a normal dose. Unfortunately Docteur Comte is indisposed, but I will need someone to verify for me who was in charge of her.'

Steinlen had just tied a knot in the twisted sheet. He pulled it tight, utterly unaware of what his hands were doing.

James prodded the Chief Inspector and pointed. Durand's mouth dropped.

Vaillant was still staring at the brain. He took his spectacles out of his pocket and slipped them onto his nose. 'Docteur Marquand is quite right, Steinlen. This is shoddy work. I have taught you to do better than this.' He peered. 'And are you sure this is the brain of the patient in question?'

Steinlen's hands were tying a second knot. He shuffled his feet. 'I'm sorry, Professeur. It's that I cut up Mlle Arnhem's brain. I didn't like to say in front of these gentlemen. I didn't think it would be needed any more. I . . . I wanted to weigh the separate hemispheres, to get a precise calculation.'

'And whose organ have we here then, Steinlen? Speak up.'

'I . . .'

'I can tell you whose organ it is.' Chief Inspector Durand leapt into action, interposing himself between the two men. His shortness was made up for by the belligerence of his stance. 'Robert Steinlen. I am taking you in for questioning in connection with the suspicious death of Judith Arnhem and for the vandalizing of the grave of her sister, one Olympe Fabre. On our way to headquarters you will lead me to your locker, or wherever it is that you keep your personal possessions. We will also make a short stop at your lodgings.'

Before the Chief Inspector had finished speaking, Steinlen made a break for it. He dodged between the pallets, tipped a stool, threw a jar from one of the shelves in the path of the pursuing Chief Inspector and a slightly slower James. It splintered as it hit the floor releasing a foul smell and a slithering gob of innards. Both of them skidded, only righting themselves with difficulty.

From behind them, the Professeur was shouting, 'Steinlen, I order you to stop. I will not tolerate such behaviour from my students. I will not have my school brought into disrepute. Stop, I tell you.'

Steinlen didn't stop. He was already at the door. The look he cast back at the Professor mingled sorrow and fear and something else, something which was unmistakably arrogance.

'Hold him, lads. Don't let him go,' the Chief Inspector shouted as the door opened.

Two men in blue charged at Steinlen. He struggled, somehow managed to escape them, his thin limbs slipping through their hands like some ghostly shadow. They raced off in pursuit, dodging passers-by, upsetting a trolley. Only at the front door, did they manage to get a proper grip.

'Get some handcuffs on him, lads, and hold on tight. I just want a quick word with the Professeur.'

James felt Steinlen's gaze on him. Beneath the thick black brows which stretched seamlessly across the narrow face, the eyes were malevolent. He suddenly spat in James's direction. 'Jew,' he hissed. 'I knew you were poison from the minute you stepped in here.'

After the initial shock, James felt a smile crease his face. So Steinlen had recognized him, after all. If not altogether for what he was.

When he stepped back into the lab, Durand had his most commanding voice on and seemed to have grown a foot taller. 'And there's another thing, Monsieur le Professeur. How long has this young man been in your service?'

'Almost a year now.' Vaillant was shaking his head. 'And he seemed such a promising student. A passionate researcher. I can't but feel that if he is responsible for all you say, there will be some good explanation.'

'We'll see. Meanwhile, I want your records for any deaths that have occurred over the last year. I want you personally to go through them before they are handed on to me.'

'Of course, of course.'

'And Docteur Marquand will do a thorough investigation of your laboratory. I trust you will help him with anything he needs.'

'I am at your service, Docteur.'

Steinlen's locker was padlocked. He tried to make a run for it, while one of the uniformed officers searched his pockets for the key. But he only managed a few steps. His lips were set in a grim line as the men pushed and prodded him back towards the Chief Inspector.

James had a moment's worry as he imagined how easily one could get lost in the maze of corridors and buildings. The men must have had the same thought, for they now held on to him as if he were a wild beast poised to spring at any instant.

Steinlen had good reason to want to flee. When they finally opened the locker, apart from an evening suit, two hats and some grimy trousers and soiled shirts, they found a large canvas drawstring bag, the kind sailors use. Inside it, was a good-size spade and a small medical saw.

Durand's eyes gleamed as if he had unearthed a treasure chest. 'Get him into the wagon, lads. We'll help you with all this. And then Monsieur Norton and I will pay a little visit to his quarters, while you get him safely behind bars. Don't lie about your address, Steinlen.' The Chief Inspector dangled the ring of keys in front of the man's nose. 'It'll just make things harder on you later. I want you singing, tonight, wrapping up all our little problems. Well, go on. What is it?'

'Seventeen Rue Jeanne.'

'In the Thirteenth?'

Steinlen shrugged.

'Walking distance, then. Do you live with anyone?'

He didn't answer.

'Never mind. We'll find out in due course. But I warn you, Steinlen, when I come and see you in your cell later, I want co-operation. Full co-operation. Think it over. You can't hide behind Vaillant's reputation. If he has to, he'll drop you into the lion's den faster than a piece of rotting meat.

Take my word for it. Faster than I can put these mud-stained trousers into this sack here.' He illustrated his words with speedy action, stuffing trousers and soiled shirts into the drawstring bag which contained the spade and saw. 'Let's go.'

Steinlen shot them a last look as the men prodded him into the black police wagon. There was desperation in his eyes. For a lightning second, pity flashed through James. He wondered at the depths to which Steinlen's ruling passion had brought him.

'Not a bad day's work, if I do say so myself.' The Chief Inspector was chuckling. 'I almost feel like stopping off for a celebratory drink.'

'Let's go and visit his quarters first, Chief Inspector.'

'All right. We can walk. It's not far. But you don't seem happy, Monsieur Norton. Yet your hunch paid off. I shall have to make you an honorary member of the Judiciaire after this. What's troubling you?'

'I'm not sure.'

James was taciturn. They walked in silence along the Boulevard de l'Hôpital and then turned into the small shabby streets of a worker's quarter. Haussmann's reconstruction of the city hadn't extended here. The houses were higgledy-piggledy, thin or squat or tall, with no overarching symmetry. Garbage reeked in the gutters. Dark-clad matrons sat on stools in front of doors and shelled peas or attended to sewing.

'You know, when I first agreed to letting you work alongside me, I was certain that all your efforts would lead us directly to your brother, perhaps simply as somehow complicit in Olympe Fabre's suicide. Don't look at me like that. I gave up the idea of a mesmeric pact soon enough.'

'And in the event . . .'

'In the event, I was proved wrong. Though we can't be altogether certain yet, can we?' The face he turned on James was inscrutable. 'Ah, number seventeen.'

A woman with sunken cheeks sat in front of a two-storey house which had lost much of its stucco. She was threading a needle, holding it a good distance in front of her. On her lap lay a pair of worn socks.'

'Madame.' The Chief Inspector tipped his hat. 'We're from the police.'

She sat bolt upright. 'Something's happened to him!'

'To whom, Madame?'

'To my husband.'

Looking at her for a moment, James thought she might be Steinlen's mother. His heart sank.

'Not unless your husband's called Steinlen.'

'Robert. My husband's nephew. By his first marriage.' She stood up shakily. 'What's Robert done? I told Michel he was a strange one. Always so secretive.' There was panic in her face.

'We just wanted to have a look at his room. He's given us the keys.' The Chief Inspector dangled them.

'It's on the second floor at the back. I'll come up with you.'

'No. No, that won't be necessary.'

'Has he stolen something?'

'Only in a manner of speaking. Thank you, Madame. No need for you to worry. We'll make our way up.'

'That's why he always locked the door. Bought his own lock, he did. Installed it himself.' She shook her head wearily. 'And all those fine manners. Made us think he was too good for us. He goes to church regularly, mind. Every Sunday when he's not working. Regular as clockwork.'

'You carry on with your sewing, Madame. Don't trouble yourself with us.' The Chief Inspector was already halfway up the stairs.

Steinlen's room was a small, dark den. Burlap curtains covered the windows. The light came in through slits at the side. Durand pushed the curtains aside to reveal a space of impeccable tidiness. The sheets on the narrow bed might be greying, but they were tucked in with geometrical precision. Above the bed, hung a cheap crucifix. A small, obviously self-made bookcase, at its foot, contained an assortment of medical texts. What clothes there were hung on hooks behind the door. Beside the bed, an upturned crate with one side removed served as a table. Inside it, hidden by a cloth, lay a small assortment of socks and underclothing and collars, as well as a clean shirt. A small, old kitchen table by the window served as a desk. There were papers on it, neatly ranged, a quill and an inkwell.

While Durand busied himself with the papers, James opened the single drawer. It contained more quills, a magnifying glass and two bound notebooks. He opened one. The writing was tiny and filled the entirety of each page. It was all but unreadable. He tapped Durand's shoulder and showed him.

'We'll take those. And the magnifying glass. We'll need it. And maybe these papers. Look.'

The unbound sheets held anatomical drawings of great precision. Sheet after sheet depicted brains of varying sizes and convolutions. James suddenly remembered what Steinlen had said to him in the lab on their first meeting. The brain was an undiscovered country, a mysterious region waiting to be charted. Was it this and only this that had propelled Steinlen into his misadventures? A sadness stole over him.

'He's got a cupboard in the hall, too.' The woman's voice surprised them. She was looking round the room with open curiosity. 'He pays extra for it. Just a little, mind. And he keeps that locked too. If you don't find what you're looking for there, then he doesn't have it.'

They followed her onto the landing. The Chief Inspector tried one key and then another without success.

'It's not here,' he said in consternation. 'He must have kept it in his pocket.' He held back a curse.

'Let's check that drawer again.'

They looked in the drawer and in every other conceivable place, but there were few hiding places in the small room.

'We'll have to force it.' Durand grimaced. 'I'm sorry, Madame. We'll need a crowbar. Or a large knife if you don't have the first.'

She looked at them sceptically. 'Maybe we should wait. Michel won't like the damage.' She smoothed her skirts with thin, nervous fingers.

'We'll pay for the damage.' The Chief Inspector's temper was running short. 'Now run along, quickly.'

'I'm not a girl, Monsieur,' she muttered, offended. But she left them and came back minutes later with a thick-handled knife. 'This is the best I can do.'

'Thank you, Madame. This should do the trick.'

James sensed that his politeness was forced. Like him, the Chief Inspector wasn't looking forward to what they might find in the closet.

James imagined severed limbs, hunks of cadavers.

At last Durand managed to prise the catch open. The door opened on a large pannier, the kind in which market vendors kept their fruits and vegetables. With a shrug, Durand beckoned to James and together they pulled the basket from the closet. The woman stood by, her face eager.

A checkered cloth covered the top of the basket and as the Chief Inspector lifted it aside, James closed his eyes for a moment. When he opened them, he saw Durand bent over the pannier. He was shuffling through something. He stood up to thrust a pile of pamphlets at James. 'No cadavers. Just these. Lots of them. Too many for any single idiot.'

James looked down at the leaflets.

'The sacred texts of the Anti-Semitic League. Just what you've always wanted to pore over on a summer's night.' He stuffed a few into his pockets and gestured to James to help him move the pannier back. Behind it, they now saw a pair of boots, a folded winter coat, and a heavy jacket.

'He was always running off to their meetings,' the woman scoffed. 'Made Michel come with him sometimes. You'd think he had nothing better to do.'

'Thank you, Madame. You've been most helpful.' Durand reached into his pocket and took out some loose change. 'This is to get your door fixed with. I don't imagine your husband's nephew will be back very soon.'

The Chief Inspector and James sat in a café near the Palais de Justice, drank brandy and scanned Steinlen's notebooks. They took turns with the magnifying glass.

'He can't have much money, the way he fills these pages,' Durand grumbled.

'One more thing to hold against the Jews. His parents should have taken him off to visit Arnhem when he was young. It would have taught him not to believe this swill of propaganda. You agree that it's pigswill, don't you Chief Inspector, pages and pages of it?'

'I guess,' the Chief Inspector shrugged, 'most of it. It obviously addled his brain.'

'And Vaillant didn't help with his theories. Wandering Jews. Left hemispheres. Hereditary taints. Our biology is becoming dangerous, Chief Inspector. Soon our doctors will be killing off the weak and the lame in the interests of the survival of the fittest. Or whomever they diagnose as weak and lame.' James shook his head. 'I almost think one should lock Vaillant up along with Steinlen — as a preventative measure.'

'Don't be ridiculous. This is a free country. One is allowed one's ideas. One is allowed to speak them.'

'But not to act on them. I guess that's something.'

'Nor, if the electorate so deems it, to institute them as law. Look at this.' Durand's voice grew suddenly triumphant. 'Here, I'll read it to you. Right near the end of my notebook. The writing is suddenly bigger just for this one phrase. It obviously excited him. "Her sister's dead and she's begging to die. It will be an act of mercy in the cause of science." We've got him, Monsieur Norton. We've got him. Garçon, another brandy. We're celebrating tonight.'

James studied the page. He felt sullied, as if the demented words had risen up to implicate him. So much hatred. So much false power. He was silent. He watched the waiter pour golden liquid into their glasses. They drank.

'Now all we need to do, Chief Inspector, is find the equivalent entry for Olympe Fabre.'

Durand's face lost its cheerfulness. 'And you don't think we will.'

James shrugged. 'No, I don't honestly think we will.'

'Which leaves us exactly where?'

'I don't know, Chief Inspector. I really don't know.'

TWENTY-EIGHT

The image the mirror gave back of the two brothers had the aura of a tinted photograph taken to mark a family occasion demanding memory. They were posed in tense stillness. Raf stood tall, his features dramatic, dark eyes flashing. James was a step behind him, cooler, older, pensive in his self-containment. Through the open window, the bells of Saint-Augustin tolled the hour.

Raf gave his tie a final tweak and turned to face James. 'I can't altogether believe I heard you say that.'

'But I did Raf. We've come to a dead end. We've followed all the possible leads, uncovered a mass of foul doings in the process, but none of them lead to Olympe's murderer. You can see that yourself. Steinlen did for Judith and two other patients at the Salpêtrière, and yes, he rifled Olympe's grave, but he didn't kill her. Marcel Caro is responsible for a great many crimes but we have no evidence to tie him to Olympe's death, and less motive. So we have to conclude that unless she was killed by a random passer-by who has disappeared once more into the labyrinth of the city, she chose her end herself.'

'There's Bernfeld. You allowed yourself to grow soft on him and let him off the hook.' Raf reached for his whisky glass.

'If you'd interviewed him yourself, you'd see. Go and talk to him, if you like. As for me . . .' James shrugged. 'What I never managed to tell you, because I thought it would distress you is that Olympe was clothed at the time she plunged into the waters. The boatman decided to profit from her corpse and stole the garments. She was wearing a frock coat, trousers . . .' He watched Raf's face closely. 'I didn't tell you because I thought it would distress you even more. You . . . you cherish a particular image of her.'

Raf's laugh was abrupt. It contained nothing of humour. He turned to look out the window so that James could no longer see his face. He said nothing.

'On top of that, when Marguerite examined her daybook, she discovered that Olympe had almost certainly been to see a doctor some ten days before her disappearance. So more likely than not, she suspected her pregnancy. That might have been what tipped her over the edge. Maybe she feared that you'd reject her.'

'I'd offered to marry her, Jim.'

'Who knows what goes through women's minds?'

Raf's low-voiced reply held a gritty determination. 'Well, I'm not giving up, even if you and the Chief Inspector call it a day.'

'I had hardly expected otherwise.' James grinned, despite himself. 'I guess it's as good a way of mourning as any. And it saves you from having to come home . . .'

'Don't be daft, Jim. I wouldn't be coming home in any case. I've got to see this whole matter of Dreyfus through. His ship will be landing soon. And then there'll be the tribunal. I wish you'd stay, too. You've been . . . well, you've been a good brother.'

They looked at each other in silence. This time James broke it. 'Careful, I've got rather used to being here and I may just change my mind. There's a certain attraction to the easy morality of this town. You might just end up having me round for longer than you like.'

'I'll risk it, Jim,' Raf smiled. 'I'll risk it.'

In that smile, in that openness to risk, James once again felt Raf's teeming energy. Despite everything that had happened, despite the pain, his brother glowed with life. It was probably Raf's very capacity for living life to the brim which he had always envied in him. Perhaps, now, some of that had rubbed off on him. Yes, it felt like his brother's gift to him. Something in Raf, something in these past weeks, had shown him that life in all its passion and complexity and absurdity was valuable.

'We'd better get over to Ellie's, Raf. It's her big night.'

The apartment was filled with the heavy scent of flowers. Every available surface sprouted elaborate bouquets. There were roses and ranunculus and giant peonies as vivid as faces. Either Harriet or Ellie herself had determined that Ellie's good-bye to Paris should have its appropriate requiem.

The salon was already lively with voices. Violette, in a lace-trimmed apron, proffered canapés. A sleek young man, who had evidently been hired in for the evening, served drinks with a café waiter's panache.

Regal in creamy silk, her hair piled high, her face flushed, Ellie presided, apparently quite in control. Beside her sat Marguerite and Docteur Ponsard, looking like nothing so much as a genial farmer hosting a family dinner. His presence surprised James, as did that of the painter Max Henry. He had gone no further than imagining Charlotte and Mrs. Elliott and, of course, the ever-present Harriet, who was in a tête-à-tête with the painter now. They made an odd couple, he so sultry and Mediterranean in aspect, she taller, straight-backed, her gaze clear and direct and so unmistakably American.

'Raf, Jim, at last,' Ellie called out to them. 'I was beginning to think we had lost you to . . . well what was it, politics? Detective work?' She didn't give them a chance to answer. 'You know, Docteur Ponsard,' she switched to French, 'my brothers are half in love with death. It's such a vast and shady region to roam around in that they've quite given up the living for it. But you, of all people, must understand that.'

'Oh no, no, Mademoiselle. I find quite enough mysteries on this side of the divide to occupy me.' The doctor rose to shake James by the hand. James introduced him to Raf and went round the room to greet each of the guests in turn.

When he had reached Harriet and Max Henry, Ellie's voice hailed him back. 'I don't know if I mentioned it Jim, but the great Max Henry did a portrait of me. It was Olympe's idea, of course.'

'Really?'

'Yes,' Ellie's laugh cascaded. 'It was months and months back, even before Raf met her I think. And he painted me as a riding mistress, complete with whip. Well the face is mine, in any case. Imagine it, Jim. No, no, you can see it. I shall make you a present of it.'

'It was an inspiration, Monsieur. Your sister impressed me as so strong, powerful,' Henry fumbled. 'Like Diana, the huntress. Or an Englishwoman,' he finished lamely, unable to prevent himself from glancing at Ellie's wheelchair.

'She is that, too.' Harriet consoled. 'Hello, James. It's a lovely evening. Would you like to see the picture now? I can take you to it. It's in Ellie's bedroom.'

'No, no, later will do.'

'I'd like to see it too,' Charlotte was suddenly beside them. 'Mother refused to allow me to have a portrait done. She said it was a vanity for women and should be allowed only for men. We're so happy to have Elinor sailing with us, Mr. Norton. It was Mother who convinced her, you know. She said she would be utterly desolate were I to abandon her for so very long. It would quite kill her.'

'Your mother is a woman of great feeling,' Harriet murmured.

James wasn't sure if he had caught an irony in her voice. He looked at her again, but her expression was serene.

'Elinor wants us to go through, I think. Shall we? And she wants both you and Raf next to her. She's missed both of you.' A slight frown creased her forehead. 'She told me the other day that childhood had been the happiest time of her life.'

James lowered his voice. 'Has she been taking quantities of her latest medication?'

'Only in moderation, today. I kept it from her. She's been quite well, really. A little melancholy, but that's only to be expected. I'm so glad Docteur Ponsard was able to come. His presence is calming.'

Raf was wheeling Ellie into the dining room. The table had been lavishly set. The guests took their places as Ellie indicated. Marguerite was at the far end with Dr. Ponsard and Max Henry at either side. Mrs. Elliott sat between Harriet and Raf, while James had Charlotte for a neighbour.

Between them, there was an empty chair, though a place had been set. He wondered who the late arrival would be.

'Don't you think, James,' Ellie whispered as he sat down, 'that Charlotte's charm tonight lies in her having disguised herself as a corpse?'

'Hush, Ellie.' He grinned despite himself.

'It's quite becoming, really.' She clicked her knife against her glass and the voices fell away. 'I'd like to thank you all for coming,' she began in English 'and to raise a toast to all of you, my dear brothers, my dear friends. And to Olympe, the sweetest absent one.'

Raf's sharp intake of breath was audible around the table.

Ellie paid him no heed and half-emptied her glass.

'And we drink to you, Elinor,' Marguerite rose to the situation. 'Paris shall miss you. I shall miss you.'

'Why thank you, Marguerite. Coming from you that is a true compliment. I shall clasp it to my bosom like a shield throughout the journey ahead. It shall fortify me.' Ellie's smile arched across her thin face. 'It was you who introduced me to that darling girl and watched over our friendship. For that, I shall always be grateful.'

James watched his sister with something like dread. He wanted to deflect her from her chosen topic. She was turning the evening into a wake. Raf's face had grown contorted. Harriet was holding her glass as if at any moment she might crush it between her fingers. It came to him, too late, that the empty chair beside him awaited Banquo's or rather Olympe's ghost. He pushed it back a fraction and plunged in to try and save the conversation. 'We must invite Madame de Landois to visit us in Boston, Ellie. She might find it interesting.'

'Invite her by all means.' Ellie threw him a coy look. 'But I don't really think Marguerite will find it very interesting after Paris. Boston, in fact, is of no interest at all.'

'Elinor!' Mrs. Elliott chastised. 'How can you say such a thing? One of our great cities. Why we have our university, our symphony, and the aspect is quite glorious.'

'And I dare say Raf and Jim's joint presence would make it more so. But I fear they have too much to fascinate them right here. Isn't that so, Raf?'

'Yes, Ellie,' Raf muttered, then reprimanded. 'I do think your choice of topics is quite tasteless. If you're trying to draw me into an argument, you may yet succeed.' There was a muted threat in his voice.

'Tasteless. I have grown tasteless, Mrs. Elliott. You shall have to coach me. Ah the food, let's hope it's less tasteless than I am. On parle du goût,' Ellie translated in case Ponsard and Henry hadn't understood.

'Taste is a strange human faculty,' Dr. Ponsard began while the soup was being served. 'I have patients who complain of having lost all taste. Yet I can find nothing at all wrong with them.'

'So you hypnotize them into taste, Dr. Ponsard. I can see the theatre of it now. You put them to sleep and you tell them that when a lemon comes their way, they'll screw up their faces and their mouths will shrivel. Or this soup, you tell them it's smooth and creamy and as soothing as the memory of mother's milk. But what do you do when your patients have lost their taste for life?'

'Ah, that Mademoiselle, that is a question. I think I might tell them to take a walk through this city of ours, so extraordinary on the eve of a great new century. And to look, to watch, to observe carefully, to see all the things they haven't seen yet. The progress of science has been truly remarkable of late, let alone the progress of technology. Think of it — electricity, the telephone. A bright world where the most distant is close. In the coming century, technology will . . .'

Ellie cut him off. 'And if your patients can't see?'

Ponsard's genial face wrinkled in sudden laughter. 'You bring me back, Mademoiselle. You are quite right. Back to the ordinary, to the human. All right. If a patient is incapable of seeing, I would tell her to listen, to listen to the stories people tell. Why just yesterday, I was in the market near the Saint-Germain and this woman came up to me to beg for a sou and she told me the most intricate story — of the great house she had worked in near Bordeaux, of the master's son, who was a little slow, but who had seduced her, so that her mistress sent her down, and how the son had promised to join her in Paris, but had never come, though she was certain he would. Meanwhile . . .'

'Stories are always stories of woe.'

'It is possible to intercede to make them otherwise. I told this woman that if she presented herself at my house on Monday, my butler would be interviewing for a new chambermaid. I shall put a word in for her. But the point is that by approaching me and speaking, this woman began to alter the course of things.'

'You are a kind man, Dr. Ponsard. There are not many like you. My brothers are kind, too. They will always help a poor woman in distress. It is when the woman reaches out for equality that they lose their sight and their hearing, and perhaps even their taste.'

'Elinor.' This time the reprimand came from Harriet.

Ellie shook her head. 'I'm always shocking you, Harriet. I promise that I do not intend to.'

Marguerite's voice rose from the other end of the table to engage Mrs. Elliott in English. James hoped it blocked out the sound of Raf's low hiss.

Tears leapt into Ellie's eyes. 'Let's be friends, Raf. Just today. Just before I go. Just for a few hours.'

'We're all friends, Ellie.' James patted her hand. It was ice cold. 'We love you very much.'

She was looking at Raf. Grudgingly, his brother patted her other hand. 'It's true,' he mouthed.

After that, Ellie behaved. James made sure he showered attention on her, prodded Raf to do the same. His brother was taciturn. He kept stealing glances at the empty chair. He only moved into conversation when prompted by Marguerite, who wanted to know how he thought the new military tribunal would conduct itself over Dreyfus.

To James's relief, no sooner had the cheese platter gone round, than Ellie pleaded fatigue. The guests soon took their leave. Only Marguerite stayed for an extra moment. She hugged Ellie and whispered something into her ear. For a moment, Ellie's face turned as stony as one of the statues in the Luxembourg Gardens. Then she recovered herself and gave Marguerite a coy little smile and bade her adieu.

'The rest of you mustn't go yet.' Ellie held onto Raf's arm. She laughed, suddenly cheerful. 'I just wanted them away. But the night's still young and I want to go out. I want you all to take me out. For my last stroll through the Paris streets. It's a beautiful evening.'

Raf looked at James, who nodded.

'All right sister, we'll race you through the boulevards.'

'Not the boulevards.' Ellie's eyes grew dreamy, her face serious. 'The Tuileries. And the river, I want to see the river with the lights twinkling at its edges.' She paused, her voice dropping to a murmur which was nonetheless a command. 'I want to say good-bye. Good-bye to Olympe.'

Silver streaked the dense foliage of the gardens, silent but for the rustle of leaves and the crunch of gravel beneath their feet. They didn't speak. They proceeded slowly. Hypnotized by Ellie's injunction, their small party had taken on the aura of a funeral cortège. She herself sat in a capsule of unbreachable stillness, like an icon they were moving towards the altar in some darkened church. Her head was poised in solemnity, her expression mournful and unchanging. One gloved hand crossed her chest to fold over Raf's who was pushing her chair. The other tensely clutched at her skirts.

Moonlight illuminated a couple clasped in embrace beneath the arching branches of a tree. At the sound of the procession, they tittered and fled into deeper shadows. James expected one of Ellie's sharp asides. It didn't come. Perhaps she hadn't seen. He met Harriet's gaze. It was full of silent intelligence. She, too, had been expecting an outburst. Something like fear crossed her face and made her lips move. But no words emerged.

At a gesture from Ellie, they turned into a path on their right, avoiding the arc of the Carrousel. It was darker here beneath the tunnel of trees, the sound of their footfall louder. James was glad of the sight of the Quai and the sudden brilliance of lamps. They crossed towards the river. Raf stopped at the edge of the balustrade so that they could all watch the choppy flow of the waters, scudding and silver-tipped.

After a moment, Ellie mutely urged them forward and when they reached the Pont Royal, she waved them onto the bridge. It was deserted. As they crossed its lonely expanse, James had an odd sensation that Paris itself had become a ghost town, abandoned by its inhabitants who had left behind homes and boats in an emergency departure. The water rushed beneath them, charcoal black and angry where the moon hadn't graced it with light. He found as he looked down that his fists were tightly clenched in he didn't know what emotion, but suddenly he had a vision of Olympe hurling herself over the stone balustrade, no higher than his waist.

It was at that moment that Ellie's scream punctured the stillness.

'What is it? What is it?' He bent to her at the same time as Raf.

She stared at them, her eyes huge. 'My purse. My best purse. I must have dropped it.'

'We'll find it for you, Ellie. Don't worry.'

'It can't be far. I would have noticed. Back there.' They were some three-quarters of the way along the bridge and she pointed back towards the right bank. 'Yes, it must have been where we stopped just before.'

Raf was already walking, his eyes glued to the ground.

'Go with him, Jim. You, too, Harriet. You know he never notices anything. It's the small, pretty one. My favourite. Father gave it to me.'

James met her eyes. They glinted oddly. He knew better than to gainsay her in that kind of mood. Yet he hesitated.

'Go on, Jim. I'll be fine. Really, I will.' She reached out to pat his hand. 'Really.' She gave him her sweetest smile.

He turned his back on her and followed the others. He could feel her eyes on him and he turned round once, but she waved him on. She was still smiling.

The sound erupted in the night air and inside him with the force of an explosion. A muffled underwater detonation like a boulder hitting water at speed. He knew instantly what it was but his mind refused the reality. From his point near the end of the bridge, he looked back fully expecting her smile. Instead he saw the chair, empty, and in the swirl of the waters, some pale silvery substance which might have been moonlight, but was a flurry of skirts. For a moment, everything froze. There was only that empty chair, the whirl of light on the river and his shout.

'Ellie,' he screamed. 'Ellie.' And then his limbs moved. Raf, he saw, was ahead of him, racing down the steps to the embankment, plunging into the river. He took the opposite course, simultaneously shouting at Harriet, 'Find a doctor. Quick,' as he ran past the empty chair to the far quay and, shedding jacket and shoes, dived in.

The waters were icy, the current a fierce tug which willed him away from his destination. When he reached the point where she had plunged, there was nothing there but blackness. He saw Raf heading towards him, saw him gulp air and dive, disappearing for too long. James let the river carry him where it would and then went under, too. He fought to keep his stinging eyes open, but there was only darkness visible. He came up for air, looked for Raf and dived again. At the fourth attempt he saw it, some billowing substance mushrooming white at a distance beneath him.

Raf reached her at the same time and together they tugged her back to shore. Her skirts were so heavy that they seemed to act as a sail, relentlessly pulling her away from their joint strength. At last they managed to hoist her onto the bank. With a grim determination which had little to do with reason, they turned her over and in a repeat of the childhood life-saving games they had practised on each other in Atlantic waters, Raf straddled her and began to pump water out of her lungs with rhythmic tenacity. It had little effect. Ellie's will had always been stronger than theirs. It could be no different in the implementation of her death.

Only when Raf's eyes met his own in desperation, did James see that tears mingled with the water on his face. He, too, was crying, he now realized. He put his arm round Raf and in the same instant, like a man waking from anaesthesia, became aware of the light shining on them and of the small crowd that had gathered.

A figure in a ragged suit was holding a lantern above Ellie and shaking his head. Dim lights glimmered in neighbouring houseboats. There was a blanket round his shoulders and another round Raf's. Harriet emerged with a policeman who muttered something incomprehensible. Nothing in the ensuing commotion made any sense, neither the arrival of a sleepy doctor and more policemen, nor the journey to a Commissariat and the dilatory filling out of reports. Nothing had any substance. The only substance lay in Ellie's smile as she said to him, 'I'll be fine. Really I will.' And then, in that sodden, breathless body, that pale skewed face, over which the smile still seemed to hover.

He had known, James thought. That part of him which was attuned to his sister had known. She had wanted to die. What else but that had she spoken of in one way and another since his very arrival in this city? He also, he realized, knew why she had wanted to die, why she had chosen that very spot in which to end her days. Above his grief, it was that knowledge which terrified him. How long had he kept it at bay?

Later, on Harriet's insistence, they went back to Ellie's apartment and drank hot coffee spiked with brandy amidst a silence none of them seemed able to break. Their eyes kept darting towards the divan where she had lain propped on her cushions. The heavy perfume of the blooms Ellie had filled the space with now took on an added significance. So dense was the room with her presence, that it seemed impossible she was no longer there.

Harriet's sudden movement startled them. Her face convulsed, she launched herself towards the divan and began to throw blankets and cushions to the floor, one after another, with machinelike frenzy. When there was nothing left to fling, she picked up the velvet coverlet itself and stripped the divan down to pale, pristine linen. There was a thud as something heavy dropped from the cover's folds. They all stared. On the floor lay two thick leather-bound notebooks, the very ones Ellie had ceaselessly scribbled in during her delirium.

Harriet bent to pick them up, but stopped midway as if some higher authority forbade her motion. Tears streamed down her face. She turned away from the two men and bundling cushions and blankets in her arms, carried them out of the salon.

James reached for the notebooks. 'Shall we?' he asked softly.

Raf shuddered. 'It doesn't seem right. She always so insisted on her privacy. And her journal was her most private possession.'

'I think she meant us to find these. Otherwise she would have destroyed them. The plunge wasn't a whim, Raf. I know it. Know it with a certainty I've rarely had about anything.'

'But how did she do it? I still don't understand that. She hadn't stood up for months. How could she . . .?'

James cut him off. 'She could walk, Raf. At least the bodily part of her could. I saw it myself, when Dr. Ponsard hypnotized her. It was uncanny. Maybe his treatment enabled her to do so when she was more aware . . . I don't pretend to understand any of it. But she could. The sorry fact is that she did.' He fingered the notebooks. 'Let's try and quiet Harriet and go back to your place. I think we need to read these.'

'You read them, Jim. I can't. Not yet. Not yet.'

James lay on the bed in Raf's spare room and scanned Ellie's journal. The script was sometimes neat, sometimes florid, sometimes altogether illegible. Several people seemed to inhabit even her writing. Except for the occasional note of a Monday or Wednesday, there were no dates, nor in this scramble of varying handwritings could he even be certain that the entries were sequential.

He skimmed, hoping that his eyes would fall on what he was looking for. There was so much here, too much for any single reading. Entitled 'Paris — Days and Ways', the journal began with Ellie's impressions of the city, its people, the books she had read and plays she had seen, and even included some acerbic political commentary. The spark and bite of her wit were in ample evidence. Gradually, other darker notes crept in — an agonized cry of loneliness, a wail of pain, outpourings which took on a delirious quality.

He didn't want to pause over this intimate matter. It felt like an invasion. He didn't want to know about Ellie's cloying love of Raf, the catalogue of her passionate longing for his continuous presence, the secret torment his comings and goings stirred in her. He tried to race on, but the leeches of her emotion had attached themselves to his skin, draining his lucidity. He found himself immersed in the whirlpool of her warring thoughts, the howls of rage and desire which lived just below the surface of the Ellie he thought he knew. Her ardent wishes were so out of keeping with the possibilities her life offered or she felt able to act on, the accompanying resentment so intense, that he felt breathless, trapped in the very paralysis which had eventually afflicted her body.

When had this war in her begun? What had caused it?

Dizzily, he leafed pages, until his eyes were riveted by a passage about his father.

'Thinking on it, I have begun to understand that he had long hated her. He shouldn't have. Her. Our mother. All those black moods, those splitting headaches. She was at their base. At the end, he wanted only me. Me to tend to him. I loved him, yet now I sense that I hated that poor, pale body with its sagging skin and distended joints. How I loathed the washing of him. Yet his need spoke louder, until it swallowed me up, cutting me off from life, leaving only a husk barely able to withstand the disgust of it. Only Raf was left to me.'

James felt his stomach churning. He forced himself to read on, half looking for he no longer knew quite what. A passage in Ellie's swirling script leapt out at him. He read it twice.

> *He has stopped talking to me, stopped telling me things. Why? Why did I ever introduce them! I fear the worse. When I said, oh so lightly and trippingly, that he was only attracted to her because of his passion for the Dreyfus case and the one over, so would the other be, he stormed from the room. He has not come back. He cannot have her. Mine. The only mine.*

James's mind reeled. He forced himself to his feet and tiptoed to the kitchen. He poured himself a glass of water and drank it thirstily, following it with a second. The last entry had bludgeoned through the locked door of his perceptions and now threatened havoc. Olympe. Olympe and Ellie. He must have missed an earlier entry which named the girl.

He took the notebooks from the bed to the small desk in his room and switched on a brighter light so as to concentrate better. A quick leafing backwards produced no mention of Olympe's name. On a whim, he turned to the second notebook and there, on the third page, he found it — the description of a visit to the theatre with Madame de Landois and the remarkable talent of a young actress, Olympe Fabre, who was this munificent woman's friend. Three pages later, came a second report, this time of a musical tea at Marguerite's house. Here Ellie sang the praises of the talented Olympe Fabre, who seemed so very much her own person, who had a refreshing air of freedom about her. The entry finished with an emphatic declaration of how wonderful it was to have found new and admirable friends, women who were untrammelled by their sex, women who had thought and read, but, unlike her, had also acted on their desires.

He skimmed more pages, but Olympe's name had now disappeared from the entries where the writing was legible. James was mystified. Had all his recent suppositions been utterly wrong? He had been so certain over these last days that somewhere in the cryptic recesses of Ellie's mind lay the essential clues to the mystery of Olympe's death, but now at a rough scan he could find no mention either of her death or her funeral.

The first pale greys of morning already trickled through the window. With the light, it came to him that if there was no methodical chronology in the way Ellie moved between the two journals, she must, nonetheless, have left some kind of suicide note. Her leap into the Seine could hardly have been unplanned. With a racing pulse, he turned to the last page of the notebook in front of him and took a deep, ragged breath.

> *He hasn't come back to me. I took a terrifying gamble and nothing has come of it. Oh Raf, my lost darling. Now I must pay. Yes, I must die. We will be united then, perhaps. She and I. She. I am not afraid. It is so very easy to write 'The End', when the middle has only been turmoil and the beginning lacklustre.*

He read this statement several times. The boldness of it both shocked and moved him. Like some antique Queen, re-imagined by a great tragedian, Ellie had confronted both her perverse passions and their consequence. He stared out at the courtyard and felt the walls transform themselves into those of a suffocating fortress — a prison of conflicting emotions condemning an Ellie riddled by jealousies to only one possible escape. She had taken it. He bit back a sob and forced himself to return to the pain of the journal.

If Olympe had become simply Ellie's unnamed 'She', he would have to read very carefully. He leafed slowly backwards. The last lines in this journal had been in Ellie's neat, finely honed script. But the preceding pages were filled with a loose, disjointed and all but illegible scrawl, the exclamation points so thick that they cut through the paper.

The handwriting worked on him with the same insinuating resonance as her voice had in the hours of her delirium. He felt he had been set adrift on stormy seas in some flimsy uncontrollable vessel poised to capsize at any instant. It was only with a gigantic effort of the will that he didn't succumb to despair and kept himself on course.

Maisie's name accosted him. Why had she surfaced at this particular juncture in his sister's jumbled mind? He made out the word *stupid*, but the rest of the sentence was unreadable. Or perhaps he didn't want to read. To know. To know any more about the embroidery Ellie had dropped on the stairs which hastened Maisie and their daughter's end.

He shuddered away the insidious thought. That way lay madness. He turned pages hastily until he reached a clear section, the script as balanced as Ellie at her best.

> *She hasn't abandoned me. My soul-mate. My sister. My second love. She is coming to see me later tonight. She has promised me a surprise. I can guess what the surprise is. I pray that I am right. She knows how I have suffered from her absence, knows that it has robbed me of all power. It was wrong of her to seduce him, to metamorphose him into a great doting noodle with only one interest in the world. It was wrong of her to give him the one thing I cannot and so to take him altogether away from me. And take herself away in the process. A betrayal of both of us. I dare to hope that she has recognized her wrong. Yes. And now they will both be returned to me. I feel it. Already I feel the rush of blood in my legs, the strength returning.*

A savage drummer beat at James's temples. He rubbed them slowly, willing himself to read on and somehow decipher the jumble of the following pages. The writing was a scrabble, the words back to front. They swam before his eyes, bringing exhaustion in their train and with it a kind of emotional numbing, so that he felt a distance growing between himself and these pages as if they no longer belonged to his sister, to poor, dear Ellie, but to a stranger who had encoded a puzzle he had to solve.

It leapt out at him like a sudden illumination that his difficulty in reading the scrawl came from the fact that a good proportion of the words were in French, though accentless and randomly spelled. Simultaneously, he made out the words *pantalons et frock.* He began to translate a little randomly, filling in as he went, jumping over the impossible, the countless repetitions.

> *She came in trousers and a frock coat. For me. My actress. My own little man. Took me out for a caper. How we laughed. Laughed in the Tuileries. Giggled at the lovers. Then the Seine. Turbulent. Dark. Darkest night. He has proposed, she said. You're really to be my sister. How dare. You can't. Sapphic. Jewess. Slut. My brother. Never. No. No. Never. She calls me silly. Bête. Me. Bête. All that is my inflamed mind. She loves him. Only. Only. Nononononono. I won't let him. The scheming. Shrew. She pushed too fast. The bridge. The bridge of dreams. Her dreams. Her love. Him, him. Only him. America. His child inside her. Never. Really. Never. Can't allow it. Can't allow it. A child. The horror. The horror. Never. Ram. Push. Hit. Ram. Hit. Over and down. Down. Down. Over.*

James's breath wouldn't reach past his strangled throat. He thrust the journal in a drawer, covered it over and threw himself onto the bed. He didn't know how long he lay there or whether he slept, but his mind produced a rapid and repetitive blur of images, bleached out, like those leaping scenes at the cinématographe. Instead of the train coming towards him, it was Olympe's falling body, propelled over a balustrade by the sudden wild heave of Ellie's unexpected motion. He saw the savagery of his sister's eyes, huge, beaming. He saw Olympe tumbling into the cold waters where he swam unable to save her, unable to save the body that followed hers in quick succession either. Olympe, then Ellie. Olympe, then Ellie, in a demonic unstoppable flickering repetition.

When the images faded, it was only because the sound of insistent knocking had replaced the endlessly recurrent splash.

'Jim, Jim. It's late. And Durand's here. He heard about Ellie. Come and talk to him.'

The Chief Inspector stood by the French windows and gazed out on the spectacle of the streets. He rocked slightly, balancing first on heels, then on toes, while his crossed hands rested on his stomach. Everything about him drooped, even his moustache. The expression he turned on James was lugubrious.

'My sincere condolences, Monsieur Norton. Your sister was a fine woman, if a troubled one. It is a great loss. A great loss.'

'Thank you, Chief Inspector.'

'Arlette is just bringing coffee. You'll join us?' Raf looked as haggard as James felt. His eyes were glassy, encircled by soot. He seemed to have slept in his clothes and have dreamt what James had been reading.

James waited until the coffee was poured and the croissants served. He still hadn't determined quite what he would say to either Raf or Durand. He sipped the scalding liquid and reached for his pipe. Raf was watching him like an accused man searching out a judge's verdict from telltale details — the lift of an eyebrow, the flicker of a nostril. James cleared his throat. It felt raw, as if he had been howling for hours at an ill wind.

'Chief Inspector, I have spent the night perusing my sister's journal. It is a strange document, intimate in the extreme, sometimes utterly incomprehensible. I fear she was even more tormented, more confused than any of us had imagined.' James paused. His skin felt clammy. He was betraying Ellie. But it had to be done. For the sake of truth, if not of the law which had no jurisdiction over the realm to which she had fled.

He rushed on. 'You remember that at an early point in your inquiry, you were convinced that Olympe Fabre's death was the result of a crime of passion. You were right. You were only mistaken as to the source and nature of that passion. From what I can make out from my sister's palpably delirious jottings, Olympe Fabre spent the last hours of her life with her. They went out together. Olympe pushed Elinor in her chair along the Pont Royal. I imagine she pushed her up to the very point Elinor chose for her own leap into the river.'

'What?' Raf's coffee cup clattered, spilling grainy liquid into his saucer. 'Say that again.'

James stilled him with a wave of the hand.

'The two women argued. It seems they argued over the pregnancy Olympe had just confessed to our sister and over her clear intention to accept Rafael's proposal of marriage. They must have argued vehemently and though it may seem startling, I believe that Elinor rose from her wheelchair and lashed out at Olympe. The unexpectedness of the attack, the surprise of it must have led to Olympe's toppling backwards over the bridge. The balustrade on the Pont Royal is not a very high one, as you know, and our sister is . . . was . . . a tall woman. My sense is that after that, Elinor propelled the event out of her mind. Developed an amnesia. It was not altogether unusual to her, as Docteur Ponsard will testify. When the scene came back to her, she set out to take her own life and to do so in the same place. Perhaps she saw it as a just punishment.'

Raf's mouth had dropped open. The Chief Inspector tsked beneath his breath.

'I shall give you the journal if you like, Chief Inspector. Much of it, as I say, is illegible. The rest in English.'

Durand was visibly embarrassed. 'I shall have to look at it, Monsieur. Only the relevant passages. For our records, you understand.'

'Of course.'

'But I am certain the investigating magistrate will agree. The case of Olympe Fabre is closed. Accidental death.'

'Thank you, Chief Inspector.' James met Durand's eyes in understanding. 'Thank you.'

Raf's mutterings interrupted them. He was running his fingers through his hair, pacing, talking as if to himself. 'I should have known. I didn't read the signs. She told me. Made it clear. A double jealousy. She didn't want us together. I had intruded on a special friendship.'

'Believe me, Monsieur Norton . . .' The Chief Inspector, too, rose. 'In my experience, it is almost impossible to prevent such explosions. They are like storms. One can sometimes see them coming, but we have no power to stop them. They take their own course.'

'Still, I could have . . .' Raf's eyes were black with sorrow. His lips trembled.

James had a sudden scalding memory of Maisie, his raging helplessness at her death and their child's. He thought of the hidden coils which charged all their relations. He thought of his own unshaped and murky suspicion of Raf, fuelled by childhood jealousies which mirrored Ellie's, but had none of her force. He had discounted her, whether because of her illness or her feminine frailty, and all the time it was Ellie who had harboured the real secrets, who had been the engine of their grief and her own.

'I don't know if you could have done anything, Raf, short of altering history or changing the world we live in.'

'It needs changing,' Raf snapped at him.

'As for that, Messieurs, we are in agreement,' Durand intervened. 'Perhaps in our new century . . .' A small smile lit his face, so that he suddenly looked like a satisfied politician. 'And may I remind you, my friends, that together we have made a little difference, perhaps accidentally, but it is a difference nonetheless. Our vice squad will be a little more wary of corruption. We have one white slave trafficker less, maybe more than one. That is not nothing.' He bowed. 'I leave you, Messieurs. Once more, my condolences.'

TWENTY-NINE

The ocean liner gleamed white against the indigo sea. Gulls circled its prow, inspected the proud chimneys and with a shriek, swooped towards the waves. Little Adam pointed and marvelled and pointed again, his cries more excited than the birds'. Her mouth a perfect circle, Juliette held on tightly to her father's hand. Arnhem, his beard and hair freshly trimmed, was wearing a new suit and he nodded sagely at his children's squeals, though his eyes held a similar awe. All around them, people clustered, shook hands, waved, kissed, wept.

Marguerite, stately in a dove grey suit, her face beautiful in its melancholy, leaned on her parasol and looked on. James approached her. 'I guess it's time for a last good-bye.'

She gave him her wry laugh. 'I'm glad you say last, James. Because I sense you've been trying to say good-bye ever since you arrived.'

'I haven't been quite that bad, have I?'

'No, no, not at all. And, despite the circumstances, your company has always been a pleasure. Not once have I felt a yawn stealing upon me.'

'Coming from you, I'll take that as a compliment. And you, you have taught me many things. Paris has taught me.'

She lowered her gaze and traced a pattern on the ground with her parasol. Her voice lost its banter. 'I haven't had a chance to say this before, but I am deeply sorry about Elinor. I console myself with the thought that she chose her own guillotine. That is something. Who knows whether when the moment comes we shall be as brave.'

He nodded.

'I shall miss you. Arnhem and the children, too. I had grown very fond of them.' She met his eyes, her own troubled. 'I hope this notion of taking them to America was not simply your way of settling family debts.'

'That too, of course. But if you had seen Arnhem's face when I suggested it, your mind would be at rest. He wants nothing more than a fresh start. A fresh start for himself and his children for the new century was in fact how he put it. He added that Rachel wanted it, would have wanted it. When I told him I could facilitate the necessary papers, he was rapturous, though he insisted that all monies were to be understood as a loan which this time he would make certain he honoured.'

He paused, his voice catching as he looked at her. 'We all shoulder our guilts as best we can. And our lives have become intertwined, willy nilly . . .'

His glance strayed towards the children.

She followed it. 'Yes, I can see that. I can see that clearly. Perhaps you are right. That, at least, is for the best.' She moved towards him and kissed him on both cheeks. 'Come back, James. You've made many friends here.'

'You, the most remarkable of them. But I leave my brother in your capable hands.'

'As for that . . .'

'What are you two smiling at?' Raf was suddenly upon them, Harriet in tow. 'Everything's in order.' He handed James a sheaf of papers, then gripped him by the shoulders. 'Thanks for everything, Jim. You'll plead my case to Mother.'

James embraced him. 'That's one I'm never sure of winning.'

'Never mind. Harriet will have a go. And she can explain Ellie to her. Tell her, as she told me, that she was a heroine before her time. I guess Olympe was too.' He looked out to sea, his handsome face sombre. 'Maybe you'll pass Dreyfus's ship on its long homeward journey. Wave to him for me. Tell him far more of France is glad to see him back than was sorry to see him go.' He gave James a lopsided grin.

The ship's horn blared, filling the air, scattering the gulls, demanding attention.

'It's time, James.' Harriet glanced up at him with shy excitement, then ran to shepherd the children and Arnhem.

Watching her, James had a glimmering sense that his future might no longer be altogether behind him.

His brother met his eyes in understanding and nodded, though nothing had been uttered. It had taken too many deaths and misadventures, but Raf and he seemed at last to be in tune.

After another flurry of kisses and handshakes, the travellers scrambled on board to stand on the deck and look out on the diminished figures of those left behind.

'Do you think the new world really is better than the old?' Arnhem asked with sudden solemnity.

'I don't know,' James murmured. He lifted Juliette into his arms so that she could see Marguerite more easily. They both waved, a wave that for James encompassed not only Raf and Marguerite, but Ellie and the Olympe he had never met and her sister and even the Chief Inspector. 'I don't really know, Monsieur Arnhem. But we make of it what we can.'

'I like your "we" Monsieur Norton. I like it very much.'

Notes and Acknowledgements

My lifelong fascination with the James family — Henry, William and Alice — and their extraordinary work, has played its part in the making of *Paris Requiem.* To them I shall always be in debt.

The *belle époque* is a period I have explored since my PhD research first led me to Marcel Proust. Of particular use in creating the world of the novel were books on the medical science of the day, as well as on policing, on the Dreyfus Affair and on the situation of the Jews. Amongst my favourites were: Frederick Brown's monumental *Zola: A Life* (Farrar, Straus & Giroux, New York, 1995); Jean-Martin Charcot's Lectures, published in various forms but also in *Clinical Lectures on Diseases of the Nervous System,* translated by Thomas Savill (New Sydenham Society, London, 1889); Michel Drouin, *L'affaire Dreyfus de A à Z* (Flammarion, Paris, 1994); Georges-André Euloge, *Histoire de la police et de la gendarmerie* (Plon, Paris, 1985); Alan Gauld, *A History of Hypnotism* (CUP, Cambridge, UK, 1992); Michael Graetz, *The Jews in Nineteenth Century France* (Stanford University Press, Stanford, 1996); Ian Hacking's *Mad Travelers* (University Press of Virginia, Charlottesville and London, 1998); Ruth Harris, *Murder and Madness* (Clarendon Press, Oxford, 1989).

Much of my research consisted in reading newspapers of the period, which provide a fertile, if sometimes lurid, account of the thinking and events of the time.

Needless to say, no other writer can be held responsible for what my imagination has made of these sources.

I am deeply grateful to my first and always critical reader, John Forrester, who is also my sometime co-author — *Freud's Women* (Penguin, London, 2000) — and who had some links to the present novel. Caradoc King, my second reader and agent, along with his assistant, Martha Lishawa of AP Watt, deserve special thanks, as does Kim McArthur, my inspired Canadian publisher and her wonderful team at McArthur & Company.

LISA APPIGNANESI is the bestselling author of seven novels and ten works of non-fiction. Raised in Montreal, she now lives in London. One of her recent mysteries, *The Dead of Winter*, was shortlisted for the prestigious Arthur Ellis Award. *Losing the Dead*, her memoir about growing up in Montreal, was shortlisted for the inaugural Charles E. Taylor Prize.